Duplicity

Secrets of a Decadent Double-Life

Nicky Webber

Media Publishers Ltd

PRAISE FOR DUPLICITY

"Webber shows intelligence and empathy, dealing with this topic. Taking a real story and bringing it to life with action, dialogue and intrigue. Recommended." Sue Armstrong

"High risk and desire with heart-stopping tension. Really pulled me into Sophia's life." Heather Fisk

"I had low expectations but once I read the first page, I couldn't put it down. Brilliant insight into a socially unacceptable life." Brian Stanton

"Totally absorbing. Taut with emotional tension and intrigue. I got totally absorbed in the character's lives." Rob Eden

"Well written with unexpected twists and insights into an intriguing life. I was hooked from the start." Jayne Farrier

"A cleverly delivered story where Sophia miraculously gained my empathy. Great read!" Mary Harrison

"Gripping from start to finish." Lyn Fields

Duplicity is inspired by the true-life story of an educated,
wealthy high-class call girl.

DUPLICITY – Secrets of a Decadent Double-Life

Note from the Author

Years ago, I worked as a magazine journalist and stumbled upon a story about an intelligent, wealthy high-class call-girl. A hooker in anyone else's vernacular. It took many months of assurances and rearranging private interviews before I was able to meet her in the flesh. It was one of the most astounding interview sessions I had ever encountered. This information forms the basis of this true-life story, DUPLICITY.

For this reason, I have changed names, dates and some of the details to protect her identity. I also have not set this story in the original geographical location and have minimised content that could result in exposing her. I believe the story provides some insight into the psychological makeup of people who choose this lifestyle. She is, of course, a rare exception and bears no resemblance to the majority of broken women who are hookers plying their trade on city streets and in brothels. This compelling book explores the reasons why this attractive, university-educated daughter from a well-established, wealthy family pursued this decadent direction.

"My objectives justify my actions."
Sophia Hawkins, on the meaning of her life.

PROLOGUE

The Dressing Room - 2017

Sophia dries herself in the bathroom of her Sydney penthouse apartment. Her cheeks are flushed from the hot shower and her long auburn hair shines in the overhead light. It's tied up in a knot on top of her head where tendrils of damp hair escape, falling to her shoulders as she leans forward to dry her legs. She flicks on the extractor fan and walks briskly into the adjoining master bedroom.

She carefully selects each piece of evening wear with Willem's preferences in mind. First a French lace and silk pair of knickers, with a matching bra clutching her firm breasts to the best advantage. Sophia catches her reflection in the full-length mirror, elegantly positioned beside the 16th-century dresser with its beautifully turned legs. The smooth curves of the antique has matching pearl handles. Handcrafted before the industrial revolution when mass production swamped the world, this magnificent dresser has small imperfections which only an expert would notice. Like Sophia, none of its flaws are immediately evident. The exquisite design with everything perfectly aligned across the six highly polished drawers reinforces her sense of order and organisation, which she relies on to ensure the perfect functioning of her private and professional life.

She smiles at herself, knowing Willem will find her irresistible. Sophia walks through a connecting archway into her dressing room where racks of designer clothes and imported shoes, hand-made from the finest calf leather, crocodile and snakeskin, await their next outing. But first, she carefully pulls a silk slip over her head before selecting an indigo dress from the second set of mirrored wardrobes.

Each cupboard is fitted with handcrafted teak compartments,

stacked with personally inscribed books, expensive gifts, artefacts and souvenirs from her travels around the world. Some drawers contain jewellery and silver-framed photographs in careful order, positioned above a series of glass-fronted drawers which hold specific pieces of imported lingerie, a wide selection of designer sunglasses and memorable items from shared holidays. The other side of the double wardrobe contains a collection of imported garments tailored to Sophia's exacting requirements.

Mirrors line the walls on two sides of the dressing room, allowing her to make specific refinements to her attire. She turns in her private enclave, critically assessing her reflection. The hem of her organza cocktail dress hangs demurely, softly hugging Sophia's long legs.

Opening an ornate jewellery box, she retrieves a diamond bracelet. Draping it over her wrist, she turns her hand as the light plays on the exotic setting. She clips the clasp, hooking the small security chain to its opposite link and lets her arm fall at her side. Glancing down, the sleeves of her dress linger at her wrist, partially obscuring the sparkle on her arm.

She casts her mind back to Willem Van Howan and the evening he presented her with the gift over dinner. The box was wrapped in black velvet with two black tulips from the Netherlands, intertwined with a satin ribbon securing the offering. It was unexpected, and more so, when Willem let slip its extravagant value, and insisted on covering the insurance cost. Not bad for a gift and, so far, it beat all others.

Smiling at the memory, glimpsing the shimmering diamonds on her wrist, Sophia looks forward to seeing him again. She runs her fingers across the gold bracelet. Each fingernail finely coated in three layers of soft peach, matching her expensive lipstick and strappy heels.

Sophia turns her body one last time, pleased with her appearance. She knows Willem, with his Dutch conservative upbringing, can easily be provoked into a jealous outburst. Unacceptable as it is, in a fully-grown man, she's reassured he is unlikely to ever stray. At twenty-nine, Sophia easily manages him with calm compliance, enjoying his conversation and charm.

An hour later, Sophia has almost completed her subtle make-up. She dusts a powder blush to her cheeks and the arches of her outer eyelids, completing the demure look she wishes to convey. Her long, dark eyelashes and full lips maintain an understated pout, enhancing her arresting almond-shaped eyes. She knows, from experience, her flawless, angelic appearance will be near impossible for any man to resist. She deliberately cultivates an innocent look, her guileless eyes wide with non-comprehension. In public, most men stare at her, fixated by lust, only to be crushed seconds later as she smiles and walks on by. She is meticulous in her choice of lovers.

Reaching towards the wardrobe shelf, Sophia selects an imported perfume before squeezing a fine spray into the room and walking into the fresh flower-scented mist which settles over her body. Again, she smiles at herself in the full-length mirrors and concentrates on her personal rating system. Running through her list of professional objectives, Sophia allocates herself a resounding nine.

With her head held high, she grabs a small leather handbag and walks through the Carrera tiled entryway. Sophia grabs the Audi's key-fob from the hallstand and sashays to the elevator. She presses the lift-button taking her down to the basement parking area. The driver's door of her imported German two-seater R8 sports car automatically opens as she draws near. She slips into the driver's seat, resting one hand on the soft leather steering wheel before pushing the starter button. The turbocharged Lamborghini V10 engine roars into life.

Sophia glances down at her wristwatch, a beautiful piece of Swiss-made jewellery, only outmatched by Willem's bracelet on her opposite wrist. With a rippling shockwave, she hears her dead mother's unbidden voice ringing in her head: Better get a wiggle on. Sophia's momentarily disturbed by her deceased mother's influence over her conscious thoughts, particularly after being secured in her grave for more than five years. She presses her foot to the accelerator and races out into the tree-lined street, past the Point Piper Yacht Club and heads towards Sydney Airport.

Dutch language had been one of Sophia's core subjects at

university twelve years earlier, along with German, French and Japanese. Like a chameleon, her ability to seamlessly adapt and compromise, tailoring her behaviour and attitude, enables her to become whoever her lover wants her to be. To Sophia, it's not merely a job. It isn't work. Her career path is driven by her passion for pleasure, indulgence and, of course, money. She executes her professional approach to the level of an art form. It's a gift, a skill unknown to many, and Sophia plies her natural talent to perfection.

Even though Willem seems possessive at times, in a strange way, she likes the fact that he's in control and often takes charge, ordering her food and wine in restaurants without any consideration for what she may prefer. As she speeds towards the airport, she tries to analyze what it is about him that she finds attractive. He's an alpha male, confident, in control and can also be loving and gentle. Other times he's demanding, questioning what she wears or where she's been.

She thinks about how outwardly self-possessed and assertive Willem is, and yet if she scratches the surface, he's a young boy, desperately clinging to her apron strings, craving attention. But aren't most people like that? Is it a mother thing? Surely not. Not Willem, he's way too secure and confident.

Sophia is happy to handle him again. How long has it been? Close to four weeks. Willem always makes love to her with enthusiasm, sometimes taunting her, teasing her to climax. He's the playful cat to her cute, furry mouse. She laughs out loud. In bed his nick-name Wim comes easily to her lips. Willem. Always engaging and intellectually challenging. Sophia loves that about him. All these qualities make it easier for her to appear devoted to him during the moments they share together.

She knows Willem imagines he's the only one. Sophia's lover is none the wiser, utterly oblivious. She believes some men hold a willing suspension of disbelief, desperate to convince themselves Sophia loves only them. She explicitly cultivates everything her lover needs or wants, reinforcing each man's belief in her absolute devotion. Each man with no inkling of anything other than what he believes is plainly visible. A gorgeous, intelligent young woman with eyes and thoughts solely for him – the ultimate flattery.

CHAPTER 1

Living Doll - 1993

In the summer of 1993, chestnut-haired Sophia enjoys pushing her doll's pram across the terracotta pavers on the extensive outdoor veranda. Her favourite doll is tucked inside, snuggled under a pale blue blanket. Talking to her baby doll is one of the six-year old's happiest moments.

'Look, Mummy, look at me. My baby likes the pram,' Sophia begs. Her soft curly hair glistens in the early morning sunlight as she gazes across at her mother and father eating breakfast. They sit in comfortable white wicker armchairs positioned at a linen covered table.

'Yes, darling. Have you had enough to eat?' Sophia's mother asks, barely turning to cast her languid gaze at her eldest daughter.

Sophia nods, disappointed at her mother's lack of interest in her baby doll. Abigail Huston glances up at her husband Michael, seated opposite. She casually pushes a strand of blonde hair behind her perfect ear. This small innocuous movement seems to be a coy act of shyness, but, in reality, is a pretense masking her abject uninterest in both husband and child.

Sophia gazes across the long driveway as it swings past a double-line of neatly trimmed cypress trees which frame the Tuscan-designed stone mansion. Established trees stand like bold sentries, guarding the driveway to one of Sydney's most luxurious Point Piper homes. The triple-storey residence straddles the manicured gardens surrounded by ivy-covered stone walls securing the Huston family in their palatial enclave. Tall French doors swing open onto a wide veranda enclosed by concrete balustrades where breakfast is served every morning.

'Mum,' Sophia repeats but knows her mother is more interested in her cell phone. It's no use. They're talking now and ignoring her again. There's no point in shouting or demanding as they will call Nanny and remove her from the terrace. Crestfallen, she walks back to the doll's pram and picks up her baby, cuddling it against her body.

She holds her mouth against baby Bella's moulded ear. 'It's all right,' she whispers. 'I love you. OK. You're OK.' She gently strokes the fine blonde hair on the doll's plastic head, letting her parents' conversation wash over her. They're always talking or arguing, sometimes shouting. Maybe they don't like me? Sophia's brow furrows. I'm not good enough to talk to. They never listen. She glances up hoping to catch her mother's attention.

'Do you think we should go back to Antibes this summer?' Sophia's father asks, his gaze still fixated on the newspaper he's reading. 'We can extend our holiday for ten more days. I can push back meetings into August. Isn't that a better idea?'

With straight hair pulled tightly into a chignon at the nape of her neck, Abigail peers up from her eggs Benedict and thin slice of toast, smiling at her handsome dark-haired husband. 'Sure, why not? It won't matter if Soph misses out on school.'

'What about my friends?' Sophia interrupts still cradling the doll on her shoulder. 'I don't want to go on holiday.' Abigail briefly peers at Sophia, uncomprehending, and returns to the conversation with her husband.

He nods at his wife. 'What about the baby?' he asks.

'Teressa can remain with Nanny or shall we take them both?'

'It's up to you,' responds Michael, not too fussed about whether the children come with them or not. He glances down at the newspaper spread-eagled across his lap and frowns at economic predictions of interest rate hikes. Michael presses his linen napkin against his thin, determined lips, pushes his chair back and stands up to leave.

Without any parental response, Sophia returns Bella to the pram, carefully tucking the small wool blanket around her, before kissing both of her cheeks. Bella is her best friend. They talk together, enjoying afternoon teas in the nursery or out in the garden. At night she often takes Bella to bed, resting her small arm over the doll as they sleep. Sometimes she dreams of having a baby just like Bella, with a smiling face, loving eyes and curly blonde hair. Her father's irritated tone interrupts her thoughts.

'Well?' Michael is only marginally interested in his distracted wife's response.

'We might as well take them both,' Abigail says glancing up at Michael. He gets up from the table and bends forward, briefly kissing Abigail on the forehead.

'I'll be back at four.' He retreats from the table, pulling out his cell phone and calling the chauffeur. 'Bring the car around Myles. I'm leaving in five.'

As he walks through the French doors into the great hall, his wife swallows her last mouthful and reaches for her cell phone. Sophia has left her pram and is standing behind her mother, listening.

'He'll be gone in twenty,' Abigail sounds slightly breathless. 'Sure. OK. I'll meet you there.'

As she clicks off the device, Sophia's voice intrudes. 'Where are you going, Mum?'

Abigail carefully places her phone on the white damask tablecloth beside her half-eaten breakfast and takes a sip of fresh orange juice.

When her mother doesn't answer, Sophia begs, 'can I come? Can I?'

'I won't be long,' she lies to her anxious daughter, 'and besides, Nanny says she'll take you to the park. As long as you're good.'

Some months later, Sophia recalls dozing on her bed during a warm afternoon worrying about her parents. She's no longer sure what day it is, and it no longer matters, but she remembers her father being overseas on business. Her mother is home alone with her two daughters. Maybe it's a Sunday as Nanny is nowhere to be seen. As Sophia drifts in and out of sleep, exhausted from swimming and playing with her younger sister in the garden, she hears her father's muffled voice. She sits up, listening.

He sounds close. Are Mum and Dad in the guest room? Why are they there? Sophia swings her body from the bed; her bare feet touch the carpet as she slowly tip-toes towards her closed bedroom door. It wasn't shut when she climbed into her bed for an afternoon nap. Mummy knows she hates the door being closed. Clasping it with both hands, Sophia struggles to turn the large metal doorknob, eventually opening the door. The voices are clearer now, and they aren't coming from the guest wing but from the spare room two doors along the corridor.

Daddy must be home. She smiles with excitement. He's got my present. I hope he remembered. He's forgotten a couple of times, but last week he promised. Elated, she runs down the hallway towards the spare room. She stops a few metres from the closed door. Dad hates it when she runs through the house.

Standing at the spare room door, Sophia presses her right ear against the painted finish, listening to muffled voices. Is that Daddy's voice? But there's also the distinct tone of her mother, giggling. They're having fun and chatting. Maybe Daddy bought Mummy a present too? Sophia uses both hands to turn the doorknob, easily opening the door this time.

To her surprise it's Daddy's friend Giles, naked in bed with Mummy. She stands inside the bedroom doorway, frozen in horror and disbelief. Giles Hamilton's head swings around and both adults scramble for the bedcovers.

'Uncle Giles! Are you mating with my mummy?'

CHAPTER 2

Wayward Years - 2003

'I wonder what my future husband is doing, right now?' Teressa asks as they head towards Bondi Beach on Saturday morning.

'Heavens. What made you think of that?' Sophia smiles with mild amusement, constantly astounded at the inane stuff her sister thinks about. Sophia's never considered marriage, but she plays along, anything to avoid bickering on such a lovely day.

Sophia moves with natural elegance, her abundant hair falling in waves across her shoulders. Fixated on maintaining a mask of polite discretion, Sophia rarely raises her voice. In contrast, her younger sister, Teressa is prone to angry outbursts of hysteria, if life isn't going her way. At sixteen, Sophia is aware of the sibling disparity, with rivalry shifting from mild battles between the pair to all-out war. Sophia practises the power of silence and clear-cut, unemotional utterances when dealing with her sister. As part of a truce, she agrees to take Teressa to the beach for an hour before she goes back to swotting for mid-term exams.

'Watch the guys on surfboards over there,' Teressa says excitedly, pointing at the small black specks of bodies on boards, rolling in on the surf. 'Look at them. Both our husbands could be surfers or maybe friends, and we don't even know them yet.'

Sophia snorts with contempt at her sister's naive ramblings. 'I won't be marrying any of them.'

'Well, I want a farmer or a businessman for a husband, and he's probably only seventeen and riding those waves.' Teressa points to the distinctive azure curve of the bay surrounded by hot powdered sand. 'Don't you think it's a bit weird to think about our husbands surfing those waves right now?'

Turning to glance at the ocean and across the crowds on the beach as they stroll along the grassy edge, Sophia responds with a broad smile. 'No, I just think you're a bit strange.'

Teressa falls silent, miffed by her sister's harsh assessment. Sophia stands still, peering more closely at the young girl beside her. Is Teressa related to her? With a brain full of air and a perspective on life so diametrically opposite. It isn't hard to see how Sophia can easily provoke an episode of angry sulking from the twelve-year old.

With a sigh, Sophia examines her younger sister's face. 'Sorry,' she says, wanting to avoid the inevitable. 'Let's not fight. I don't see a white picket fence and two point two kids in my future. But if you do, then why not?' She smiles disarmingly. 'You'd make a brilliant wife and mother.'

Teressa is immediately pleased. 'Don't you want to have children?' she asks.

'Of course, I do,' Sophia laughs distractedly, worrying about a doctor's appointment she has next week. 'But there's plenty of time and fun to be had before the serious business of being someone's mother. What a thought! Besides I'd rather adopt and give two unwanted children a chance than raise more humans on this overpopulated planet.' As the self-righteous words escape her lips, Sophia glances at Teressa, modifying her language. 'You know what I mean. I want to do some good in the world.' *Lofty idea,* her critical mother's voice speaks up.

Teressa sniffs, her mouth contorting into a crooked smile, but she has nothing more to contribute.

'Get us a place on the sand over there.' Sophia indicates the left side of the beach. 'I'll get the ice-creams but wait for me before you go in the water.'

'Yeah, definitely,' Teressa says as they separate.

Sophia finishes her high school year with straight As, bright, effusive and vivacious, everyone loves the teenager. A year later, Teressa attends the same private girls' high school. The teaching staff soon realise the younger sister bears no academic talent and absolutely no resemblance to her older sister.

Teressa struggles in Mathematics, English and Science, even with the advantage of private lessons in nearly all subjects, and both parents despair of their youngest daughter. She barely makes the grade in the second year when Sophia enters her first year of university. While Sophia has pity for her sister, she regards Teressa as a shadow person with limited personality and a strained sense of humour, favouring melodrama as a *modus operandi* to get her way. The only thing in common is their mutual love of hit songs from Savage Garden after they skyrocketed up the charts two years ago in 2001. Blasting music out from the living room while lounging around the outdoor swimming pool proves common ground, and a shared pastime they both enjoy.

Eight months earlier Sophia stopped menstruating, initially unconcerned, until her mother insists on seeing a specialist. 'You're not pregnant, are you?' Abigail's off-hand remark shocks Sophia, who rolls her eyes and doesn't respond.

After various medical interventions and exploratory tests, her gynecologist calls Sophia and her mother to his private North Shore rooms. It's a modern high-rise building with four floors of medical specialists. Each level has shared reception and waiting areas. Sophia and Abigail take the elevator to the third floor before being ushered into the specialist's clinical office.

After initial pleasantries, glancing from Abigail Huston, well-dressed and dignified, then to her daughter, bored and totally disengaged, Dr Kingsley, middle-aged and balding, appears distinctly uneasy.

Dr Kingsley leans forward peering over the top of his rimless spectacles. 'Unfortunately, I have some bad news,' he says, his voice hesitant with something more serious to impart. Abigail raises her eyebrows, mildly astonished.

'Have all the test results come in?' she asks with concern.

The doctor nods, glancing down at a few papers on his desk as the two women hold their breath. Now Sophia concentrates her attention too. His eyes move to his laptop, and he scrolls up and down a couple of times considering how he should broach the subject.

'First of all, most of your blood tests have come back negative,' he says with a weak smile looking from one expectant face to the other.

'And this means?' Sophia interrupts.

'That you're mostly healthy and normal,' he responds.

'Mostly?' Abigail frowns.

'Look there's a physiological issue here …' he states. 'And a hormone problem.'

'OK,' Sophia acknowledges as her mother sits speechless. 'Spit it out.'

'You were born with a condition called premature ovarian failure,' he explains. 'It means your ovaries no longer produce any viable eggs.'

Abigail gives an involuntary gasp.

'I'm sorry.' Dr Kingsley looks at the pair sitting across from his desk as if the diagnosis is his fault. 'Also, your estrogen levels are low which is part of this condition. There's an added complication too. Unfortunately, Sophia's uterus is abnormally shaped and tilted the wrong way.'

Abigail frowns, leaning in closer, processing the information. 'So, what does this mean for Sophia?'

He turns, looking directly over his glasses into Sophia's eyes. 'I'm afraid it means you can never have children. Even if you did manage to get pregnant, it's highly unlikely you could hold the pregnancy to full term.'

Abigail stares at Dr Kingsley's face as her hand automatically reaches out to her daughter, clutching Sophia's forearm. 'I'm sure there'll be medical advances,' she says to the doctor and as an afterthought adds, 'or she could adopt.' She turns to look at her silent daughter but can't tell if Sophia is upset or doesn't fully comprehend the impact of the conversation.

'Have you got any questions Sophia?' Dr Kingsley asks.

Sophia shrugs, and all three sit in the soundless space between awareness and understanding. Finally, Sophia speaks.

'I thought one day I'd get married and have a child or maybe adopt one or two,' she says almost inaudible. 'It doesn't matter.'

The adults in the room exchange a concerned frown above Sophia's bent head. Her hands clasp together and release a few times before resting in her lap.

After several sleepless nights, the ordinarily even-keeled Sophia erupts into anger, followed by a shouting match with her parents on Sunday morning. She convinces them that it's not the harsh fact she will never have children.

'It's the fact that I have no choice,' she shouts. 'There's no choice for me. One day I want to be a mother.'

Her parents' exasperation is magnified by their inability to salve her suffering and provide some support. She gets louder, as if dialing up the volume will create more empathy and understanding between her two useless parents.

Their solution is counselling, and after three drawn-out therapy sessions with a tired and uninterested psychologist, Sophia refuses to attend anymore appointments.

CHAPTER 3

Head Cold - 2003

Sophia had already fired off a text to Florian Fabre, her best friend, confirming her life would remain childless. During the same evening Florian calls as Sophia lies sprawled across her bed. On hearing his concerned voice, she stands, gently closing her bedroom door.

'Well?' he asks, 'what gives?'

'Excellent news.' Over the cell phone Sophia sounds like her regular effusive self. 'I'm cured!'

'I think the cure is worse than the crime,' he jokes. 'Who the hell wants kids anyway?'

'I don't. Well, not for a few more years,' she says. 'I mean I'd prefer to adopt when I'm older.'

'So … ahh …' Florian treads carefully, not sure how to progress the conversation. 'Are you saying you can have kids?'

'No.' She releases a strained laugh. 'The good news is that I can't! My offspring won't be burdened by my poor nurturing skills.'

She has never experienced failure. Her achievements and successes during her seventeen years are overshadowed, let down by her own imperfectly formed body. What had she done to cripple her reproductive organs? Beautiful on the outside but an inner rot, cells refusing to create a womb that works, ovaries distorted and ineffective. Why? Was this a price to pay for being attractive and intelligent? The full burden of sterility was so final. There's no wiggle room, no alternative option. There was no escape, no solution, not even a workaround. Grappling with the concept of never feeling a baby wriggling in her belly, a new life, a part of her own and the man she would love one day. An unforgiving bitter pill to choke down in tears late at night.

She studied hard to pass all exams, won the attention of those around her, was the leader of the high school debating club and sat on the school council. She's good at everything except the very reason females are born, to procreate, to be a mother, to raise children. She pulls her thoughts back to Florian. Suppressing her angst and the irony, always raving about saving the planet and her devotion to adoption. *Be careful what you wish for*, her mother's voice reverberates inside her head.

'Talk about a win-win!' Florian says.

'For sure!' Sophia responds half-heartedly, masking her inner distress. 'But I'll probably be away for a few days.' It's a lie. But she wants time to absorb the full impact of her diagnosis. She makes an easy excuse. 'I'm coming down with a damn head-cold.'

Florian smells the smoke before he touches the screen. 'Come on, Soph, you can level with me, you know.'

He listens to her talk as she berates her childless lot in life before cajoling her into being grateful for the good things evident in her self-indulgent existence.

'Look who's talking,' she challenges. 'Mr. Fabulous Fabre who can do no wrong. Life's pretty good to you too!'

'Hello?' Florian counters, 'I'm gay, so there's only fifteen percent of the population to play with. How's that good? You've at least fifty percent, so I say eat my damn shorts!'

She remains silent, and Florian decides to try another angle. 'Imagine being Schapelle Corby sentenced to an Indonesian jail for twenty years, for smuggling drugs she knows nothing about.'

'All right, I get it. Things could be worse. In a way I'm OK with being childless,' she says. 'I haven't had time to even factor kids into my world, let alone not have them before they're even a blip on the radar.'

'You've got a lot to live for Soph, lots to do and see. Don't let a thing like this hold you back.'

'It won't,' she replies resolutely. 'It merely confirms with the trajectory of my career, children aren't featured in my future. It's a sign I need to pursue a hard-core career,' she laughs falsely.

'Yeah, you've got much better things to focus on and get ahead while you're still young,' his chuckle sounds awkward.

The next day a transformed Sophia emerges from her locked bedroom. Florian has convinced her to be the driver of her own destiny. These recent events are the beginning of Sophia's challenging attitude towards her parents, who associate her poor reaction to her medical diagnosis. It makes perfect sense, to them, but for Sophia, there's something more subversive swirling around in her thoughts which creates a deeper undercurrent in her life.

CHAPTER 4

The Lie of the Land - 2004

Teenage Sophia easily deciphers the machinations of the men in her life. By the time Giles starts taking an interest in her, she has already learned plenty about how men operate by joining her father and his six-man crew in regular sailing sessions. Her intelligence and a quick wit make the seventeen-year old her father's favourite. She knows intuitively which levers to pull and constantly manipulates him to acquire almost anything she wants. Spirited and vibrant, young Sophia is a force of limitless charm.

Her father's 14-metre classic yacht, *Trojan Eagle*, won the Admiral's Cup several years ago, inspiring her to join the crew. It quickly becomes a regular sport, and she rarely misses any of the training sessions held on Thursday nights. Twin-masts with a triple-skin kauri hull, the Sparkman & Stephens New Zealand-designed boat stands out from the other competitors in its class.

The enthusiastic crew meet at the Cruising Yacht Club for training races in Sydney Harbour, preparing for the Australia Day Regatta. Initiated to mark the arrival of the First Fleet in Sydney Cove on 26th January 1788, the regatta attracts 168 classic and modern yachts, including historical replicas as the focal point of annual celebrations racing offshore in Botany Bay.

Sophia loves the competitiveness and the thrill of the ten-ton steel keel slicing through the ocean waves at a thirty-eight-degree angle. Fear and excitement mingle with the fresh sea air as they race ahead of the pack. With the stainless-steel gunwales submerged underwater along the port side, the crew cling to the higher side of the deck or lean out over the bow to balance the boat as it powers through deep water.

Racing against other yachts over the years exposes Sophia to the characteristic secretive signalling between sailing companions.

Being the only female onboard it is imperative she keep up with the action. She wants to be as good as any man, swift and responsive to the Skipper's every command. But often instructions were soundless and perplexing for the teenager.

In the beginning, she is at a loss to understand how each sailor knows precisely what the Skipper is thinking. Did they share some alien talent for Extra-Terrestrial Perception? What super silent sensors sent coded responses between each male mind? It was only with concentrated observation, on her part, she finally understood the secret exchanges between the male crew. This activity contributed to their highly proficient racing machine and success on the water.

'Leo,' her father shouts from the helm, squinting into the piercing sunlight, with the vast white sails billowing into the oncoming wind. The crew spring into position, gripping ropes, hauling in the sails, moving the boom and mainsail in symphonic unison. Then the finely tuned facial language kicks in. The lift of a left eyebrow and two men begin turning the double winches, grinding for their lives, sweat quickly forming on their foreheads, dripping onto the teak deck.

A subtle nod of the Skipper's head to the right and adjustments to the mainsail-traveller are made to maximise lift in the bracing breeze and swing the elegant yacht to port before tacking into the next leg of the race. Within seconds the huge yacht inches ahead of the others, comfortably establishing the lead position. Tension unites all seven crew as they push forward with every centimetre of sailcloth and length of uncoiled rope running hard, taut against the competing southerlies. Her father makes every intimate sign count towards maximising the win they almost always enjoy. This regular achievement fosters much good-natured banter with the crew in contrast to annoyance from their competitors after *Trojan Eagle* takes the whistle at the finish line again.

It takes about a year for Sophia to fully appreciate the universal signalling skill which she observes equally in the boardroom or during private functions. A lift of an eyebrow or an almost imperceptible nod, communicating volumes about sailing manoeuvres or favoured proposals at meetings or adding specific emphasis and direction during private discussions, while others remains oblivious. She quickly grasps men's silent language and soon deciphers each secret signal to her own future advantage.

She assumes some male behaviour lingers from the ancient Paleolithic Period when cavemen hunted in packs, and soundlessly communicated to ensure a good kill. They still do, she thought to herself with a wry smile. Sophia observes loosely affiliated groups of hungry stalkers at men's clubs and gatherings in bars. Silent interaction is still relevant in the predatory pursuit and chase during the contemporary hunt in today's crowded urban landscape.

It was around this time that one of her father's business associates and family friend, Giles Hamilton paid particular attention to Sophia. Uncle Giles always had a low-key presence in her childhood, but he now seems more interested in Sophia's opinions as she advances into her teenage years. She recalls a blurry image of him in bed with her mother many years earlier. The childhood memory of shocked expressions on both Giles and her mother's faces brings back the pain of her mother's infidelity. Sophia's heart aches with the cold realisation that her parents were always more interested in their private lives and lovers than in their own two daughters. The dynamics of her mother sleeping with Giles, a good ten years younger than her father back then, makes sense of her mother's surreptitious flirting with the man, beyond the earshot of her father but keenly observed by Sophia.

By the time she was ten, Giles seemed to ignore the Huston household, only attending rare family celebrations where she would exchange a few polite words with the man. What happened between Giles and her mother? There was scant contact with Giles during those interceding years. Was it a lover's tiff? Had her father discovered the pair as she had years ago? The lovers remained unperturbed and never discussed their affair with Sophia. Where was Giles? Her mother's answers were always off-hand, and she avoided any further discussion on the topic.

Giles was still a keen sailor with the same strength and endurance of his youth, even though he sometimes felt the full weight of his thirty-three years. He re-joined the *Trojan Eagle* crew and renewed his friendly banter with Sophia. Giles'

19

relationship with her father was healed, and the helmsman shook Giles' hand, pulling him in for one of those close bear hugs, laughing cheerfully. Glancing at her father's expression, she could tell that all was forgiven. Maybe one day she'll find out what drama had banished Giles from their lives for more than five years.

She watches Giles' fun-loving expression. Still good-looking with an open-faced charm and energetic wit, he comfortably held his own with the younger men on board. He meticulously maintains his firm muscular frame with daily bouts at the gym and evening runs often exceeding ten kilometres a day. Sophia could easily see why her mother found Giles so attractive all those years ago. His curly hair blowing wildly about his face enhanced his ageless appearance. His bright eyes were always smiling, even when his voice turned mildly irritable. Even-keeled Mr Hamilton was back in from the cold. Glad to have him on board again too, Sophia smiled, inwardly grateful for his natural charisma.

In his youth, Giles thought life was a game and women were a sport. Married several times, (at last count, three ex-wives), he still manages to fascinate women of all ages; a kind of sexual allure radiates from his charming attitude to life and love. His sultry voice and direct eye contact fools a woman into believing she is the only woman on the planet. Women flock to him at every public event. This ignites raging jealous outbursts from ex-spouses. In later years he learns to curb his engagement by keeping his hands firmly in his pockets.

CHAPTER 5

About the Boys - 2004

The relationship with Giles began innocently enough. 'What are you drinking?' he asks at the yacht club on Thursday night after another sailing win. The room is crammed with men, joking, laughing and enjoying heated discussions over the movement of sails, the building pressure of wind and the advantage of local ocean currents.

'Lemonade thanks,' Sophia says.

Giles frowns. 'Come on, we came in first. You have full rights to celebrate.'

She leans forward, grabbing Giles' shoulder, pulling his head down to where she sits. Above the noise in the crowded clubhouse, Sophia speaks into his ear, not wanting the humiliation of anyone overhearing.

'I can't drink. I'm only seventeen.'

He tilts back regarding her at arm's length. 'Who the hell cares? No one here does. Besides you could be at least twenty-five,' he adds with a broad smile.

She looks at him in silence, pulling a non-committal face.

'Are you telling me you don't drink?'

Sophia smiles. 'No. I drink,' she explains, 'but just not in public. I'm underage and don't want to get anyone in trouble.'

'What about a Sav?' he offers. 'No bastard here's going to dob you in, or they'll have to deal with me.'

Minutes later, he presents her with a chilled glass of white wine, brushing off the legalities of underage consumption.

'As long as you drink with an adult,' he grins, breathing deeply through his nose in a dismissive gesture. 'That's quite acceptable under the statute, you know.'

'You're very convincing with your persuasive argument to flout

Australian law,' Sophia says.

Ignoring the bait, Giles compliments her on her appearance, offering to take her to the beach with her sister, Teressa, so he can learn more about her interests, away from her distracted parents.

Giles Hamilton, an investor in her father's business, and for many more years, apart from the silent years of noticeable absence, is part of the Huston family. He watched her grow up into an elegant looking, intelligent teenager.

More recently he's been fantasising about Sophia, contemplating an affair with her. Initially, he dismisses the idea as too risky, given his business relationship with her father. But Giles enjoys her company, believing their sixteen-year age difference is barely noticeable in public. She makes him laugh and feel young. Being near Sophia invigorates him, making him alive with anticipation. He recognises how enamoured he is with Sophia, captivated by her charm and humour.

The following weekend Giles calls Sophia's cell phone.

'Feel like a coffee?' he asks unexpectedly. 'You mentioned wanting to work at the UN after you graduate ...' He hesitates. 'And I thought we could discuss it a bit more. I have a few contacts in diplomatic circles.'

'Wow. OK, that would be great.' At last, she has a chance of getting in front of someone with clout, a contact to pull strings and secure a position in the diplomatic corps. 'I have to take the dog for a walk,' she explains. 'Are you happy if he comes along?'

'A dog? That's news! How old is he and what's his name?' he asks with enthusiasm.

'He was only a two-month old miniature schnauzer,' Sophia responds. 'A rescue dog from the SPCA about three months ago. Such a sweetie. I can't believe he got dumped. His name's Loopy, a kind of bastardisation of the French word for *wolf*.'

'I see,' Giles says. 'It's so good of you to adopt a dog, but I thought your dad didn't like dogs.'

Sophia snorts. 'Yeah it was a battle of wills so you can tell who won the war,' she giggles. 'Is it OK to bring him?'

'Of course, no problem. I'll meet you at the dog park.'

While Giles and Sophia stroll side-by-side, engrossed in conversation, the fluffy cream and grey schnauzer runs off the leash, bounding freely over the neatly mowed lawns.

Giles is keenly interested in determining Sophia's sexual status, wanting to find out if she has a boyfriend and if they have slept together. But he registers it's not the kind of time or place for such penetrating questions. He considers potential ways to gradually nurture Sophia towards his direction, believing a little patience and selfless consideration may improve his chances. During their casual conversation, Giles braces for the right opportunity to ask more intimate questions in the hope of garnering closer contact.

'You talk a lot about this guy Florian,' Giles says and throws a small rubber ball for Loopy to fetch as they walk along the concrete paved pathway.

'Yeah, he's my closest friend,' Sophia says, distracted by Loopy skipping back towards them with the ball firmly clenched in his small jaws. 'I can tell him anything.'

'That's impressive. You mentioned earlier Florian's not your boyfriend,' Giles says.

'No,' she remarks without further explanation.

Frowning, Giles turns to look at Sophia's face. 'You must have a boyfriend by now,' he says, watching for a change in her expression.

Sophia shrugs. 'Nah. No one's interested in me. It's the story of my little life.'

'I find that very hard to believe,' Giles says, raising his eyebrows. 'Firstly, you describe your life as *little*. I would've thought a gorgeous girl like you would be hounded from morning 'till night.'

She sighs, glancing down at the ground.

'What is it?'

'Boys don't like me,' she says. 'I'm not sure why but they avoid me, and no one ever asks me out, except Florian. I've told some of them that Florian's my boyfriend, so they don't think I'm a complete loser.'

'Oh no,' Giles interrupts. 'Teenage boys have got no bloody idea. They must have rocks in their heads. Any full-blooded male,

24

and I count myself in that group, can see you're a lovely young woman. Surely, by now, they must've tried to get you into bed?'

'Compliments will get you nowhere,' she playfully chides. She had fantasised about Giles paying her hard cash for sexual favours. Sophia knew about his reputation with women, recalling his affair with her mother years ago. There was no doubt in her mind, he was sussing her out. So obvious. The way he was talking galvanized her into giving him his money's worth.

'Duly noted.' Giles grins, registering that she is no fool.

'One guy did try his luck.' She laughs. 'But he was the ugliest guy in the school. There was no way!'

They burst into laughter.

'Poor sod. So are you saying you're still a virgin?' Giles attempts to hide the astonishment in his voice.

'Yeah, I am,' she replies. 'So what? I guess it'll stay that way for a while.'

'It seems crazy. Maybe boys your age are overwhelmed and frightened of you.' She looks at him with surprise, and so he elaborates some more. 'Because you're way out of their league,' Giles suggests.

This is a concept she's never considered. Sophia falls silent as they walk on, and Giles continues throwing the ball. Loopy is already tiring and insists on holding the ball in his mouth instead of dropping it at Sophia's feet.

Sophia contemplates if Giles is playing her, asking unexpected questions, alerting her to his potential interest. She considers this option carefully and future implications – rich food for thought.

Eventually, the conversation resumes, and Giles continues listening to her teenage angst. He silently commits to assisting her, helping her navigate through these turbulent teen years. He convinces himself patience is a gift, and he will happily wait until Sophia is a little older.

CHAPTER 6

Parental Control - 2004

Sophia continues to cause upset on the home front and challenges her parents at every turn. To control Sophia's wayward conduct, Michael and Abigail Huston agree to restrict her finances. Her regular $800 weekly allowance is immediately stopped until she shows more decorum in her dress and more grace with her language. Her parents promise to gradually increase the money back up to the original weekly sum once she meets a list of acceptable behaviours.

This restriction on her allowance incenses Sophia. She believes it unreasonable and unjust, but no amount of negotiating or manipulating on her part makes one iota of difference. She riles against their demands, which further infuriates her parents.

'This is simply unfair,' Sophia states, struggling to keep anger from her voice.

'You'll get to learn life is unfair Sophia,' her father says firmly. 'Besides, you're virtually ignoring us and carrying on like a bit of a tart.'

'Whatever do you mean?' she replies, rearranging her facial features into a mixed expression of shock and surprise.

'You have to admit your dress sense has much to be desired. You're asking for trouble!'

'Quite frankly, my dear,' interrupts her mother, 'you looked like rape-bait in that skimpy outfit you wore last weekend.'

'Some of your conduct on the boat is cause for concern too,' her father interjects, trying to stick to the high ground and avoid an all-out battle between the family females.

'What are you talking about exactly?' Sophia demands, sensing rising humiliation at her father's accusations.

'You, flirting with Campbell on the boat last Thursday. He's almost twice your age, and it's embarrassing,' he retaliates. 'You're making a fool of yourself in public!'

Sophia's passive face belies the glint of intolerance and anger at the direction of their challenging conversation.

'I think the pair of you need to reconsider your focus on morals,' she announces. 'You talk to me about morality while you both indulge in a series of short-term unacceptable affairs. Your marriage is a joke, making this discussion redundant, don't you think?'

Her mother gasps and her father's eyelids flutter in shock. It was almost imperceptible, but Sophia feels confident she has them both on the ropes.

A sarcastic tone has crept into her voice as she carries on. 'Don't you two think moral fortitude should start at home?' She calmly shrugs her shoulders before grabbing her car keys and flouncing out of the front door.

During this same timeframe, Mr Hamilton begins lavishing Sophia with considerably more attention than is warranted. It makes sense for Sophia to make a play for Giles, to see if he will pay for her attention too. She saw a movie once, where a concubine in ancient Egypt virtually ruled the country through the money and status she derived from her relationship with the king. It didn't seem that inconceivable that Giles would pay her hard cash for favours enabling a work-around with her parents' tight purse-strings. She could have plenty of money and buy what she liked without their knowledge or consent. This plan had real appeal to Sophia.

One day when they are walking along the waterfront promenade with Loopy, she finds herself complaining bitterly to Giles about her parent's maltreatment and the unreasonable nature of their financial control.

'It's about power,' Sophia explains. 'They think they can regulate my behaviour, and I'll become more compliant under their financial control.'

'Well, Sophia, your parents, I guess, are at a loss and are trying

28

the age-old, classic money-control approach.' He grins. 'Money restrictions work for divorce, so why wouldn't it work with reining in your behaviour?'

'I've got other plans and intend to earn a living for myself,' she announces proudly, pulling herself up straight to face him.

Giles smiles, charmed by her energy and confidence. 'Please tell me you aren't going to take a job as a supermarket cashier or some waitress in a burger joint.'

'No way.' She laughs. 'I've much bigger plans than that!'

'I see.' He laughs with her. 'Let's hear them all. You now have me intrigued.'

'Compliments might get you somewhere,' she flirts, laughing.

'Really? Well, I may just try a bit *harder*,' he says, smirking at his innuendo as she laughs louder.

Giles is stunned with surprise; clearly, she's a virgin in body only. Sophia is a little more worldly-wise than he anticipates, and then he recalls the time the six-year-old caught him in bed with her mother years ago. Embarrassed, he blocks out the memory.

'What exactly are you planning then?' he asks.

'I want to pay my own way, and I guess you're aware that all is not well with my parents,' she says regarding the look on his face to see how far she should go. 'There's been a few marital conflicts, and financial issues with Dad's business.'

'I see,' he says, recalling several tense conversations with her father over the holding company's financials.

She rolls her eyes in mock disapproval. 'I'm going to look after myself. I don't need their money,' she says firmly. 'I want to earn my own.'

He nods, impressed by her determination. 'How do you propose to achieve this?' he asks.

'Let me put it this way, Giles, I'll do almost anything to earn my own money.'

'Truly?' he says in disbelief but is secretly excited by his prospect volunteering her services. 'Do you mean anything? Are you offering what I think you are Sophia? I don't think your parents would be too thrilled.'

'It's nothing to do with them. I need to earn money to enjoy my life without being beholden to their demands on my time and whereabouts.'

'Right.' Giles smiles again, contemplating his next move. 'Does this mean you could be exclusively mine, or am I reading too much into this?'

'You can read into it what you like, but if it's a private arrangement between you and me, well ...' Her voice trails off, and they both stop walking. Facing one another, she continues. 'I promise, Mr Hamilton,' she states boldly, 'if you pay me six hundred dollars a time, I'll happily be at your service.'

A rush of adrenaline powers through Giles' body as he considers the incredible opportunity she presents. This is far more than he could ever have imagined, and she's handing it to him on a platter!

Almost speechless, Giles hears his own voice say, 'OK.' He knows he needs to play this cautiously, needs to slow things down and find something to stall the conversation while he tries to gather his thoughts. Instead, bold words escape without his permission. 'Would you come to my bedroom?' he asks audaciously, unable to contain his excitement.

'Whatever do you mean?' Sophia's face transforms into complete shock, her mouth opens in disbelief. 'I'm talking about being a personal assistant,' she says, every word loaded with serious intent also conveyed in her rigid body language. 'Your comments are very inappropriate!' she states, pressing her lips together in anger.

Blood rushes into Giles' face, he feels heat moving up through his reddened neck. He battles to maintain a calm exterior. The thought of her discussing this conversation with her parents finally makes him gasp in rising panic.

'I'm so sorry. I don't know what I was thinking ...' Giles blurts.

Sophia's stony face is deadly serious, without a hint of any childish immaturity. 'My only requirement,' she stands tall, regarding him intensely, staring into his tormented eyes, 'is that our arrangement is kept strictly private and confidential between us.'

CHAPTER 7

Outrageous Proposal - 2004

She burst out laughing, not able to contain her serious pose any longer. 'Don't worry Giles, I'll never drop you in the shite, especially not to my ignorant parents.'

Her voice belies her youth. Sophia grabs back the power and control. 'Oh, and there's one small thing.' She pauses. 'Our agreement does not include sexual intercourse,' she announces with growing assurance. 'But obviously, I'm willing and able to perform anything else, you may wish, for a small fee.'

Giles Hamilton, now gob-smacked and simultaneously relieved, struggles with his sense of disbelief over-riding his excitement. He can't find the right words to express his delight at her incredible offer. Sophia holds her silence too, as Giles works through her outrageous proposal. After about two minutes strolling along the promenade, he stops and stands still beside her. He is the first to break the silence, turning to face her, his voice more serious and considered as if negotiating an investor contract.

'Exactly how do you envisage this working Sophia?'

'Well, it certainly couldn't take place in my home, obviously,' she states matter-of-factly. 'And I assume it couldn't happen in your home, with your wife and children under the same roof.' A faint flicker of a smile creases the corners of her voluptuous lips. Sophia knows how these things work. She has eavesdropped and spied on her parents most of her life, being privy to their clandestine arrangements with lovers over the years. It's simple.

'So, like everybody else involved in a clandestine affair, a hotel of your choice is the best option. Naturally at your cost.'

Breathless with anticipation and the effort of processing her words, Giles finally responds. 'Forgive me, Sophia, but I'm a bit taken aback. It's quite a lot to absorb and an intriguing proposal.'

She steadies her gaze directly into his blue eyes and smiles. She has the air of a woman who knows exactly what she's doing and has every confidence Giles will pay, in more ways than one, for the pleasure of her naked body.

Arrested by her daring, he notes that she has the same mischievous look on her face as his ex-wives. A momentary glimmer of concern graces his face as he realises Sophia's self-assurance is common among empowered women. Giles is a fluffy lap dog being brought to heel.

'I do appreciate what you're saying, and don't get me wrong, I'm indeed, very interested. I want to make sure you're clear about what's on offer and how this whole thing is going to operate. You use the word *affair*. Of course, it wouldn't be an affair. It would be a straight business arrangement which is fine with me, as long as that's fine with you?' As an after-thought, he asks. 'But why not have sex?' He's convinced once he's had her body in his assertive hands, she will be begging for more.

Sophia smiles, holding his attention, eyeball to eyeball. She can see he is serious, and she knows exactly what to say next.

'Giles, I'm no child, and I've known for some months you've been grooming me for this specific task. Let's stop pussyfooting around, pardon the pun, and get on with it. In terms of my virginity, I wish to keep it. As simple as that. I'm not willing to compromise the value of being a virgin … at this stage.'

Giles nods, understanding, but it won't stop him from trying. She pulls him back to the conversation again.

'It's a bit unsavoury to bring this up …' She hesitates. Giles raises one eyebrow, questioning, but doesn't say a word.

'What about protection?' she finally asks.

He nods. 'Yeah, I believe you can get pregnant from foreplay, you know.'

'Little chance,' she smiles demurely before glancing back up directly into his eyes. 'I'm sterile, so you're safe with me. But am I safe with you, Mr Hamilton?'

'Of course,' he says. 'I'll get a medical certificate if you like.'

She shakes her head, and with the formalities out of the way, he sighs with relief. Giles is over the moon with delight and excitement. 'How do you want to play this?' he asks.

'A strict business arrangement suits me fine too,' Sophia says self-possessed. 'And like all agreements, we need to review the terms and conditions regularly. I imagine as I grow older, I'll move on and don't want any upset or drama when the inevitable end takes place.'

She notes with some pleasure that Giles' face is a picture of absolute lust, masked and controlled, but she can tell he is spellbound, hanging on every spoken syllable she utters.

'If you agree to these terms, then text me the time and place, and I'll be there. But no more than twice a week. I only need six hundred dollars a week to cover my extra costs, my petrol and a few drinks over weekends. And remember, if I take on a boyfriend, you need to keep out of it. Ours is a private arrangement. I don't want anybody else to know, including any personal love interest, I may or may not have. Are you clear about this? Do you agree?' She turns away from him, ready to walk after Loopy, who has wandered some distance ahead.

Giles can't help letting out a small chuckle as he considers her bold demands, while they continue along the promenade. He still can't believe his ears.

'Sophia, you are beautiful, intelligent and incredibly savvy, but I never imagined I'd enjoy the luxury of this generous arrangement. I absolutely agree with your terms. Let me look at my calendar, and I'll give you a date, time and place now. If you change your mind, that's fine. But if you turn up, I hope this can be a regular engagement. Twice a week is perfect for me,' he says.

She regards him carefully and smiles, holding out her right hand. He clutches it, firmly shaking her hand and says, 'It's a deal then.' She nods in acceptance.

This agreement persists, and Sophia happily meets Giles Hamilton at several different five-star hotels scattered throughout the city. On one occasion they travel further afield, booking into an exclusive boutique bed and breakfast in the remote countryside outside Sydney for an overnight stay. During all the hours their naked bodies move together, Sophia remains the virgin while the older man fails in his best attempts to alter her sexual status.

To avoid any gossip or questions from nosey hotel guests and management, they contrive a credible story. Sophia becomes Giles Hamilton's *daughter*, humbly camouflaging their sixteen-year age difference. This proves to be a reasonably plausible explanation, satisfying most suspicious enquiries. They enjoy delicious dinners on several occasions, before returning to their private hotel for the enjoyable indulgence of her nakedness against his. They eat at the most expensive restaurants and dine on exotic seafood washed down with vintage French champagne. Sophia quietly listens and learns very quickly how to handle herself in the company of other well-heeled, savvy businessmen.

Giles can't get enough of her and begs Sophia on several occasions to meet him three times a week, which she refuses, reminding him of his verbal obligation. Giles quickly concludes it's unwise to push his luck.

Late one afternoon, naked in their luxurious hotel bed, Giles is face down, with Sophia straddling his back, massaging his shoulders and neck. She feels the tension in his body ease, as she reaches for more almond oil from the bedside table. Her hands move firmly over his skin, he closes his eyes and exhales. Within twenty minutes she has massaged his back and shifts her naked body on top of his upper thighs as she firmly works her fingers down his lower back, using her knuckles to smooth the rigidity along his spine. Using the heels of her hands, she works the strain from his muscles, her fingers gliding smoothly over his oiled body. She listens carefully to his breathing, confirming he is completely relaxed, so relaxed, she wonders if he's fallen asleep.

She gently wakes him up, intent on sharpening his senses, leaning her breasts forward, shifting her legs and moving her hands to the bed on either side of his torso. In this way the surface of her body slowly moves along the full length of his back, sliding herself up and down his almond oiled skin, her nipples hardening against him. His breath quickens. She smiles to herself amused at how Giles playing dead has encouraged her pace. She moves her body beside him, urging him to roll over onto his side, to face her.

'Sophia,' he breathes in a harsh whisper, kissing her mouth with

35

a familiar intensity. She responds, reaching her hand to his groin. He is already hard, and like a magnet, his member is drawn into her oily palm beseeching her for release. Not yet. She knows precisely what Giles wants and how he wants it. Snugly held and comforting, she begins to move her hand. Giles reaches for her too. She's already wet with expectation, and their breathing works in concert, slowly at first, then faster, breathless, gasping before they both moan with profound relief. She smiles at him, and he kisses her lips with quiet gratitude.

Both lay sprawled across the bed, content in the afterglow of mutual satisfaction without going the full distance. Sophia can't help joking about Clinton's legal defence making total sense.

'I did not have sex with that woman!' she mimics, laughing out loud. With her virginity still intact, she argues, Giles could therefore *not* be considered an adulterer.

'Umm, I wonder if that defence would work nowadays,' he smiles. 'Are you hungry?' he asks as Sophia giggles at the double meaning of his words.

Having consumed a salad for lunch, Sophia had complained earlier that she was still starving.

'So, you aren't going to become a vegan then?' he jokingly asks, rolling towards her under the white cotton bed sheet.

'I might,' she teases grinning at him. 'I think healthy eating maintains a robust body and an agile mind.'

'Well, maybe I should become a vegan too.' He chuckles.

'Just a thought, do vegans give head?' She frowns, and he laughs before she continues. 'Surely they can't if you logically follow their philosophy of never eating anything with a heart-beat.'

'Thank God you're a carnivore,' quips Giles, amused and still surprised how her mind seems to act in contradiction to her angelic-looking face.

She leaps out of bed. 'Have you seen the time? I've gotta go!'

Giles' head falls back on the pillows. Listening to her showering, he remembers how annoyed she gets with his persistent attempts to crack her unrelenting grip on her virginity. His original plan of taking full advantage of her has backfired. Giles holds a faint suspicion that he is being played. Snorting at his own pun, he recalls how she is so immovable on giving up her over-valued virginity.

Giles isn't sure how much longer he can resist before he grows bored and takes on another woman as his lover. There are plenty of keen candidates out there in the real world. But for some reason, he still can't let Sophia go. Her youthful energy and vibrant personality make him forget the limits of his body and transports him back to his teens.

He senses softening of his upper arms, imagines more creases surrounding his thirty-three-year old eyes which are not apparent to others. But he's beginning to feel uneasy about it being only seven short years before he hits the big four-zero. He expects his once solid six-pack will have morphed into a spongy rounded paunch. He wonders if his future one-pack belly will sometimes obscure his ability to see his own genitals.

He must stop himself thinking like this. He's still young. Of course, these thoughts only swirl around because Sophia is only seventeen. It's ridiculous. But those things aside, he's still attractive to the opposite sex and has most of his hair, not grey yet. Yes, she allows him to forget his age and personal shortcomings. She's forever tempting him with an innate addictive quality about her which he simply can't resist.

CHAPTER 8

Down A Peg - 2004

Much to their delight, Abigail and Michael Huston notice how their eldest daughter is suddenly cooperating. She's polite and easier to communicate with, happier in herself, making her trouble-free to manage. They believe it's their *tough-love* approach to financial control which brings Sophia to heel.

But Sophia has a sixth sense about privacy. She's cautious about spending her hard-earned cash on anything obvious like expensive shoes or clothes. Avoiding unnecessary attention from her parents or unwarranted interest from Teressa remain top of mind. Prying questions will force Sophia into more lies, complicating the web she has already woven. Her philosophy to keep things clean and straightforward, to garner enough money to buy the lifestyle she wants necessitates being polite and indifferent towards her parents and younger sister. They remain oblivious, so she is free to pursue her chosen path.

Teressa gradually grows into her expanding teenage mind, consciously scheming to manipulate those around her and considers ways of bringing Sophia down a peg or two. Waves of raw jealousy soak into Teressa's thoughts. Sophia's ability to attract anyone's attention, especially Uncle Giles', who seems to continually defer to her older sister in conversations, irritates the younger sister. Teressa is consumed by jealousy and resentment. She becomes more daring in her attempts to garner Giles' interest, and one day, when her *uncle* is sitting in the living room waiting for her father to return to the house, Teressa grabs her chance to wreak revenge.

'Would you like coffee?' she asks Giles who glances up from the newspaper he's reading.

'Thanks, Teressa. Yes. I'd love one. God knows how long your father's going to take,' Giles answers affably, shaking out the newspaper before scanning the young teenager. 'How are things going at school? Got a boyfriend yet?'

Teressa snorts. 'No. Not really,' she says innocently. 'But Sophia has an older guy from uni she's seeing.'

'Lucky Sophia,' Giles replies, slightly annoyed. While Teressa prattles on, he wonders at his resentful response. Why else would she mention confidentiality and then expect him to tolerate a boyfriend? The little minx. Playing him for a fool and using him as a source of income.

'Well, do you?' Teressa repeats again, interrupting Giles with growing exasperation.

'Sorry. What was that?'

'Do you take milk or want your coffee black?' Teressa asks with disarming politeness.

'A dash of milk, no sugar,' he replies, distracted.

'Anything wrong?' she asks.

'Nah, just hoping we win the Tri-Nations against the All Blacks. They say it's highly likely given we're hosting it this time. About bloody time too.'

Two days later, Giles calls Sophia. The conversation is abnormally restrained, and Sophia frowns, trying to fathom what could be wrong.

'I don't quite understand. Is there a problem?' Sophia asks.

'It's simple,' he repeats. 'I thought we had an agreement of trust and you would tell me if you were sleeping with another guy. It's none of my business but …'

'I'm not seeing anyone. Who told you that?'

He falters, not sure if it's worth exacerbating the situation and then relents, his annoyance at her behaviour overrides his good sense. 'Teressa mentioned your sex life to me over coffee a couple of days ago,' he announces, immediately regretting his exaggeration.

'She told you that?' Sophia's voice is electrified.

'Yes, and she implied, that she thought you and I had an unsavoury association,' he adds, deciding to test her integrity and

40

commitment to their arrangement.

Having pulled the pin with Sophia, he held his breath, waiting for the explosion.

'That bitch!' Sophia hisses into the mouthpiece.

CHAPTER 9

Listing to Port - 2005

Late one Thursday afternoon, Sophia joins the sailing crew down at the yacht club for another training session. Campbell, eight years older than Sophia, with thick dark hair, has already indicated an interest in their only female crew member. Sophia, wary this time after the confrontation with her parents, plays coy, almost ignoring Campbell's overtures as they motor out into the bay.

While the crew set the flapping sails, tidy the deck, secure the winch-handles and coil ropes ready for racing, Campbell considers his chances at making a move on Sophia. He gingerly steps across the deck, carefully positioning his feet as the boat rolls and pitches against the waves. He unceremoniously plonks himself next to Sophia on the starboard bow of the boat, their legs dangling through the wire railings with sneakers almost tip-toeing on the rising swell.

Her father switches off the diesel engine as a fresh gust of wind fills the mainsail. The wire stays clink against the masts to the musical rhythm of the restless breeze. The powerful underwater currents swiftly carry *Trojan Eagle* out into the darkening ocean as the boat heaves towards port. Silence falls as the skipper, Sophia's father with his feet spreadeagled, stands rigid on the foredeck clasping the stainless-steel wheel and squints into the distance looking for the racing start-line in the fading light.

'Over there!' shouts Campbell, his arm outstretched, a decisive finger pointing towards the starting buoy rising and falling on the ocean tide.

'Roger,' yells Michael Huston, turning the chrome wheel and realigning his sights. One eye momentarily on his daughter notes her apparent disinterest in Campbell for a change.

'Had any luck with those job applications to the government?' Campbell asks innocuously. 'Overseas trade missions and diplomatic corps will be screaming out for someone with your … er …multi-lingual skills.' He leers mischievously.

'Nah, apparently not,' Sophia responds, cool, calm and ever so collected. Somehow Campbell has lost his appeal. 'I'll have to wait until I graduate. Apparently, there's a long waiting list, and the embassies very rarely have vacancies.'

'A girl like you could get a job doing anything,' Campbell responds enthusiastically.

'Umm, maybe,' Sophia says, looking out towards the moving horizon. 'I want to earn well and get ahead in the world. Not easy when you're my age.'

'I know a couple of mates,' Campbell winks at Sophia. 'They could keep you gainfully employed in the meantime.'

She turns to face him, and he plants a full kiss on her mouth. She pushes him backwards with both hands as he fumbles to keep his balance.

'What do you take me for? You jerk,' she shouts above the roar of the violent wind. His lustful expression confirms she has been a fool. What an idiot to have flirted with Campbell in the past few weeks. He had made it plainly obvious that he wanted sex for his good favour. Dad's right. It is as if a veil has been removed, an opaque bucket from her head, allowing her to truly see, for the first time, the brutal, lecherous transaction Campbell represents. She fleetingly glances towards the helm to make sure her father has not seen the incident; the mainsail obscures the pair, and her father is concentrating his gaze at the next tacking mark.

Anger rises into Sophia's throat, as Campbell, rejected, skulks towards the bow of the boat and joins in a conversation with two other crewmen. What is he saying? It's impossible to tell. She watches the three men and wonders if Campbell, like Giles, can afford her. She gives a shudder. Campbell, uncouth and crass, is definitely removed from any potential client list.

CHAPTER 10

Sister Teressa - 2007

Sophia is sprawled across the sofa in the family room watching a local documentary recapping the Dr Muhamed Haneef affair. Wrongly accused of being involved with terrorists who attacked the Glasgow Airport earlier in 2007, Haneef is going to be deported back to India.

'Can you believe this?' Sophia turns to her mother, texting on her phone in the armchair opposite. Abigail lifts her head, looking blankly at her eldest daughter.

'Mum. The Glasgow terrorists. You know?' Sophia waves her arm towards the sizeable flat-screen television hanging flush on the wall. 'Apparently one or two of them are Haneef's cousins, so we get heavy-handed with a doctor living here with no criminal history? It's crazy. We're no better than terrorists ourselves. Haneef works bloody hard in the local hospital and has no criminal record, but they treat him like dirt. They step up, cancel his visa and arrest him without charges. It's unfair. It's insane.'

'Yeah, you get that these days,' Abigail says dismissively and walks from the media room. Sophia watches her mother leave, understanding that while she is graduating at the end of the year, she will still be forced to remain living under the same roof as her parents. How long was it going to take for her to accumulate enough money to move out? Her parents couldn't show less interest if they tried. She sniffs dismissively, attempting to suppress repetitive thoughts and avoid rising frustration. Patience. It's a waiting game, and in time Sophia knows she will enjoy a life of her own without their continual interference.

At the same time, Sophia hears voices, people talking in the entryway. Sophia mutes the television, straining to listen to the conversation between her mother and someone else.

'Darling, so pleased to meet you.' Her mother's fake voice, rich with platitudes, is the first Sophia deciphers.

A deeper voice responds. 'I'm very pleased to meet you too, Mrs Huston.'

'Please call me Abby.' Her mother's voice sliding like oil over the conversation. 'We don't stand on ceremony here, Ben.'

Rising from the couch, Sophia strolls into the entryway, and Teressa immediately introduces Ben Wilson, her first serious boyfriend, to her older sister. He's in his final year of college. Ben is a handsome, shy and anxious eighteen-year-old, frequently glancing down at his own large feet, shifting from one to the other when introduced to her father.

Teressa has made herself fair game. Sophia bides her time until she can wreak revenge on her wayward sister's interference and lies. Here it is, right under her nose, a boy for Sophia to torment and teach sixteen-year old Teressa a memorable lesson.

Taller than both sisters, Ben's athletic body belies his quiet, unassuming attitude. Dark wavy hair encircles his pale skin, and Sophia is sure she can see his thick brown eyelashes blink as he surveys the great hall. They stroll outside and sit on the adjacent terrace enjoying early evening drinks before dinner.

Sophia instantly assesses Ben as having further potential for closer inspection. Teressa reaches for Ben's hand and walks him to the edge of the terrace overlooking the manicured lawns as Abigail and Sophia listen to Michael lecture them about the limitations of the electoral system. Sophia has already glazed over, struggling to restrain waves of boredom from registering on her face.

She glances behind her father's nodding head, at the young couple several metres away, quietly talking. It's evident Teressa is besotted with the boy. More to the point, what is he doing with Teressa? Her sister appears bland, a pale dust jacket to the sleek black slacks Ben wears for the evening. Her sister barely wore make-up. Careless at the very least if she expects to keep Ben at her side. Handsome Ben, lacking in confidence, his broken inner workings generating a need fulfilled by her fragmented feral sister.

Sophia recognises the opportunity to play the game she and Florian so happily engage in. Like a tiger in the wild, she can now

48

single out her prey. What a high target Ben makes providing the opportunity to torment her sister. Too easy. An unexpected opportunity. Sophia stands and carries the bottle of wine from the table and saunters towards the engrossed love birds. Within seconds she places her body between her sister and Ben.

'I can see you two need a top-up.' She smiles agreeably from one face to the other as they automatically hold their empty wine glasses towards Sophia for a refill.

'Thanks.' They both nod at Sophia before taking a sip.

'Any plans for university next year?' she asks, concentrating on fresh-faced Ben.

His eyes flicker with surprise. 'I'd like to study oceanography,' he says with growing confidence.

'Why?' Sophia asks, finding his answer unbelievable, unless she has misjudged his silence as ignorance when, in fact, a genetic inability to communicate indicates a brilliant scientific brain pulsating behind those bovine brown eyes.

'I want to help the planet, and I love fishing,' he blurts, caught off guard. Was he the kind of person who was ever on guard? He struck Sophia as a go-with-the-flow kind of guy. No drive or ambition, and yet his words conflict with her initial assessment.

Sophia glances at her sister's anxious expression, a warning in her eyes for Sophia to watch her step. 'Fascinating,' Sophia says, glancing back at Teressa who takes the gap.

'We're going for a walk around the garden,' Teressa announces, grabbing Ben's elbow and directing him to the wide paved stairs down into the garden. 'Can you text me when dinner's ready?'

'Sure. Have fun,' Sophia smiles with wide suggestive eyes.

Teressa ignores the implications and moves as far away as possible from her conniving older sister.

Later, during dinner, as they all sit around the dining table, Sophia snatches every opportunity to gaze directly at Ben, smiling and asking several innocuous questions in a carefully modulated voice, interspersed with her lilting laughter.

'Do you have any brothers or sisters?' Sophia asks, smiling at Ben sitting opposite.

'An older brother,' he responds.

'I guess you two are pretty close.' Sophia tries to encourage the shy teenager to talk more about himself.

'Sometimes. He's setting up his own business.'

'That's great.' She smiles warmly. 'What type of business?'

He hesitates, searching for the right words and sensing increasing anxiety within himself and also radiating from Teressa sitting next to him. 'It's online retail. I sometimes help him with stock and freight in the holidays.'

'That's good,' Sophia coos.

'So you must get on reasonably well with your brother if you manage to work together,' Abigail interrupts.

Sophia leans back in her chair, as the conversation moves around the table; finally, her eyes drift to Teressa's reddened face. Sophia's unwarranted focus on Ben is irritating her younger sister. It doesn't stop there. During dessert, Sophia's conversation continues to saturate the young man with flirtatious charm, much to the ire of tight-lipped Teressa who silently seethes with rage at Sophia's manipulative tactics.

CHAPTER 11

Dearest Sibling- 2007

Later that evening when Ben disappears home, Teressa flounces off to her bedroom without a word. Sophia takes the opportunity, knocking tentatively on her sister's bedroom door. Teressa opens the door, reluctantly allowing Sophia into her luxurious double bedroom.

'What exactly do you want?' Teressa demands, her words clipped, still miffed at Sophia's flirtatious tactics.

'My, my, so very tetchy,' Sophia says, her eyebrows raised and lips in a sarcastic grin. It was apparent to Sophia they both shared the same mother, but it was more evident than ever, her younger sister must have a different father. Teressa is so utterly unlike Sophia in every way. It would be no surprise to learn the genetic score didn't quite add up between the pair.

'How the tables turn,' Sophia says. 'I only came in, dear sister, to ask how you managed to meet that gorgeous looking Ben boy.'

'It's none of your business!' Teressa shoots back, already angry at the way her boyfriend seems so enamoured with Sophia.

'Well, dearest, it is now that I've met him. I mean, who could ever forget him?' Sophia says, ratcheting up the torment. 'Remember darling, all's fair in love and war.'

'So, it's a war you want?' Teressa spat at her confident older sister, 'or shall I tell our parents about your raging sex life with Mister high-society Giles Hamilton?'

Sophia pulls herself up tall and sneers down at her shorter, plainer, plumper younger sister. 'Don't be ridiculous!'

But Teressa's small-rutting, animal instincts can tell she's hit a nerve. There's certainly something there, some seed of unease in Sophia's expression.

'You seem to spend an inordinate amount of time with dear

51

Uncle Giles,' the younger sister scoffs. 'What do you think everyone is saying? One of my friends saw you having dinner with him and told me you were Giles' *daughter*. His daughter? Are you kidding?'

Sophia hesitates, regarding her sister as a risky provocation.

'Try your damnedest,' she says with a calm, measured, coldness. 'Gossip is rife, and it's an absurd suggestion. Do you think I'd even look at a man that old? He's in his thirties, almost twice my age!'

Teressa considers the reality of her suggestion. 'For once I'd like to put you in your place,' she smirks. 'Back off or I'll cause more trouble for you than mere gossip.'

'Nothing you can do will make the slightest difference to the inevitable outcome.'

'We'll see!' Teressa says, desperately wanting to maintain the upper hand.

'Why are you bothered? Your trite little affair with Ben is meaningless!' Sophia can't help belittling Teressa. 'I'm very aware of your lies. Did you think for one moment it wouldn't come back to me?'

Her younger sister's bottom lip trembles, and tears brim into her eyes. She is no match for Sophia. 'Get out of my room, you selfish bitch,' Anger and frustration flushes her face and stings the air between them.

'Remember darling sister, you get to have children and I don't!' Sophia says, hardened by the reality of her future childlessness. Comments like this prove valuable capital, leveraging her sister back into second place. A painful lesson for her younger sibling to swallow.'

Teressa falls silent, blinking back tears and biting her lower lip. 'That's no excuse. Get out!'

'You'll always be on the back burner.'

Sophia turns on her heels and strides from the bedroom, gently closing the door behind her. She thought of slamming it hard, rattling the door frame and echoing the anger, downstairs into the lounge where her parents sit oblivious. But Sophia is never predictable.

A week later Teressa's best friend tells her about seeing Sophia with Ben in the back of a parked car on the previous Saturday night. Infuriated, Teressa tackles Sophia when she returns home in the evening.

'Keep your fucking voice down,' Sophia says in a harsh whisper, clutching her sister's upper arm while trying to march her down the hallway towards their bedrooms. Fortunately, the sisters' rooms are positioned on the opposite wing from their parents which assured them some privacy.

'Think about it,' Sophia states in hard staccato clusters as if instructing a wayward child. 'Ben was so easy to pick off!'

Teressa yanks her arm free from her older sister's grip. 'Who the fucking hell do you think you are?' Teressa challenges.

'Someone with a few more clues than you have!' Sophia shoots back inflaming Teressa's hysteria. Sophia almost frog-marches her sister into the wide corridor, leading to her own bedroom. She attempts to muzzle Teressa's loud, over-active response.

The battle lines are drawn again, but little is resolved. Within five minutes, the younger sister screams in frustration and flees from Sophia's room, slams the door behind her and runs to the sanctuary of her own bedroom.

CHAPTER 12

Magnetism - 2007

With Sophia's rocky teenage years behind them, her parents congratulate themselves on their exceptional parenting skills. Their worthwhile investment in an exclusive private girls' school education has finally paid off. Sophia is convinced her career and future success is guaranteed. Full of enthusiasm, she sets her heart on being a translator for the United Nations or working in the Australian diplomatic corps. She charms her parents with future job prospects and becoming a wife to an ambassador which delights them both.

'I could travel the world, meet interesting people and get to understand different cultures and languages,' Sophia explains, looking from one parent's delighted face to the other.

'For this reason,' she reveals,' in keeping my future options open, I'll graduate with an A-grade pass in Japanese, Dutch, French and Italian languages. The pleased expressions on her parents' faces sealed her determination to exceed expectations.

'I'll be top of my class,' she says with confidence. Both parents silently applaud one another with an exchanged expression of triumph, having little doubt Sophia will apply herself with every fibre of her being. Keen to eventually cut the feted ties of family bonds and suffocating wealth, she single-mindedly applies herself to ensure success.

For the past few years during annual university holidays, her father has generously sent Sophia overseas to Europe and Japan, giving her every advantage.

'Immersion in different languages, countries and cultures,' Sophia explains, 'gives me the best chance of speaking like a native-born local.' Sophia's parents beam with gratification. Finally their eldest daughter will contribute dignity and pride to the family name.

'I'll support anything to help Sophia enter into the diplomatic corps,' Michael tells his wife later that night.

Within two years of her university study, Sophia speaks in the vernacular of all four languages, easily picking up slang and becoming completely multi-lingual. She stays in private homes in Amsterdam, Utrecht, Paris, Avignon, Rome, Verona, Tokyo and Osaka. Each summer holiday Sophia works hard on building relationships with locals, some were colleagues of her father's and his business associates, others were complete strangers, entranced by the young woman. It isn't long before she is worldly-wise and able to hold her own in any situation and conversation.

A major bonus from her university years is the chance meeting with her old school friend Florian Fabre, a gay student who shares her Italian class. This tall reed-like Adonis marches around the university campus dressed in skin-tight black denim, leaving nothing to the imagination. Favouring flamboyantly coloured body-hugging shirts and exotic Arabic designed jewellery, Florian stands out from the crowd. Every female crossing his path gazes at the blonde-haired young man with unbridled adoration, but he remains utterly unaware.

At first, they share revision exercises, listening to recordings of Italian lectures and repeating foreign sentences back to one another, amid laughter at questionable pronunciation.

During the gruelling weeks of study during the last semester, swotting for final exams and hurriedly completing assignments, Florian and Sophia cement a much closer friendship.

'We need an emergency word,' Sophia suggests one morning after the last Italian tutorial as they walk across the concrete paved quad on campus. By the time they arrive at the university cafeteria she is grinning broadly at her perplexed friend.

'You know, when one of us says the word, we'll know to make moves to escape from the conversation or the situation.' She peers into Florian's puzzled face. 'We need the kind of word that you don't often say, but you can weave it into normal conversation.'

He shrugs, placing two coffees on the table in the student lounge, but is already happy to play along. 'What kind of word or phrase do you mean?'

Sophia leans back on her chair and gazes into the distance behind Florian's head.

'What about, *congress tart*, she says with bravado. 'It's crazy, but it would stand out as an alert if one of us said it and no one else could figure out any coded meaning.'

Florian bursts into laughter and several students at the next table glance over at the pair. 'How the hell do you work *congress tart* into a normal conversation?' he asks, bewildered, still chuckling at her madness. 'And what the hell is that kind of tart anyway?'

'It's just a name for a small pie. I love them. Almond and raspberry cake mixture in a shortbread-type base.' She watches Florian subconsciously licking his lower lip. 'I'll bake you some one day.'

'Yeah right!' He chuckles. 'So how do I weave this into an emergency conversation Soph?'

'OK,' Sophia hesitates. He can see the cogs whirring inside her mind.

'Say we're at a gathering and I'm stuck with two other couples who are waffling on and I want to move onto to someone else. You know, there's a fascinating man on the other side of the room and I need an introduction.'

Florian inhales, quickly visualising the scenario. 'Yeah,' he says slowly, watching Sophia closely.

'That congress tart is the best I've ever tasted,' she says exulted by her efficient delivery. 'I'm going to order another congress tart for your birthday.'

Florian frowns. 'In a random sentence like that?'

'Well, no, I'd normally make some initial comment about the food and then roll out the congress tart,' she smiles innocently.

'Good. You keep the emergency phrase in the first half of the sentence so it immediately puts me on red alert!' he laughs. 'I'm still not sure if this is ever going to work.'

CHAPTER 13

Stranger Danger - 2007

For the first time in her life, Sophia feels safe to say whatever's on her mind. Her trust solidifies with Florian, so does the depth of their shared understanding. Neither has sexual desire for the other, so it is a perfect friendship, without expectations and completely unconditional. Sophia is relieved there are no emotional or financial demands from Florian. She loves him like a brother, someone she can always depend on to rescue her from any tricky situation. Strangely he makes it easier for her to take risks because she firmly believes he will always have her back. Sophia knows they both understand and accept one another's boundaries. It's a relaxed, comfortable and uncomplicated friendship, which she will value for the rest of her life.

With a similar take on the world, the pair become close confidantes of one another. There's something about her that attracts Florian. He can't quite nail it down but soon realises there's an unusual emotional detachment about Sophia, a remoteness he finds appealing. She never gets overly excited or upset or even angry unless extremely provoked. He likes this even-keeled, intelligent young woman.

In their final year at university, Sophia begins to open up to Florian about her life and the struggle she has at home with her family and particularly her parents. It's easy for Florian to listen and advise. He offers homespun psychology during their discussions, explaining that her state of mind reflects her life experience, and is a response to the emotional rollercoaster she's already lived.

As Sophia grows older, she becomes more striking, but Florian finds her even more intriguing to talk to. She makes razor-sharp observations with an acerbic wit delivered with astonishing charm.

Her intellect is beyond anyone he has ever met. Florian shows enormous respect for her opinions and her burning desire to take on the world.

Sometimes on a Friday or Saturday night, the pair meet in a local bar and enjoy a couple of drinks together. Occasionally a young stud in the room garners enough courage to approach Sophia. Some are arrogant and cocky, believing every girl will breathlessly accept any advance, while others are drawn to her angelic beauty, desperate to hear her voice.

One evening a tall man in his mid-twenties saunters up to the two friends standing at the bar. The unexpected stranger shifts his feet, slightly uncomfortable, before interrupting Sophia.

'Sorry to bother you both, but I want to say you are the most beautiful creature I've ever seen,' the young man blurts out to an uninterested Sophia.

Florian has observed this scene play out numerous times before and takes a step back allowing Sophia to respond. She stares at the interloper and says nothing.

The stranger continues anxiously. 'Can I buy you another glass of champagne?' He smiles disarmingly.

'No, thank you,' Sophia responds firmly.

On some occasions, the culprit nervously hovers nearby, not quite sure what to do with himself. Florian steps up, suggesting he move along, after explaining the girl is with him. Instant confusion suffuses the stranger's face. Florian's colourful attitude and appearance have already convinced everyone in the bar that he must be queer.

'Come on, honey,' Florian admonishes the young imposter. 'Time to move along. This gorgeous young woman is with me.'

'Ah … are you her boyfriend?' Some question, their eyebrows raised, incredulous.

A slight smirk on Sophia's lips replicates the mischievous glint in her blue eyes, a voyeur in her own tactical game of life.

'I'm her special friend,' Florian announces with sarcastic emphasis. 'And I'm a boy, but I'm happy for the two of us to share a drink together if you like, sweetie.' Florian leans in towards the male's face, making it perfectly clear with his penetrating brown eyes he's capable of dating any man.

This often proves to be the fatal straw for any wayward suitor. Later the pair giggle, laugh and carry on drinking, dissecting the evening's incidents at the bar. They often gossip in Italian to avoid drawing anyone else into their conversation and confidently express absolutely anything they like without prying eyes and ears. A public display of this nature usually frightens any other would-be lover from attempting to communicate with the gorgeous young Sophia.

For her part, Sophia is often oblivious to the surrounding adulation of the male population. She knows she has magnetism, and if Sophia puts her mind to it, she can easily make any man compliant. But at this stage of her life, she isn't fully conscious of how far she can ride this personal gift-horse. As the years trudge on, Sophia leaves a host of broken hearts in her wake. But for now, her haughty, no-nonsense attitude combines nicely with tight-fitting, sexually advantageous clothing, giving her the upper hand and continuously drawing attention to herself.

Florian remains astounded at her ability to flirt with stealth, wordlessly using her eyes and the upper half of her body, sometimes even her feet, to entice the attention of an innocent man to worship at the altar of Sophia Huston.

CHAPTER 14

Game On - 2007

'That's incredible,' Sophia says between mouthfuls.

'What is?' asks Florian, pressing pause on the remote.

'That Haneef guy. The Muslim doctor. He's been awarded compensation. A substantial amount. Whatever that means.'

'Yeah well they treated him badly, racist stuff I reckon,' Florian says as Sophia nods, glancing back at the flickering television screen.

'Lucky it's been kept confidential or the government would have Joe Public queuing for pay-outs,' she comments.

'How long has this guy had to wait?' Florian asks.

'I think it happened three or four months ago,' Sophia responds, taking another bite from the roasted chicken leg held in her fingers.

'So all that stuff about him being a terrorist or a *risk* of being one because of some cousins is straight bullshit? Want another drink?' Florian asks raising his glass.

'I said it was bullshit back then and I'll say it again. That poor guy lost his job, his reputation and think about all the media hype and emotional stress. Yeah, pour me another one.'

During the final months of university Florian and Sophia develop a predatory drinking game. They often share a drink or two on a Friday night at a favourite local bar. Noisy with crowds chattering and laughing above the music, the large open-plan bar room is crammed to the rafters with drinkers relaxing after a long hard week. On entering through tall double doors, Florian scans the assembled revellers and considers a potential victim on the far side of the bar. He immediately knows this unassuming man will prove a challenging target for daredevil Sophia.

Florian singles out the forty-something, drab-suited businessman who wears a wedding ring. There is no doubt the target is married and evidently sits next to his wife at a table directly in their line of sight. The couple are engrossed in conversation with friends. He observes their lips almost touching as they try talking above the clamour. The man's paint-brush moustache sends a shiver down Florian's back, but this doesn't stop him testing out how far Sophia will go.

Sophia orders their drinks as they take up positions along the highly polished timber bar.

'See that guy over there in the corner.' Florian indicates moving his head slightly to the right. 'The one sitting with his wife in a grey-spotted dress. Let's see if you can reel him in.'

Sophia leans forward. 'Too easy,' she says, her mouth against his left ear.

Florian gasps with delight. 'I'd go straight for you, darling,' he grins. 'But I don't think Mr Moustache over there is gonna be easy. Check out the ring on his companion's left hand. Let's see if your unrivalled magnetism is strong enough for this minnow.'

'Game on.' She giggles, stepping away from the barstool. 'Carry on talking to me while I kick-off the match.' She smiles persuasively, an impish glint in her eyes.

He launches into a conversation about shoes and brands that work and why. Sophia moves to the side of her friend, adjusts her expression and appears slightly bored. Her body language conveys a distracted and uninterested demeanour. She peers around the noisy room until her eyes rest on the selected victim. He doesn't notice her at first, but within seconds he's looking straight at her. She smiles openly, her eyes signalling a more enticing story.

His distracted wife, flat-chested after collective years of breast feeding three children, continues chatting to a woman opposite. Sophia immediately registers the husband's attention. His mouth smiles, imperceptible to everyone else in the noisy bar, apart from Sophia, who indicates instant recognition. Has the target acknowledged her? It's difficult to tell. Looking away, back towards Florian and nodding as if she is part of his conversation, she glances up directly into the man's staring face. Now confirmation is absolute. The brief flicker in his eyes gives open affirmation. Sophia lifts the wine glass to her lips and slowly takes a sip without moving her eyes from his face.

The man's wife pulls her beige cardigan across her wash-board front, and says something to her husband, chatting briefly, before swinging back to the original conversation with her friend. Sophia touches the side of her hair and slowly drags a few stray strands behind her ear. All the time, she holds his gaze and smiles at the stranger. He is utterly mesmerised, and she knows it.

She whispers to Florian, 'the fish is on the hook.'

Sophia walks away, down towards the other end of the bar almost out of her target's sight, delicately clutching her empty glass. She stands casually at the bar, waiting to be served. It could take a while. Several thirsty patrons huddle a couple of metres from her, desperate to pay for the next round. Sophia places an empty glass on the surface of the bar. With her back now to the man, she waits, but he makes no attempt to walk across the crowded room. This fish requires a little more encouragement.

Sitting at a long wooden table on the opposite side of the jam-packed bar is a boisterous throng of sports fans celebrating a win. Their deafening laughter and noisy chatter are no hindrance to secretive Sophia's silent gestures. Her victim understands and responds, acknowledging her with a subtle lift of an eyebrow. Her well-honed predatory instincts are confident he has deciphered her communication. All doubt dissolves between them both, as Sophia's eyes continue to tease out more flirtatious signals to her naive male target. Both hearts race a little faster but each for entirely opposite reasons. Sophia desperately wants to win the game and prove herself to Florian.

She turns back to the bar, letting her prey stew for a few minutes. When she's sure his frustration is peaking, she swings around again, facing him before taking a step away while keeping one hand securely resting on the bar. She looks at him while her right-hand clasps her gold chain necklace, and with her thumb and forefinger she gently strokes the delicate gold pendant. She smiles at the people around her. She dare not look at Florian, several metres away, leaning on the bar, appearing to ignore her, or she risks bursting into uncontrollable laughter. Taking a sip from her fresh drink, Sophia gently moves her beautifully manicured fingers

65

up and down the chain-links of the pendant. The weight of the oval gold locket allows it to fall enticingly between her breasts. She slowly caresses the chain several more times, seemingly distracted as she surveys the crowd.

Her male victim's smile immediately evaporates. She can tell, from the corner of her eye, even at this distance, that he is breathing a little harder and faster than usual. His wife stands up from their table, and Sophia glances back down at her half-empty glass when the barman offers her another refill. She nods, aware of the air displacement against her skin as the woman walks briskly behind her, towards the bathrooms at the back of the crowded bar.

Within seconds the fish is not only on the hook but miraculously finds himself standing right next to this angelic-looking beauty. The fact that Sophia is way out of his league doesn't cross his mind for a moment. On the contrary, he believes she is obviously smart enough to notice a stud when she sees one. She clearly indicates, out of this entire crowd, she wants to get to know him better. He's not surprised by her blatant invitation.

'Hi there. You look a little bit unhappy standing here all by yourself,' the strange man says smiling, knowing he has to quickly get her name and phone number.

Sofia smiles at the interloper. 'Before you ask. Yes, I do come here often.'

'Well, now we've got that sorted,' he says, mildly amused, 'may I offer you a drink?'

'That's very generous. Thanks, but I've already ordered,' Sophia says as the barman places a tall glass of vodka and orange juice on a folded paper napkin in front of her.

'Can I have your number?' he asks nervously, looking behind Sophia, at the bathroom swing doors on the back wall at the opposite end of the bar. His wife will surge back into the room at any moment, a tsunami to destroy his best-made plans.

'No,' she says firmly. 'I'm here with my boyfriend.' She casually waves her open palm towards Florian, who stands nearby, watching them both. Amused, Florian raises his eyebrows, tilting his head with a confirming grin.

'You're with him?' asks the confused man.

66

Sophia nods. 'Yes. I'm sorry.'

Bewilderment merges with disappointment, contorting his face as he takes a step backwards. At the exact moment, his wife suddenly appears through the bathroom swing doors and walks right up to her husband.

'Hey honey.' She's applied a new film of bright red lipstick, drawing unwarranted attention to her thin lips set in her beige face. 'You're off to the bathroom too?' she asks without waiting for an answer. 'Want another drink?'

The man nods, dumbstruck and walks off towards the bathroom doors still flummoxed about what just happened.

Florian and Sophia exchange a secretive smile and continue chatting at the bar before leaving an hour later.

Once outside in the cool evening, the pair break out into convulsive laughter.

'You win!' chuckles Florian.

'Again!' she giggles. 'But I do think we should stop this stuff now. I need to move onto much bigger fish!'

Both believe the game is only a game and neither take love, lust or the occasional leer very seriously. It's late and they're both hungry so they catch a taxi back to Florian's flat and reheat some leftovers on toast.

'Oh, do you now?' he laughs. 'What exactly is the plan then?'

'I've written a great CV according to Giles,' Sophia says.

'I bet he was helpful,' Florian interrupts. 'Didn't he have contacts in the diplomatic corps? He said he could pull a few well-heeled strings.'

'Yeah.' She sounds despondent. 'He's been a huge help and has copied me into emails with my CV attached to the foreign ministry and a couple of ambassadors but so far no luck.'

'Give it time Soph,' Florian says. 'They run things like a PTA committee with umpteen sign offs and discussions to select candidates. Have you applied for any actual advertised jobs yet?'

She nods.

'And?' he asks.

'No response. I don't even know if they've opened my email or read my CV.'

'It's frustrating but they're probably waiting until you officially graduate. You know that magic bit of paper is supposed to make all the difference.'

'Yeah, I know,' she sighs. 'I'm beginning to wonder. I guess I need to curb my enthusiasm. There's something else I've thought about too. I might need a cover story, and I thought your new interior design business would be simply perfect.'

'Whaaaaat?'

'Yeah!' she says. 'I could be working for you and dealing with your clients.' She smiles in that oh-so-Sophia kind of way.

'Don't try that trick on me, girl!' he chuckles. 'I'm only starting out. I can't afford to employ you.'

'Who needs employment! I want to pretend that you employ me so I can get on and make some real moolah all by myself!'

He nods, certain if anyone had a plan that would work, it would be Sophia.

'Tell me more.' He grins and as she hesitantly describes a possible option, elaborating on an alternative career plan, his expression grows more concerned.

CHAPTER 15

Dumped - 2007

Sophia stretches out on a lounger next to the lap pool, basking her statuesque body in the early summer warmth. With eyes closed, she ruminates about her naive sister scoring a guy like smart attractive Ben. Her thoughts turn to Giles. Maybe she's the fool? The thought of Teressa enjoying the pleasures of a virile young guy raises questions about her path to fulfilment. But the money. Ben can't give her sister the lifestyle, the gifts and probably not the pleasure Giles offers. Who knows? The boy is probably a virgin. This idea explains a few things.

Teressa appears at the other side of the pool and stalks towards her older sister. 'I heard you dumped Ben.' Teressa's red-faced anger is outmatched by her shouting at a bored Sophia. 'Is that true?'

'*Dumped* is a bit over the top,' Sophia replies. 'Besides he's too young for me. Remember you pretty much alluded to this in your gossip to Giles? I was too young for him? Ring any bells with your lying and conniving. I've had a very humiliating and embarrassing conversation with Giles. No apology dearest?'

Teressa makes a scoffing noise. 'That's the last thing you'll ever get from me! You can't go around abusing people!' The pitch in Teressa's voice rises an octave as she fights to keep her emotions in check.

'Isn't that what you wanted? You instructed me to step away, and I have.' Sophia states nonchalantly. She doesn't remove her sunglasses or turn her head to regard her agitated sister standing next to her. 'What the hell do you want, dear sister? Like, what exactly?' Sophia asks, her eyes still closed beneath her large designer sunnies.

'You make my blood boil. You darn-well know what I'm

talking about!' Teressa's words soaked in frustration barely hit their mark.

'Stop being so obtuse, Teressa. I'm outside, by the pool dozing in the sun and simply have no idea what you're ranting about.'

Sophia wishes Teressa would evaporate and leave her in peace. The lesson's been executed along with dear boring Ben. Giles is never boring and always generous. A much better proposition. Disappointment in Ben's performance gives her pause for thought. The fumbling of a virgin. Yes, the sorry saga is hardly worth the pain of listening to the ravings of this lunatic sister.

'You dumped Ben in some patronising stunt last night,' Teressa shoots back, hot with rising anger.

'So what?' Sophia sighs. 'That's life. He'll get over it.'

'But why? Why flirt with him in the first place?' Teressa's voice almost whines, as she attempts to comprehend the ruthlessness of her older sister. 'You steal him from me, and then dump him within a week. What the hell's wrong with you?'

'Listen Teressa. He's a child. What's worse, he's a boring child and simply not up to the calibre I'm used to.'

'So you ruin my life and relationship with him just for fun? I loved him.' Tears spring into Teressa's eyes as she struggles to speak. 'You took unfair advantage of him and me.'

Sophia has underestimated her sister's emotional attachment to the boy. Read that one wrong. A feeble sense of guilt encroaches on Sophia's resolve.

'Think of it this way. I did you a favour. He's weak and dull.' Sophia hesitates, considering the harshness of her attitude and relents. 'I'm sorry. You know nothing went on, so how could I dump him? There is nothing to dump,' Sophia says with some remorse. 'Anyway, he's all yours now!'

Teressa lets out an exasperated shriek of sheer despair before turning and marching off. Moments later Sophia, eyes closed, basking in the warm sunlight, with her earbuds playing her favourite music, is suddenly doused by a large bucket of ice-cold pool water. She leaps up shrieking in shock as Teressa races back inside the house.

In the late afternoon, Abigail Huston arrives home slightly tipsy, carrying large shopping bags from a series of exclusive inner-city boutiques. Myles, the chauffeur, mostly obscured by the bulky shopping, carefully positions the bags and boxes on top of the beautiful highly polished rosewood dining table.

'Anything else?' he asks, keen to get back to the car.

'No, Myles, thanks. That'll be all. I need to sit down.' Abigail struggles breathlessly.

She turns to place her handbag on the rosewood chiffonier and catches sight of Sophia peeling an orange through the archway into the living room.

'Have you seen your sister?' she asks as Sophia lifts her head in response. 'We had a short conversation, and she sounds quite distraught over some breakup drama with Ben.'

'Yeah, she was a bit tense with me too, but she's always upset and hysterical over something,' Sophia responds, off-hand, as she walks through to the kitchen sink to rinse the sticky fruit juice from her hands.

'She's young... she'll ... get over it ...' Abigail says haltingly, gasping for air.

'Are you all right?' Sophia frowns with concern, moving towards her mother.

Abigail waves her hand dismissively. 'Yeah. Yes. Yes ... I'm OK,' Abigail says almost to herself as she slumps onto a dining room chair.

'I'll get you a glass of water,' Sophia offers.

'No. No. I'm fine. Just let me catch my breath.'

'Too much effort overworking your credit card,' Sophia smiles.

Her mother gives a weak grin, the colour draining from her thin face. She stares hard at Sophia. 'You need ... to do ... something with your ... hair.' She battles to get the words out between short breaths.

Sophia sighs with annoyance. 'It's still damp from the pool.'

'Oh, I didn't know you'd been swimming,' Abigail says still breathless.

'You look very pale.' She rests her hand on the back of the chair, taking a closer look at her mother's face. 'Let's go to the sofa, and I'll make you a nice cup of tea.'

Abigail nods and smiles at her daughter. 'Thanks, that sounds wonderful. I think I must've overdone things or maybe I'm coming down with some virus.'

'It's OK,' Sophia says, looking concerned as she helps her mother walk to the living room and slide onto the two-seater. 'Put your feet up if you like. Shall I get a blanket?'

'No, no,' Abigail responds, lying across the couch.

'Just rest here, and I'll bring the tea in a sec.'

CHAPTER 16

Carla's Confrontation - 2007

During those dark, cold early morning hours where her mind drifts in a half-sleep into a twilight zone, between darkness and reality, Sophia wonders if she has a distorted perspective on life. Maybe she has it wrong and it isn't some kind of game but a more deadly serious pursuit to the bitter end. She turns over, pulling the sheet over her ears, squeezing her eyes shut as waves of anxiety roll into her consciousness. Maybe it's all a mistake. An error of judgement. She depends too much on Florian too and needs to get another female's perspective. Someone trustworthy.

After two hours of fitful semi-sleep she drags herself out of bed, reassuring herself life isn't as bleak as she imagined. She resolves to meet her old friend Carla Fitzsimmons for lunch and run things past her.

Carla is alert, smart, and perfectly formed with voluminous red hair hanging in thick curls framing her freckled face. Sophia has grown closer to Carla and has confided in her more readily in recent years.

Animated and good-natured, Carla has a Catholic upbringing and while she isn't critical or judgemental of Sophia, she manages to deliver hard advice when called for, with tact and integrity.

Over a large porcelain pot of English breakfast tea, Sophia delivers a sanitised version of the confrontation with her sister. To her surprise, instead of siding with Sophia, Carla accuses her of being stunted with an EQ of a four-year old.

'I think that's unfair,' Sophia retaliates. 'My emotional intelligence has little to do with hard reality.

'You're talking about Teressa here, your one and only sibling,' Carla explains. 'Put yourself in your sister's shoes. She loves this "boy", as you call him. You consciously mess up her relationship with Ben without seeing the bigger picture.'

'But what about her lying to Giles? He's a long standing family friend. I felt humiliated and embarrassed,' Sophia says almost pleading for some allegiance in the inflexible world of waring siblings.

'Come on. What does he matter?'

Sophia pulls a face and looks directly into Carla's questioning eyes. An oversight on Sophia's part in withholding how close Giles was to her makes Carla take an impractical course in her thinking. She doesn't dare tell her friend she's involved in a clandestine sexual arrangement with Mr Hamilton. A barrier too high to breach in a conversation about her sister. She should have thought things through before she raised the issue with Carla.

'I guess Giles doesn't matter so much,' Sophia says, lying.

'If you can't interpret the emotional state of your own sister then how do you know the best way to react?' Carla challenges. 'I hate to tell you this, but I understand why your sister is so furious with you.'

'Yeah,' Sophia responds remorsefully, feeling guilty, but not quite sure why Carla is taking Teressa's side.

'You need to think before you speak,' Carla points out. 'It's not about your level of intelligence. It's about compassion and understanding for others. Sometimes your arrogance and inability to read the room makes you sound like a hard-nosed bitch.'

Sophia sits in shocked silence as if reprimanded by her parents. This is familiar ground, immediately bringing anger and retribution to mind. Sucking in air through her nose, Sophia glances up at Carla. She's right. Carla reaches for her friend's hand.

'I only tell you this because I regard you as a close friend and want you to be a better person,' she says with a sympathetic smile. 'Sorry, I don't mean to sound harsh. Your sister is four years younger than you. She needs your support and understanding and of course it means tolerance on your part. I know you're a better person than this.'

Being called a *bitch* twice in a matter of weeks was pause for thought. Sophia accepts the notion she needs to soften, be more compliant and less provocative. She believes she only behaves badly when dealing with her uncultured sister. The solution? Maintain polite indifference as much as humanly possible when dealing with family members.

One Saturday evening when Sophia intends leaving the house to meet a small group of friends at a local bar, she walks into the living room to tell her parents she's out for the evening. It's one of her domestic obligations, agreed to as part of her ground rules, for living under *their roof*. Her father rouses from his cell phone as she stands in the doorway and frowns at his daughter.

'You're not going out dressed like that are you?' he asks.

'What's it matter?' she replies, rummaging around in her stylish leather clutch-bag for the keys to her red sports car.

'Sophia!' Her mother's voice rings out with indignation. 'Don't you dare talk to your father like that.' Abigail leaps up from the sofa and stands next to her husband. Both parents' eyes are fixated on their daughter's disenchanted face.

Sophia glances up, clutching her car keys and regards their disgruntled expressions. She immediately falls silent, knowing it's the best option, prompting her mother to intercede again.

'Your father's right. You can't be serious about going out with all that makeup plastered on your face. You look like a thirty-year-old. It's way too much, and the false eye-lashes make you look like a hooker.'

Sophia sighs. Seriously? Please. Not this again. Her eyes roll up towards the French crystal chandelier hanging from the centre of the ceiling. She huffs, turns her back on the adults and marches through the front door without a second backward glance. What do they know anyway? Who the hell are they to make judgements about my appearance? They are both morally corrupt, sleeping with other people and then daring to call me out. It's laughable.

She refuses to allow the incident to occupy any part of her mind and knows she'll soon be out of their view and beyond earshot. Little do they know, Sophia is doing whatever she likes with their dear and close family friend and trusted business ally, Mr. Giles Hamilton.

While driving to an uptown hotel for her secret rendezvous with Giles, she muses over the alarm on their faces when she eventually tells them what's really going on. A wide grin spreads across her face. Too bad for them. She pulls herself together, hearing Carla's words repeating in her head. *Avoid combat and conflict. Be a little more compliant and understanding and less like a spoilt brat.* The word *arrogance* and *bitch* still reverberate in quiet moments.

In the milky, cool light of early morning Sophia mulls over the previous evening's argument with her parents. A surge of deep remorse over fighting with her mother and sharp-edged guilt at abruptly leaving the house after the angry exchange makes for bitter remorse. Maybe her parents are right. If she expects to enjoy a high-class lavish career, the need to refine her appearance and attitude is critical. Both Florian and Giles could advise her on how to draw less obvious attention and help her garner more understated appeal. She picks up the tacky false eyelashes from her bedside table and flings them into the waste basket next to her dresser. She won't be wearing those ever again.

Sophia resolves to deliver breakfast to her mother and offer apologies for her childish outburst and unruly behaviour. She replays the wording through her mind several times while making a tray of tea, toast and a bowl of fresh fruit. Her mother usually sleeps in her own bedroom, so it's easy to sneak in and ask for forgiveness before Sophia works on placating her father.

She balances the tray on one arm and gently taps on her mother's bedroom door. Not surprising, there's no response. She taps her knuckles a little louder with the same result. Sophia carefully places the breakfast tray on the antique sideboard next to her mother's bedroom door, clasps the door handle before slowly pushing the door open. The heavy drapes at the tall French windows are sealed shut. In the gloom Sophia barely makes out her mother's sleeping body under the blankets in the middle of the over-sized, intricately carved rosewood four-poster bed.

'Mum?' she whispers softly and then repeats the word with increasing volume. Initially, Sophia walks gradually towards the windows and with one arm slightly pulls open one side of the drapes. Her mother doesn't move. She must've got trashed last night after Sophia went out for the evening. Sophia moves to the side of the bed, reaching her hand towards her mother's shoulder and gently shakes her. Her mother rolls over onto her back, her pale face motionless and her eyelids closed. At first Sophia leans across her mother in stark disbelief.

'Mum?' she asks, still expecting some response.

No. No. This can't be happening. A surge of adrenaline races through Sophia's body, and her hands begin to tremble. Had her mother taken sleeping pills with the booze she consumed last night? Maybe she's only unconscious? What the hell is going on? Sophia feels for a pulse along her mother's exposed neck. Abigail is already cold. Sophia moves her fingers into several different positions, struggling to find a heartbeat. There's no pulse. None.

Sophia's entire body shakes uncontrollably, gasping for air, trying to control her reaction. This reality didn't match up with her normal expectation about life. How could this be so? Surely it's some kind of sick joke? She gazes at her mother's pallid face as disbelief turns to horror. She quickly jerks her hand away from the lifeless body. A small guttural sound escapes from Sophia's throat before she runs from the room and races downstairs to her father.

A few hours later Abigail Huston is pronounced dead by her local GP. Painful shockwaves echo around the family, throughout the neighbourhood and across the higher echelons of Sydney society. An autopsy the next day reveals a massive coronary has stolen the forty-eight-year old's life.

CHAPTER 17

Ashes to Ashes - 2007

Sophia sits unmoving in the front pew of the overcrowded church aware of the packed congregation sitting behind her. Detached, feeling like a cardboard clone of her real self, unaware of the soft murmurs, occasional tears and nose blowing of the assembled mourners. Abigail Huston's untimely death is a shock to the gathering on this wet spring Wednesday in 2007. It's the first day of rain in many months and the overcast weather echoes the heavy sadness permeating the mourners at Abigail's funeral. Melancholy sharpens the chink in Sophia's hardened heart as she struggles to maintain normal composure. The sombre congregation fall silent moments before the priest arrives at the stone carved pulpit. Several prominent friends and extended family members speak of the wonderful character and vivacious personality of Sophia's dead mother.

Michael Huston looks grey, matching his grey silk three-piece suit, as if he has aged ten years in as many days. He is unable to talk at the funeral and is barely audible as members of the congregation offer their condolences. He slouches, silently severed from Sophia and Teressa who stand alongside him in the front pew. Teressa continually weeps and sniffles into a series of damp tissues before shoving them into her coat pockets as the voices in the front of the alter talk glowingly of her mother.

Florian stands on the other side of Teressa, clearly bereft of the ability to comfort his weeping friend's youngest sister. It seems that standing, sitting and following the predictable funeral routine fulfils most requirements. Their grandmother, Edith Hawkins, dressed in black, stands with stoic forbearance on the other side of Florian. Her face bleak as she lifts her face and catches Sophia's sad eyes.

Later, as the mourners gather at the Sacred Heart Cemetery for the burial, Sophia observes the crowd, standing isolated towards the back as Teressa clings onto her wretched-looking father, tears rolling down her pale cheeks. After the service, Michael remains inaudible, barely able to respond to people at the gathering offering their condolences and shaking his hand, and nodding weakly at those who approach him.

Afterwards an array of refreshments is served with plenty of alcohol available in the community hall adjacent to the stone church. Sophia leans against the back wall and overhears two older men trussed up in dark suits discussing her mother.

'I remember when we were students,' the tall thin stranger pauses, recalling a time, many years ago. 'Abby had a magnetic aura about her.' He runs a hand through his wild hair. Thin rimless glasses seem precariously balanced on his long nose as he peers solemnly into his whisky glass. 'When she talked to you, she completely drew you in. She was incredible. Captivating.'

The shorter bald man nodded sagely. 'Yes, I remember the first time I slept with her. I was completely shaken. It almost brought me to tears,' he says in a methodical clear voice. Sophia keeps her head down but leans in towards their backs to listen more closely.

The tall man nods. 'I know. I've never felt anything like it, not before or since. Remarkable woman.'

They pause, both considering their past, saturated with nostalgia for a wild youth recklessly spent.

'I thought I was going to have a heart attack one time. Sensory overload.' He smiles at the memory.

'I don't think I could take it either,' says the bald stranger sipping from his drink. 'Imagine being married to her. I used to get bitter and twisted every time I took her out. Other guys leering at her or frozen in awe, dumbstruck by her appearance. It put me off.'

'I hear you. I ended up spending most of my time fending off unwanted advances from other guys too,' adds the taller man. He inhales deeply, considering his next comment. 'You know, I trusted her at the time, but it eventually got too stressful. Guys hitting on her. There was something alluring and mysterious about Abigail.'

82

His friend nods and mumbles something incoherent. Sophia remains dead still, intrigued at the commentary about her own mother. It was unbelievable, but clearly Abigail must have been something amazing back in the day.

'I considered it a lucky escape when we broke up. Although now and again, I'd reminisce and get all nostalgic reliving the few months we spent together.' The tall man sighs and takes a large gulp from his glass of watery looking whisky.

They both glance across the room, silently observing the other mourners chatting and chuckling, telling stories from the past. Sophia takes the opportunity to slink along the wall and walk her way towards a long table laden with food while she processes her ill-advised eavesdropping on the strangers' conversation. For some unfathomable reason she feels uneasy, learning her mother was some kind of siren in her youth. Maybe her mother was not that different from her eldest daughter after all. Sophia considers their similarities but stops herself. The pain of comparison brings her too close to unwanted tears.

It was astounding to hear how her mother had a similar magnetic attraction, men falling over themselves to be with her. Thinking about this and Carla's words combine to resonate, giving her an understanding of her mother's profound detachment from both daughters. A conscious emotional exclusion from connecting to her daughters' lives. This is exactly how Sophia treats others. An emotional barrier, an immovable wall reducing her chances of being hurt by remaining remote and unavailable.

Was she an introvert? It seems a ridiculous premise. But she acts at being outgoing and happy for the sake of others in her life. It's easier, less complicated than playing her true self. Reality is something more complex. Emotionally locked. That's how she copes with Giles. Playing the mistress, fun loving and shallow at times. Suppressing who she really is. It's difficult to see how Sophia is a genetic replica of her mother. Could Sophia be taking detachment to the next level? A useful attribute to cope with the men in her life. Sophia's use of her body for money while imprisoning her heart in an inflexible cage, an impenetrable prison, making too hard to scale the ramparts of resistance, shields herself from emotional reality. If she went ahead with her business strategy, in a weird way, sleeping with several paying clients could be a form of compensating for this brokenness, her inability to deal with sentiment from those closest to her. The flip-side offers advantages too. She could act the part of coquette, lover and confidante but maintain a poignant detachment from clients. She now wishes she hadn't stood there frozen, listening in fascination to her mother's ex-lover's commentary.

Sophia didn't shed a tear, not then at the funeral, nor the long dark days before. Every lonely night afterwards she jolted awake, seeing her mother's dead body, slack-jawed and lifeless, tormenting her sleepless nights. She wept and occasionally wailed into the darkness before whimpering into a short, fragmented sleep.

Some weeks after the funeral, while sitting in Florian's minimally furnished apartment, Sophia confides her concern at being tormented and numb, in equal measure.

'Maybe it's the sudden way events took place? She died three weeks after your graduation,' Florian explains. 'It's supposed to be a time of celebration and relief from the hallowed halls of academia,' he quips half-heartedly. 'You know, the Class of 2007, looking to the future and all that.'

'Yeah for sure,' she says stiffly. 'But I do wonder if there's something wrong with me. Because, Fab, I'm not sure I feel anything. Sometimes I don't give a damn but alone at night I get so upset, almost hysterical. It's simply not me.'

He nods and rubs one open palm across her back, attempting to offer some comfort. But she moves away, carrying her half-filled glass of sauvignon, and sits opposite in his old tartan patterned armchair.

'Most of the time I feel nothing,' Sophia repeats then hesitates, thinking more deeply about her feelings. 'You know what? If I'm entirely honest, I have a slight sense of relief she's gone.'

He nods again, uncertain how to respond. 'Maybe it's something you have to come to terms with. You know, it was totally unexpected. You're probably still in shock.'

Sophia says nothing, contemplating the limitations of her inner emotions and her innate difficulty in analysing feelings.

'Umm,' he finally mumbles wordlessly under his breath and they sit in shared silence without any need to talk. Tears begin to pool in Sophia's eyes and he reaches out for her hand pulling her towards him, enveloping her in a hug as she sobs uncontrollably against his shoulder.

'I'm sorry,' she repeats. 'Sorry. I didn't mean to ... cry.'

'It's OK, Soph,' he soothes. 'It's all right.'

'I didn't mean to be such a bitch,' she laments between sobs.

'Oh darling, you aren't a bitch at all.' He strokes the back of her hair and hugs her closely. 'It's OK.'

'I've been such an idiot.' She sniffs and pulls away from Florian who passes her a couple of tissues.

He stares silently at her tear stained face stricken by grief and loss. 'Why are you talking so harshly about yourself?' he finally asks with deep concern.

She haltingly explains the arguments with her mother, the comments from Carla and how she needs to find a better way of handling Teressa.

'Darling you are beautiful and clever. What more do you want? More to the point what more does that dysfunctional family of yours want?' He smiles sadly, trying to throw his best friend a life raft but unsure about the way forward.

'I need to change the way I think and act. I've been treating those around me the way my family treats me,' Sophia explains. 'The very things I despise in others are the very same ways I operate.' She sighs heavily, looking at Florian. She has to compartmentalise the pain and hurt, lock it away so she can focus on getting on with a life of her own making. A world occupied by the beat of her own drum.

This was getting all too psycho-babble for Florian to handle. He felt sympathy for Sophia. Over the years she had resisted awkward displays of true emotion, her survival technique. He danced on thin ice between unemotional listening and supporting her with carefully balanced empathy.

85

'Remember I love you,' he simply says.

'Me too,' she says with tears in her eyes, irritated at her inability to show him in every word and deed.

CHAPTER 18

False Freedom – 2008

One morning things feel different to Sophia. What's changed? Nothing much except her energy and enthusiasm has finally returned. Out of the doldrums, she smiles at her reflection in the bathroom mirror while brushing her teeth. Freedom beckons, it's so close she can almost touch it. Her decision to move out of the family home, and find her own rented flat, uplifts her spirit. Teressa and her father will remain home alone, rattling around in the Point Piper mansion.

Turning twenty-one a few weeks ago and securing her own rental home lifted her sense of autonomy. Sophia is determined not to ask her father for any more money. Instead, she's entirely focussed on securing her financial independence. She chants the words *freedom and independence* under her breath while driving, walking and falling asleep. She scrawls the two words on Post-it notes, as if they are a mantra directing her destiny, sticking them to her bathroom mirror, her laptop screen and inside her make-up drawer. With enough savings now she can finally step away from the wreckage of her family and secure her own flat and future.

Later that day, Sophia uses her keys to enter the Point Piper home, locating the housekeeper dusting the antique furniture in the great hall.

'Hi, Anna. Is Dad around?' she asks, striding into the room.

'Well, how are you, Sophia?' The housekeeper's face crumples with concern. 'Feeling any better?'

'Yeah. I'm going to be OK. Is Dad here?'

'He's not good,' she says, her pale face ingrained with distress. 'He spends most of his time in bed and refuses to get dressed, preferring to stay in his room most days.'

'Oh, I really need to talk to him,' Sophia says.

A grimace graces Anna's thin lips.

'I'll be moving out of here next week. I've found a small flat to rent in the city but want to explain to Dad first.'

'Oh,' she responds with surprise. 'You go up and talk to him. He'll want to see you. It's been tough going. I'm trying to organise tasty food and special treats he used to enjoy, but he's still not interested. It's been months now,' she explains anxiously, wringing her knobbly hands in front of Sophia. 'I'm afraid he's not well, but he refuses to see a doctor.'

Sophia huffs in brief annoyance, raising her eyebrows in tandem with the shocked expression on the housekeeper's pallid face. The woman's short dark hair is plastered to her tiny head, positioned on a well-rounded, squat body supported by flat, sensible leather walking shoes.

'Don't you worry Anna,' Sophia announces. 'I'll go up and shake some sense into him.' She grabs the bannister, about to ascend the sweeping staircase when the alarmed housekeeper grasps Sophia's forearm as she grips the railing.

'Oh, no, Miss. I think you should be more careful.' The housekeeper's voice pleads for mercy on her father's behalf. 'He's grief-stricken. Show him a bit of compassion.'

Sophia inhales deeply before racing up the stairs two at a time and marches towards her father's bedroom-wing. She comes to a standstill, facing his closed bedroom door. Sophia pulls herself upright, sucking in another deep breath and gives the bedroom door a couple of hard, determined knocks. With no response, she grasps the large brass handle and boldly pushes her way into the darkened musty room. The place gives her the creeps. Flashbacks of her mother's death in the bedroom down the corridor invade her thoughts, but she refuses to allow the images to taunt her. This is daytime, and her father is very much alive.

She strides up to the crumpled mound covered in bedclothes. 'Good morning Father!' she says in a raised voice which is greeted by a weak groan from under the covers of the impressive four-poster bed. Sophia marches across the expansive room to the large double windows and rips open the heavy brocade drapes. She unlatches the casements and flings open the windows allowing sharp streaks of hard light to slice across the bedroom carpet.

A louder, more conscious groan escapes from the four-poster bed. Sophia stands at her father's bedside. 'Really? Is this what you're up to now?' she asks.

Her father doesn't respond. He has suffered a night of fitful sleep with tormenting dreams before finally succumbing to the effects of three sleeping pills washed down with a tumbler of single malt whisky around 2.45am. He's in no mood to communicate, least of all with the demands from his eldest daughter baying at the edges of his consciousness.

Sophia waits, silent for a minute before taking another tack. 'For heaven's sake! Don't tell me you're mourning the death of Mother in this ridiculous display of guilt and remorse?'

He rolls under the covers and curls his legs up in a foetal position, grabbing one of his pillows and holding it over his head in a vain attempt to block out Sophia's penetrating voice.

'You didn't even like each other!' she announces, challenging him to a duel. 'Your behaviour is pitiful under the circumstances. Why in God's ruptured green earth would you display such a degree of grief over a lost love? Are you kidding me? It would've been more acceptable if the two of you had displayed any affection when she was alive. Is this a fool's joke?' Anger creeps into her voice, she tries to control her annoyance with a modulated edge of irritation. For God's sake, come on,' she finally pleads, realising she needs to keep her voice under control. But it's too late.

Suddenly he throws his arm out from under the bed linen and bolts upright into a sitting position.

'Fuck off!' he shouts, red-faced with rage, his voice reverberating around the room. This outburst would, no doubt, be shattering the pristine housekeeper's chastened ears where she anxiously stands, surreptitiously listening at the base of the ground floor stairwell.

CHAPTER 19

Demise - 2008

Michael Huston dressed in a beige silk suit strides through the tall revolving glass doors of Sydney's largest casino. It didn't take much for his risk-taking genes to quickly convert him into an avid gambling addict. With no business demands to attend and few people interested in talking to him, Michael plans to win his wealth back at the black-jack tables. But first, he needs a drink.

'Triple single malt.' He orders from the attentive barman who is dressed in a white shirt and black bow tie.

'Sure Mr Huston.' The barman knows this customer well.

'Not very busy tonight,' Michael observes, casting his eyes around the VIP lounge. None of the high rollers appear anywhere in sight. More chance with Lady Luck, he smirks to himself.

'It's early for a Wednesday.' The lanky barman grins and passes the large tumbler of whisky to his customer.

Michael swirls the ice in his glass before gulping it down in two short bursts. 'Another,' he instructs, shoving his glass unceremoniously onto the bar.

The barman nods. He's seen this guy drunk, passed out and late one evening three weeks ago, slumped at the bar weeping and slurring incoherently. After a bit of an incident, he managed to call Mr Huston's daughter, Sophia, to pick the customer up. A combo of horror and embarrassment played out on her face as Sophia walked into the bar, her eyes falling on her father's drooping body barely balanced on the edge of a bar stool. This time, the barman delivers a gentle reminder.

'Go easy on the drink, mate. I don't want to contact that daughter of yours again.'

'Nah. Thanks, mate,' Michael says, grabbing the second drink and swigging it down in quick succession. 'Once is enough with

Sophia on my case,' he grins sheepishly. 'Wish me luck.'

The barman smiles and nods as he watches Mr Huston saunter through the double doors towards the gambling tables. He carries a compact black leather bag, with a zip around three sides and a handle he loops over his wrist. The kit, crammed with casino chips he won the previous evening, gives him tremendous confidence. Tonight's his best chance of doubling his money.

Michael grabs a seat at his favourite table and places ten thousand dollars' worth of chips in two neat little stacks on a split between black and red. Two other desultory patrons barely glance at the new player. The croupier makes the call, dusts the flats of her hands together and swiftly deals the cards to the four patrons keenly watching her every move.

Several hours later Michael takes a break, heading for the bathroom. After using the urinal and without washing his hands, he shoves open one of the individual toilet stalls, enters and locks the door before sitting on the seat. Michael unzips the leather bag, now half-empty, rummages around and pulls out a small plastic zip-lock bag. He gingerly pours a little white powder on the back of his trembling hand and leans forward snorting the cocaine into his left nostril. He hesitates momentarily, and closes his eyes, luxuriating in the buzz before repeating the exercise with this right nostril. It's a hit. He's a thousand times better after losing at the tables. He's bullet-proof. He'll go back for more and is absolutely convinced he'll swing a bold win tonight.

In the early hours of the morning after the barman cautiously pours Michael his very last drink, the anxious man insists on calling a taxi to take Michael home.

'Please man, not Sophia again,' Michael pleads, slurring at the young man clutching him as the pair stagger outside to the waiting cab. In the back of the taxi, Michael dozes, in and out of consciousness. At one hazy point in what seems like an extraordinarily long journey home, he registers how haphazard life has become. How depressing and chaotic. It abruptly dawns on him that he must be coming down. Bugger. Thank God he's going home. There's booze, and he's pretty sure he can remember where he hid a tiny stash somewhere in the library. But inside which book? When he finally gets to bed, he has another epiphany. Hang on. What was the first one again? His life kept floundering on the lost shores of expanding confusion because he was sick. Maybe a doctor? He knew there was something wrong. He needed more drugs. Should he stop drinking? Nah. That's idiot talk.

The pale dawn light stretches across his bedroom floor and half-way up the opposite wall when he wakes up sobbing, still drunk or stoned or both. In his befuddled mind, Michael remembers weeping at intervals throughout the night, abandoned and completely isolated. His daughters rarely talk to him anymore.

In a drunken, stoned rage six months after Abigail's death, he fired his loyal housekeeper and lied to his daughters about her leaving on holiday. The next day Michael acknowledged Anna's loyalty over the years, paying her three months wages in lieu of her length of service. He accepted too, his obligation to pay her one week's wages for every year she had worked, as stipulated in her contract which she signed twenty-three years earlier.

He has a few thousand left in an overdraft, so he reluctantly pays her out in full. He wants to be left alone in his rambling home. The kitchen, lounge and study become his domain, while his bedroom, which he keeps locked, is in a far worse shambles than his daughters could ever imagine.

Michael regularly orders fast food, asking Myles to collect the meals at all times of the day and night. The chauffeur is too terrified of his employer's erratic behaviour to question or even make suggestions about healing Michael's obvious pain. Fearful of losing his job, Myles also proposes helping around the house when permitted, which is rarely during these dark self-destructive days of deep decline.

Mr Michael Huston's friends quickly abandon him. Like swallows migrating for winter, they are scarce after his wife's funeral. Social invitations dry up for the middle-aged man, alone with a questionable attitude and risky business investments. Gossip is rife, fuelling the withdrawal of many so-called friends, who once surrounded him with grasping adulation.

The wives club and their husbands are all too wary of inviting the wounded business titan to soirees, public events or their private homes. His membership is cancelled. Michael's aggression and foul language interrupts the pristine confines of high society and confirms their merciless fears. He camouflages his disgrace by gambling more often. He tells himself he can stop gambling and drinking any time, but he doesn't want to. There's a buzz about the casino, making him important again, relevant and alive. But the stakes are sky-high, and he takes special care to conceal his risky activity from everyone, even himself. He loves the laughter, the glitz and his new *friends* who gather around the casino tables encouraging him to play hard and high. He finally discovers a sense of belonging and meaning in his narrow life.

After waking in the middle of the day, he stumbles into the kitchen and pours himself half a glass of whisky, not bothering with ice this time. He gulps and swallows, squinting at the intense sunlight stretching across the countertop and bouncing off the tiled floor. What was that thing he thought of last night? *Satori?* It doesn't matter. It'll come to him later. He empties the glass down his gullet in one swoop and slams it on the surface of the stone countertop. The loud noise startles him to his senses. He shuffles into the great hall dressed in baggy stained pyjama pants and an old faded t-shirt. Music will shift his mood. Block out the failures of the night before.

The unholy dregs of booze and drugs give some momentary relief, cushioned by blasting music as he dances and sings out loud at high noon, alone in the open plan living space. Finally, he lurches back to bed, pulling the covers over his head to block out the full sunlight streaking through his partially-closed curtains. Michael wakes up several times in the mid-afternoon, before dragging his shadow-self aimlessly around the house, remaining obliterated for the rest of the shortened day.

He had recently acquired a reputation for swearing in public or breaking into songs from the seventies at inopportune times. Michael Huston is a liability that even his personal assistant, who calls his cell-phone every lunchtime, has learned not to question and not to call more than once daily. But she's also gone down the gurgler along with his entire life, after discovering he could no

94

longer pay her salary. Without her, Michael is completely adrift.

It dawns on him as he attempts to sleep off his drugged haze that he's rudderless. Without a strong woman at the helm, he is entirely at sea. A mere piece of flotsam tossed around dangerous oceans with no safe harbour in sight – a dark and stormy sea containing limitless barbs of humiliation and trauma. Isolation and misery are his default positions. He can't carry on like this. He's tried, on a couple of occasions over the previous three months, to pull himself together. It's proved fruitless. Is he suffering a self-induced midlife crisis? Like Pavlov's conditioning technique, Michael Huston still assumes he can buy anything he wants, but the irony is, he doesn't want anything money can buy.

Sophia calls his cell phone once a week, but their stilted conversations are short. There's a niggling sense of disaster lurking in the background when she listens to her father's overly positive responses about his business, which deepens her unease. She keeps her fears to herself, waiting for the right time to discuss face to face with him, needing to understand some hard facts.

Once or twice, Michael talks to his chauffeur, who listens carefully, not quite grasping the ramblings of his boss. Myles reassures him *this will also pass*, but Michael can't find a way forward. Soon a barrage of emails and official-looking letters from the bank threatens foreclosure after numerous phone calls about defaulted payments are simply ignored.

On Tuesday Michael, dressed in a corporate uniform, navy suit, silk tie with subdued blue and grey non-descript patterns and a matching swatch of fabric in his breast pocket, endures a lengthy and frustrating meeting with his lawyers and company accountants. After twenty minutes, he slams his fist on the board room table.

'Listen to me.' His voice is taut with anxiety. 'What the hell am I going to do then?'

Exasperated, his company lawyer speaks in direct, unembellished language. It's the only way the message is going to resonate with Michael Huston.

'Basically you're fucked,' the older man states.

Michael shoves his head against the back if his office chair as if the force of his lawyer's remark has punched him in the face.

'But there must be something we can do?' His voice is almost whining like a disbelieving child. He turns towards the chief accountant, a thick-set man bound up in a pin-stripe suit with a hard, irreproachable attitude.

The man shakes his head. 'You're out,' he says, pulling a disgruntled face. 'I don't see any way around this. The company is gone, your shares are gone, and you owe everything else to the board and the bank. You must cash up, and fast, to get out of this mess. Let's face it, this is the same conversation we've had with you, Michael, for the past four weeks. The outcome remains the same. It's over! You need to sign these documents and sell your properties, or the banks will do it for you,' he says, shovelling a sheaf of typed documents towards Michael's stricken face.

Michael leans onto his elbows resting on the large polished boardroom table and covers his face with his hands. He glances up at the four stony-faced men seated around him.

'The overseas properties too?' he asks weakly.

'Yeah,' the chief accountant reiterates. 'Everything must go, and after that, you'll still owe money to the bank.'

In the long months leading up to this crucial meeting, Michael, bankrupted global businessman, casino high-roller, and ex-bon vivant has also run up a casino tab of three and a half million dollars. His executive team of advisors are unaware of this additional debt which he has simply no way of servicing.

He decides to say nothing. Confession is for pussies.

CHAPTER 20

Downturn - 2008

Her cell phone rings for the second time. Teressa calling again.
Sophia switches it off and stands motionless in her penthouse
kitchen staring at the screen. She freezes for a moment
contemplating if she should have answered the call. Before Sophia
has a chance to thrust her phone back into her handbag, it buzzes
again. The shrill persistent sound can't be ignored.

'Yeah?' she says, emotionless.

'Why don't you answer your bloody phone?' Teressa's voice
demands shrilly.

'What is it?' Sophia refuses to be lured into another argument.

'It's Dad. I was around there yesterday, and he's adamant that
he's been working in his study for three days.'

Sophia snorts. 'So what? Leave him to it. At least it's a
reasonable distraction.'

'We talked for over an hour, I had to go because it was getting
late, but he seems pretty agitated.'

'What do you think we should do? He's getting worse but I'm
not sure how we can sort this out.'

Already impatient Sophia wants to get off the phone. She
shouldn't have answered the call.

'He keeps repeating he's in some kind of trouble. It sounds like
financial problems,' Teressa pauses and Sophia remains silent, so
her younger sister continues. 'Last week when I saw him, he
looked grey and ill. Then he started mumbling, almost to himself,
that he was going to lose everything.'

Suddenly Sophia is paying attention. 'Are you sure?' she asks
flatly, keeping alarm out of her voice.

'Yeah,' Teressa answers. 'He wants us both to meet up and
discuss things with him this weekend. He said Giles had been

helping him and the company accountant gave him some advice but there wasn't much they could do.'

'Do about what? Sophia responds. 'What's going on exactly?'

'That's my point,' Teressa says with mild irritation. 'I simply don't know. I've had less contact after I went flatting. He won't elaborate until we're both together so he can talk it through with us at the same time.'

'Sounds ominous,' Sophia observes almost to herself. 'But I'm sure it's nothing major. Let's meet him at the house on the weekend and he can get it all off his chest,' she says attempting to reassure her sister but feeling uneasy.

Both sisters arrive in separate vehicles on Saturday afternoon at their family home. They are shocked by the upheaval inside the house and brace themselves for their father's unkempt appearance.

'Mum would never allow things to get as bad as this,' Teressa says, upset.

'Yeah,' responds Sophia, 'but we're dealing with an entirely different species here.'

Teressa gives her tactless sister a dirty look.

Most of the full-length drapes are closed with only a few thin streaks of sunlight cutting across the great hall. The once luxurious room is now crammed with used plates and cutlery, empty wine glasses and bottles. Clothing is draped over various antique armchairs as if discarded while passing through while some indeterminate items are flung over the armrests. The back of the dining chairs are carelessly misaligned without any concern for their position around the long dining table.

Folders, files, old newspapers, colourful magazines and documents litter every surface. It appears Michael has used scissors and cut out various articles from documents and newspapers scattered across the far end of the table. In the dull light, ominous shadows are stamped against the back wall as if blankets, cushions, fast-food packaging and possibly shoes lurk behind furniture obscuring the full horror.

'In here,' shouts Michael Huston's compromised tone. The command and strength in his voice has disappeared and in its place is a feeble attempt by their father to sound as if he remains in charge. The sisters exchange a look and for once they silently concur that no comment or reprimand will be expressed to their dishevelled, distressed parent.

Both sisters are initially shocked at the sight of their fragile father as he ushers them into his study and moves folders and documents from two chairs so they can sit down. He makes his way around to the large leather office chair behind the desk and faces his two daughters. Framed by a large window behind his head, his stooped shoulders convey it all. Both girls remain silent, saddened by this grey old man seated before them.

'I wanted you both here.' He coughs, blows his nose with a tissue and shoves it into the desk drawer. 'There's been a bit of an inconvenience and I thought it best to talk to you both at the same time, so we're all on the same page about the situation.' A short guttural cough escapes his lips again.

He glances from one studied set of eyes to the other but both young women remain expressionless. He pours more whisky into the closest glass at hand. There are several other grimy looking glasses scattered across the surface of the large desk where strewn papers, pens and his smudged reading glasses sit precariously balanced on the edge of a folder. Michael appears a decade older than his forty-eight years. There are dark rings under his eyes and his thinning hair dances in the weak lamp light which warms the exotic timber lined study walls.

Sophia is certain her father's left hand is trembling slightly when he reaches for the glass and takes a furtive swig. He then swallows another gulp in short succession. It's unbelievable that this pale facsimile is her father. His shirt-collar looks grubby in the dim light and clearly food of some kind has dribbled down the cotton front, staining his white shirt below the third button.

When Teressa stands up to pull back the drapes her father shouts at the top of his voice, 'NO! Leave them!' She immediately obeys. The sisters exchange another look and acknowledge their private agreement of not inflaming an already difficult situation.

As their father begins to explain, his voice rises and falls, sometimes almost inaudible.

'Sorry, Dad can you repeat that,' Sophia asks. 'I can't quite understand how this has suddenly come about.'

She holds her breath as her father launches into a convoluted explanation. It's confusing and she suspects her wily father is trying to hide the facts and real details. It's unbelievable. Sophia sits stunned, trying to unravel the impacts this will have on their future lives.

At times Michael seems near tears but both girls remain seated in stony silence allowing their father to speak unencumbered by interruptions. After almost an hour, he slows, and his rambling voice finally stops. He leans back into the comfortable leather office chair, regarding the astounded expressions on both his daughter's pale faces.

Sophia is sure Michael thinks he's covered all the bases and can carry on regardless. There's something unsettling about his matter-of-fact demeanour.

Sophia speaks first, summarising the situation. This is mostly due to Teressa's tearful state which has left her speechless at the dire consequences of her father's poor judgement.

'So if I'm to get this straight,' Sophia frowns, hesitating, 'are you saying your share prices fell during the GFC and global equities fell further impacting the Australian market. These conditions killed off your entire business?' She can't keep the incredulity out of her astounded voice.

Michael nods, his eyes trained on his eldest daughter. 'I was stretched with property investments and then when the dollar fell, I had no cashflow to meet business obligations.'

Sophia purses her lips, unimpressed by the eyewash. There has to be more to the story. He's hiding behind the GFC and she knows Australia hasn't been hit that hard during the economic downturn. How bloody convenient. The pact she made with Teressa meant she shouldn't tackle him while he's down but the sly way he presented the situation has the stench of corporate bullshit, *socialising the rat into the global framework.* Her jaw automatically clenches, restraining her desire to slap her father across his alcoholic face. Yes, alcoholic. She'd guessed for some time but now it's all come down to this. It was unfathomable. She tries another angle, wanting to clarify reality for them all.

'Dad, are you talking about the holding company or the board members of your property development businesses?' she asks with a sinking feeling, hoping he doesn't mean both entities.

'The bloody board.' he mutters

Teressa can't quite comprehend the discussion around hostile takeovers and lack of investor funding. She struggles to understand the financial crisis in which the family now find themselves.

'You're no fool Dad and have made more than a fortune over the past twenty-four years,' Sophia states. 'So how could everything be obliterated so quickly?' Her father always said he would never hold less than fifty-one percent as a stakeholder in each investment company. There is a strained silence between the tense trio.

Michael clears his throat uneasily before attempting to explain further. 'We can discuss the ins and outs all evening, but the fact is everything I own and have worked for all my life, is lost. Everything's gone forever.' His words were halting, tortured as more silent tears escaped down Teressa's cheeks which she intermittently dabbed with a tissue scrunched into a damp ball in her hands.

'So, Dad, let me try and understand,' Sophia continues. 'You're saying that the board and the shareholders have voted you out of your own business?'

With an ashen face, heavy with guilt and humiliation, Michael slowly nods a wordless affirmation.

'There's no more cash or equity left in any of the business investments or the holding company?' Sophia asks in disbelief. 'Am I understanding you correctly?'

He nods again, his lips a crumpled line across the bottom half of his face. 'I over-extended myself and put the business at risk. It gave the board the perfect opportunity and ammo they needed to cut me out.'

'I see,' Sophia says, glancing sideways at her wounded sister. 'I know the economic downturn hit you hard, but it still doesn't fully explain how there is not a bean left on the table.'

Michael looks down, dejected. He had hoped to use the demise of the holding company as the most plausible explanation. It was clear that his eldest daughter was not so easily fooled. He glances from one daughter to the other and remains silent.

'Well?' Sophia asks with barely concealed annoyance. 'You have the two holiday houses, this house and cars, plenty of assets you could liquidate.'

He exhales, his elbows bent on his desktop and drags both hands through his hair.

'I'm so, so sorry but there's nothing,' he mumbles. 'All those assets are part of the bankruptcy and must be liquidated to clear the debts.' He holds his face in his hands, not wanting to see the expressions on his daughter's faces.

Sophia frowns, confused. 'But hang on a minute, surely they can't take our family home too? It's in a trust!'

Alarm rose in her voice for the first time. At the mere mention of bankruptcy Teressa whimpers, pulling out another tissue from her pocket to wipe her eyes as she continues weeping.

Their father nods as he sucks in a breath.

'But how? How can this possibly happen?' Sophia asks, alarmed by the inevitable.

'I moved the house out of the trust to raise funds for the bank. I needed the equity. I thought, at time, I could pull things back together.' He hesitates, contemplating how far he should take things and then grimaces, remembering his shaken inner voice saying, *Mate, you've got nothing more to lose.*

'Yes. The house is part of everything,' he says almost incoherently and reaches for another gulp of whisky. 'I'm so deep in debt with creditors threatening legal action. The shareholders and directors made an offer for my fifty-one percent which I've accepted. They've taken the business over and are considering if they can rescue it with more investors' involvement.'

'At least you've got that pay-out Dad,' Teressa says weakly.

'Trouble is the debt is more than the pay-out and has also gone into paying off the creditors. There is literally nothing left. I'm still in shock myself. After all these years of hard slog, and at this point in my life I'm left with nothing.' He sighs heavily before continuing hesitantly. 'I need to explain where a large portion of the accumulated debt comes from … I'm not sure how to put this,'

103

Michael confesses. 'But I've been gambling almost every night since your mother's death.'

Sophia's face hardens with contempt. 'You're completely unbelievable!' she spits venomously. 'Don't you mean for the past three years, *before* our mother's death?'

Teressa reaches out, grabbing Sophia's forearm in a simple signal to keep calm. Let it go. No use crying over spilt milk.

Both sisters watch their father's slow nod, looking down at his hands resting on the desk. He won't be telling them any of the details. There's nothing more to discuss, and Sophia believes no point in talking about the curdled milk.

Moments later the sisters bid their father goodbye and leave him standing forlorn at the front door as they scuttle to their cars and without a backward glance both disappear.

Back at her compact flat, Sophia is struck with an overwhelming sense of exhaustion, a wave of fatigue permeating through every part of her body. Unlike her normal routine, she is too tired to shower or remove her makeup. Instead, she brushes her teeth, removes her clothes and falls into bed. Her bedside clock shows midnight. Within a couple of minutes she escapes into a nurturing sleep.

Shattered by stress and financial worry Sophia wakes in the middle of the night after dreaming of being chased by hordes of creditors, screaming and shouting her name. She finally falls asleep again and dreams she's pushing an overladen supermarket trolley, bulging with plastic bags and an heirloom oil painting randomly jammed in amongst the strange collection of old boxes and papers, folders and books she pushes along busy Market Road, past the State Theatre in downtown Sydney. She squints down at her grubby feet jammed into a pair of old rubber thongs. People in the crowd shove her while some sneer and abuse her.

'Git off the bloody street you loser,' shouts an angry businessman who looks uncannily like a distorted younger version of her father.

Several women cross the road, preferring to dodge the traffic rather than pass by her on the same pavement.

Sophia turns towards a large shop window that reaches from

104

ceiling height to the ground. She halts. Her reflection is an older woman, a filthy, scruffy looking bag-lady. In mute disbelief she raises her hand and the reflected image does the same. Terror courses through her body with razor-sharp accuracy as her heart races and beads of perspiration form on her forehead and upper lip.

'It's me,' she repeats to herself over and over. 'It's me,' her own voice echoes into the street and everyone peers at her. Sophia's minimal clothing is dirty, torn pieces, scraps of filthy rag barely clinging to her body. Humiliated and horrified, she looks away, glancing downwards at her filthy clothes. Two pouches barely clinging to her short, faded cotton skirt have something in them. She rams her hands inside the dog-eared pockets and touches a few coins. She has to get out of there, catch a bus or a taxi back home. Her cell phone is missing. She's gripped with rising panic. Withdrawing her hands, she sees four coins amounting to a single dollar sitting in the palm of her grimy hand.

Thirsty and hungry with no way of getting help, her sense of horror and isolation overrides her ability to think. No money. She has no money and knows with every cell in her frightened body that without money she has nothing.

A policeman slams his uniformed hand on her shoulder.

'Where do you think you're going?' He shoves her roughly, forcing her to stumble. Gripping her upper arm, he drags her back up onto her feet before she falls hard onto the rough concrete footpath.

'I need to get home,' she begs. To Sophia's surprise her voice sounds submissive and whining.

The officer sneers in disgust. 'It ain't here, so move along,' he says in a thick outback accent, unmoved and uninterested in the pleas of another homeless vagrant.

'Please, please help me,' she tries to appeal to him.

Ignoring her, he shoves Sophia backwards and she stumbles against the trolley. 'Git going and stay away from here.' His voice rises in anger. His right hand reaches for his gun, resting in a leather holster which Sophia hadn't noticed before. Suddenly he points the black metal barrel between her petrified eyes. She screams in long soundless agony and shocks herself awake.

It takes a few seconds for her to realise she is in the safe confines of her own rented flat. Breathless with horror, she reaches for the bedside lamp and flicks the switch. Her heart still thumping in her chest. She inhales deeply through her nose and tells herself she's all right, that everything is OK. She's safe. But she registers her darkest fears of the future are enacted in this nightmare.

CHAPTER 21

Nose to the Coal Face - 2008

Sophia's growing frustration at rejection emails from job applications in the diplomatic corps leaves her disheartened. All the good positions are over-subscribed with every keen young thing clamouring for an internship. Her chances are limited, especially after background checks reveal her father is a high-profile bankrupt. Private conversations between key players in the upper echelons of corporate business and political influencers ensure the doors of opportunity are firmly locked. Sophia has rent to pay and reluctantly accepts a receptionist job at a travel agency after fruitless months of job hunting.

It isn't long before she resigns in boredom at the menial tasks, low wages and irritation with the inane chatter from those around her. There must be a better way to secure an income and quality of life she justly deserves. She blames her parents and their wealthy indulgence during her childhood setting a high benchmark. She's determined to breach the barriers of relative poverty to gain financial independence. There is an easier way lapping at her consciousness. But how to get there?

Sophia understands her father can no longer support her or help subsidise her lifestyle during the years it will take to establish her career. Even if it were possible, landing a job and working at it for years to accumulate enough funds makes this option a dead end. She doesn't have the luxury of years to wage a career war. She needs income fast.

The kernel of an idea which has washed around in Sophia's busy mind the past couple of months holds some opportunity. Unexpectedly, she realises her unique position. The business arrangement with Giles is working perfectly. Maybe she can expand this into a fully-fledged operation? At first she struggles with the concept. Is she crazy? Her disappointment at being overlooked by the diplomatic corps brings her need to earn a living into fresh focus. Her multi-lingual talents could be put to good use, for a non-negotiable fee, way beyond the reach of most. The critical reasoned part of her argues relentlessly: Are you insane? After all those years of university study you choose to become a high-class call girl.

She replays last months' tense conversation with her father, clawing at the scab of absolute fear and poverty. A wave of utter terror seeps through every pore as she considers surviving penniless in the real world. The implication of her father's demise almost brings her to tears again. She rolls to the other side of her bed, pulling the quilt up over her shoulders. Reality hits home. The impact of financially supporting Teressa and her father for some years is her responsibility. Who else? Who can help the family now they're penniless? Who would be willing to carry the full burden of her father's stupidity? She has to step up and help but how can she fast-track an immediate income?

What of Grandmother? Her father can't contribute to Edith's retirement care anymore either. None of them are capable of scratching out a living. Their livelihoods all depend on Sophia. But how can she generate enough to support the family? Her father was furious when she suggested he talk to his brother for a loan. After all the misery and angst he is still too proud to approach any relative for help. She needs to focus on her mad flicker of a business plan and get some constructive strategies in place. Could it be a real money-making opportunity instead of hot air intermittently blowing through her mind, going nowhere? She must talk to Florian, and somehow override his resistance. He wasn't too keen eight months ago when she vaguely intimated her course of action.

What if I take on other well-heeled men, like Giles? Sophia begins to daydream about a couple of wealthy lovers. Ruminating about the credibility of each man paying for her company had its own difficulties. There's lots to consider and she can't ever risk anyone finding out. But at the same time, she needs to talk to someone, to see if this new business model can stand real scrutiny.

110

She fleetingly considers Giles as the most obvious advisor, but if he hates the idea, he could make her life impossible. There was no way she would accept charity from him either. If he knew what she was up to, in her private business, he could withdraw completely from the family and sever any future chance of earning income this way. He's also inappropriate given his affair with her mother years ago. Sophia isn't sure why she hasn't confronted him about this either. An instinctive aversion, her gut warning her not to tackle him has stopped her mentioning the past to Giles. He evidently thinks she was a child at the time and would probably not remember him *mating* her mother that summer afternoon back then. She suspects his long friendship and business connection with her father are contributory factors, triggering alarm bells every time she considers raising the issue. Why rock the boat? There's been enough disasters already in her short life. Why set herself up for more?

Even-keeled Giles may be angered at the very thought of sharing her with another man or maybe two. Is this like being an escort or a call-girl? What's the difference with other people who have ten or more lovers in a lifetime? She simply wants to manage her lovers along business lines. Why not? Was that even a thing? The trick will be keeping her clients private from the world and secret from one another.

From her sailing experience Sophia intuitively understands male needs, accepts every client will desire her full attention, utterly and absolutely. One paying lover is not enough to support her family. She will need a few more. But how will it work?

If she maintains a monogamous subterfuge with each client being the only lover, then she has an ideal excuse to charge each one a monthly retainer. This would offer some job security. A wide grin spreads across her face. It is cunning, she acknowledges and if she can only swing it into cold hard reality, her financial problems will evaporate in one erotic heartbeat.

Within a matter of months, her father has sold their magnificent Point Piper family home along with the other properties in Australia and overseas. Instead of freeing him from anxiety and

111

fear, Michael Huston deteriorates, retreating further into the past. He finds solace in the familiarity of his successes of twenty years ago. Michael announces to anyone listening that the proceeds from the sale of his family home allows him to escape the ghosts of the past and provides enough additional funding for investment in an exciting new business. None of this bears any semblance to Michael's reality, adding to his daughters' public embarrassment and humiliation.

He tells everyone he is paying off some minor debts and will soon announce a new confidential business deal. He explains over the past six months he has been working tirelessly to secure a fantasy business buy-out. This fast-growing, imaginary business offers him a significant shareholding, a company that would take the market by storm. His future success is assured.

Both sisters and some of his business associates know this is nothing but hot imaginary air. He has already torched and burned his own credibility, similarly he had smoked the relationships with venture capitalists, investors and shareholders alike. There is no future business potential in the newly minted husk that is the current Michael Huston. He has scorched many alliances and business relationships over the past year. No one will touch him with any kind of pole. His likely future is fast-tracked into obscurity, but for now, his daughters humour him by never daring to ask any penetrating questions.

'Leave him to his dreams,' Sophia comments to her sister over lunch one day as their father excuses himself and stalks off to the bathroom with the determination of an armed warrior readying himself for another boardroom battle. 'Why bring him back to reality, when his life is charcoal and ashes?'

Teressa nods silently, watching her father slowly exit the room.

A week later the two sisters help him move the remaining furniture into his newly rented flat. Most items had been auctioned and sold to defray his ongoing expenses with lawyers and creditors howling for blood. His humiliating move into a small one-bedroom apartment in Paramatta should have bought him closure, but there is little acceptance of reality on his part. The sisters agreed to take turns visiting him twice a week. Their gaunt father, looking frail, continued to voice his empty plans and hollow business proposals. Nodding in rare agreement, the sisters privately refuse to confront their broken father.

Three weeks after her father's move into the cramped confines of his new abode, Sophia knocks on his apartment door. No answer. She calls out to him several times, getting louder, finally thumping with her fist on the green painted metal door.

His neighbour, a middle-aged matron with curly purple hair, pokes her head from the adjoining apartment.

'He's not been too good,' she says. 'I talked to him yesterday, and he said he was feeling poorly. He looks pretty crook to me.'

Sophia nods with concern. 'Is there any way I can have a key and get inside? It's unlike him not to answer. I saw his car downstairs in the parking lot.'

'He's there,' confirms the middle-aged lady, walking towards Sophia. 'He doesn't feel like answering.'

'Oh,' Sophia looks confused. 'Why not?'

'He told me he was over it. Over everyone and wants to be left alone. So, I have.'

'Have what?' Sophia asks frowning.

'Left him alone,' the older woman says. Sophia looks down and notices the faded pink slippers the woman wears have two holes where the toenails of her two big toes have worn their way through the top of the fabric on both shoes.

'When did you last see him?' Sophia asks, shifting her face towards the woman's rheumy blue eyes.

The woman shrugs. 'I dunno. Maybe two or three days ago.'

Sophia frowns again, unsure about how to progress.

'Here, I'll give it a go.' The woman offers and rummages around in her baggy cardigan pocket, pulling out a bunch of well-worn keys. 'I used to be able to open the door with a hairpin, but I don't use 'em anymore,' she says in a broad Australian twang.

'Please,' Sophia responds, stepping back from the doorway and indicating with her right hand. To her amazement, the neighbour opens the front door in under two minutes.

Sophia thanks the woman and without hesitation marches

through the open front door. She calls out to her father a couple of times as she walks through the cluttered kitchen and into the small adjoining lounge. Saddened by the single two-seater sofa taking up the majority of the space, her fear of being penniless nips at the fringes of her reality. A stark warning as she glances around the cramped room. She calls her father again. There is no response. The flat stinks of sweat, alcohol and old rotting food. She notices the overloaded kitchen bin and guesses this is the main culprit. All the windows are tightly closed, some of the curtains pulled shut, making for a dingy, claustrophobic space.

Quickly glancing around, Sophia walks into the bedroom. The unmade double-bed is crammed into the small room, covered in various pieces of clothing, hangers, and some folders and papers balancing precariously on piles of washing. The sheets and yellowing bed pillows look filthy, with both side tables cluttered with rubbish, side plates, half-eaten pizza, and mugs and glasses with small amounts of unconsumed liquid. Shoes and underwear, belts and socks litter the bedroom floor. Sophia is repulsed by the entire experience but has no time to consider any solution before marching into the small bathroom.

With disbelief she sees her father lying awkwardly on the floor, his head wedged between the sink and the base of the unflushed toilet. Before she can react, the female neighbour lets out a shriek. She has followed Sophia through the flat and can't help being horrified by the state of Mr Huston lying awkwardly sprawled on the grey linoleum floor.

Sophia crouches, gently turning her father onto his back. With growing horror and a sense of déjà vu about her mother's death, she fears her father has died too. She frantically presses her manicured fingers against his neck and then leans in close to assess if she can feel his warm breath against her cheek.

'Is he OK?' asks the neighbour, refusing to move from the bathroom door frame.

'No!' responds Sophia without hesitation and urgently commands 'Call an ambulance now!'

CHAPTER 22

Maternal Love – 2009

In her suburban flat, Sophia is surrounded by half a dozen packing boxes from her parents' old house neatly stacked up along the hallway and several in one corner of her small bedroom. She opens two sealed boxes containing some personal items, but the others are crammed with memorabilia and old books collected over many years by her dearly departed mother.

After phoning her father about bringing a few of her mother's boxes to his apartment, she receives a flat refusal.

'Are you OK?' she asks.

Over the past year her father has gradually managed to semi-control his diabetes; if only he could stop his excessive drinking. He still has the scar from the large gash to his forehead after falling unconscious in the flat. Teressa and Sophia take turns over weekends to visit him. With the way Sophia's new life is unfolding she wants to bury the past. She isn't sure what to do with her mother's things and Teressa indicates even less interest. Sophia fears opening her mother's boxes, wary of what she might find, and the risk of emotional upset delivered to her from beyond the grave.

'Yeah,' her father responds, his voice weary and heavy with indifference. 'I'm fine. I don't need any more rubbish cluttering up my place.'

'OK,' Sophia says. 'I'll sort it out. Teressa said she would pop over on Saturday morning.'

Her father grunts in response which Sophia believes sums up her father's life. She says goodbye and clicks off the phone.

His self-absorbed capacity for narcissistic navel gazing is the one trait the demise of his fortune has not altered. Sophia sees him for what he is, a boring, irritating and frustrating old man. The less she has to do with him the better. How had she ended up with two narcissistic parents? What were the chances? Both parents lacked a genuine sense of love for their daughters and for one another. The knock-on effect for both sisters has proven emotionally catastrophic. She wonders if Teressa's recent religious obsession relates to similar dysfunctional territory, failed love and a sense of loss.

There's nothing worse than a new convert, who constantly quotes Corinthians and damnation in the face of Sophia's cynicism. Her Achilles heel is impatience as she battles to maintain an air of tolerance with her neurotic sister's ramblings. It's the least she could do given Teressa suffers from the same love-less upbringing. She is convinced Teressa sought God to assuage her wounds from a compromised upbringing.

Their mother's incapacity to love has harmed them both and probably her father too, although he deserves it. No wonder Abigail, emotionally broken and wounded, died young. Always looking for lovers, Abigail pursued transient affairs and failed every time, neglecting to secure love with any sense of permanence. These thoughts swirl around Sophia's mind as she grabs a kitchen knife and begins slicing through the brown packing tape securing the top of her mother's first storage box.

There's something satisfying about slicing open her mother's life, rummaging through her past, with old books, papers and ornaments unwrapped, exposing memories. Sophia is impressed. Some of the items may be worth a lot of money. Getting them appraised by an antique dealer will be a priority. One sculptured piece of an ape sitting under a palm tree has a silver stamp underneath and appears to be signed by Buccellati. It will be simple enough to have it valued. But there's no provenance or sales bill with the piece. Sophia estimates it could be worth more than seventy-thousand dollars.

'Thank you, Mother,' she whispers into the air, placing the sculpture on top of the kitchen counter. Rummaging amongst the crumpled newsprint in the box, Sophia unearths an eccentric looking statue signed by Frank Meister. She smiles at the thought of adding this to her coffers. She will have to split the proceeds from any auction with her sister. Did she really have to? Teressa has no idea about these items and shows even less interest in their mother or art of any kind. Sophia also places the piece on the kitchen counter and considers them both. How to handle things with Teressa. How could she work around any obligation to split the earnings with her younger sister? She decides patience, a wait and see policy, making sure she gets a valuation of each piece before any auction takes place. Fleetingly, she accepts there's one antique for each daughter. Maybe that's a better way, a token, a memento from their dead mother to each of her bereft daughters. She makes a mental note to hold onto the most valuable item of the pair. *Teressa need never know.*

Returning to the unpacking, there are unwrapped piles of old books which she stacks neatly next to the boxes in the small hallway along with other folders stuffed to breaking point with nondescript documents. She slices open the fourth box where she finds several personal diaries lying on top. As she selects the first dark leather-bound notebook, a folded piece of paper falls to the floor at her feet. Sophia picks it up and carefully unfolds the fragile hand-written note. It is a personal letter in her mother's distinctive scrawl. Strange, maybe she never posted it. There is no envelope with the name of who it may have been addressed to.

Dearest
After my mother's funeral I've been awash with melancholy, racking over my past. I realise I never really knew her. All those wasted years of anger.

In the end, I learned to live with the hurt. It's sad that I wasn't what she wanted in a daughter. I was never enough. I too was therefore unable to give her the love and respect she desperately wanted.
As I look back, now that I have two small daughters of my own, I understand that I've transferred the burden of being emotionally cut-off onto the next generation. Learned behaviour, I guess. Conditioned to treat my daughters at arm's length too. I still have that mantra repeating in my head:

If I am not perfect, no one can love me.

Perfection, how insane is that? No one is ever perfect, and least of all, myself. Looking forward to seeing you Sunday.

Abby x

Her mother's words, written all those years ago about her own mother, were pause for thought. Were her decisions and actions a result of a loveless approach to relationships? A life lived with an innate brokenness, handed down from mother to daughter, for generations to come.

Never mind the sons of the fathers. It was the daughters of the mothers who impacted Sophia's ability to live a happy, fulfilled life in a well-adjusted relationship.

Sophia jumps, startled by a knock at the front door. It's Florian holding Chinese take-aways and bursting into the flat with his usual upbeat enthusiasm.

'Thought you'd be hungry about now,' he says. 'Sorry I didn't call. My battery's flat.'

'Glad you came over. I was about to get all upset and maudlin over Mother,' Sophia says, grabbing one of the paper bags from Florian's hands.

'Oh, darling what's wrong?' he asks, concern in his voice. 'You do know your mother is only human.'

Sophia sniffs, giving a weak smile. 'Been unpacking boxes to chuck out and found some interesting things.'

They sit at the kitchen counter, eating and chatting about the two sculptures. The conversation ebbs and flows, as it does with close friends working through recent issues and updates. Florian is slightly surprised by Sophia's heartfelt candour. She isn't often so emotionally honest and open. He cuts to the chase and expresses the real reason he suddenly popped over unannounced.

'Have you had any more thoughts about your new business strategy?' he asks, smiling with keen interest at his friend munching through the last vestiges of their shared meal.

She nods, swallowing a mouthful of delicious chicken fried rice.

'Yeah, I've got nothing to lose. What are your top three tips, Mr. Florian Fabre, for nurturing my angle within?' she asks, raising her eyebrows and effortlessly playing the coquette.

'No use trying your tricks on me, darl,' he laughs. 'I have a few ideas to focus on which may help.' He pauses, inhaling through his nose and leaning back in the kitchen chair. 'You need to always pay attention. Always maintain eye contact. You need to concentrate all your attention on the guy you're with. He's the centre of your universe for as long as he's paying.'

They both chuckle. 'Yeah. I get that,' she says before grabbing a bottle of wine from the fridge. 'Do you want a drink?'

'Sure, Sav's great. How many clients are you thinking about?'

'Maybe two or three, including Giles.'

'If you're taking it this far you may as well go hard.' He chuckles. 'Why not five or six clients?'

'Really?' Sophia falls silent considering the complexities.

'Go for broke,' he advises.

'I've spent a lot of time thinking this through. I don't want to take on just any guy off the street. I firmly believe a select group of dedicated men who appreciate the finer things in life are the clients I need.'

'No doubt they'll want to enjoy the finer things, like your good self,' Florian smiles.

'Exactly!' she says, triumphant.

CHAPTER 23

Like A Virgin - 2009

'Your father's definitely not himself,' Giles tells Sophia as they wait to be called for dinner. He elaborates a little more, explaining how his friend and business associate has lost all motivation and appears to be sleepwalking through life.

'I suspect he's been severely depressed for some time,' he offers, recapturing her attention.

'How serious do you think it is?' Sophia asks, confused by the unexpected direction the conversation takes.

'He's made a few crazy decisions. Evidently not in his right mind,' Giles explains. 'I've tried talking to him, but it's useless. I've offered help and some financial input, but he calls me patronising.' Giles sighs. 'He's not who he used to be, and no one wants to deal with the new Mike!' He inhales deeply, raising his eyebrows. 'If he was open to getting help, your father could get back on his feet,' he concludes. 'But what about you? I hear you've chucked in your first job.'

'It's so boring.' Sophia responds, downcast. There's no way she's going to complicate their relationship by risking a discussion around her new potential business. Feeling remorseful and guilty at withholding her true calling is one thing but jeopardising her plans is one step too far. Giles is older and a bit more conservative. He could go off like a box of crackers if he knew what career path she is considering.

'I thought I was going to scream,' Sophia says.

'You don't want to be doing that unless you're safely in bed with me!' Giles grins as Sophia snorts and rolls her eyes.

She's used to his double entendre and quips about sex. Surprisingly Sophia hasn't surrendered her virginal status, and Giles still hasn't given up trying. Sophia's learned nearly everything she needs to know from their pleasurable hours of foreplay and flirtatious conversation.

After nearly two years under Giles' tutelage she's well equipped to know precisely what men want and how to deliver. No longer the apprentice, she still insists on the sanctity of virginity, much to Giles' frustration. Part of him is grateful, better to have her in his bed than not, so he doesn't push his luck. No point in upsetting the status quo for an unassailable target which she refuses to relinquish. He has utterly underestimated her in every conceivable way. He grins as he listens to his young companion chatting about her life.

While waiting for their table they're directed to the long bar in one of Sydney's world class hotels. Both are seated in rich black and gold brocade armchairs, sipping their drinks to the refined tones of a grand piano situated in the corner of the well-appointed room. A classical musical genius, dressed in a white collared-shirt and formal black trousers, gracefully plucks at the keys and lifts his handsome head to smile openly at Sophia. She doesn't acknowledge him, looking away back towards Giles relaxing in the ambience of the sumptuous room. The pianist is about her age, young and fit with thick dark hair that almost covers his bright eyes. His shoulders shift and swing to the rhythm of the slowly building movement of Ennio Morricone's adagio in the famous musical film arrangement, *The Mission*.

Sophia sips from her glass and smiles warmly at Giles, making sure she maintains eye contact, confirming he is fully engaged with every word.

'Florian said he would keep an ear to the ground and put me in touch with some of his contacts. I might be able to help him in his new start-up business too,' she babbles, concerned Giles may sense something is not quite right.

'That's good. Maybe I can help? What does Florian want you to do?' Giles asks, mildly interested.

'Interior design and admin work. He already has three clients. I believe he needs a perfect personal assistant.' She beams, pointing her index finger back towards herself. 'Moi, of course.' She laughs, breaking the sexual tension between them.

124

'Of course! He'd be a fool not to take you on board, darling,' Giles responds with mock surprise. Should he reactivate the conversation again about her status and his desire? He ponders other ways he can attack the issue. Sophia is on her second glass of French champagne which usually makes her pliable. Why not? There's nothing to lose.

Leaning back in the comfortable armchair, he regards this young, gorgeous woman sitting opposite fondly gazing at him.

'So are you still a virgin?' he asks in a harsh whisper, holding his glass close to his mouth in a feigned attempt at a hushed confidential tone.

Sophia inhales through her nose, looking steadily at the older man opposite. 'You never give up, do you, Mr. Hamilton?'

'No,' he admits, grinning.

Why would she hand over her virginity for free? It's a commodity like any other service she intends to ply in her new business. Some of her research showed wealthy men bidding online for virgins with prices sky-rocketing in some cases. Mercenary? Who? Them or me? Virginity's the only thing which I can make a fair chunk of cash from and who knows how long I'll have to wait until I get my business off the ground. I need cashflow and a safety-net to cover family expenses. If I play my cards right, there's no reason why I can't sell my virginity for a small fortune. It's chicken feed for Giles and wealthy men like him.

They both eye one another, uncertain which way the conversation is going. Giles is confident she is, for the first time, thoughtfully considering his request.

But she isn't, not unless he's prepared to put real money on the table. Mind you, there had been several times lying naked in bed with the man when he had driven her wild with desire. Very nearly, on two separate occasions, she almost threw caution to the wind, allowing him access to her most sought-after asset.

He is the first to break the impasse. 'I'll pay top dollar and show you a good time,' he grins broadly.

'I'm sure you will, but my top dollar is probably out of your reach,' she teases.

He smirks. One thing he's learned about Sophia is her

unmitigated delight in the taunting game. It's an art form with her, and he's keen to play if it finally means she willingly commits her virginity to him.

The banter back and forth continues for a few minutes before he grows mildly irritated.

'Come on, Sophia, for heaven's sake,' he says, exasperated. 'What's it worth?'

'You tell me,' she smiles playfully, concentrating on the electrifying tension between them.

'Say twenty-five thousand dollars,' he states, deadly serious.

'How did you know?' she mocks, and he bursts out laughing.

'You little minx,' he chides.

But Sophia ignores the taunt and carefully lays out the structured payment plan to maximise her returns on his investment.

'Let me finish, darling,' she smiles adoringly at him, and his racing heart contracts with anticipation.

'This arrangement is obviously outside your original obligations,' she explains.

'Of course,' Giles repeats, with a poker face, almost holding his breath and nodding his head a couple of times, desperately trying to contain his excitement. He knows she's a sharp operator and must keep his wits about him.

'There will be two payments,' she announces matter-of-factually. The first twenty-five beforehand and the second twenty-five within twenty-four hours after the momentous event,' she boldly says with a mischievous expression.

Giles' mouth falls open in disbelief. Fifty thousand dollars! He's hoodwinked again. He concentrates on slowing his breathing and maintains a business-like pose during the tough negotiation. After all, this is as far as she has ever taken this discussion before. His requests have been rebuffed numerous times over the preceding years.

'Well you're truly on form,' he says calmly, 'but let's say I make the first payment and refuse to hand over the second.' He has plenty of money and they both know it. He will let her have a little fun bartering over the deal.

Sophia expects this kind of challenge and lifts her chin, haughty with confidence. 'Let's say losing fifty percent of my fee will result in permanent isolation.' Her face is deadly serious, even the playful glint in her blue eyes has diminished. 'That's not playing nice now, is it Mr Hamilton?'

Her mock sadness and dejected appearance give him pause. He doesn't want to be on the wrong side of her, that's for sure. But Giles wouldn't put it past her to notify his wife. No fool like an old one. Let's face it, she hasn't demanded double that amount. He would've easily coughed up a hundred grand for the full pleasure of consuming her gorgeous, lithe body. He smiles on the inside while maintaining an expressionless face. Rule forty-six, in any negotiation, don't let the opponent read your thoughts.

But as if reading his mind, she says in the same no-nonsense business-like voice, 'For each week you withhold the second payment, I'll be doubling the fee. I can easily, and happily, make my fortune this way.'

He chuckles and holds out his hand to her, shaking it. 'It's a deal,' he surrenders. She always knew he'd comply.

Giles can tell from the thinly disguised look of triumph on her face that she had him from the start. Damn it!

In the guise of a bit of fun, Sophia tests out her personally written client contract. 'We should enter into a binding agreement,' she announces with authority, although it's a bit of a lark and neither takes it too seriously. She hands him a two-page draft closely typed. They laugh and joke about her dubious wording, and numerous bullet points.

'So, does this mean I'll get more bang for my buck?' he asks as they both roar with laughter, drawing attention from the surrounding patrons at the exclusive five-star bar. A waiter appears, interrupting their joviality, and walks them to their table for the evening.

Giles watches Sophia absorbed by the piano music and the surroundings, admiring her as if watching her from afar. He knows her 'contract' won't hold any water but decides to humour her.

'What happens from now on, if we're having sex every week?' He frowns. 'I hope you don't have any intention of hiking your rates. Thirty-five thousand dollars a year in retainer fees is a bit steep too.'

Sophia doesn't miss a beat. 'Oh darling, for you it'll always be mate's rates!'

He laughs, charmed by his young companion's attempt at company law and the ability to browbeat him into submission. Without another word he pulls out a pen, signing the contract.

Sophia makes a mental note to never give Giles any real legal document. One day she will get an official contract drawn up if she can figure out a way to secure more paying clients. She briefly entertains the notion of Giles introducing her to well-heeled businessmen, but then dismisses the idea as a conflict of interest on his part and hers.

'You do know this is now legally binding,' Sophia teases, 'even though you've scribbled changes all over this brilliant piece of contractual documentation.'

'Nice cigar, darling.' He chortles while sipping his wine.

'Well, you wanted to reduce your contact with me to once a week and it only seems right to make it official,' she says.

'It's an official deal then,' Giles leans in closer to his young lover. 'Once a week is good enough for a wayward married man in his thirties,' he whispers to his mistress.

CHAPTER 24

Members Only - 2009

Sophia initiates several exhaustive online searches throughout the global and local sex industry. Maintaining her anonymity by clicking on incognito mode, avoids alerting anyone else to her internet activity. Much of the information is sordid, unappealing and boring. Finally, she contacts Florian, her trusted confidant, to work through the finer details of running a potential business in the high-class call-girl industry.

They agree to catch up in the next few days, and she makes a mental note to side-step dubious details in her conversation. Sophia spends several nights scribbling in a notebook, spelling out her objectives, a calculator at her elbow working through various fee structures. The idea of each client paying a monthly retainer makes perfect sense. It will smooth out her cashflow and keep her clients locked and loaded. She punches in twenty-five hundred dollars each and then tries thirty-five hundred before realising the retainer needs to be a lower base rate. She runs several estimates over the nightly fee, using a range of figures, finally accepting five to six thousand dollars per booking. She will firm up final figures after her investigations are completed.

The bigger issue is finding the right type of high-end clientele. It's going to take smart planning and good contacts to foster introductions amongst the well-heeled. She fantasises about a few scenarios, wondering if her approach is realistic. The business must be strictly under the radar. No one will ever know, and her clients will never find out about one another.

The monthly retainer is necessary to maintain her comfortable lifestyle. Each man will think he is paying a retainer to contribute to her living costs, and she will always be available to him. She smiles to herself. It's a convincing argument and makes perfect business sense. She plays a conversation with one of her imaginary clients in her head. Sophia considers objections and problems like double bookings or a client arriving unannounced. She thinks of every eventuality and mentally scripts a series of slick responses.

After a few more calculations, adding up retainers and overnight fees she settles on the number seven. Giles plus six other men will make up her clientele. She begins to imagine her future career and how it must function like clockwork. Seven wealthy men who believe she is their exclusive mistress. Her cover as an interior designer working for Florian is perfect, but she appreciates discussing her business plans with him will need to be in a little more detail than she first divulged.

In an ideal world, each client will be married, with demanding work commitments and regular overseas travel. For this reason, he'll happily pay a monthly retainer to secure her in the exclusive lifestyle she is destined to enjoy. Over time, Sophia wants to own a beautiful penthouse apartment and acquire a separate private suburban home.

Seven is a lucky number, didn't the Bible tell us so? Or should it be ten? No. Seven has a good feel about it. Seven men's preferences will be kept in seven separate wardrobes lining a locked room in her imaginary luxurious penthouse. She visualises a beautiful, teak and mirror-lined dressing room. Behind each timber panelled door are the items belonging to each lover. Each client will be assured she has eyes only for him because she will always wear items, perfume and clothing to suit his preferences.

She stops day-dreaming for a few minutes, considering how often each man will want to sleep with her, given they are often overseas on business and have family commitments too. Her imaginary clients are allocated two sleep-overs a month each for the sake of business forecasting. Conservatively this gives her a monthly income between fifty-five to over eighty-seven thousand dollars. She scribbles and recalculates the numbers again.

It's highly unlikely she will see all seven men in the same month. With their combined fees she can afford to spread them out across the working weeks. She snorts out loud into the darkening living room. She clicks her cell phone. Already 7 pm! She gathers up the papers and scribbled notes. Food. Sophia reminds herself it's dinner time. Stepping away from the kitchen island, Sophia, pours herself a chilled glass of wine from a half-empty bottle in the fridge door. She flicks on the overhead lights and takes a gulp from her glass. Her mind is now racing with so many elements to her business plan needing focus. The phrase *call-girl* sounds so simple, a basic transactional, uncomplicated arrangement. In the real world, Sophia knows there's a wide range of issues to overcome.

Her father's business lawyer, Ruben Swersky, is ideal for drawing up the private business contract. She acknowledges lawyers have a code of confidentiality, so she assumes she's safe from any sensitive information becoming public. Confidentiality is her mantra. It's also one of the key benefits her clients will fully appreciate, over and above her services.

Securing paying lovers as clients, she contemplates, will prove the most difficult aspect of the entire business. Giles Hamilton is the obvious candidate as an entrée into the league of businessmen but how can she keep the contractual sex-for-money option away from Giles? She needs wealthy men who prefer uncomplicated sex and enjoy a bottomless well of money to finance their predilection. While Giles has agreed to pay fifty thousand dollars for her virginity, Sophia needs to rethink the complexities of their arrangement. What if she could convince Giles to buy her a penthouse apartment for life-long sex with a first option of her buying him out within five years? This proposition is outrageous, but the entire thing is crazy, so why not give it a go?

She scribbles more details in her notebook:

August 18th

Objective: Seven clients or more?
   1. Each client will never know about the others.
   2. This secures their devotion and continued retainer payments and the privilege of sleeping overnight.
   3. Need a world-class apartment (business operation) and a private suburban home (personal life) to maintain

complete separation between both aspects of my life.
4. *Need two identities to gain complete separation from business and personal life.*
5. *How to meet potential paying clients?*
6. *Don't let greed get in the way!*

Finding wealthy clients is the most significant issue Sophia faces but by playing her hand right, Giles might unknowingly assist with introductions. She calls him the next day.

'I have a proposal,' she says.

'Haven't we already agreed on this Soph,' Giles responds with annoyance in his voice, anticipating her reneging again on their fifty thousand deal.

'Well yeah, but I have a much better idea.'

He sighs. 'You do? I'm waiting to hear what diabolical approach you're now offering. I feel like I've got one hand on the devil's staircase and the other on speed dial for the underground.'

'Giles, please. Don't be a grumpy man,' she teases.

'Out with it then. I feel the last few months have added twenty years to this poor devil's shortened life.'

She snorts with amusement. 'What if you and I went fifty-fifty into sharing a beautiful city side penthouse apartment? As a property investment,' she hurriedly adds.

'Umm,' he says into the phone.

'I get to live there, and you have my full attention and my entire body twice a month for the rest of your life.'

'Y-e-s,' he says warily. 'Why not once a week like we agreed? 'What's the catch?'

'I have the first option to buy you out in five years or review it if we're both in agreement.'

After a pause, Giles answers, 'All right, but once a week would sweeten the deal.'

Sophia smiles to herself. 'OK,' she says reluctantly. 'Agreed.' She knows Giles feels he's won the upper hand, but she's given nothing more away than what was originally agreed. Merciless, she says to herself, smiling broadly, before ending the call.

In the end, the pair purchase a beautiful four-bedroom

penthouse apartment overlooking Sydney Harbour. Giles insists the property be held in a Trust with both as equal beneficiaries and his lawyer as executor. Sophia is delighted and immediately talks to Florian about decorating the place over the coming months. Giles agrees to carry the costs of the renovation work too and books her for a weekend in the penthouse once she's moved in. Sophia secures her five-year buy-back clause in the legal documents, so both parties are happy and go out to celebrate on Thursday night. Party night, Giles insists on calling it.

After a couple of drinks at an up-market restaurant near Darling Harbour, he leans forward and whispers in her small shell-like ear. 'Sophia, I know you can't still be a virgin.'

'I am,' she says indignantly, 'and I assure you, you'll get our money's worth.'

'I'm sure of that.' He smirks across the table at his beautiful mistress before walking her to the elevator up to their luxurious hotel room on the twenty-fifth floor. He swipes the security card and locks the door behind them.

'Remember I'm still a virgin,' Sophia says walking into the plushly decorated bedroom.

'Me too,' Giles laughs, 'with you, of course.'

She makes an indistinguishable sound. 'I hear the best approach is to get it over with as fast as possible.'

'What?'

'That's what I heard from others at school years ago.'

He frowns and raises his eyebrows without saying a word.

'Don't hurt me,' she says.

'I mean to hurt you as much as you hurt me!' Giles can't maintain a straight face and chuckles. 'I plan to get my fifty thousand dollars' worth! Not to mention the painful years waiting and the agony my wallet feels every time we meet.'

'It's OK,' she says. 'I'm not going to hurt you anymore.'

He grins. 'It's about time you assumed that position.'

'Ever the romantic.' She sniffs, removing her clothes and jumping into bed.

Within seconds his naked body is beside her. She knows him well. Years of sex-less play takes away some of her anxiety. But

134

Sophia isn't sure. What is she to do, exactly? Giles starts as he always does, gently stroking her back and thighs.

She runs her fingers over his shoulders, down his back and reaches for his groin.

Giles pulls away. 'No, you don't,' he says. 'This is my game.'

'Let's have a test drive to see what the fuss is about,' she jokes.

'Believe me, I know what the fuss is about. No need for a test run. Now stop talking.' He hesitates and regards her face. 'Are you nervous?' he asks, a fleeting look of concern in his expression.

'No ... not much.'

'You are. Dear Sophia, it's never great the first time, I hear tell,' he quickly adds, 'but I'm sure you'll enjoy it from here on in.'

'Very funny.'

'Shhh.'

She lies still wondering how he's going to manouvre to get their body parts aligned. She has a rough idea after watching a porn video years ago but didn't watch it all the way through so is still a little naive. What was she thinking, basing a business proposal on a product she hasn't even tried herself? The mechanics is mind-blowing. Who the hell designed things like this? It all seems so comical. As a child, she remembers seeing two dogs hard at it in the park and she just wanted to laugh. Maybe she'll have to get on all fours? She frowns.

'Something wrong?' Giles asks.

She shakes her head. 'No. Nothing.'

It's unbelievable how tense she's getting, uncertain what she should be doing, especially as he's stopped her contributing any foreplay.

Moments later his naked body lies facing hers, erect and breathing heavily, side by side. He reaches down between her legs, like a keenly trained athlete, his muscle memory guides his hands, his fingers knowing the comfort of her warm, hidden secret place. He's at home in her familiar landscape and easily brings her to climax as his own eagerness strains for self-control.

She softly moans against his ear, relaxing after the wave of ebbing pleasure eases. This is nothing more than she has always enjoyed with Giles over several years. As the warm sensation suffuses throughout her body Giles moves on top of her. She rests her arms around his shoulders, running her right hand smoothly down towards his thigh. At thirty-eight he still has a firm muscular butt, his hard erection pressing against her. Aroused by his excitement, she squeezes his thigh. Moving, he slowly guides himself against her.

The feeling of his member, the head at the entrance but not much more, as she senses something crucial is about to take place. His entire body part is somehow, miraculously going to shove itself into that tiny dark space. She has often looked at his erection and wondered how something of that size could fit inside a female's body. Her friend Carla had laughed at her when she asked that question. 'Don't you worry.' She chuckled. 'It'll fit and once you start having sex it'll be impossible to stop.'

Sophia's annoyed with herself, it's unlike her to be so distracted. He holds his breath, saying nothing. Not sure what to do Sophia remains still and unmoving. Breathing again, Giles begins to move, pressing himself further into her. There is a tiny sharp pain as he moves deeper inside. She gives an unexpected muffled yelp, through closed lips and holds her breath, her body tense. He stops and kisses her, saying nothing before slowly moving inside her again.

He stops. 'Why aren't you moving?'

'Oh. I wasn't sure what to do ….'

'You're supposed to move with me, together,' he says with consternation.

Later, after showering she smiles at him spread-eagled in bed. 'Was it worth it?' she asks feeling somehow older and wiser.

'Absolutely.' He smiles at her. 'But I owe you an apology. I was wrong. I didn't believe you could still be a virgin.'

CHAPTER 25

Members Lounge - 2009

'Not that I'm an expert,' he hesitates, 'but if you want some background ... I have a friend whose aunt runs a brothel near the CBD.' He watches her closely. There isn't a flicker of consternation. 'Actually, she's an aunt of mine. Most of the family have very little to do with her.' He pauses, cautiously waiting for a response.

'You kept that secret very quiet,' she accuses with a wide grin. 'What's the brothel called?'

Florian shrugs uncomfortably. 'It's called the Green House on account of the glass-domed conservatory in the centre with the roof painted deep green. I helped two years ago, with the interior *décor*.

'Oh,' Sophie says, startled. 'Why didn't you mention it before?'

'I didn't think it was something you'd be keen to hear about.'

'Go on,' she insists, brushing her hair back from her face. 'How does it all work?'

'Hang on, Soph,' Florian looks disturbed. 'You aren't going to become a regular call-girl, are you?'

'No!' she almost shouts. 'That's insane. I'd never do that, but I do want to understand more about the business side. Do you think I could meet and talk to your aunt?'

'OK. That's a relief,' Florian responds, still feeling uneasy about where the conversation is leading. 'In the past you've mentioned saving unwanted children, adopting a child and giving it a loving home and better life.' He hesitates. 'That dream would be impossible if you go down this track Sophia,' he cautions her as if paying for sex is an antidote for living happily ever after. She smiles to herself at his earnest naivety, mildly surprised by his concern too.

'I can be a romantic at heart and maybe one day before I'm

forty I'll retire from this and find true love,' she says. 'The more I think about it, the more I'd like to adopt or foster a child.

He nods, saying nothing, pondering this unlikely fork in the road of Sophia's life.

'You don't look like the type to hang about on the corners of King's Cross,' Celeste comments, sniffing the air and looking down at the young woman. She glances furtively at her nephew, Florian, who merely nods and introduces Sophia to his aunt.

A waitress ushers the trio to a table for Victorian high tea in the gardens park cafe. Moments later a waiter delivers a large pot of English breakfast tea, three porcelain plates, cutlery and a fine china tea service, carefully placing it on their linen covered table. He disappears, quickly returning with an elaborate looking three-tier cake stand loaded with delicious savouries, cream covered chocolate slices, and sweet miniature petit fours.

Celeste's well-worn face belies her age. Slim and in her mid-fifties with fast-moving, beady eyes darting around the room from face to face before she sits down. Her short, bleached hair is on-trend with the trimmed edges obscuring her drooping earlobes. Heavy fresh-water pearl and gold stud earrings drag her ears down against her cheeks.

Surprisingly, she wears minimal make-up and takes care to dress in designer label clothing which screams upper middle-class. You'd never know she was a madam. Sophia notes how this woman could merge seamlessly into any crowd without drawing attention, until she opens her mouth. Her face is animated, and she continually smiles at Sophia, who worries Celeste sees her as a future source of income. Sophia immediately plays along, encouraging the older woman to reveal as much as possible.

'Florian delivered a brilliant job at the Green House. I wanted the interior to look like an old Southern American plantation mansion, tall palms, pineapple lights and crystal chandeliers. You know the kind of thing.' Celeste smiles warmly, holding Sophia's gaze, scrutinising the young woman. 'He knows his stuff, does our Florian,' she continues disarmingly. 'A brilliant interior designer. He told me you were thinking of working for him. What's changed your mind?'

Sophia glances across at her friend, who is about to laugh, so she quickly looks back at Celeste, waiting expectantly.

'I'm not sure yet,' Sophia says. 'I'm hoping to find out what's involved. My family's in a spot of trouble, so money has now become a priority.'

This seems to satisfy Celeste for the moment. She is the youngest of eight siblings, the *runt of the litter*, she often jokes. Born of Irish Catholic immigrants, Celeste's street-wise, pragmatic approach to religion and compromising moral fortitude doesn't prevent her from hiring twenty-eight women who work twenty-four hours a day across three rostered shifts.

'I built the call-girl business up from nothing, and I make damn sure they're all well looked after,' she states proudly. 'I started out working Kings Cross with the other poor losers and drug addicts thirty years ago. Finally, I saved enough cash, with the help of a silent investor, to buy the Green House and look at me now!' she laughs. 'Girls like yourself are coming to me all the time looking for regular work and a secure income.'

Florian's right, Sophia thinks, his aunt is brash and outspoken, but she finds Celeste likeable with a down-to-earth, direct approach. He's already explained how Celeste's name means *heaven sent*, but she was definitely the ugliest in the family who regarded her lifestyle as one foot in hell and the other sliding down a slippery slope. Her appearance is no drawback, and over the years Celeste has endured every cosmetic intervention known to the free world, transforming from an ugly duckling into a celestial swan with an appetite for men of biblical proportions.

With a bulldog obsession, Celeste tirelessly focuses on the success of her business. 'It's a calling,' she explains with reverence, 'which provides me with a very comfortable lifestyle. Thank you very much.' She grins and leans across the table. 'Listen darl, let's get real here. Where the hell would we be without men?'

'No worse off.' Sophia chuckles. 'I have one question, so I can get my head around the rates and payments. Can you please explain how it all works? It must be tricky at times?'

141

This query pleases Celeste no end. She's confident Sophia will be a great little earner once she's learned the ropes. Discussing rosters, business targets and expectations along with pulling in pre-qualified clients is the kind of business talk Sophia relates to.

'No one likes talking about money,' explains the Green House madam. 'The first thing we serve customers is an elegant menu of expensive drinks, from imported champagne at over eighteen hundred dollars a bottle to wines and whisky of all kinds and qualities, just like the service my girls offer.'

Florian lets out a low whistle. 'I'm so glad I'm not straight,' he chuckles. Both he and Sophia are dumbstruck at the cost of alcohol, but Celeste responds quickly, dissuading them of any assumptions on that front.

'Champagne costs a lot.' She grins deviously. 'But it also includes the full service, if you get my drift?'

'Oh,' Sophia says, surprised by this revelation. 'Is this for the whole night?'

'Don't be ridiculous!' Celeste replies. 'I don't want my staff sleeping on the job. It's work, hard bloody graft and clients pay for the service. It can take somewhere between ten minutes and two hours depending on the John.'

She observes the confusion on the two young faces across the table. So naive, it's like leading a lamb to slaughter. 'Look, it's dead simple. The champagne costs eighty bucks, the balance is the fee for the girl for an hour, and if it's longer, they pay another hour's fee whether they use up all that time or not. This is the fee for my top girls of course, and there's only about eight of them. The others work a John over in ten minutes and he pays his three hundred bucks and walks. It's like a production line, you could be stuffing beans in tins at a canning factory. The girls call the open lounge *the snake-pit*, for obvious reasons, it has a high turn-around, and they make a good living.

'I offer this two-tier service, and of course, other specialities, for a bigger fee for those who can afford it. I'm able to capture the best part of the market.' Celeste pauses, sipping tea, and glances from one astounded face to the other. 'You've gotta cater for everyone love, you know, or you'll be out of business before you've got their pants down.'

'What money do the girls make' Sophia asks.

'It works out at about forty per cent,' explains Celeste, 'but it does vary. If she's good and can turn the business around and service more clients, and they love her, well, I'm open to negotiation. Remember I've the overheads of the house costs, maintenance, upkeep, and insurance.'

Sophia nods, 'I see.' She quickly calculates she could potentially make three thousand dollars or more a day, which motivates her next question. 'What about tax and other costs? Do you charge anything to the working girls?'

Celeste's impressed, not your average dumb hooker, she thinks before replying. 'I run a licensed business, so I have to pay for that and pay for their regular weekly health checks. The girls pay tax and, you understand, some of them are in the top bracket so pay thirty-two percent or more in tax annually. My accountant runs the books and makes sure they meet their Australian Tax Office obligations. It's all above board,' she continues elaborating. 'Prostitution was decriminalised back in 1979 and owning or managing a brothel is legal. But, the weird thing is, making a living from earnings as a sex worker is illegal!' She laughs. 'Go figure. The madness of men in power. I reckon we've got a higher ratio of morons in government than in any other part of our economy.'

Sophia and Florian laugh in agreement and nod in unison without saying a word. Celeste launches into a rambling commentary about the poor state of politics and the associated limp wristed leadership yo-yo-ing around decisions and foreign policy. 'Look at climate change,' she says. 'How far have those politicians got their heads up each other's arses?' She catches her breath and takes another gulp from her lukewarm cup. 'It's gonna take more than prayers to get us out of this mess. I know they separated politics from religion years ago, as hard as that is to believe, given the number of political evangelists that can't see the fake truth from reality. I should know. A lot of these blokes are my most committed customers.'

Florian interrupts. 'The whole world is in a sorry state, and I lay

143

most of the blame at the PM's door.'

'Yeah well, don't be like that darl. He makes some idiot moves but the idiots we have in power still tap dance to his tune. We need to separate politics from sex, then maybe a few of those leaders could think straight and make hard decisions.' She grabs her serviette and presses it against her lips. For the first time, Sophia notices how thin and fragile Celeste's hands seem, papery skin taut across the bones of the back of her tiny hands. Celeste must be at least a decade older than Sophia initially imagined.

'All the bloody shagging around that goes on in our parliament. It's like sleeping while Rome burns,' she continues. 'We've got the sleeping and the burning all humming along nicely but the cost to the bloody country it's ...'

A waitress wanders over to the trio deep in conversation. 'Would you like anything else?' she politely interrupts.

'No, thanks,' Florian states after checking with the two women sipping from their porcelain cups. They hardly ate anything from the delicate cake stand, and now take the opportunity to select a few more tasty morsels before continuing with their conversation, once the waitress is out of earshot.

'What do you think?' Celeste asks Sophia as she bites into a slice of carrot cake. 'Interested in joining the team?'

'I need to think about it and work a few things out,' Sophia says, savoring the icing, pressing the sweet buttery topping against the roof of her mouth as she considers how to communicate her non-committal response to Celeste.

'I forgot to mention the house rules. Things like no kissing on the mouth, no exchange of any personal information and of course you need a fake identity. A name the men can call you. We like to keep your private life completely separate from your work. Besides it's much safer that way too. I'll give you a print-out if you decide to sign the contract.'

Sophia nods but has already made up her mind to avoid going down this track, at least, in this particular way. She already has a more sophisticated plan in mind.

Celeste stands up, and the other two do the same. 'Lovely to have met you.' She offers her hand to Sophia. 'You would be a

144

real asset to my business. I hope to hear from you in the coming week, and we can discuss it in more detail. No pressure.' She chuckles as she grabs her handbag from the back of the chair and flings it over her shoulder. She leans closer to Florian giving him a hug. 'Lovely catching up with you too, darl,' she says. 'Must do this again soon.' Before Florian responds with the usual platitudes, Celeste turns on her heels, striding towards the exit.

They face one another and smile.

'What are you thinking?' Florian asks as the back of his aunt retreats towards the parking lot outside.

'The thing is,' Sophia grins, 'hooking like that is going to be pretty hard on the member's lounge, if you get my drift!

CHAPTER 26

In the Know - 2010

During the next six months, Sophia works for Florian twice a week in his new interior design offices based amongst the trendy café scene of Sydney's Surry Hills business district, crowded with terraced houses, fashion boutiques and a vast array of eateries. Florian merges into the creative vibe of the area, connecting to the vibrant local community. They work together like clockwork. Sophia's energy and eye for detail proves invaluable as she types up proposals for new clients. She attends functions with Florian and is occasionally mistaken for his girlfriend, which neither of them bother to remedy.

'Let them live the dream.' Sophia giggles. 'There's a whole lot more they don't know and the more confusion, the better.'

'Yeah and let's keep it that way darling,' Florian warns.

Within two months Sophia has taken possession of the new contemporary penthouse on the top floor overlooking Sydney Harbour with expansive views across the seawater towards the north shore.

In quick succession, Sophia organises a series of builders and tradies to renovate and redecorate the apartment. In fulfilling her dreams, she converts one of the bedrooms into a walk-in dressing room. Giles happily pays for the upgrade without so much as a whimper. After all, Sophia argues convincingly, any investment in the property will increase the value of his share. It takes carpenters nearly five weeks to install the seven highly polished, teak double-doors. The cabinet maker finishes them to a high standard, pleasing Giles and Sophia in turn. They also fit out a separate walk-in robe for Sophia, off the master bedroom and ensuite bathroom. Sophia charmingly explains to Giles how she intends to store her shoes and clothing across both areas.

'You have to agree, Giles, there is simply not enough storage in this place, and the rooms are huge, so it makes sense for us to have more cupboards and shelving,' she says convincingly.

The ensuite bathroom has a large oval, marble hot tub installed. Exotic timber and luxurious tiles replace the old flooring throughout Sophia's new home. Scattered deep-pile fine silk and wool Persian rugs are prudently positioned across the floors of the living room and bedrooms.

Once the newly tiled bathroom is completed and the hot tub fully operational, Sophia spends several hours with Giles soaking and massaging his back, neck and feet on the first lazy Thursday afternoon they share together for several weeks. It only seems right, she explains with a determined pout, that they both christen their second-best investment.

Sitting naked in the bath opposite his young lover, Giles grins. 'What's my first?' he asks.

'Me, of course, Mr. Hamilton!' She laughs, sitting up, flirting with him from the other end of the bath as she pulls a handful of hair up from the back of her neck to the top of her head, exposing her smooth breasts above the soap suds. Giles admires how she replicates an ancient Greek goddess, her glowing porcelain skin and dark hair, a playful twinkle in her eyes that never leave his.

He frowns, teasing her too. 'So not this multi-million-dollar home you've acquired through nefarious means?'

'Oh darling.' She giggles and teases. 'What can I do for you to ease your pain?'

The following morning, she arranges to meet with, Carla, who phoned Sophia out of the blue to have coffee at a nearby café in Surry Hills. After ordering and sitting down at a small table in the *avant garde* little Mozart Café, Sophia glances around the eclectic mix of artworks scattered on brightly coloured walls.

Carla starts talking almost immediately, infused with excitement about her new job and her latest boyfriend. Another one has already passed through the revolving doors of Carla's love life since they last spoke. The café possesses that mid-morning buzz of a few discreet businesspeople, immersed in critical discussion. On the opposite side are a pair of colourful and casually dressed musicians with several writers and artists hunched over surrounding tables chatting and laughing with one another while sipping the best coffee in the world.

Carla frequently brushes her thick curly hair away from her eyes as she chats with growing enthusiasm. Her layered look is an attempt to disguise her lengthening fringe, which is growing out and now aligns with the tip of her nose, irritating her as she talks to Sophia. Carla lived in Germany for several years as a teenager and speaks with a subtle foreign accent having acquired a few guttural expressions and Germanic mannerisms from her past.

She often waves her hand dismissively at Sophia if she disagrees with her friend's comments. Always dressed to perfection Carla wears the latest branded shoes and flawless clothing. Her blue eyes rest on Sophia's as she listens intently to her friend. They were never very close at school, but after graduating from university, they now maintain closer contact. Sophia wonders if she should divulge anything about her private business arrangements, or for the sake of privacy, keep Carla in the interior design business camp with other friends and family. *Probably smarter.* Still, she trusts Carla and knows she wouldn't judge her and has proven in the past that she can keep a secret.

'Did you hear about Tom Jenkins?' Carla leans into the centre of the table, lowering her voice. 'You know he had that affair? I thought it had blown over.'

'Really? I was sure that so-called romance had burnt itself out, especially given the twenty-year age difference,' Sophia interrupts, leaning towards her friend in a conspiratorial gesture.

'He's no longer lecturing at uni. I think he got fired because of the affair with Vicky the Vixen.'

'What happened?' Sophia is keen to hear the details but knows Carla will want to draw the story out and make it more salacious than it is. 'Do you think it's inappropriate, a lecturer shagging a student? Even if the student's already twenty?'

Carla leans back, pulling her cropped cashmere cardigan across her breasts, regarding Sophia as she sips her coffee. 'I don't know if this is gospel, but I heard from Darren that Vicky accused Tom of rape.'

149

Sophia's eyebrows shot up in surprise. As a rule, she wasn't easily shocked by any human intrigue, but this caught her off-guard.

'But that's insane!' Sophia blurts. 'How's that even possible? She's been sleeping with him for years.'

Carla is enjoying this. 'Well,' she says, 'it may have been years, but they broke up ten months ago, and their paths crossed at some city club.'

'Hang on, what about his wife and kids?'

Carla laughs. 'Small potatoes darling. You are behind the eight ball. Tom's wife divorced him!'

'Now that's incredible. I always thought Tom would divorce her. How the stomach churns!' Sophia smiles at her friend's smugness. 'How did things swing into sexual assault then?'

'That's just it.' Carla hesitates for dramatic effect. 'They both got drunk, shared a taxi, she got out with him at his flat, and before you know it, they're going for it like rabbits.'

'So where's the rape factor in the drunken debauchery of two inebriated consenting adults?' Sophia asks, mildly amused.

'Exactly!' Carla sighs. 'It's a mess, and the police are involved now in some tit for tat thing.'

Sophia rolls her eyes and shakes her head in bored disbelief.

'Who the hell cares what people do with their sex lives?' Carla states. 'The two of them need their heads smacked together!'

'Umm,' mumbles Sophia. 'Maybe I do too?'

'Why you?' Carla asks.

Sophia gently unpacks her plan, carefully explaining how her paying lovers will contribute to her coffers, ensuring there is no compromise in her wealthy lifestyle.

'What do you think? Am I completely crazy?' Sophia says, looking closely at her friend, who moments earlier, had already sworn strict confidentiality.

Carla presses her lips together, considering how to respond and as the seconds stretch into a minute, Sophia begins to regret mentioning her career plans.

Suddenly Carla reaches across and grasps Sophia's hand. 'It's none of anyone's business and least of all mine,' she says. 'I get it,

150

and when I was tight for cash a few years ago it crossed my mind, so I do understand.' She pauses. 'As long as you're safe and don't get any weird aggressive psychopath clients.'

Sophia chuckles. 'Hell no! I'll be double-checking and vetting every single one. My biggest problem is how to find these well-heeled men who would pay for me to be their mistress.'

'Interesting. I recently heard a podcast interview on the wealthy New York party scene. Several people, big noters of course, kept name dropping. I'll find the link and forward it to you. With a bit of research you could suss out their credibility and interest in your offering darling.' Carla smiled warmly. 'It's all about close connections.'

'Sounds like a plan. At least it's a start. Thanks.'

'But my immediate thought is, what would your mother have said about this career path?'

'That's a non-issue. Mum's dead.'

'What about your grandmother then?' Carla asks.

'Darling they're never going to know. The only people that do know are you and Florian.'

'I don't want to sit in judgement,' Carla repeats. 'Part of me thinks it's a bad idea. You're smart, gorgeous and have everything going for you. You could get into all kinds of trouble.'

Sophia nods. 'Yeah, I've already thought about all eventualities,' she simply states, and within seconds they both walk off the topic catching up with other news and gossip from past associations.

CHAPTER 27

Legally Binding - 2012

The petite blonde personal assistant to Ruben Swersky, a high-powered corporate business attorney, emails Sophia to confirm an appointment to review the terms of her client contract.

Within five minutes of arriving at his high-rise glass and chrome clad building, Sophia is ushered into his sizeable office. Swersky stands as she enters his office, moving around his commanding glass-topped desk, and reaches out to shake his new client's hand. He's deep in his sixties with penetrating hazel eyes which quickly sum up the young woman standing before him. They had briefly spoken on the phone and exchanged emails over proposed contract drafts. The final draft document was emailed to Sophia the previous week. This morning's meeting is to go through each clause and ensure she is entirely happy with everything he has included.

Swersky admits to himself that Sophia is way beyond his expectations, far more elegant and refined. He imagined some rough diamond, a good sort, a caricature of a brothel manager. But now, finally setting eyes on Sophia, he understands how a woman like her can pass for a credible business associate or love partner with any well-heeled executive.

The real surprise is how disarmingly beautiful and charming she seems. At first, he concocted an image of an over-zealous sex addict and after talking over the phone for the first time, he modified his imaginings to include a more intelligent, cunning and hardened youth. But shaking her hand and assessing her from top to toe, he concludes she is none of these things. He smiles, mainly at his own ignorance. The beautifully coiffured, well-dressed young woman standing before him is utterly beguiling.

Sophia sits in the upright leather armchair opposite her attorney and begins reading through the draft clauses of the contract.

'I want to amend one or two things. And there's a couple of items I want to discuss and see if they should be included,' she explains without glancing up from the tightly spaced fourteen-page document.

'No problem,' Swersky smiles, his large hands clasped together on the yellow writing pad in front of him.

Sophia looks up with an innocent smile. 'I've asked your secretary, but would still like to confirm this contract is absolutely confidential, legally neither you or any of your staff can divulge anything about my private life or business affairs?'

Swersky shifts back into his black upholstered office chair, his large upper torso strains against the small shirt buttons, pulling the white fabric taut across his stomach. Sophia pretends not to notice and stares directly into Swersky's sharp eyes.

'I assure you, nearly everything we deal with here is strictly private and confidential,' he says in a reassuring tone. 'Our practice prides itself on always maintaining the security of our clients in every way.' He clears his throat. 'The very foundations of our relationship with our high-profile clients is based on trust.'

'Good,' Sophia says. 'There's one other thing I want to make you aware of, off the record, of course. Are you open to hearing this?'

Swersky remains tight-lipped. Here we go, they all have something similar to say. It must be the anxiety and fear he brings out in new clients. He rearranges his features to appear more concerned and raises his open hand to indicate for Sophia to continue.

'You'll appreciate my business places me in a vulnerable position,' Sophia states and Swersky nods. 'I intend to enter into this agreement with somewhere between three and ten clients. Each one is signing a mutually exclusive agreement with me. Paying monthly retainers and special fees are one thing, and I think the clauses you have drawn up are perfect. No change there. But I want to ensure I safeguard my position to the utmost, and of course, protect the security of all my clients too.'

This isn't the normal preamble Swersky is used to. His

furrowed brow indicates he's listening intently. He briefly wonders if Sophia would take him on as one of her trusted clients. She could be the answer to world tension. At the very least, he deserves a test run …

'…so I'm only wanting to do this for my utmost sense of security you understand,' Sophia says noting Swersky seems a little confused.

'Sorry, Ms. Huston, I didn't quite catch that last sentence. I was momentarily distracted about the header on the agreement.' He's lying and she knows it.

Sighing, Sophia places the draft agreement on Swersky's desk. 'I was simply explaining, off the record of course, that I intend to make copies or take photographs of any incriminating material I find on my clients, in order to use it should they become difficult or refuse to terminate the contract on request.'

'I'm not quite sure what you mean,' Swersky interrupts.

'Off the record then, I shall repeat myself,' she responds.

'Apologies,' he says, blinking at the rebuke. 'But please explain in a bit more detail.'

'I'll take an incriminating in-house video, if you get the literal picture? I'll photograph any documents they bring to my home, which I think may assist. If a client becomes unruly, rude or demanding I will show them this evidence to ensure they back off or I'll threaten to expose them to their wife or global online media. Their choice.' As an after-thought Sophia adds, 'the information I accumulate on each client will be kept in a bank security deposit box. Once the contract is terminated, on agreeable terms, I will destroy the unsuspecting client's subversive evidence. But if there is any trouble, I have enough information to obtain immediate compliance.'

She sits back in her chair and a lengthy pause ensues as the older man considers the criminal impacts of such activity versus the obvious desire for absolute co-operation from Sophia's own paying clients.

Swersky pushes his fingers through his thinning grey hair and Sophia notices a Masonic gold ring on his middle-finger. Odd, she thinks, convinced Swersky is Jewish, but then who really knows without digging a little deeper.

Swersky holds Sophia's gaze and she remains silent, returning his challenge. After what feels like a lifetime, Swersky sighs. 'Let's say I didn't hear any of that,' he grimaces, 'on or off the legal record.'

She nods. 'There is one other item I'd like to include in the contract. I realised yesterday if one of my client's die I'll be out of pocket.'

'I probably will be too.' Swersky smiles, to break the tension.

'Yes, I'm sure we share a few clients,' Sophia grins unconvincingly. 'But can I put in a three-month stand-down period? In other words, if a client dies, they have to continue paying their monthly retainer for three months after their death, so I have time to secure a replacement.'

If he wasn't looking at this gorgeous female while she spoke those words, he would never have believed the level of ruthlessness coming from her beautiful lips. It was disarming and disturbing all at the same time.

In the absence of any response, Sophia speaks again. 'Think of it as a notice period. At least that could cover my associated expenses during the shortfall.'

'How many clients are you planning to kill in that penthouse?' Swersky grins.

'Only those who don't pay.' She laughs.

CHAPTER 28

Angel of Innocence 2012

On the weekend, Giles invites Sophia to attend a charity ball. He hands her a credit card instructing she buy something unique and gorgeous to wear on the special occasion.

'I want every man in the room to be envious,' he says, handing over a credit card with her name stamped boldly beneath the metallic security chip.

She flips it over, glancing back at Giles. 'Wow, this is for me?'

'Yeah. My monthly payments will automatically transfer into it, so we need never discuss filthy money again.'

A wide smile creeps across her delighted face. 'How can I ever thank you?'

'You already have,' he chuckles. 'You saved me fifty grand, and it was worth every dollar,' he jokes.

'I know!' she says, looking mischievous. 'It's the least you can do for me!'

On Saturday evening, Sophia stands resplendent in a French Oscar de La Renta haute couture ballgown with hand-stitched gemstones around the bodice and hem, looking expectantly at her lover. Her hair is piled high on top of her head, and delicate sparkling diamond earrings reflect Giles' delight. He's speechless.

'You are breathtakingly beautiful,' he says in a gruff voice, straining with emotion. In the same moment the chauffeur calls, confirming he is waiting outside. The pair enter the elevator down to the ground floor, and Giles warns Sophia not to touch him during the evening.

'We don't want any unnecessary upset with the hordes, and we don't need my wicked other half to get wind,' he concludes. He will introduce Sophia to numerous friends and business associates as his *niece*. Sophia respects his wishes and follows them to the letter. As the evening progresses, she maintains constant eye contact with him from across the room, reinforcing in his mind, he's the only man she adores.

It pleases him no end, and he chooses to ignore the intrigues of female wiles. He's enjoying the best years of his life. Giles intermittently glances over at Sophia, recalling the electrifying feeling of her naked body, writhing in pleasure beneath his, her soft lips and warm breath against his ear when he makes love to her. It's an experience like no other.

He can never get enough of her. She inspires and motivates him; she drives him wild with desire within hours of having spent himself. He's convinced he has the animal instincts of a young buck, a bullet-proof lover, and he's certain she can't get enough of him either. She's worth every cent and then some. Giles scans the crowd in the auditorium and glimpses Sophia looking back at him with love in her deep blue eyes. It's enough to take his breath away as he reluctantly turns back to the conversation with two middle-aged investment bankers.

After dinner, Giles introduces Sophia to a thirty-one-year-old New Zealand businessman, Hugh Rixon, who owns an international electronics business based in Australia. The easy-going Kiwi often travels worldwide, resolving logistics and complex systems issues. With a palatial home in the Bahamas, Hugh also has another off the coast of Italy, France and several family homes in Sydney and Lake Wanaka in New Zealand's South Island.

His tall, muscular frame belies Hugh's real charm along with his wry sense of humour. He reaches out and shakes Sophia's right hand. The constant sparkle in his eyes triggers sexual tension with Sophia. She'll pursue him, saving the hunt for a later date. She's not going to risk her relationship with Giles for the sake of a possible Kiwi contact.

While chatting politely Sophia hands him her personal card. Her private cell phone number is elegantly scripted on the back of a plain white card with *Sophia Hawkins* embossed on the other side. The simply designed card reveals the understated elegance Sophia lives by. Florian designed and printed only 30 business cards as a temporary solution while Sophia sources potential paying clients.

As Hugh takes Sophia's card and flips it over, he smiles longingly at her. 'I'm divorced and single,' he states without any hesitation. 'Who cares?' she replies nonchalantly with the innocence of an angel, wondering if Hugh likes the perfume she wears.

Hugh's eyebrows spring up like a cat leaping after a bird. He winks and tucks her card into the top pocket of his hand-tailored silk and merino wool suit.

Sophia slowly takes a sip of her red wine and holds her hand out. 'Nice to have met you, Hugh. I hope we get to catch up soon.'

He nods, speechless, as she turns on her heels and walks back across the room, closer to where Giles stands talking to a small group of businessmen. With every confidence, Sophia is sure Hugh will be calling before the week's end.

The following day Giles retreats to his family home to spend some limited time with his wife and three children. Sophia escapes to the calm and peace, relishing having the penthouse to herself. During the late morning, she calls Florian over for lunch.

At high noon Florian arrives with a bottle of dry Sauvignon from New Zealand, of course. This is an in-house amusement the pair often play. Sophia has already mentioned her short conversation with a Kiwi businessman from the previous night. Florian can't resist the temptation of a little vino reminder.

'So, girlfriend, tell all,' he says as he flops onto the comfortable four-seater sofa which dominates the spacious lounge.

It doesn't take long for Sophia to outline her future business strategies, explaining how it will all hang together, but she needs his considered input.

'You don't think Celeste's business is the way to go? With one foot in the bordello door it could mean you learn a lot more first-hand.' He chuckles. 'Pardon the pun.'

'The whole brothel business is sleazy somehow, and I can't face sleeping with gross men,' she explains. 'I plan to hand-select my targets and manage the whole process for myself. I firmly believe I don't need any madam to push me around and take the lion's share of my earnings.'

'OK,' he says reluctantly. 'I don't want to see you land up in trouble. It's a risky business, especially on your own.'

'Think about the average streetwalker, they're often alcoholics or stoned or both and barely make a living. That's exactly the opposite of what I want to do.'

'Tell me how,' Florian asks, and Sophia picks up her notebook from the sizeable glass-topped coffee table. The pages are crammed with scribbled notes and are almost entirely filled with diagrams, clauses for contracts and various lists of financial calculations and options.

'Look I'll never underestimate what you want to do. You've already managed to get this beautiful apartment out of Giles.' He concentrates on Sophia's face. 'It's amazing. You seem to have a magnetic force field around you. I have no doubt you can do this. But what about in the long term? Where do you think your life will end up?'

Sophia gives a sigh. She has considered this question many times and knows it's a short-term career. 'By the time I'm thirty-five, I'd like to be married and living happily in suburbia,' she states matter-of-factly.

'What?' Florian snorts. 'That's the last thing I'd ever have thought I'd hear from those lips. Are you still wanting to adopt thirty desperate kids?'

'That's a bit over the top Mr Fabre. I'm a realist. I know time will pass and I'll get beyond any male interest,' she responds. 'There's a lot of men keen to part with their money out there, and I intend to maximise my potential as they say in the corporate world. Add value to the customer experience and socialise the bloody concept into my business framework.'

They both laugh at the corporate jargon and take a sip from their glasses. The conversation waxes on about political shortfalls and economic suicide, the potential impacts of bird flu, global warming and the failures of future plans, driven by short-sighted politicians obsessed with living in the past.

After enjoying lunch, they continue chatting and finally Florian offers to introduce her to a couple of his clients who may be

161

interested in her business offering.

'I'll make myself tax-deductible.' She giggles, heady with three glasses of wine coursing through her bloodstream.

'Hell yeah, especially if you're in an apparent consultant meeting with them overseas. Part of their tax-deductible business trip too, don't you know!'

'You're a bloody genius,' Sophia announces, and they clink their wine glasses together for the umpteenth time.

'When's Giles coming back?'

'He's away for three weeks now. A trip to London and France. This gives me the chance to rekindle my business objectives!'

Finally, at 4.32pm Florian heads off home and Sophia showers before crashing onto her king-sized bed, falling into an uninterrupted sleep.

CHAPTER 29

Geisha Girl - 2012

Over the past few months Florian has offered Sophia's services to a few of his wealthy clients. A couple have indicated serious interest. As winter lurches into early spring, Florian introduces Haruto Tanaka, a Japanese ship's captain, to Sophia. They share several cellphone calls and an hour's private conversation in a local up-market hotel room before finalising their verbal agreement. Sophia gives the handsome captain a draft copy of her official contract, carefully explaining the terms of their arrangement in fluent Japanese.

'You need not sign it now.' She smiles. 'If you agree to the terms you can contact me for a booking and bring the signed copy to our next *official* meeting.'

Haruto grasps the document and bows his head acknowledging acceptance of Sophia's approach. She refuses to email the contact, wishing to avoid any misuse or breach of security. She waits, anticipating some negotiation from Captain Tanaka, but the tall Japanese man needs little discussion and quickly agrees to her contractual terms, promising to bring the signed contract back on his next visit. Married with two young children, Haruto is her first Japanese client.

Sophia doesn't count Giles as one of her patrons. They agreed on a cashless arrangement as part of their penthouse transaction. She recently signed the Trust documents, confirming the five-year buy-out in her favour. Sophia moves swiftly and definitively to secure ownership of the magnificent *business* premises within the stipulated time-frame.

Haruto represents her initial foothold in the seven-step business plan to achieve financial independence. Polite and formal, Haruto treats Sophia with the utmost care and consideration. He asks for little, other than requesting a back massage, on his return to Sydney. He is entranced with the expectation of relaxing in the deep-water hot tub in Sophia's new penthouse. Their meet and greet goes without a hitch. True to his word, Haruto pays his monthly retainer in American dollars directly into Sophia's holding account.

Sophia has already scanned through the local Japanese newsfeeds before Haruto arrives back in Sydney for their first live session five weeks later. She is attracted to her Japanese client, making her work more palatable, especially when Haruto arrives dressed in his stark white uniform with its distinct gold insignia.

He smiles and formally bows his head before Sophia pours him an ice-cold saké as they relax in his hotel room, discussing some of his interests. There were no real surprises in his reply email outlining his preferences, hobbies and chat feed interests. Haruto does seem more formal than expected, more out of shyness maybe or deference to her, than an indication he's hanging on every word she utters. He'll soon warm up. Why else would he sign up so eagerly and transfer funds within twenty-four hours? It's all been so uncomplicated. Hopefully the other five potential clients will be straightforward too. She expects after the weeks at sea he will want to get down to business.

Instead, Captain Haruto invites her to dinner where they continue their *date* at a nearby five-star restaurant. Sophia explains how she suffered a sad breakup over two years ago after a long-term relationship soured.

'The contract is necessary to protect me financially,' she explains, speaking his language. 'I lost most of my money to an ex-partner who swindled me out of my savings too.'

Haruto nods with empathy. 'I understand,' he simply says.

'My apologies for the official protocol in the contract,' she ventures. 'But I hope you appreciate why I'm being cautious.' Sophia knows this approach will feed directly into Haruto's cultural heritage. 'I assure you I will always be happy to go out with you.

Haurto smiles again, nodding his head in acceptance.

166

'The agreement means you can terminate our arrangement at any point if you are not pleased with me. There will be no emotional upset or arguments on my part.'

'Sophia-san, you are making a good geisha for me,' he says in English before his expression changes. 'I am saddened for Sophia-san's heartbreak. I fully understand your, how do you say it? *Caution*,' he smiles at the young woman seated across the table. He reaches for her hand and tries to explain in his cultured Japanese language that he will never take advantage of her. 'I will show you in every way the love and respect you deserve, Sophia. I know we don't know one another very well, but you are a beautiful woman, and I will always treat you with care.'

Sophia bows her head and gracefully thanks Haruto for his understanding and generosity, assuring him in turn of her singular devotion. 'I will always try my best to please you,' she smiles. 'I will care for you with loyalty and love.'

Haruto is pleased. He had only met Sophia six weeks ago and yet they were both so drawn to one another. It was good fortune and timing that presented this opportunity, and Sophia is confident during their conversation that he will look after her.

With great tact, Sophia diplomatically explains she's always been deeply intrigued by the geisha approach and maybe, in the beginning, he could look upon her as his very own geisha girl. Haruto laughs out loud, chuckling, his dark eyes dancing in hers.

'Sophia-san, you already are the perfect geisha for me. I am pleased with this promise,' he states using the Japanese word for commitment and fidelity. They indulge in a delicious meal of several courses, and a bottle of saké and continue talking and laughing, enjoying one another's company.

Haruto is astounded at her grasp of the Japanese language, her quick wit and effortless charm. He can't believe his luck. She teases him about politics and torments him with the prospect of the fun they'll have once he drums up the confidence to seduce her! She explains how she has tried to overcome her shyness and promises to happily massage and scrub his handsome body in the hot tub once she moves into her new penthouse.

'But this time I'll remain in your hotel room. I hope you

understand?' She glances up at him coyly, then looks down in an act of obvious piety. 'I wish to know you a bit more' Sophia explains with a small white lie. 'I have a personal rule. I never sleep with a man on the first date.'

He smiles weakly, a flicker of a frown conveys his disappointment. 'I understand, Sophia-san. 'I have a wife and two children at home. I know the way of a good woman. We will know each other first,' he says with a mixture of disappointment but appreciation for the moral stance this European girl expresses. 'But remember, I've been five weeks at sea, it is a stressful job, so I do need some help to get some peace.'

'Would your wife be happy with this?' she asks coyly, looking more concerned than upset.

'Yes,' he says emphatically. 'She has children, and I have worked to pay for her life.'

'Will you tell her about me?' Sophia asks, already worrying about an irate wife from the other side of the planet hunting her down for revenge.

He roars with laughter. 'You are very funny Sophia-san,' he says almost choking on his mouthful of grilled cod. 'She will never know. Why cause pain?' He chuckles. 'She doesn't know what she doesn't need to know.'

Relief filters across Sophia's face.

'Unless you decide not to be a geisha and tell her?' he questions with mocking concern and an overblown deep frown.

Sophia laughs, reaching out and clasping his forearm, leaning closer to Haruto's face. 'That is something I will never do!'

'Good,' he replies nodding and smiling. 'We are clear about the things we will never do.'

Three hours later, after making love to the ship's captain in his hotel room, she dresses, and bows farewell to Haruto at the hotel room door. He politely drops his head in acknowledgement before turning back into his room.

Sophia catches a taxi home to her small suburban flat, confident that Haruto will be a long term client. The real dilemma is finding four more clients without Giles or her family finding out.

168

CHAPTER 30

Sibling Remorse 2014

After first meeting Matt Simpson nearly a year earlier, their grandmother, Edith Hawkins called Teressa's new love interest a *wide boy*. Edith was something of a suffragette in her day and invoked her substantial feminist rights by refusing to take her husband's surname, Huston, all those years ago. She is quick to assess Matt as being self-indulgent, arrogant and ignorant, all in the same breath.

'What the hell does this mean?' Sophia asks, knowing the expression, *wide*, is meaningless to both sisters.

The older woman sniffs, looking from one expectant face to the other. 'I don't want to be disparaging,' she says.

'But you're going to be,' responds Teressa looking uneasy.

'He's a bit of a smart Alec. A man who will wheel and deal, pull any stunt to get ahead in the world,' Edith continues.

Sophia is impressed by Edith's words which state out loud the same sentiments Sophia has about Matt. He is the kind of guy who keeps all his sporting trophies and medals crammed into shelves displayed in his lounge. His skin seems taut across his face as if he's been outdoors in the sunlight too long. The critical glint in Matt's eyes convinces Sophia he can't be trusted.

'That's ridiculous!' Teressa blurts out to her grandmother. 'You've barely exchanged two words with him. Give him a chance before you both pass judgement.'

Edith pulls herself up straight. 'I don't need to exchange words with the man. I simply watch and listen. To put it in language you girls will understand, he's a bullshit artist.'

Awe struck by her grandmother's directness, Sophia smiles inwardly. Right on the money Granny! Matt is not smart enough and doesn't put any meaningful effort into driving his career. In a short conversation with Sophia, he was unable to explain what he did for a living. His words were like shifting sand, accumulating, reforming and disappearing, leaving Sophia perplexed about Matt's credentials and even more concerned about his credibility.

She notices the trimmed edge of his t-shirt sleeve rising and falling as he moves, exposing a prominent scar twisting like a keloid snake around his upper arm and into obscurity under the fabric. It could easily have been a knife wound. Alarmist? Maybe a car accident. Did he even have a car? One thing was sure, Teressa's limited intellectual capacity matches her boyfriend's non-existent academic prowess. While Matt is ordinary looking, his eyes are forever scanning the environment, which Sophia suspects is Matt's method of assessing who and what is worth his attention, working the room for his advantage, and it makes her uneasy.

Teressa raises her voice, arguing with Edith, which penetrates Sophia's thoughts, bringing her back to the tense conversation.

'All I ask, Grandma, is that you don't judge,' she says in a higher pitch, stifling controlled anger. 'At least give him a chance. Be fair.'

Their grandmother smiles and nods in acquiescence. There's no point fighting a battle when this flimsy relationship is doomed to die on its feet.

Months pass, life rolls on, and Sophia makes excuses to avoid contact with Teressa when Matt, who is now Terresa's fiancé, is around. During down time she watches re-runs of the popular television series *Rake*, amused and absorbed in the acerbic humour of this hard-bitten city barrister. Florian manages to weave some of Rake's one-liners into their conversations, making her laugh and they joke about the degradation of Rake's personal and professional life.

After months of limited contact Sophia finally agrees to meet Teressa for breakfast on Saturday morning. On a call the previous night, Terresa mentions wanting to bring her older sister up to speed with her impending wedding plans.

'I have something significant to tell you,' she announces during the phone conversation.

Please, God, she's not pregnant was Sophia's first thought during Teressa's phone call. She couldn't face more drama with her family, but there was no way of avoiding the conversation. In some ways it was expected that Teressa would choose a jerk to marry. Why should she be surprised? She's not. But she makes up her mind to avoid being obstructive. It achieves nothing other than more distance and remoteness in her relationship with her sister. No matter how hard she ventures with Teressa, there's nothing gained.

The sisters meet at their local café, crowded at this time of day. Fortunately, a couple are leaving, so the sisters grab their table positioned in a reasonably quiet corner of the restaurant for an uninterrupted discussion.

'Matt reckons we should bring the wedding celebration forward,' Teressa starts explaining.

'Why not wait?' Sophia says as she glances across the café to read the breakfast menu chalked up on the back wall.

'There's no point,' her younger sister says. 'We both want to get on with it now.'

'As long as you feel certain. It's a big step,' Sophia says, trying to remain calm. 'You've only known Matt for a few months.'

'Eleven and a half months actually,' Teressa corrects.

'Oh, wow,' Sophia says, genuinely surprised.

'We're both a hundred per cent committed, so there's no point in hanging around.'

As they drink black coffee with fresh croissants stuffed with lashings of sweet plum chutney and crispy bacon, both sisters talk about the details of the ceremony. Sophia knows she can't change her sister's mind. Teressa is immovable.

'You need to trim the guest list,' Sophia advises. 'It's too many people, and how are you going to pay for all of this?'

'Well, I can't,' Teressa states bluntly staring at her sister. 'I was hoping you could help us out?'

'I'm not sure that I'm in any position at this point, but I …'

'I'll try and cull the guest list' Teressa interrupts, 'by about thirty. Matt has everyone including the kitchen sink turning up. I

173

need to discuss it with him.'

'Is Matt's family going to chip in?' Sophia asks, waving her arm at a waitress for a coffee refill.

'Well, he said he would cover the drinks for the guests of course,' Teressa says weakly.

'Does he know the situation?' Sophia demands. 'He'll have to cover a bit more than drinks. What sort of money are you talking about for the entire wedding? Including that expensive-sounding dress you mentioned.'

'I could get a less expensive dress,' Teressa offers reluctantly.

'How much?'

'Well, as it stands, thirty-five thousand dollars,' she replies.

'Are you out of your mind? This cost is insane, given the financial stress we're all under.' Sophia sighs and wonders about what kind of cuckoo-land her sister inhabits.

As naive and frustrating as Teressa is, Sophia also feels, at the same time, very sorry for her. Compared to Sophia, Teressa was only a child when they lost their mother, which could account for her over-emotional reactions. Teressa deals with their father more often too. Sophia feels guilty but unsure why, until she remembers the boyfriend she had *stolen* from her sister all those years ago. She was some teenage bitch back then with no regard for the boy or her sister.

There were a few moments of silence as the sisters consider the worrying wedding dilemma.

'Look I'll loan you twenty thousand, not a penny more and I suggest you get catering and venue quotes to cut your budget back,' Sophia states as if she were convincing a board of directors during a tricky business meeting.

Teressa leaps from her chair and grabs Sophia around the shoulders, tears of gratitude filling her eyes. 'Oh, thank you, thank you. I can't tell you how grateful I am. I promise I'll pay you back,' Teressa blurts out between tears of relief.

'Yes, you will!' Sophia insists, unmoved by her sister's emotional display. 'I'll type up a payment plan. I'll also announce your divorce if you default on the repayments.' She smiles and then hesitates. 'Do you want to call Matt and see if he agrees with this? I assume he'll be contributing to the repayments?'

'Yes, of course,' Teressa says, pulling herself together, her face reverting to a sombre expression

Sophia silently considers the wayward Matt Simpson, medium height, average appearance as if butter won't melt, but something is unnerving about the guy. She warned Teressa months earlier but can't quite express why she's still uneasy. 'He seems untrustworthy,' she explains.

'Oh really?' her sister shoots back. 'How the hell would you know? You've hardly exchanged half a dozen words with him during the entire time we've been going out.'

The resulting argument does nothing much to ease either sister's concerns, and now Sophia is offering to finance this union nurtured in hell. She must've lost her mind too.

Two weeks after their shared breakfast, Sophia receives the wedding invitation in the post. Opening the envelope, she looks at the pink and gold scripted font and immediately considers the extravagant cost of its design and printing. 'Calm down. It's not your wedding,' she says as she strolls back inside her suburban flat.

Looking at the wedding date brings the firm realisation that she can't face attending the ludicrous marriage ceremony. Teressa fawning over Matt, her father drunk. The whole thing will be like some crass sit-com she wants to fast-forward.

The next day she calls Teressa.

'Thanks so much for the beautiful invitation,' Sophia offers.

'You like it?' Teressa asks, pleased with the acknowledgement.

'Yes, of course, but I have a problem with the wedding date. I hope you'll understand.'

'Oh no,' Teressa's voice sounds hollow, bracing for a well-known let-down or excuse from her sister.

'I'm so sorry, but I have to fly to Lyon that week for a client. I'm doing that high-end interior design project with Florian. I didn't think there would be a clash. I am …'

Teressa cut her off. 'Can't you change it? Push it back or forward a day or two. I want you to be there.'

175

'I can't. The client leads a busy life and specifically demanded these dates. I'm so sorry. I'll make it up to you when I get back, once you're back from honeymoon. We'll go up the coast for a weekend together. Just you and me.'

Teressa doesn't respond.

'Are you still there? Sophia asks.

She hears her sister huff into the phone before speaking. 'I knew you wouldn't come,' she says flatly. 'You had no intention. How can I explain your absence to Matt's family, my friends …'

'Tell them exactly what happened. It can't be helped. You don't have to lie or make anything up,' Sophia says reassuringly. 'I'm sure they'll understand.'

'Well, I don't!' Teressa spits.

'Hang on. Remember I'm the one financing this …' She is about to say *fiasco* when Teressa hangs up on her.

No pain, no gain, Sophia thinks but is brutally aware she's better off out of it.

Giles happily remains in bed on alternate Thursday afternoons. Their contra-deal works like a well-oiled machine with both parties savouring the advantages. On the first night Sophia walks through her newly renovated penthouse apartment, filled with joy. The renovations are so much better than she first visualised, the spacious rooms and quality finishes are faultless.

'Perfect,' she murmurs to herself, walking into the master bedroom where the soft dove-grey walls and deep pile carpet have created a sumptuous room. An adjoining Italian tiled ensuite with a large oval porcelain hot tub as the centre-piece almost takes her breath away. She's absolutely delighted as she strolls down the hallway into the converted third bedroom, commandeered as the fully-fledged dressing room of her dreams.

CHAPTER 31

Signed up - 2016

It's a hot day in New York city where Sophia walks along the sidewalk. She's in a hurry to meet Giles for lunch at his preferred bar and grill six blocks away. It's the first time he's invited her overseas and, so far, it's been three exceptional days.

During the daytime he's wrapped up in meetings, allowing her freedom to visit art galleries and museums. One day she takes a ride to the top of the Empire State building and then spends harrowing hours strolling through the National September 11 Memorial and Museum situated on the site where the World Trade Centre once stood. The enormity of nearly three thousand names listed on the monument is gut-wrenching. How frivolous and inconsequential her life seems. She must find something meaningful and worthwhile. Pursuit of money is a means to an end, not a means in itself. But what else can she do? What should she do?

Her phone beeps. Startled, she glances at the screen as she signals for a yellow cab. Giles is waiting. A cab pulls over to the curb and she grabs the passenger door. Out of nowhere, Rafe Le Monde, a distinguished looking fifty-year-old, manages to shove Sophia aside and pitches his body across the back seat, leaving Sophia stunned on the sidewalk.

Rafe turns to look at his opponent, running his hand through his thick mop of curly hair. Within an instant, he realises the error of his actions and begins to apologise profusely. His thick French accent is an obvious giveaway, but Sophia struggles to understand his broken accented English. In his panic, he desperately tries to communicate without the correct vernacular being immediately available.

'Am I going or what?' interrupts the gruff voice of the agitated cab driver.

Rafe reaches across from the back seat with his left hand and touches the man's shoulder. 'A moment please, just sorting this out,' he instructs.

Turning to look up again at the beautiful woman standing on the street flush-faced, he fully grasps the error of his poor judgement.

Sophia, with an expression of mild amusement, interrupts him before he responds. She rattles off in fluent French her assessment of the situation.

'Monsieur, you can see I was here first, and you used unnecessary brute force, almost pushing me into the gutter. I am shocked by your rough conduct. I am astounded at this poor behaviour from a man of France,' she says, embellishing retort, knowing she can pass for an original Parisian. There is a slight sense of amusement playing in her gorgeous blue eyes.

He remains speechless, dazzled by this young creature who addresses him formally in his mother tongue. Rafe quickly tries to regain his composure and holds out his hand.

'Please. My most humble apologies,' Rafe says with deep sincerity engraved in his expression, thankful that he can use his own language with this beautiful stranger. 'I cannot say what came over me. Share the cab with me. Please, I absolutely agree with you and my unruly, vulgar physical abuse of such a refined young woman is unacceptable. Apologies to you again.'

Sophia smiles graciously and clasps Rafe's right hand, sliding effortlessly onto the back seat beside him.

'Rafe Le Monde,' he says, kissing the back of her hand before finally letting it go.

'Almost pleased to meet you,' smiles Sophia demurely. 'Sophia Hawkins,' she adds by way of an introduction.

'Where do you wish to go, Ms Hawkins?' Rafe asks.

The driver signals and launches the cab into the busy city traffic. Twenty minutes later, Sophia has Rafe's business card and promises to call him before the week's end.

A visitor to New York, Rafe Le Monde explains he's lived on the historical outskirts of Paris with his wife Vera during their twenty-four tumultuous years of marriage. With no children, Rafe is the last in a long line of wealthy ancestors over several centuries, living a life of extreme indulgence. His family inherited and accumulated land-owning rights and property investments over the past two hundred years, making him one of the wealthiest billionaires on the planet. But no one would ever know. He doesn't need to impress; he dislikes branded shoes and clothes and fancy cars. He hates crowds and *events* of any kind. Steel-willed and decisive, he carefully cultivates an exterior image of a slightly disheveled university professor.

Within a few weeks, Rafe has arranged to meet Sophia in Sydney. The night after he arrives in his private Lear jet, he happily signs the terms of her agreement, becoming her newest paying lover.

Weeks later, back in her Sydney suburban home during a lazy mid-morning, Sophia sits on the couch, sipping black coffee and reads through the newsfeeds on her cell phone. Distractedly stroking Loopy's grey furry head, then scratching him under the chin, Sophia begins talking to her devoted dog. His eyes never leave his mistress's face.

'If only you could talk.' Sophia kisses him on the head and returns to her cell phone newsfeed. 'Ah, I know what you want,' she says to Loopy who's wagging his enthusiastic tail. Sophia picks up his dog bowl from the nearby laundry floor and loads it with strips of raw beef. She smiles and laughs at Loppy's frenzied excitement as she sets the stainless dish on the tiled floor. His tail wags vigorously as he eats his meaty breakfast. Thank God for Florian who lives in her house, more often than not, looking after Loopy, feeding him and taking him for walks while she is working with her business clients in the penthouse apartment. It's a relaxed arrangement which Loopy barely seems to notice. He wags his tail and is delighted to see Sophia and Florian in equal doses.

Her cell phone vibrates on silent. It's Florian, full of excitement over some juicy gossip.

'Got back from the gym,' he says breathlessly. 'I caught up with Gazza. Remember him?'

'Yeah, of course, the guy with one eye who loves fishing,'

Sophia replies. 'Come on what's the juice?'

'It's that wayward brother-in-law of yours …'

'Spit it out Mr Fabre, I haven't got time to second guess. Give me the shit. There has to be plenty where that guy comes from.'

'And surprise, surprise. There sure is!'

'Yeah.' Sophia's tone indicates it's enough of a beat-up.

In a rush of enthusiasm, Florian divulges the whole story. 'Gazza's sister's been having an affair with Matt for over four months, and she caught him in bed with another girl a couple of weeks ago. A cousin of Harold's. She's some alcoholic gambling loser. You won't know her.'

Sophia remains silent.

'Are you still there?

'Yeah,' she says into the mouthpiece frowning. 'But you know what? Is there any way you can get me hard evidence?'

'I'm way ahead of you darl,' he almost squeals into the cell phone. 'I've got pics on my phone!'

CHAPTER 32

Lucky Liaison – 2016

'Yes. Pour me another. Thanks' Sophia smiles disarmingly at the tall foreigner, holding a bottle of imported champagne.

'I have a strict policy,' he says with a thick Dutch accent. 'I don't offer women drinks without knowing their name first.'

She immediately flips into fluent Dutch answering the astounded man in his mother tongue.

'Sophia Hawkins,' she says, holding out her hand. 'Pleased to meet you. I'm here to listen to the miracle of commercial bank forecasting.' She regards the stranger more closely as they shake hands. He's attractive in an alpha-male way, a strong man who knows his worth and his mind, what he wants and how to get it. She tilts her head slightly as he calls over the waiter to refill their almost empty glasses.

'How did you manage to get one of these platinum invitations?' she asks, wanting to place him amongst the well-heeled crowd.

He chuckles, charming Sophia, who already pegs him as a potential client. 'Willem Van Howan,' he states, calculating how much he should explain. 'I'm a shareholder, like you I presume, or do you have a lucky husband lurking in the background?' He scans the crowd before glancing back at Sophia.

Sophia grins, deciding to play the game. 'I'm only twenty-seven. Way too young for a husband, Mr Van Howan,' she says in informal Dutch. He's hooked and knows she has significant wealth or critical contacts to be present in the room.

She knows he's impressed by her fluid grasp of his language and understands the subtleties of Dutch slang.

He insists she calls him Wim, as his friends do back home in the Netherlands. Surprisingly Willem Van Howan confesses to being a member of parliament in his home country. Sophia imagines this makes him vulnerable to public scrutiny and criticism. She reconsiders if he is a likely client given the risk factors.

Being a leading figure in the Tweede Kamer, the second chamber, Willem explains he's recently become the most likely candidate in the conservative party, the VVD, to become the party leader. Or so he tells Sophia, which she guesses is part of his ego and desire to impress. She reads global news feeds and hasn't heard his name before. She'll do some background checking over the weekend.

Sophia knows it's difficult to assess potential clients, especially at this level. He's involved in a range of high-end business interests, but politics is his true passion. Now at forty-two years, he's confident and astute enough to pursue his place in parliament.

'Maybe even governing the country,' he says. Sophia ensures her expression conveys constant admiration at his achievements.

They're interrupted by the personal assistant of the Governor of the Reserve Bank calling the audience back to the auditorium. The pleasant interlude is over. Sophia slips her business card into Willem's hand. 'I hope we get to carry on with this conversation.' She turns on her heels and walks back to her seat.

Being a married man, Willem intrinsically understands the wiles of the average female. But he quickly realises that Sophia is anything but ordinary. He manages his life by partitioning certain aspects and keeping secret Sophia as an antidote for his stressful life is a perfect arrangement. But she will have to get security clearance.

Willem's parliamentary staff undertake thorough security and background checks of Sophia before he declares her a risk worth taking. At least, that is how Willem explains it to Sophia on their phone call after the meeting. In reality, an intense argument erupted with his head of security, Johan Stiles, over Sophia's plausibility. There's some doubt about how she earns a living, and her wealth appears to be extremely private. But her high-class background, education and credentials all checked out.

'She seems to have relationships with many powerful men,' Johan states. 'With a surname that's not her father's. As if this was more grist to Sophia's demise. 'If nothing else it's enough to place a pause on this one.'

'Don't be ridiculous,' Willem instructs. 'She's a smart woman with a strong business sense. She comes from a wealthy background and had an excellent education.'

'Maybe so, but her father has some dubious dealings.' Johan chooses his words carefully, not wishing to inflame Willem's anger.

'You've done the checks, she's clean, and these things you bring up are trifling,' he says. 'I'll take my chances.'

Johan nods and leaves the office, after secretly recording the conversation on his cell phone to cover himself when the whole relationship, without a doubt, comes unstuck. He knows it will. It's just a matter of time.

Over the following months, Sophia receives a clearance card with a security chip to confirm her identity. After digging into his background online, she learns he is married. He must've been handsome in his youth, and is astute with gentle brown eyes that captivate Sophia.

Out shopping in Sydney's exclusive boutique precinct, Sophia floats home on a blissful wave of contentment. The back seat of her car is covered in new designer clothes, shoes and perfume. She swings the steering wheel into her driveway and receives a text from Florian.

'Loopy sick. Am at the vet. Call me.'

Immediately shaken from euphoria, Sophia quickly phones Florian before stepping out of the car.

'What's wrong?' she asks as soon as Florian answers.

'It's not looking good.' Florian tries to explain, upset himself at the shock, recalling the events of the morning, the frantic heart-stopping race to the vet clinic. 'All I know is that it's a blood disease of some kind.

Sophia let's out a sob of disbelief. 'He was OK this morning.'

'I know,' Florian says. 'He suddenly coughed up blood. They're giving him a transfusion.'

'I'm coming there now,' she says. The phone goes silent.

Sophia reverses the car and speeds towards the local vet clinic.

Her mobile phone rings. It's Florian again.

'I'm so sorry, Soph. It's bad news.' Florian's voice breaks. 'Loopy has just died.'

Bursting into uncontrollable sobs, Sophia pulls over to the curb and turns the ignition off.

'I'll bring him back to the house. Meet me there,'

Sophia nods but can barely speak as she clicks off the phone.

She gazes tearfully out of the window. Buildings, vehicles, street signs and distorted colours, everything seems so impossibly normal. Her thoughts inevitably rush towards Loopy, her ever-loyal, loving schnauzer. His cute face, his sensitive eyes. Clutching him closely around his neck and burying her face amongst his soft fur. Her watery eyes blink back fragmented memories, like an old black and white movie as Sophia remembers cuddling and talking to Loopy, his eyes loving her. A kind of tortuous litany of images bombards her as she weeps. It's unbelievable! Memories trigger more tears, trickling down her stricken face. On her arrival home, she bursts through the front door, but Loopy doesn't rush to greet her, leaping at her feet, excited at her return home. The full impact of Loopy's loss slams home.

Minutes later Florian arrives carrying Loopy's body, wrapped in a sheet, into the house. Crying, they both cling to one another.

'I'm so, so sorry,' Florian keeps repeating, hugging his tearful friend. 'It's too awful.'

CHAPTER 33

On A Whim - 2017

Sophia eases her first-class seat backwards and closes her eyes, hoping to sleep on the long-haul flight to Amsterdam. A few hours rest before she meets Willem will do her good. She heaves a sigh and a hint of a smile creases her lips, thinking about the raw magnetism of the man. Something complex and edgy lurks beneath his practised business-like exterior, intriguing Sophia, encouraging her to dig a little deeper next time. Astute, with gentle brown eyes, Willem has an undercurrent of something more intriguing which has already captivated her full attention.

On arriving at busy Schiphol Airport in Amsterdam, a security guard wordlessly collects her bags and drives her to a quiet country village on the outskirts of Utrecht. Sophia looks forward to their intellectual sparring and interesting conversations during the next few days of shared solitude. Sophia knows Willem is keen to indulge in their mutual physical attraction and with a flutter of excitement she's wanting to understand more about the mysterious, complex person she suspects is the real Willem Van Howan.

As dusk engulfs their quiet rural hideaway, Willem pours chilled champagne over a shot of brandy in tall crystal cut glasses, knowing it's Sophia's favourite indulgence. He drops a sugar cube into the stem as fine bubbles rise to the surface. The discreet housekeeper and chef arrive before lunchtime and are gone by 5pm each day, so their delicious meals are prepared for them to simply reheat.

The bathrooms are cleaned and serviced every day, replacing the previous day's linen with oversized fluffy white towels, and fine Egyptian cotton sheets on the sumptuous king-sized bed each night. Their indulgent evenings are enjoyed in the privacy of their own luxurious country retreat.

'This has gone straight to my head.' Sophia giggles, looking at the dregs of her champagne cocktail as she sprawls across the black leather four-seater sofa.

'Aha! My evil plan is working,' Willem responds in Dutch, chortling as he takes another swig and slumps down beside her.

'You have a plan?' Sophia frowns, slurring in Dutch. 'That's more than I've got.'

He smiles broadly. 'With you, my *Schat,* I have everything.'

'Umm, a man with such promise and calling me *darling* toooooo!' Sophia, tipsy and on an empty stomach drains her cocktail glass, taunting her adversary.

'Maybe you need to eat something?' Willem says, looking slightly concerned.

Sophia erupts into another bout of giggling. 'Is that your idea of foreplay Willem?' she teases, leaning back on the couch and provocatively crossing her legs.

A wide grin spreads across his face. 'Ms Hawkins, I am ninety-nine per cent certain that you're not wearing underwear.'

Pulling herself up straight and placing the empty glass on the edge of the coffee table, Sophia sniffs, indignant and affronted. 'What an outrageous accusation, Mr Van Howan!'

For a split-second, Willem looks shocked before laughing out loud, grabbing her proffered hand and pulling her up against him. She can feel his heart beating against the palm of her hand resting on his shirt front. He'll get his money's worth tonight. Letting him pull her down the hallway and into the master bedroom, her naked feet barely touch the carpet as she floats beside him in a blissful cocktail haze

He flings her backwards on the bed and Sophia squeals in delight. She pulls her clothes off and fights to undo the belt tightly drawn around his waist. Half undressed, he presses his body against her nakedness. It wasn't supposed to be like this. He's familiar with her and had planned to take things slowly, bring a more erotic flavour to their lovemaking.

But every time he sees her naked, vulnerable, a rush of uncontrollable lust and hunger to be inside her drives him hard with hot desire. Sometimes when apart from Sophia, distracting thoughts of her make him hard with yearning.

189

His second wife, Marit, recently joked that he must have someone else on his mind. She had no idea how right she was. Right now, right here, he doesn't need his wife on his mind either. He blocks her out. Willem is smart that way. Life is very carefully pigeon-holed, and each area safely detached from the other zones, especially the ones Sophia occupies.

In a swift automatic movement, he throws his remaining clothes across the room and presses himself against her warm, inviting flesh again. Sophia notices a shift in his facial expression, from Willem to wild animal, his instinctive need for sex overriding all other queues. Slack-jawed and stony-faced, sex is his singular focus. She breathes in the fresh sandalwood soap on his naked body but remains silent, looking at him, sexual tension increasing to an almost uncontrollable point. He presses his mouth hard against her lips, almost aggressive, before thrusting his body into hers. She moans, deliberately arches her back, magnifying his unrestrained excitement.

He clamps a hand over her mouth, firmly pressing her lips against her teeth. It almost hurt, distracting her from her work. After a minute or two Sophia is slightly alarmed. Is he challenging her? His dead-pan face, eyes not seeing her, hard to read, lust overriding all else. She makes a muffled sound, and he seems to shake himself back to the present, removing his hand and clutching her wrist in a vice-like grip.

He tries to concentrate on holding back, knowing he has little chance of lasting much longer. She turns her mouth to his right ear. 'Come, come' she whispers wanting it over. She's had enough. His aggression sobers her up. Sophia concentrates on synchronizing her body with his, writhing to his rhythm, pushing back against him, stroke for stroke until he can't stand the torment any longer. She kisses him long and hard, clinging to him, pressing her nails into his back as they climax together. As the moment passes, Sophia holds onto him, gently stroking his back as his heavy breathing gradually slows and he rolls over, away from her.

Within minutes Willem falls into a deep satisfying sleep while Sophia lies awake mulling things over. Her arrangement with Hugh Rixon has grown closer over recent years. She has no doubt

190

Hugh's feelings are more serious but worries about the tweaks she's made to her back story to convince him of her credibility. She didn't like lying to him. She dozes into a half-sleep and two hours later they're both finally awake, ravenous. They shower together before padding into the open-plan kitchen to eat their delicious dinner in their towelling dressing gowns.

As Sophia clears the plates away, Willem calls her over to the sit beside him on the sofa.

'I have something special for you,' he says with a disarming smile.

She frowns with surprise as he hands her a beautiful black-velvet gift-box bound together with silk ribbon and two tulips.

Holding the box in both hands, she looks up at Willem, expectant.

'Go on then, open it,' he says.

Sophia sits facing Willem, speechless. 'What's this for? I don't know what to say.'

'I thought we needed to celebrate.' He leans forward and longingly kisses her mouth.

'It's not my birthday,' she replies.

He laughs. 'It's twelve months to the day since we met,' he says proudly. 'Open it.'

'But I have nothing for you,' she exclaims.

Still in shock, Sophia opens the gift and lets out a gasp of surprise when she pulls out a magnificent gold and diamond bracelet. 'Willem!' she exclaims. 'This is too much.'

'I know,' he chuckles. 'But I want you to have a gift as beautiful as you are. You deserve it.'

The next day over breakfast, Sophia receives a text confirming she must leave Willem a day earlier than expected. Haruto wants to see her in four days back at the Sydney penthouse. Sophia doesn't want to disappoint. Carefully contriving an excuse, not wishing to annoy Willem, she explains her sister is upset over a miscarriage and needs to urgently rebook her return ticket. Only twenty-four hours later, with sincere regret, a single tear escapes Sophia's eye as she kisses Willem farewell and steps into the waiting taxi.

This is all the reassurance Willem needs to believe Sophia is truly devoted to him.

Once back in Sydney, Sophia calls Hurato twice and confirms his reservation. She strolls into the dressing room of the penthouse and surveys the eight full-length built-in cupboards lining the walls and whenever a client books her, she makes sure to wear the selected items the client has gifted to her. Sophia swaps out photographs of herself with each client so her entire home reflects her client's preferences. Sophia picks up the framed photograph of Giles, turns it over and deftly slips the photograph out of its frame, replacing with it one of Haruto.

This action she repeats for every client, making it plainly apparent that Sophia has eyes only for them. She never crosses wires or allegiances. Each man maintains the belief that she is theirs alone. Sophia says nothing to disavow them of their dream. At times she worries about their willing suspension of disbelief, but she needn't have concerned herself. Each man desperately wants to hold onto the conviction that Sophia has eyes and a beautiful body only for them. But how long can she maintain the subterfuge?

By the winter of 2017, Sophia has several clients, each man paying a monthly retainer for his exclusive rights. They happily part with additional fees for supplementary services. Still, Sophia finds each man is relatively pedestrian in his sexual desires.

When thinking about hookers, brothels and the seedy underbelly of Sydney's nightlife, thoughts go to deviant sexual activity. Bondage, strangulation, role-playing, weird and kinky sex games of all types. But for Sophia, there is nothing more demanding or taxing than relatively straight sex. The men are fond of her, in as much as they can show true affection to a female. Always polite and considerate, her clients are relaxed and happy, free from domestic and work demands. They enjoy her sense of humour, well-read intelligence and good conversation. Over time, her clients respect and appreciate her as more of a glamourous companion, with special benefits, for which they gladly contribute towards her expensive monthly upkeep

CHAPTER 34

Clandestine Contacts - 2017

'You don't mind if we only talk this time?' Sam Baxter says.

'No problem,' Sophia smiles. 'But you do realise you've said this to me every time you've been here?'

'Have I?' Sam says, perplexed. 'It doesn't seem possible.'

'I know,' Sophia says not wanting to challenge the fragile thirty-two-year-old and create more angst.

Sophia met her fourth client at a children's charity event, several months ago, while sipping premium quality wines from the Barossa Valley. Sam Baxter, an over-indulged son from a long line of wealthy Australian entrepreneurs, accepted Sophia's business card and called her the very next day. Over the following weeks they met four times, but her new client isn't interested in any physical contact. He merely wants to talk. She quickly learns to listen, saying nothing but making affirmative noises as her client rambles on.

It surprises her. Surely psychological therapy cost a lot less than her fees? But Sam, irritable at the suggestion, explains he's tried everything to no avail. Being with Sophia assuages his spirit and improves his confidence. Although difficult, Sophia accepts this, especially when Sam pays her generously after every visit.

Prone to depression, Sam is hounded by debilitating loneliness. His parents, like Sophia's, were more concerned with themselves and their impression on the world than loving their children. Sophia immediately recognises his need for touch, love, listening and admiration. *Poor little rich boy* is the refrain which springs into her head after their first meeting.

Their night-time conversations often extend into the early morning hours before they both fall into a profound sleep. Suffering from insomnia, Sam makes no overtures for any other service offered by a disconcerted Sophia. Lately, she believes her new client must be asexual and simply not interested in sleeping with her. Maybe there's something wrong with her? It's unnerving after all these years to be rejected, and for the first time in her life she understands the upset, heartache and misery of not being good enough. Part of her knows Sam doesn't mean it in this way, but it's still disconcerting and makes her feel guilty about the bar games she and Florian used to play on unsuspecting strangers.

'What can I do for you?' she asks yet again, during a lull in the conversation.

'Would you do anything I ask?' Sam says grinning.

Sophia's delighted. At last there's something he wants. 'Yeah, within reason, of course.'

'I'm not here for sex Sophia,' he says. 'It's of no interest to me, and I can get sex anywhere and with my family money I can get it from nearly anyone I want.'

'I see,' Sophia responds, never feeling so helpless in her life.

'I love being with you. Talking to you.'

She proves to be an invaluable source of personal attention and infinite understanding, hours of conversation which he tirelessly pursues. He had told his brother Sophia was better than any therapist but refused to give her contact details to his younger sibling.

So enamoured by Sophia, Sam Baxter invites her to his parents' estate positioned close to her old family home in Point Piper. It is a small gathering of around a hundred well-heeled guests celebrating Sam's parents' wedding anniversary.

On arrival, Sam introduces Sophia to his father, Maxwell Baxter, closer to sixty and no ordinary man.

'Pleased to meet you,' Maxwell says, taking her hand and kissing it firmly while his dark eyes penetrate Sophia's, assessing and analysing this new woman in his son's narrow life.

'Nice to meet you too Mr Baxter. Sam has told me a lot about you,' Sophia politely acknowledges the older man.

'I can see Sam has finally lifted his game.' Maxwell raises an eyebrow, smiling directly at Sophia.

196

The father presents a more lucrative option than the son but it's too late for a directional change, Sophia thinks. Maxwell's thinning dyed dark hair falls forward as his slightly puffy eyes survey his new guest. With a body bordering on paunchy Sophia finds something charming about the man.

Maxwell's hard-bitten, confident, quick-witted manner is the kind of challenge Sophia enjoys. But should she? She'll save him for later. Sam walks Sophia out onto the expansive patio overlooking the vast manicured exotic gardens where the exclusive guests sit drinking and chatting around a large heated swimming pool. Domestic staff deliver drinks and canapes on oval silver trays, a selection of exotic cocktails, champagnes and spirits of all kinds are also available at the bar on the main terrace.

A five-piece band play music and as the early evening wears on people swim and dance, some naked and some not. Some watch, some participate, but whatever goes on, Sophia maintains sober control over her demeanor. After some deliberation, Sophia believes Maxwell Baxter may be too big a fish to land, not to mention the complicating factor of his navel-gazing son. But if one of her paying lovers withdraws, Sophia could approach Maxwell directly with her client proposal. It's risky, but not much more than ones she takes almost every day.

Later that evening Sophia is touching up her lipstick in one of the powder-rooms off the main corridor to the open plan entertainment area. She notices the sound-proofing of the room is exceptional. All she can hear is the lower base tones as the music is amplified by large speakers to the outdoor gardens.

The bathroom door-handle clicks and Sophia glances from the mirror towards the doorway, her lipstick still held in her right hand. Maxwell Baxter steps forward out of the shadows into the full light of the exquisitely tiled powder-room. Surprised, Sophia starts to speak and, in a heart-beat Maxwell has grabbed her upper arms, forcing his mouth onto hers. She flays and tries to wriggle from his grip.

'Come on, be a sport,' Maxwell slurs, struggling to kiss her.

'Mr Baxter!' Indignant, she manages to stab his face with her lipstick, its soft red colour crushes onto his cheek and bleeds in a crooked line down his face.

In shock at the unexpected response from the girl, Maxwell steps back, rubbing his hand over his check, momentarily alarmed at the blood this wanton female has caused.

Frowning, Sophia is breathless from the adrenalin rush but notes the perfect circular outline of the metal lipstick casing embossed on the man's chubby cheek. She bursts into uncontrollable laughter.

Maxell turns his thunderous face to the mirror and sees bright red grease over half his reflection with a blotch on his shirt collar too. He swings back to Sophia, laughing hysterically and storms from the room.

CHAPTER 35

Willing Suspension - 2017

It's Saturday night and the foreshore near the Sydney Harbour Bridge is heaving with young party revellers. Sophia drives her sports car right up to the security barrier outside the Overseas Passenger Terminal, where the guard smiles acknowledgement at her familiar face and raises the barrier-arm, ushering her access to the substantial ocean-going passenger liner secured to the wharf.

Within minutes she notices Captain Haruto Tanaka, master of one of the largest ocean-going liners, dressed in his crisp white uniform marching down the gangplank carrying a small leather hold-all. A flutter of excitement ignites her evening as she watches him stride towards her parked car.

Mysterious and handsome, Haruto seems to command the entire wharf as he catches her eye. She smiles, relieved to see him again, but he gives no acknowledgment, although she observes the sway of his shoulders gives him away. She can tell he wants to run to her but, always in control, Haruto casually moves forward, ignoring several other crewmen who bow their heads as he passes. Butterflies of excitement are swirling in Sophia's stomach, but she will let Haruto set the tone, taking his lead, not wanting to spoil his game plan for them both this weekend.

Without a word of greeting, the uniformed man opens the back door and flings his tog bag onto the back seat. He opens the door and climbs into the passenger seat. He smiles and briefly plants a kiss on her lips. He speaks in fluent Japanese about how delighted he is to see Sophia, after a gruelling three-month round trip, sailing through international waters. She responds in the captain's mother tongue, smiling warmly before reversing and driving back through the security gates, giving a casual wave and nod to the security guard on duty.

Sophia has a sense of satisfaction knowing Haruto is always aroused by the mere sight of her. Electrified with anticipation, he will be struggling to maintain his self-control. She smiles inwardly listening to him breathe a sigh of relief at returning to his favourite Antipodean shore. He feels grateful for the two short days and two long erotic nights before his inevitable departure back to Genoa where he disembarks before sailing another ocean liner home to Tokyo Bay.

'Let's go out and have a celebration,' Haruto suggests after arriving at the penthouse.

'Why? Is it your birthday?' Sophia asks, prepared for every eventuality in managing her client's requirements.

'Yes. I am here with you.' He grins. 'Tetsuya's for dinner!'

'All right. Give me five minutes and I'll be ready,' she says.

'I need twenty,' he chuckles, 'to get out of this uniform.'

After they shower and dress, Sophia offers Haruto a flute of chilled Taittinger Champagne as a prelude to their evening out together. He is in particularly good spirits.

'Apart from dreaming of you on my journey over here. I've been wondering what you've been up to.'

Sophia smiles and sits down on the sofa next to her Japanese client. 'Working on projects with Florian. We're tendering on a residence in New York. One of those luxury apartments. All of the interiors need upgrading.'

'Sounds like a big project,' he says.

She nods. 'It is. Kept me off the streets while you were sailing the high seas. Nose down, bum up drawing up the schedules and helping Florian with the plans.'

'Is that all?' he jokes

'No.' she replies primly. 'I took a short break to watch Miss Universe in Tokyo. That Hotel Chinzanso looks incredible.'

'Ahh. Did you see Momoko Abe crowned?'

'She's beautiful.'

'A little,' Haruto shrugs seemingly unimpressed.

'The champagne? Are we celebrating something?'

He smirks, not that his face was ever used to classic smirking.

'What?' she questions. Haruto is always up to something, and she plays along. 'Tell me. What awful plan are you hatching?'

'You're magical,' he says and leans forward with one hand on her cheek and kisses her longingly.

'Well, Mr Tanaka, I see things are getting serious.' Sophia puts on a languid voice and gives a small laugh, her eyes dance in his, playing her very best coquette-geisha impression.

'Maybe,' he says, taking a sip from his glass before placing it on the coffee table.

'We will lose our reservation if we mess around any longer,' she states, looking at her cell phone.

'Huh!' he laughs. 'They wouldn't dare!'

'OK then.' She smiles adoringly at her Japanese lover and stands up, reaching out her hand, pulling him from the sofa. 'You better make it quick.'

'My dear Sophia, you know I am not for quick.' He snorts with derision, highly amused by her sexual overture. The Japanese translation cannot be fully honed for English conversion. He hooks her into his own game, and she has no idea where this is going but plays along. He refuses to move from the sofa, instead, he pulls her back down to sit beside him.

In a single swift manoeuvre, she positions herself on his lap. He laughs out loud, wholly absorbed in the energy between them and silently holds her gaze.

'Well?' she asks, her brow slightly furrowed with consternation.

He reaches his right arm into the cushions behind the couch and produces a small gift box. Haruto has elaborately wrapped the present in hand-painted Japanese paper, surrounded by a broad silk ribbon. Written in calligraphy along the length of a narrow white card, Haruto bestows love and good fortune in three Japanese symbols, slotting it under the silk binding. He hands the gift to Sophia. It is her turn to be shocked into silence.

'This isn't what I expected,' she says, a little flustered by the turn of events.

'I know,' he responds. 'You always think sex is the objective Sophia. It is not this time. Go on. Open it.'

She wriggles on his lap and turns to unwrap the beautifully presented gift. When she lifts the white lid off the small box, a small shriek escapes from her lips. Lying on the deep blue velvet lining is an emerald and diamond necklace, jaw-dropping in its simplicity and contemporary design.

'Oh, Haruto, this is too much. It's so beautiful,' she says breathlessly as he lifts the necklace from the box and carefully fastens it around Sophia's elegant neck.

'Why?' she asks, astounded by his generosity.

'Because you are so beautiful,' he says, smiling warmly at her as they kiss. His fingers linger at her neck and move gracefully over her body, tracing the curve of her back. She stands and walks towards the marble kitchen counter. Haruto obediently follows her silent direction. She turns to face him with her lower back resting against the white and pale grey marbled kitchen island and reaches up to the dignified Japanese man standing in front of her.

Sophia pulls him down towards her mouth and kisses him with greater intensity. Can she distract him enough, convince him to make love here, on the kitchen counter-top? It's a game, a tormenting play for his physical touch. This is a test of his will and she knows the odds are in her favour. They usually are. Grateful and loving, he's drawn into the pleasure of her touch, the sensuous promise of more to come.

He steps back and holds her chin in his hand, gazing into her warm blue eyes. 'Not here,' he gruffly whispers.

Sophia tilts her head, a playful look in her eyes.

'Not now,' he says more clearly, pulling away from her.

She steps up to him and kisses his neck and then gently bites and nibbles his ear, sending erotic shock waves through Haruto's body. Sophia presses herself against him, moving her hips against his. She can tell he's keen, his breath quickens against her neck. He groans, grabs her upper thighs, lifting her off the floor and turns her towards the kitchen countertop.

Sophia clutches the smooth stone surface of the benchtop, bending over with her feet apart. It was an invitation impossible to resist. Haruto steps up against her back, runs his hands over her thighs, reaches under her green silk dress and swiftly pulls down her panties. She bends further forward, stretches out her arms and positions her feet to maximise Haruto's pleasure. Within seconds

204

he is naked, the weight of his hard, engorged erection moves against her naked buttocks, teasing her, stroking between her legs.

Ripe with anticipation, Sophia still worries about being late for the dinner reservation. She leans forward, her head between her arms, resting on the marble surface as Haruto moves his fingers between her legs, his breathing growing louder, more breathless as excitement overtakes his senses. She arches her head, thick auburn hair falls across her naked back as he continues to touch her, gently, then harder, softer, then slower. He knows she is wet with arousal and ready for him.

He is a master all right. Sophia grins. 'Put it in,' she murmurs breathlessly in English.

He leans his weight against her back, his penis, taut with desire pressing against her buttocks and responds in Japanese.

'I don't understand,' he says with impressive self-control.

She pleads in his mother tongue, and he grabs a handful of her long hair, gently twisting her head to the side. Haruto tenderly bites along the delicate edge of her ear, distracting her with the sensation, before thrusting his member home. They both surrender to the delicious, blissful immersion of their senses in pleasure and delicate pain. Moments later, they are both spent, but there is no time to waste.

Now running twenty minutes late, the taxi finally pulls up at the curb outside the Japanese restaurant in Kent Street. The driver races around to open the passenger door. Haruto emerges from the back seat dressed in an ivory linen suit and holds out his hand for Sophia who moves out of the vehicle looking majestic in her new emerald and diamond necklace. Sophia is resplendent in a vibrant green silk sheath which clings to the curves of her body, revealing only her naked arms and ankles as she steps from the car and holds onto Haruto's proffered forearm. Sophia's intoxicating aura is only overshadowed by the sparkle of precious cut-stones resting on the half-moon shaped curve of her porcelain skin exposed by the modest cut of her neckline.

She resists the temptation to kiss him as he looks at her with approval as they stand on the pavement. Holding hands, they stroll towards the restaurant. For a fleeting moment, Sophia thinks she recognises someone on the crowded footpath. It's a busy evening, with couples and families bustling along the jam-packed street. She turns her head glancing in the direction again and is convinced it's the retreating back of Willem Van Howan's head. Is it likely that he's in Sydney? It wasn't noted on his itinerary and she knows he has a booking in three weeks' time.

A shot of adrenalin races through her body as she swings back to smile at Haruto. Had Willem seen her? Was it even him? Unlikely. He's not even in the country! She laughs nervously as they walk through the double doors of Tetsuya. Maybe it wasn't Willem and if it was, he may not have caught sight of her in the crowd. If he had, there was no doubt, he would confront her on his next visit.

Haruto frowns at Sophia. 'Are you OK?' he asks in colloquial Japanese.

She smiles weakly and squeezes his hand. 'Yes, I am very OK.'

But the more she thinks, the more she fears Willem has seen her with Haruto. He's supposed to be in the Hague. He had a series of meetings. She takes a deep breath. Willem will challenge her. Call her a liar, or far worse. Surely it wasn't him. It can't be. Her thoughts yo-yo back and forth. Sophia tries to repress her anxiety. Compressing it into a tiny, hard kernel at the back of her mind. Let it go. There's nothing you can do. Haruto is your focus now. She turns and smiles warmly at him as they are ushered to their table.

CHAPTER 36

Bigger Than Texas – 2017

'You know how it is, the local designers all start copying one another, and similar styles seem to merge,' Frank Horner explains at a chance meeting in the first-class bar on a return flight to Sydney from Amsterdam.

Frank's a well-built American ex-navy SEAL who Sophia guesses to be in his late forties. 'I want some fresh ideas, and I can tell, just looking at you Sophia, that you have a bucket of fresh ideas!' He chuckles, his words captured in a rich southern drawl. His eyes dance above a broad grin. 'You need to come on down to Houston and see the property for yourself,' he suggests.

'That can be arranged.' She smiles demurely. 'I'm sure we can transform the place into a real home.' Sophia takes another sip from her cocktail glass.

'I want a wow factor in the entryway. I'm keen to see what kind of magic you can do.'

Sophia is sure he's keen but is he willing to commit to her business arrangement? Immediately she clicks with him. He's worth incorporating into her stable of clients, if he can play by her rules. A faint smile plays on her face as she keenly listens to Frank's chatter.

'It's a lot of work and taken over three years to build,' he says, explaining the construction of his new multi-million-dollar family home nearing completion outside Huston.

His easy manner and hazel eyes draw Sophia in like a laser beam. 'We could use your help but come and see for yourself. Let me know what you think.'

Always a shrewd businesswoman, Sophia maintains a considered and noncommittal response. 'I'll be delighted,' she says. He could, of course, be anybody. Men like to talk big, but who knows, maybe he'd make a suitable client? She makes a mental note of observations and preferences Frank alludes to during their two hour in-flight conversation. Sophia opts for some research before she formally approaches Mr Horner.

'I don't mean to sound hesitant, but I've been away for a fortnight and want to check with my business partner, Florian Fabre. I'd like him to come along too,' she says calmly. 'He's an interior design genius with colour and placement.'

They swap contact details, and three weeks later Florian and Sophia are on a flight to Houston. The friends enjoy several dinners together with Frank while Florian works on the interior plans, the perfect opportunity for Sophia to tactfully offer her services to her new target.

Late one evening in her luxurious bedroom, Sophia sits glued to her laptop searching Frank's background online. It proves difficult, even in incognito mode. He's a man who's carefully covered his tracks in an attempt to remain anonymous on various boards. With a quick phone call to an old university contact with a master's degree in IT, she discovers Frank's an oilman and has a name synonymous with heart-stopping wealth. Investments in business and property have multiplied his equity and quadrupled his assets in the past few years, making him one of the Rich Listers of America.

A few days later Mr Horner signs up with Sophia and pays six months retainer upfront, and the two friends are awarded the house interior design contract too.

Frank is delighted and makes his first booking with Sophia for a trip to New York, where he has a business meeting with other board members. 'Always so boring and I often try and wriggle my way out of these round-table waffle fests,' he explains.

'I can imagine,' Sophia responds, rolling her eyes skyward in mock disinterest.

'To have you waiting for me back at the hotel,' he chuckles in disbelief, 'will make it damn hard ... for me to attend those boring boardroom meetings.'

She grins with that look in her eyes, concentrating on Frank's face. 'Now I do have ground rules, and work comes first. I never want to come between a man's means of income and his wife,' she says, suddenly looking serious.

He guffaws loudly. 'Don't you worry darlin' the only place I want to be is between your beautiful thighs.' He bursts out into hearty laughter at his own joke.

Sophia discovers a few wives in Frank's background but says nothing. Unbidden, during a phone call, he readily confesses being a serial monogamist,.

'Only one wife at a time. It's all I can take,' he grins again.

With four children from three different wives, he maintains his lawyer is kept in the lifestyle he aspires to in Frank's divorce settlement fees alone.

Back home in Sydney, Sophia walks with Florian along the beachfront promenade.

Florian nods. 'Here, sit down.' He indicates one of the wooden benches along the walkway. They both sit in silence for a few moments, looking out across the harbour before Florian speaks.

'What are you going to do?'

'Have you had a chance to sort the video cameras in the penthouse? I need material on Willem. I must be ready with a strong response to his potential threats.'

'What do you mean by threats?'

'He's agitated and I know he saw me with Haruto even though he hasn't tackled me yet. It makes me uneasy.'

'OK,' Florian responds feeling apprehensive. 'He's not going to risk his entire career on a scandal involving a mistress on the other side of his political world. But how can you bring him to his senses? He seems almost jealous, obsessive. To be honest he gives me the creeps.'

'Me too.' Sophia says. 'My only option, which gives me real clout, is to photograph any documents and ID papers in his briefcase. He always brings a tog bag with clothes and that tan leather briefcase. I don't know what's in it, but a video of us having sex and possible documents as proof he's been in my company, will put me in control of a tricky situation.'

'That's easy enough,' Florian interrupts. 'The video camera in your room is in position and the WiFi data is automatically stored on the hub and replicates a back-up on your laptop.'

'Good.' Sophia has a bit more control over Willem and feels relieved she has more confidence in her plan. 'If he doesn't comply, I'll notify his wife... probably not,' she grins. 'But I'd tell him, on a long-distance call.' She forces a laugh, watching Florian's grim face.

'Really?' Florian asks. 'Is this wise? There must be some other way.' Speechless, Florian continues listening with rising panic.

CHAPTER 37

Bolt-Hole - 2018

Florian frowns. 'I don't quite understand. You want to buy a house in suburbia? Is it necessary? You already run between the penthouse and a small flat.'

'It sounds weird on the face of it, but I'll give up the flat and live in the new house, when I find it,' Sophia explains, taking a gulp of coffee as they sit in the penthouse chatting.

'Why bother?' he asks, confusion mounting. 'Stay in the penthouse and if you need to escape, go to the flat. It's less cost and drama,' he persists, dunking a second gingernut into his coffee and taking a mouthful.

Sophia shrugs her shoulders, pulling a face and realises she's raced ahead in her planning and not included Florian. No wonder he doesn't get it. 'Two things,' she states. 'I hate paying rent into a landlord's pocket, even if its chicken feed. I also want the capital gain in a family home of my own. I need to keep my business absolutely separate from my private life. A bolt-hole away from work, if that makes sense.'

'Ahh, OK. I see where you're coming from.'

'I'd love to have a garden of my own too.'

You'll pay upwards of a million dollars for three bedrooms in the 'burbs.'

She grins and leans in towards him, holding his gaze in hers. 'Don't you worry your pretty little head about it. I have the money and have been saving for over five years for this very opportunity.'

'Mortgage?' he asks.

'I only need fifty percent. I think, Mr Fabre, you have grossly underestimated my value and earning power.'

They both laugh and he playfully punches her on the arm.

Sophia explains her new private home in the suburbs will prove

211

an ideal cover-story woven together with her fake interior designer identity, camouflaging her true calling from friends and family. This new suburban home will be her bolt-hole escape to a private urban sanctuary where the intrusion of her business life and clients has no place.

After six weeks of house hunting, Sophia drags Florian to inspect several homes in various leafy, middle-class suburbs that are on her hot list.

'It has to be one of these,' she says, passing her cell phone to him over a boozy lunch at a city restaurant. 'Click the saved real estate links.'

Florian flicks through, dismisses two and hands the phone back. 'The other two look perfect. You should buy both!' He chuckles, tipsy after a long lunch. Let's go to the open homes this afternoon, but I need a coffee before we leave.'

Two hours later they enter the second house on the must have list. Several other potential buyers are milling around the interior, making muffled comments to their partners. In contrast, Sophia grabs Florian's elbow and takes him outside into the neatly trimmed garden.

'This is exactly the house I want!' Sophia announces.

'I totally agree. Where do we sign, darling?'

Another couple within earshot, standing inside the open plan living area, glance at the pair outside in surprise and titter to one another with mild irritation.

As proof to Florian that she's never impulsive, she suppresses her excitement and tells the agent she will sleep on it and contact them in the morning. That night she tosses in a half sleep, concerned about this step of buying her first property. The penthouse doesn't count, that's a private arrangement between her and Giles. This new home will be her very own. She runs through the interior of the house room by room, visualising her furniture and aspects that need some work and renovation. She imagines a housewarming party and having family and friends over for lunches. She rolls over again, squeezing her eyes tight, attempting to force herself to sleep. The house is perfect. She always desired a

212

property that wouldn't attract any public attention. It's a regular four-bedroom, two-storey dwelling with a manageable garden in the north-eastern suburbs of Sydney, less than seventeen kilometres from her central city penthouse. It's comfortable, low maintenance with a high degree of privacy from the street. Tall hedges and automatic metal gates provide the security Sophia requires. At 10am the next day, Sophia meets the real estate agent and signs the offer to purchase.

During the evening Florian arrives at Sophia's flat with a freshly roasted chicken. She quickly produces a green salad and they enjoy a shared dinner while watching the news.

'Amazing!' Sophia shrieks as the presenter announces the Reserve Bank has dropped the official cash rate to a new historic low of 2.25 percent. 'My mortgage will almost be free.'

'Trust you to always land with your bum in butter.' Florian grins. 'Let's hope it does some good for the economy and not only your unfolding life.'

'Now, now, do you mean my economic use of my bum or the butter.' She giggles. 'We're damn lucky. We've got jobs and neither of us is directly affected by the oil price.'

'Unless it's massage oil.' He chortles, throwing a colourful plaid cushion at her.

'Now down to more serious stuff,' she says pulling a memory stick from her jacket slung over the back of an armchair. 'I've the next batch of video clips saved on this.'

'Right. I'll copy them onto a drive at home and then return it, say next Tuesday week,' he says as she places the brushed metal device into his open palm.

'Great. Same as last time.' She sighs heavily. 'I don't like doing this and I hope I don't ever have to use them.'

'I know.' He reassures her, not wanting to get into another tense discussion over legalities and privacy laws.

'I do sleep better knowing I've evidence on everyone. You know what it's like if you don't cover your tracks. So, I prefer to be cautious and protect myself.'

Florian nods. 'Sure, I totally get it.'

Sophia changes direction reminding Florian of his promise to create phony collateral to support her two identities. One as an interior designer and the other a private penthouse business owner. Something to keep her clients secure and also maintain the ruse of being a successful interior designer to appease her grandmother, father, sister and a few quizzical friends and associates.

Developing a false identity for her business results in a nod to her family surname, Hawkins, her grandmother's maiden name. Sophia knows she will automatically respond to the old family surname if it is called out in public. She also likes the natural, unassuming simplicity of the name, *Sophia Hawkins*. She reviews her newly designed driver's licence and realises Florian's creative talent surpasses her expectations. He opens a heavy black portfolio and produces several elegant matt finished business cards with *Sophia Hawkins* detailed gracefully embossed on top quality white linen card.

'Wow,' she says, taken aback at how subtle the business cards appear. 'One for each of my business commitments.' She chuckles, shuffling the deck of Sophia Huston interior designer cards in amongst simple Sophia Hawkins penthouse business cards.

'Who shall I be tonight, Mr Fabre?' she smiles.

'Umm, try to remember who you are when you're with my clients, darl, or we'll both be in trouble.' Florian frowns. 'Of course, you don't want to be using this replica driver's licence in the real world if you get pulled over by a cop,' he explains to Sophia as they look over the documents. 'It's proof of your Hawkins identity for your clients if you should ever need it. In reality you'll have to use your genuine passport and driver's licence when you travel overseas or if you get caught speeding downtown.'

'Sure. I'm reluctant to do anything criminal,' Sophia says. 'I'll be very careful none of my clients see my original documents.'

'I could create a fake passport too if you like, so if anyone happens to look through your handbag ...' he is interrupted in mid-sentence.

'What?' Sophia responds with alarm. 'I didn't imagine ... but it's a real possibility.'

'It is, but hopefully one that never happens,' Florian says.

'OK. Make one, and I'll ensure I keep my original passport locked up. Finding the fake one will at least confirm with anyone looking that I am who I say I am,' Sophia sighs. 'Trust and credibility are critical in this business. I can't be too careful.'

'Exactly,' Florian responds. 'Give me your original passport so I can replicate everything in it apart from the surname. I'll get it back to you next weekend, Ms Hawkins.' He grins.

Clever *re-purposing* of Florian's interior design business templates and documents enables him to create relevant plans, sketches, papers, and client portfolios. A folder of replicated interior design work, complete with Sophia's name, on occasional documents and header-sheets, provides hard evidence of her fake *employment*. This is credible proof for her friends and family too. Sophia doesn't have other close friends, but there are a few old school friends, like Carla Fitzsimmons, she runs into now and again. It helps to have a very well-rehearsed cover-story to back up her lifestyle and camouflage her real career.

Fortuitously, Frank Horner's interior design job allows for plausible excuses to travel overseas and meet with other potential clients. She's also taken lots of photographs of Frank's project, confidently discussing the interiors, colour swatches, contemporary furniture, antiques and centre-pieces, including artwork for expansive walls to enhance the overall style of his newly completed home. Sophia jokes with Florian that he's getting free interior consulting services from her as an 'employee' and she's securing Florian's business success.

'It's the least I can do given all the support you've shown me.' She smiles warmly.

While showing interior shots of Frank's palatial home to her sister a week later, she explains this new project will put her on the map with wealthy clients, and she hopes to gain more commercial work too. Everyone loves her style, she clarifies, and working with Florian proves a successful business partnership.

No one thought anything was amiss with Sophia's life until she visits her grandmother.

CHAPTER 38

Photographic Memory - 2018

It is a temperate Sunday afternoon when Sophia arrives at her grandmother's retirement unit, set in the garden of the rest home facility. Edith Hawkins moved there after Michael could no longer afford to cover her independent living costs including private care in her own home. A small gathering of family and a few close friends are crammed into the compact lounge for her birthday celebration.

Edith, the challenging focal point, holds court surrounded by adoring guests. It's easy to see her warm blue eyes once held an inherited beauty passed down the generations to Sophia. A sharp mind lies behind her wrinkled face and thinning eyebrows. Her eyes dart around the room from one face to another as she chips into the conversations and challenges disagreeable opinions.

There is a knock at the door, and a nursing assistant helps the catering staff deliver trays of club sandwiches, small apple tarts with cream and other delicious treats for the small gathering. Sophia's crumpled father is slumped wordlessly on the floral couch next to his elderly mother, and Sophia sits in an armchair opposite, watching the pair with interest.

Seated on the other side of her grandmother is another older man, Max Forsyth, a long-time friend of her grandmother's. A captain of industry, Max made his fortune from targeted investments in an array of manufacturing businesses. Now in his winter years, he happily indulges those around him with the improved tolerance he lacked during his hard-bitten business dealings. His round face tilts forward from the weight of his double chin giving him the appearance of listening and understanding the chatter. Sophia knows otherwise.

'Sophia's doing very well in her interior design business,' her grandmother says, jolting Sophia from her ruminations. Edith walks to the sideboard and grabs an envelope containing the colour photographs. 'I had them all printed,' she says proudly, smiling across the small open-plan room at her granddaughter. She shuffles back to the sofa and slowly lowers her body into position between the two men.

Sophia's grandmother passes a clutch of photographs for Max to hand around to the others in the room. Before circulating the handful, Max sifts through glossy images, barely interested until he notices a shot of Frank Horner standing with three other people after a hunting trip.

'Hey, I know this guy,' he says, thrusting the photograph across the coffee table towards Sophia.

'I doubt it,' Sophia says. 'This was taken at a new property in Houston, Texas.' Always wary of providing any details, she resists any queries regarding her client's contact information. But her heart palpitates in shock as she regards Max's eager face.

'This guy,' he says, pointing a craggy index finger at Frank. 'He's an American. I did some business with him before I retired a few years ago.'

Sophia nods, smiling in an attempt to deflect any further conversation on the topic and begins describing a new project Florian is tendering for in Spain. She clicks onto the photo gallery on her cell phone and passes it to her grandmother and Max to view more recent images. Her thoughts are racing to recall some of the new project details, and in the end, she decides to wing it. What would they know anyway? She has to do everything she can to avoid the risk of Max placing Sophia with Frank. Could he know something? Is it even possible? Max was a few years younger than Edith but barely looked retirement age. Has there been a discussion between the two old business connections? With rising fear clawing at her throat, Sophia swallows hard. Has Frank given the game away?

Max won't let the issue go and continues zeroing in on Sophia as Edith flicks through the Spanish project and asks a few simple questions.

'You're Sophia, right?' Max asks, looking directly into her blue eyes. Sophia nods and smiles politely, glancing back at her intrigued grandmother, keenly observing the pair.

'How far is this new property from Barcelona?' Edith asks.

'I'm not sure,' Sophia says. 'But the kitchen is magnificent, look at the stainless steel and marble surfaces in this photo. It's got that …'

Max interrupts, frowning at Sophia. 'Strange. Last time I saw Frank, must be about a year ago now, he talked about a mistress called Sophia, who was also an Australian.'

A cold rush of horror surges through her body, but Sophia's face doesn't convey a thing other than polite indifference.

'Really?' She smiles disarmingly. 'Quite a coincidence, wouldn't you say?'

'I love the kitchen island,' Edith interrupts. 'So big and beautifully designed.'

Sophia turns towards her grandmother and smiles, nodding in agreement. 'You should see the gardens. The landscaper had only made a start when I was last there. They'll be magnificent.'

She couldn't help herself and angles her head to see if Max is about to release his victim. But he's staring straight back at her. She blinks in shock, and he sees it. Max grins and raises an eyebrow. He knew. *Fuck.* She gives no further indication that anything is amiss, choosing to ignore him for the rest of the afternoon.

She needs to speak with Frank as soon as she returns home. Max's comments are a severe breach of her privacy and go against the client confidentiality contract. But what can she do? Cancel the contract and infuriate a man like Frank Horner. There is no way she can take him to court or enforce a penalty. Asking Frank to fix it could implicate her. Too much of a coincidence after this skirmish with Max. Agitated, Sophia makes her excuses and leaves twenty minutes later after hugging her grandmother farewell and promising to visit the following weekend.

As she steps outside Sophia inhales deeply. This is bad, really bad, and puts her whole business at risk. She'll tell Frank to contact Max and shut him up. Worse, is the prospect of having Max as a client, demanding that he join her members' club for free! There's no way she is willing to embark on an arrangement with this much older man. Max is no affable Giles. She fears demands for *free membership* is Max's ulterior motive. Once outside, Sophia quickly walks towards her parked car. Her mind races through various scenarios, increasing her sense of alarm. Maybe doing and saying nothing, maintaining ignorance and denial is the only way to handle this for now?

She swipes her ignition key-fob, the sports car beeps and unlocks. Max is suddenly standing behind her.

'Nice car,' he announces loudly as Sophia's blood runs cold.

'Thanks,' she utters, turning to open the driver's door.

'I hear you get a hefty retainer from Frank,' he elaborates.

Sophia swings around. Max is taller and slimmer than she first thought, having only observed him seated next to her grandmother on the floral sofa. His brown eyes are wide with excitement at the prospect of challenging her. Dark brown hair belies his age, but in his navy jacket and expensive designer jeans, she assesses him to be in his late sixties with the definitive look of a tenacious capitalist.

'All my interior design clients pay a retainer,' she says matter-of-factly. 'Some of my larger projects can last for over two years.' She is unwavering in her grim determination to shut Max Forsyth up permanently.

'Oh?' Max leers. 'I heard you're offering other kinds of fringe benefits to your clients.'

'Whatever do you mean?' Sophia responds, indignant with steely eyes trained on her adversary.

Silence.

Each considers the next manoeuvre in this game of truth or dare. Sophia takes control and puts this old man in his place.

'I'll have you know, Mr Forsyth, I'm a fully qualified professional, and I protect my business clients at all costs,' Sophia says morphing into full corporate speak to close this man down. 'I have no idea where you got any other impression from, but I maintain a world-class business with integrity and professionalism at all times.'

Max hears an undercurrent of anger and hard-edged annoyance in her tone. She is no longer his friend's sweet little granddaughter. He realises his hope at gaining something more from this beautiful creature has evaporated.

He hesitates and mumbles, 'Oh, I'm sorry. I misunderstood. Apologies. I did hear you've done some amazing work.'

Sophia remains silent as she watches him retreat. Her lips press together in a hard, unrelenting line as she turns, climbs into her car and drives off.

Back home in suburbia, Sophia walks around and around the house, replaying Max's guarded threat. She decides to call her closest confidant.

Ten minutes later Florian bursts through the front.

'Darling, darling,' he says, excited at the prospect of the first stage for their new project in Spain kicking-off the following month.

'Don't you ever ring the doorbell?' she asks, having opened the security gates earlier. 'I'm beginning to regret giving you keys to my houses, life and soul.'

He rolls his eyes and throws himself on a kitchen barstool as Sophia flicks on the coffee machine. 'Listen, girlfriend, I need you to come with me to Barcelona, and of course, the trip's on me.'

'I can't. I'm booked up for weeks, and I have a strict policy of keeping my word.'

'Ahh! So, so boring!' Florian says with a loud sigh. 'I'm here. Tell me what's up?'

'There're a few things stressing me out,' Sophia states. 'I had a call from Frank, by the way, and he's delighted with your proposal. He couldn't stop raving.'

'That's good news, right?' Florian responds. 'No drama.'

Sophia nods. 'Yeah, of course.'

'Is that it?' he asks frowning in surprise.

'No, wait there's more. I've got a bit of a situation. An older guy ...'

'Yechhh.' Florian interrupts. 'You told me old guys were off the client list. How old are we talking?'

'Will you listen to me for a change,' she frowns at him.

He regards her, concentrating on her casual appearance. Without makeup and dressed in an old pair of jeans worn with a grey t-shirt, Sophia still manages to look hot. And that's saying something from a gay guy.

'OK, out with it,' Florian says. 'I'm waiting. I haven't got all day, darl.'

'I met a friend of my grandmother's today, although he's at least ten years younger than her,' Sophia explains.

'That's a relief!'

'His name is Max Forsyth, and get this, he's a business friend of Frank Horner.'

Florian takes a few seconds to compute the unlikely coincidence. 'So? That isn't a dire situation, is it?'

'It could be,' Sophia replies as she relates the afternoon tea and the conversation with Max at her car.

'I don't know what to do. Should I ignore it and pray he goes away or contact Frank and tell him to fix it as he gossiped to Max about me?'

'This is tricky,' Florian says slowly, considering a gamut of possible solutions. 'You'll be damned if you do and drowning in the deep end if you don't.'

'Well, yeah,' Sophia says. 'I guess, doing nothing until I absolutely have to is a bit smarter. In that way, if Max says and does nothing, keeping the confidence, then no one gets upset.'

Florian nods. 'I wouldn't want to be demanding stuff from Frank. He can be hardcore and gets aggressive very fast. Then we both lose. He's a hothead and likely to cancel our contract for the interior work too.'

'I denied it and told Max he's got his wires crossed, so there's a small chance he'll let it go.'

'Ummmm. OK, I'll keep an ear to the ground with Frank when I'm over there again, and now I know Max's name I'll be on high alert for any mention.'

CHAPTER 39

Startling Details - 2018

Twenty minutes later, Sophia leaves the house with Florian in their separate cars. She has a booking at lunchtime with her Kiwi client, Hugh Rixon, at the penthouse, with precious little time to shower and dress before his arrival. Ten days have passed since she last saw Hugh and Sophia is keen to spend time with him again. Out of her seven clients, Hugh is the one closest to her heart. He reminds her of a younger version of Giles, so Hugh's immediate appeal is undeniable. As the weeks have flown by, Sophia has grown more intimate than she normally allows, finding the New Zealander gentle, charming, generous and kind-hearted.

While she's buttoning up the front of her silk blouse, the downstairs security doorbell rings. She marches to the front door and checks the security camera. Hugh is, as usual, precisely on time. She smiles to herself and picks up the pace to buzz him inside. Moving to the large mirror above the ornately hand-carved mahogany sideboard in the lavish entryway, Sophia leans in, checking her makeup and quickly ruffles her hair with her manicured fingertips. She is surprised at how excited she feels at the prospect of spending time with Hugh. Exhilarated like a delighted schoolgirl before the prom, she grins at her own image and stands beside the front door waiting for the doorbell to ring.

She doesn't have to wait long. The doorbell buzzes, and she counts to three before opening her door. Hugh is dressed in a dark, fitted fine merino wool suit. Although he is six years older than thirty-one-year old Sophia, he doesn't look it. He greets her with a broad grin, his brown eyes dancing, and grabs her, pushing them both back into the penthouse apartment. Hugh swings her around and plants an enthusiastic kiss on her lips.

'Good to see you too, Mr Rixon!' Sophia leans into him, firmly pressing her body against his and feels startled by their shared attraction. She's never experienced this sensation before. Sex with him was no job, not a checklist of actions to fulfil, or a means of ensuring she meets contractual obligations to every client. On the contrary, she can't wait to get him naked in bed.

Facing her, still holding her around the waist, he closes the front door with the back of his foot and clutches her hand, dragging her across the entryway, into the opulent master bedroom.

Sophia luxuriates in finely tempered anticipation at the rising sexual tension between them. This is always the way with Hugh. From the very first time he slept with her, she experienced the early stirrings of deep desire and fine-tuned pleasure which she's never before fully appreciated.

She analyses and assesses the reasons why and considers Hugh's divorced, single status with no apparent baggage could be the key to their mutual allure. On closer inspection, this holds no weight, other than grasping for some excuse dressed up as the reason for their love. Was it love? Unlikely, but then what else could it be? Most of her other clients are married, looking for an escape, but Hugh seems to make Sophia his reality and wants to immerse himself in every part of her life. With elements of disquiet, Sophia realises this relationship could become trickier at maintaining the subterfuge of mistress or girlfriend. Still, she doesn't allow these thoughts to circulate now as Hugh releases her from his embrace.

He carefully removes her clothes as she attempts to take off his. Still half-dressed he pulls her onto the oversized bed. Sunlight streams through the massive floor-to-ceiling glass windows overlooking the city where the expansive harbour bridge spans the azure ocean sensuously moving to nature's tidal rhythm. He kisses her again, longingly, not wanting the hungry pleasure to end.

Afterwards, he stretches out across the bed with his eyes closed, his imagination on replay, rousing his desire again. Sophia turns to him, leaning on one elbow.

'You're truly exceptional,' she tells him. 'I wonder what makes you so extraordinary?'

Hugh opens his eyes and looks lovingly at the beautiful woman beside him.

She wants an answer, which won't be easy. She can tell, with Hugh's naked body under the sheets, something more pressing is on his mind.

'Circumstances,' he responds. 'The lucky combo which lets an individual shine.' Hugh has answered this question many times before. 'Without the right situation and merger of good universal forces, the potential for a good man to excel remains buried in the shadows.'

Sophia smiles. 'You're as impressive in the shadows as you are in broad daylight!' They both chuckle as he talks to her about visiting New Zealand in a few weeks. He has meetings in Wellington but think they might spend a few days at the exclusive Huka Lodge near Lake Taupo.

'We can helicopter over, and I'll show you the sights.' He smiles, elaborating further. 'The flight itself is so beautiful, snow-capped Mount Ruapehu and the lake.'

'As long as you give me a few days' notice, I'll be at your service, sir.' She grins. For the first time, she is struck by the idea that Hugh would be horrified if he knew the true extent of her business arrangements. Apart from the revulsion of being a call-girl, the full impact of her daily deception would end their relationship. He would be appalled, and this horrifying perspective begins to torment Sophia, silently nagging at the back of her head and in the dead of night when she wakes with a start.

'Just how I like my concubines.' He interrupts her dark thoughts with his relentless good mood.

A tiny kernel of a potential relationship makes her truly happy, a warm sense of belonging with Hugh, comfortable ease which is new to her. At the same time, while these blissful thoughts creep into her consciousness, ugly bouts of anxiety and terror interrupt with flashes of fear that Hugh will discover her true calling, crushing any emotional fantasy.

As a distraction, to bring herself back to reality, she discusses her interior design work in Texas and Spain as well as a few local jobs, carefully avoiding any risky association with her secret indulgence. Sophia continues to play the coquette, flirting with Hugh over photographs and client portfolio images, talking about the bedroom suites and how she designs the interiors to best effect.

After Hugh leaves for the airport, she feels bereft, isolated and lost without him nearby. He texts her cell phone before his plane has left the tarmac, '*I miss you already.*'

She responds, sending him a heart emoji and a sad weeping face and long with a capital, bold X.

Sophia knows her behaviour goes entirely against her policy, but she can't help herself. She responds instantly when he contacts her and is repeatedly drawn to his every need. Sophia admits to Hugh that over the years, their relationship is growing more significant. How can she handle him with growing frequency and still maintain her clients as a primary source of income? Fear of being caught out by Hugh haunts her waking moments and continues to torture her sleepless nights.

The following morning, Hugh calls for a quick catchup.

'I can't get you out of my head,' he says, 'so I called to hear your voice.'

Sophia is secretly pleased that he is obviously falling for her. 'I'm the same,' she replies, and they continue chatting for a few minutes. She hears a vehicle pull up in her driveway. 'Gotta go, a delivery guy's arrived. Speak soon.'

Sophia has no bookings for five days and intends to make the most of it. She can't wait to nestle onto the sofa in the early autumn sunshine and immerse into a new book.

CHAPTER 40

Married to Marit. 2018

So far this year it's Willem Van Howan's third flight to Sydney and with back-to-back meetings until the weekend, he's relieved to know he has thirty-six hours slotted in with Sophia. He gazes out over the Pacific Ocean from his first-class airline seat, spacious and comfortable, the staff seeing to his every need. The thrill at the prospect of having Sophia to himself for the weekend is exhilarating. He can barely concentrate on the NATO report spread across his laptop.

Sophia, he breathes her name. Being with her makes all things seem possible. He's known Sophia for over two years. Her electrifying effect on him is in blunt contrast to his domestic love-life. Willem marvels at the comparison. With Sophia, he enjoys pleasure without any conjugal suffering. She never imposes any demands. Compliance – he likes that about her.

His brother's wife's family were diamond jewellers in Rotterdam, so last year he managed to purchase the anniversary bracelet at cost. Counting himself truly blessed, he lies back on the headrest and closes his eyes, luxuriating in the memory of the last time he held her naked body. It's been six long weeks without her.

Dozing in his comfortable aeroplane seat Willem's thoughts are brutally interrupted by memories of the previous night with his second wife, Marit. Willem knows his second wife believes she is always on the back burner. She repeatedly tells him with every chance she gets. After much resistance and brutal arguing, Marit finally seems to understand that she is only a tiny part of Willem's busy business and political life. His ex-wife and three children are a priority too, especially as Marit refuses to have children. An accomplished oil painter, Marit is on a career trajectory that offers

229

no time or attention, let alone the indulgence of having offspring. This is one thing Willem agrees on with Marit.

On several occasions in the past year, Willem has talked to Sophia about Marit, in a sad, disillusioned kind of way. Sophia knows, like most of her clients, that Willem pays for escapism.

Willem recalls the argument with Marit the previous evening. He had taken her out to dinner at a three-star Michelin restaurant in Amsterdam. It was a calm, star-lit night as their chauffeur drove them into the city. Willem hoped to smooth things over with Marit before he departed for Sydney.

As the maitre'd showed them to their table situated in a private corner of the salubrious establishment, Willem tried to elaborate again, on his reasons for returning to Australia.

'I'll only be gone for a week, then a few days in Paris and back home,' he said, casually glancing at the menu.

Marit stared at her husband, politician, businessman and multi-millionaire. 'Yes, it sounds like a small thing, but you do this with growing regularity so that half the year is spent without you,' she says bitterly.'

Willem knew she was in too deep to escape and contemplated how to progress and avoid more conflict.

Reading the flicker of antagonism that crossed his wife's face, Willem spoke again, looking directly into her distressed eyes.

'You look particularly gorgeous this evening,' he said, a little worried that he sounded unconvincing. He brandished a broad, loving smile, at least that was his intention.

Marit glanced down at the menu and spoke to her husband in a clear, uncompromising voice. 'I can smell the deceit on you, Willem.' Her cheek twitched as she clenched her molars with antagonism.

He sighed, almost feeling sorry for her. 'Marit, Marit,' he repeated her name softly. 'Let's not spoil our evening together.'

'What's another spoilt evening?' she said calmly looking directly into his remote dark eyes, even now they fleetingly seemed gentle and compliant. 'I spend my life in splendid isolation, you ignore me and are out swooping around the world engaged in foreign policy conciliations,' she stated, cold and unemotional. 'While you endure, oh so many crucial meetings at the UN, I sit alone ignored back here at home. What makes you think I have anything left to give to you?'

He looks demeaned, eyes downcast, knowing it was going to be another one of those evenings, soured by nasty comments from a spoilt wife. It dawned on him this was a pattern in his life. Marit sounded more and more like his first wife, Marieke, who lived with him for three long years. The same demands and criticism from both women. Except for Sophia, who was none of these things. She was worth every cent for the uncomplicated love and understanding she offered.

But he needed to entertain a diplomatic truce with Marit or she would fester during the ten days he was overseas. His career would never withstand another divorce, and the scandal could clip his wings in mid-flight to the premiership.

'Tell me, Marit, what do you want from me? I have a political career,' he said with a heavy sigh. 'Like we agreed years ago, it's the same demanding situation that keeps you in this indulgent, all-expenses-paid lifestyle.'

'We've been over this ground before,' she stated.

'Ja, I know!' he shot back. Marit stared at him, saying nothing. 'Look let's not argue on my last evening here. I want us to have a nice time together, and now you start with the same tired, old story.'

'I do, Willem because it's the same tired old lies that you feed me.' She put down her knife and fork and eyeballed him, anger simmering very close to the surface.

'What lies? What are you talking about?' he asked exasperated, attempting to keep his voice steady.

Marit shook her dark head slowly. 'It's a feeling, something's not right. The expression in your eyes ...'

'So you accuse me because you *think* there's a lie?'

'I sense it.' Marit tries again but can't tell, without hard facts, that she is doomed to oblivion.

Willem, with his lips pressed together, ran his tongue over his front teeth, considering the best way to handle this without igniting an explosion. 'You know, Winston Churchill made an observation during the war years. Let me quote him: *A lie gets halfway around the world before the truth has a chance to get its pants on.*'

'And your point is?' she said clearly unimpressed.

'That lies, misgivings and misunderstandings cloud judgement with everyone so you can't use it to criticise or accuse me. There's so much pointless gossip. You know, it goes with the job Marit and you need to ignore it.' He paused, considering if he'd covered all the bases. 'You can't state what the issue is, and a *feeling* is a subjective intangible. My darling wife, there is no foundation for any bad feeling. I have always loved you and always will.'

He smiled warmly at her again and reached for her right hand. She allowed him to clasp it. 'I love you too, Willem,' she offered in a weak, conciliatory voice. 'I'm always so lonely when you're so far away.'

'Ja,' he soothed, 'of course. That's completely understandable. When I'm back, we'll go to Rome for a week's holiday together. That's a great plan, ja?'

'Or ... maybe I can travel with you to Sydney. I love that city and haven't been to Australia for years,' she said feeling uplifted.

He hesitated, controlling the mild shock at the prospect of Marit inside Sophia's territorial pigeon-hole, in mind as well as reality.

Marit smiled and squeezed his hand. It was the least he could do, having given Sophia that beautiful necklace. Images of Sophia's delighted laughter ran through his mind as he exchanged a concerned smile with Marit, placated for the moment.

He was wary of his second wife, she seemed to have an uncanny telepathic energy, which often picked up on some dark undercurrent between them. It was unnerving. This repetitive conversation was usually the starter's gun for Marit's persistent dissection of their relationship. He needed to take extra care to be vigilant and extremely discreet to avoid hours of accusations lurking in the backdrop of their marriage. He said nothing, contemplating a response.

'On second thoughts, Rome is a much better idea.' Marit smiled, released his hand and took a sip from her wine.

Back in Sydney Sophia waits at the airport for Willem's plane to land. She usually looks forward to his arrival, but this time she fears a confrontation. Willem had been busy and unavailable with political demands over recent months. She recalls seeing the back of his head and shoulders visible in the crowded street. Flashes of holding Haruto's hand, him leaning in closely; and the fractional moment where she thought, or had she imagined, she saw

Willem's face turn away. Maybe it wasn't him? Willem's not the only tall, dark broad-shouldered man on the planet. She tries momentarily to distract herself and focus on the people walking out of the international arrivals exit doors.

She shakes her head, as she gazes at the crowds of foreign travellers spewing out of the gates with their overloaded trolleys, chatting and laughing. Had Willem seen Haruto with her? If he had, what excuse could she come up with? He hadn't mentioned it on the phone. He had no inkling that anything was amiss, and yet the undercurrent of anxiety still stalked her thoughts. Maybe she could argue that he was mistaken. She could easily contrive an alibi with Florian for the evening. She snorted, knowing he wouldn't believe her, dressed in that green silk, made up to the nines. Sophia glances at her wristwatch. She's twenty minutes early. Her unease at the situation compresses time, and somehow with her nervousness, she had arrived at the airport well in advance of Willem's arrival, specifically to maximise her misery. Life really does conspire to exaggerate her agony.

She forces her thoughts to change tack. There were plenty of positives, including energy, wit and fun with Willem, they shared a similar crazy sense of humour. Sophia contemplates walking into the airport arrivals, but instantly dismisses it, preferring to sit in her car instead of subjecting herself to the crushing swathes of people inside the arrivals lounge. She flicks open her cell phone and notices a short text from Matt; Teressa's husband:

'Call me ASAP.'

'What now,' she says out loud as she reluctantly returns the call. 'Hey,' she says as he picks up the call.

'Soph, I've got a bit of a situation,' Matt says.

'Have you now?' she responds with sarcasm, distinctly unimpressed.

'Something wrong?' he asks.

'Nah. I'm waiting at the airport so cut to the chase,' she says in that no-nonsense tone of hers.

'Look I need to ask you a big favour.'

There is a pause. Sophia expects Matt to carry on. When he says nothing, she asks, 'I wonder what that could be?'

'Don't be like that, Soph. We're family. I'm hoping you can give me a loan.'

'Right,' she says. 'Exactly how much are we talking about?'

'Let's put it this way, it ain't chicken feed,' Matt says.

She snorts. 'Of that, I am absolutely sure! Spit it out.'

'I need seven hundred and fifty-four thousand dollars. Before you say anything, I've the money coming to me in three weeks, so it's only a short-term bridging finance kind of thing.'

'Right.' Her voice is soaked in boredom. No surprises here. 'If it's rock-solid, why won't your bank give you a short-term bridging loan?'

Silence.

'Why do you need so much money, for heaven's sake?'

'Well, it's been about a year of gambling. I'd hoped to retrieve my losses, but lady luck has proven uncooperative. Now I've been banned from the casino, and they're after me to promptly cough up.'

Her shock turns to annoyance as she thinks of this drunken loser married to her anxious sister and continuously cruising along the knife-edge of depravity. There's been plenty of gossip from Florian about Matt, which she chose to ignore. She once responded with, *let him hang himself.* But this time the length of rope extends a little too far.

What had her father said, all those years ago, when he was still sane and in the full flush of prosperity? *Never ever be a lender to family or friends. It results in a hiding on both sides, and everyone loses.* She can still hear those words ringing in her ears.

Sophia continued. 'I haven't got that kind of money hanging around waiting to hand over to you, Matt. Besides you and Teressa still owe me the money I loaned you for your wedding. I'm in no position to hand out anymore.'

'That's not what I heard,' he sneers into the phone.

'Matt, you either go quietly and blow smoke up someone else's arse, or I'll tell Teressa about your affair. I know all about it. I've even got the photos to prove it. So, let's put our sabres back in their sheath and get on with our little lives.'

'That's bullshit!' he spits into the phone. 'Rattling the cage isn't going to make anyone any happier, and by the way, your darling sister is getting more neurotic by the hour.'

'No thanks to you!' Sophia fires back. 'Your marriage has only lasted four years. You need to borrow a huge sum of money while my sister is distressed by your behaviour and constant absences. Why would I support that? Take a moment to think clearly for a change. I caution you to be careful, very careful about threats you make to me.'

'You better watch out yourself. I know you're hooking from that penthouse in the city,' he blurts, his voice saturated with controlled anger. 'You best help me out, *sister*,' his voice steeped in sarcasm, 'so we can both keep our personal vices to ourselves.'

Sophia wants to mend the relationship with her sister. Teressa's had a raw deal with her parents and now this cheating low life husband. If she doesn't help, Teressa will completely flip out. It's a mess, and Sophia feels as if she has no choice. Reluctantly she makes a decision for her sister's sake, not her own.

'Text me the casino bank account and your membership number,' she says, in a modulated tone. 'You'll need to sign a loan agreement and a payment plan before I make the funds available. You've got six months to pay me back,' she says abruptly, her voice cold as high-tensile steel. 'You default, and I promise you'll live, if you're lucky, to regret it.'

CHAPTER 41

Bad Apple - 2019

Florian, alone in the penthouse, is repairing one of the security cameras inside Sophia's home. She regularly downloads surveillance footage of her clients' activities, creates a back-up and astutely stores the memory sticks in Zip-loc plastic bags, each with the initials of her client's name and each bag secreted inside her private dressing room in the bottom drawer of each relevant client's wardrobe. In this way she maintains complete control over each client's information and has easy access, should she ever need to manipulate her way out of a tricky situation, with any of her paying clients.

A weekend free of clients allows Sophia to take a break with Carla, where they stay in a bed and breakfast hotel along the coast. Florian continues working on securing the surveillance cameras in the bedroom and living room areas. He's playing an old re-run of a news documentary from 2012, which he mostly ignores. When the presenter details a gay sex scandal involving Peter Slipper, speaker of the House of Representatives at the time, Florian stops working and watches the images flit across the screen. Someone Ashby, Florian didn't quite catch the first name, a radio presenter, made sexual harassment allegations about Slipper and he was investigated over fraudulent CabCharge vouchers too.

Florian sniffs. 'Stupid fag,' he mumbles as he walks into the second bedroom. Carrying a compact rechargeable drill, he removes the micro camera from the frame of an oil painting opposite the double bed. He rolls it between his thumb and index finger, trying to determine if the WiFi signal is still active. Florian holds it up to the light from the window to get a closer look at the connections when the downstairs door gives a shrill ring.

He frowns, carefully placing the tiny camera inside the dresser drawer, before sliding it closed and walking into the entryway. A small light flashes on the penthouse security system. He gazes directly at the small screen where a strange man in a navy suit stands, briefly peering up and smiling into the camera. Florian pushes the buzzer and leans forward into the mouthpiece. 'Yes?' he enquires, unsure about the interruption.

'Hi,' Willem says, disconcerted at a suspicious looking stranger answering Sophia's security system.

'I've come to drop off concert tickets for Sophia. Is it OK if I come up?'

'She's not here. Gone away for the weekend,' Florian explains, but Willem won't be fobbed off.

'No problem, I'll leave them with you. Only be two secs.' Willem sounds pushy in his thick Dutch accent, determined to get his own way.

Florian hesitates then pushes the buzzer. He has about sixty seconds to tidy up the miniature tools, pliers and pocket-knife from the bedroom and brush himself down. Fragments of plaster-dust where he drilled into the walls of the hallway and bedrooms have gathered on his dark t-shirt and formed small powder mounds on the grey tiled floor.

Moments later, the front door buzzes, giving Florian a start as he sucks in a breath through his nostrils and strides to the entrance. He is caught off-guard as he opens the front door. Willem marches past him and into the living room.

Taken aback, Florian offers his right hand to the stranger. 'Yeah, nice to meet you too.' His voice drips with sarcasm.

Willem throws back his head. 'I'm sorry … er … what's your name again?'

'I'm Florian Fabre, a friend of Sophia's.'

Willem grasps the proffered hand and shakes it. 'My apologies, Mr Fabre. I am returning to The Hague and want to leave this for Sophia. She told me she was away for the weekend, but I forgot. So busy,' he says in a clipped Dutch accent. Florian watches him furtively scanning the open plan interior.

Florian immediately realises Willem Van Howan is one of Sophia's secret seven. He needs to treat this client with deference and respect. Florian feels certain Willem's motivations are suspect but he doesn't want an unnecessary argument with Sophia.

'Would you like a coffee?' Florian asks.

Willem momentarily considers the offer. 'No. Thank you. I have a plane to catch. But why are you here?' Willem asks, forthright, trying to sound mildly interested instead of annoyed and irritated by the flamboyant looking young man standing before him in a pair of pink and black floral slacks.

'Sophia generously allows me to stay here while she's away. I'm having my flat painted and, you know, the fumes and the noise of the painters with their sanding machines and boom boxes.' He is blathering on, trying to mask his anxiety.

Willem slowly moves around the open plan lounge, kitchen and dining room, glancing at the walls and bookshelves. Nothing has changed. Everything looks normal, but he continues to frown.

'Something wrong?' Florian asks.

'What is *the flat*? And a *bomb boxes*?' he asks, in broken English, looking perplexed by the young man's comments.

Florian laughs and explains what he meant. 'Do you work out?' he asks, almost flirting with Willem.

Confused, Willem makes a half-hearted attempt at being amused. 'But how do you know Sophia? Have you known her for long?' he questions with an unconvincing pretence at casual interest. Willem wants some answers from this strange young man. A real oddball.

'Ahh, well, we go back some years. I knew Sophia at school and then we met up again at university. You know the drill, she had boy problems and so did I.' He grins unabashed.

Willem inhales deeply. 'Maybe I'll have that coffee now?'

'Oh, sure,' Florian responds. 'Take a seat,' he says and walks into the kitchen and flips the switch on the espresso coffee machine.

'You seem to know your way around,' Willem observes dryly.

'Yeah, I helped with decorating the place. I'm a business partner in the interior design business. I'm sure she would've mentioned that.' Florian is starting to relax and believes he has smoothed down the Dutchman's ruffled feathers. He hands Willem a mug of coffee. They both sit in the living room, silently regarding one another.

'Interesting,' Willem says slowly swallowing a mouthful of

coffee, not taking his eyes from the younger man. 'You see, it's surprising to me as I don't fully understand the interior design business.'

'Yes we work together on various residential projects, Florian says. 'Sophia is very talented.'

An almost imperceptible smirk crosses Willem's lips. He concentrates on trying to construct a reasonable sentence in English which is devoid of emotion but still remains clear and concise. Without any prelude, Willem changes direction in the conversation 'It's good that you are here,' Willem says. 'She has often talked about the house design work. OK, I understand. I thought there was another man.' He hesitates, considering how far he should go. 'Maybe the other man is you? A good friend, ja?' He watches Florian's face for any recognisable emotion. Nothing. 'I need to talk to her about it. I think Sophia is lying to me. What do you think?'

Florian's jaw drops along with the colour in his face. He frantically gathers himself together as the adrenalin courses through his bloodstream.

'Look, it's none of my business,' Florian manages an immediate response. 'Sophia is a good friend, but I keep out of her private life.'

Willem nods slowly, glancing around the room again. He stands up carefully, placing his half-empty mug on the glass and chrome coffee table.

'Ja, I agree,' Willem replies blandly. 'It is private.'

'What makes you think she's got another man?' Florian asks out of curiosity and wonders if he can save the unlikely situation.

'Nothing much.' Willem hesitates, taking a page out of his wife, Marit's playbook. 'I have a feeling about it.'

Having regained his composure, Florian eyes the older man with interest. What is he even doing in Sydney? Sophia didn't mention it. He seemed obsessed with her. Is this guy stalking her?' Florian decides to keep quiet and not reveal too much about his own involvement in Sophia's business. He will save this for a direct conversation with Sophia on her return home.

'I must go. Thank you,' Willem interrupts in a formal tone.

Florian knows he has to respond to Willem without adding to the tension. 'Be careful around accusations about Sophia. Are you trying to upset her?'

'No, no, of course not. I… err … want to understand how Sophia operates.'

'Operates?'

Willem falls silent, looking closely at the younger man. 'Are you sleeping with her as well?' He frowns, unable to keep annoyance from his voice.

Florian bursts out laughing. 'No way!' He chuckles. 'I'm gay, but I already alluded to that earlier!'

Willem looks confused and then embarrassed. 'My apologies.'

'No problem,' Florian responds and then is struck by a brilliant strategy, 'I can assure you Sophia keeps everything very confidential. I assume you are her lover, the Dutchman, she fondly speaks about. Is that not you?'

With visible relief, Willem reaches out his right arm, and the pair shake hands. 'Thank you, Mr Florian.' Willem smiles. 'Ja, it is me. I must go, or I will be late. Please give Sophia my gift. I will call her soon.'

When Sophia returns to the penthouse on Sunday night, she is mortified to hear that Willem tackled Florian. But she's pleased with the expert way Florian handled the tricky circumstances.

'I don't get it,' she says, alarmed. 'He's not even supposed to be in Sydney. He's a week early.'

Full of uncertainty, Sophia wonders if Florian's response to Willem is convincing. She will have to somehow convince Willem that he is being paranoid and desperately trying to fish information out of Florian was not the right way to go about things. He should talk to her face to face. Sophia tries to push the elements of disquiet out of her mind about Willem. She shrugs and takes a deep breath.

'Let's go out for a drink to celebrate your survival at the hands of Mr Willem Van Howan and my survival in the hands of a masseur who tried to kill me with his thumbs!'

It's a quiet night with only a spartan number of customers scattered around their local hotel bar. They are both sipping their second glass of Veuve Clicquot.

'Has to be champagne to celebrate our recovery.' Florian

chuckles with false relief.

'Willem seemed very hot on the fact that you could have another man,' Florian says. 'The anger, just below the surface while he was fishing for information, was unnerving. Imagine if he knew your full story. He'd be the type to kill you.'

'That's a bit melodramatic, given the conversation you had with him. It's not that bad and besides, he has a reputation to protect.'

'Maybe, but his ego is stronger than any other consideration,' counters Florian. 'Please be careful.'

Sophia wants to change the conversation and starts talking about another favourite topic. Society's double standards.

'Don't you think it's reasonable for a woman, these days, to sleep with seven men during her lifetime?' Sophia asks. 'That's my intention, only seven including dear Giles, which seems pretty average for females these days.'

'Yeah, but how would I know?' Florian responds, taking a swig from his glass. 'The thing is …' he pauses, carefully considering how he can convey his response with tact and a little diplomacy.

'What?' she asks, looking across the small round table at her worried friend.

'Seven men is no big deal but having them all at once is the issue,' he says. 'They don't know about one another, so that's the tricky bit, especially when they're paying a retainer to keep you in the lifestyle to which you've grown very accustomed to, darling,' he adds, raising his eyebrows in expectation.

'It's not that much of a big deal.' She smiles at him. 'In reality, it's only about one lover a week. That's less sex than most marriages! What makes my approach more morally reprehensible than seven sequential relationships?'

'Yeah, yeah, I get it,' Florian responds, sighing. 'But I don't think the average Joe will buy that argument. It's something about the commercial aspect.'

Sophia interrupts. 'Oh, please. What do you think men do when they take out women? That's all I hear about. How they pay for this and pay for that. They often joke about the costs of high maintenance females. Remember, a happy wife, happy life! So they cough-up and complain to me about how their wife or girlfriend doesn't understand them and won't put out regularly.'

Florian wants to warn Sophia about Willem. He's a risk factor and he can imagine the dark side of Mr Van Howan being very black. But how to shift the topic of conversation and draw her back to the reason they are in the bar.

'Let's toast to our collective survival,' he interrupts, raising his glass and smiling at his friend.

'For sure!' Sophia laughs. 'Phew, it's been quite a day.'

'Soph.' Florian's thoughtful expression makes her glance up from her drink.

'Yeah. What's the matter?' she asks, concerned.

'It's Willem. I think he could be dangerous. There's something about him that makes me uneasy,' he frowns. 'I can't explain.'

'I know he seems strange,' she responds, 'but he doesn't mean to come across so brutal.'

Florian nods, not entirely convinced.

CHAPTER 42

Grilled - 2019

The extended outdoor dining table covered in a crisp white linen tablecloth stands amongst the lush semi-tropical plants of Sophia's new two-storey home. With Florian's help Sophia moves the table under two old date palms in the backyard garden. Sophia's guests arrive laden with snacks, salads and desserts, plonking them on any available kitchen surface before they stroll outside chatting and catching up with one another. The guests lounge in woven cane garden furniture scattered around the pocket-sized swimming pool. Their laughter enhances the warm bliss of the summer's day.

'Has everyone got drinks?' Sophia asks Florian.

'Yeah,' he smiles holding up an empty wine bottle.

Pleased to play host, Sophia listens with pleasure as a pregnant Teressa and Matt stand at the nearby barbeque turning steak and sausages while talking to her next-door neighbour, Rex Murphy. Matt hands the barbeque tongs to Rex, a short, hairy-chested man with thick eyebrows that appear to slice across the top half of his bald head. A scar from a lawn-mowing accident ropes its way across his nose, enhancing his Neanderthal mono-brow exterior. His appearance belies his youth. At only thirty-years old, Rex has cultivated a beaten up Humpty-Dumpty image with an easy-going pleasant disposition.

'Give it a go, mate,' Matt says, shoving the metal tongs into Rex's open hand as he strides off through the ranch-sliders into the open-plan living and kitchen area. As Matt walks towards Sophia washing lettuce in the kitchen sink, she notices Florian has disappeared into the bathroom as Matt makes a bee line towards the kitchen counter. Her heart sinks. The very last thing she wants is Matt whining in her ear. She glances up from the salad she's preparing and braces herself for another scuffle with her wayward brother-in-law.

'Hey,' he says with a beguiling smile.

Sophia looks up, disenchanted. 'You want something?'

'Well, now that you ask,' Matt says with an unnerving glint in his narrowed eyes.

'What now?' Sophia asks in a hushed voice, cautiously sarcastic. 'I would've thought you've got everything you need and are about to pay me back in full.'

'Well, it's ...' his voice weasels its way into the subdued silence of the kitchen.

She throws the paring knife onto the benchtop sink and grabs the kitchen cloth wiping her damp hands. 'I think you'll find your time is up, along with my tolerance. You owe me the five hundred and thirty thousand dollars, and I expect your transfer into my account by Friday.'

'Hear me out,' he pleads.

'Why?' Sophia raises her voice, and two of the guests chatting on the timber veranda outside look around glancing at the pair standing in the kitchen.

Matt walks around the kitchen island and stands alongside Sophia, casually smiling and glancing outside at the friendly gathering as if nothing is wrong. He leans towards Sophia's cheek, his lips close against her right ear.

'Let's keep calm,' he says softly. 'This is only a quiet little private negotiation.'

'The negotiation happened years ago,' she replies, carefully articulating each word in a clear, monotone. 'You may recall my reluctance to loan anything to you. How the hell do you think I'll react now that you've reneged on payments, not to mention the extended time frame?'

His face drops, and he scowls, concentrating on the garden party happily chatting outside, not turning his head to look back at Sophia. 'I need an extension for another three months,' he says with dogged persistence.

'So, we're clear, and to use your turn of phrase,' Sophia hisses in a harsh clipped whisper. 'No. Fucking. Way!'

'Let's not get too off-piste with this whole thing Sophia,' he says, calmly modulating his voice. He could've been describing a happy beach outing as Sophia seethes next to him. If any of the guests were observing the pair, they could only decipher the sharp blush of anger on Sophia's cheeks, and disregard the sparks of fury in the depths of her blue eyes.

'It's real simple,' he continues. 'I've the evidence and enough information to convince Teressa, your father and your grandmother of exactly what you do for a living.'

'Are you threatening me?' she spat back at him, having gone way beyond aggravation with her brother-in-law.

'Hell no,' he sighs. 'I'm stating the facts.'

'Honey, I really don't care.' She suppresses the anxiety as it rising in her throat. 'You aren't the only one who's tried this trick with me. Best you think again!'

'Well, it's your call, but you leave me no choice,' he states with unbridled arrogance and provocation. It's almost too much for Sophia to tolerate.

She inhales before speaking again and swings around to look directly into his porcine eyes, confirming her worst fears. Another reckless life lesson she's learning, but she's not going to let him get the upper hand. She should have listened to her gut instinct but her sense of obligation to her sister had scrambled her good sense and muddied her decision-making at the time. Stupid. Now she has to deal with this idiot when she should be enjoying the barbeque.

'My experience with gambling debt is that it rarely gets repaid. It's an addiction. There's no wiggle room. Remember, you signed a repayment agreement with me. You can't help playing the tables and throwing away my money to rescue your previous losses. Admit it. You're now deeper in the hole!'

'It's none of your business,' Matt replies in a hardened voice. 'All I'm asking for is some extra time to pay it off. I promise you'll get the rest of your money repaid to you in full.'

'Matt, you've already had two years with this outstanding loan! You give me no choice.' Sophia sighs heavily, slowly shaking her head. 'We're both in checkmate.' She hesitates, considering if she has the advantage. She doesn't want to upset her sister any more than her stupid husband already has. But there's no way she'll allow this prick to walk away from his debt without paying up. She's not on the planet to support him. But she feels responsible for her sister and her baby, which is due in only a few months.

She fears Teressa's lack of ability to cope. Sophia chooses her words carefully to gain greater impact and control over the conversation.

'Get this into the very narrow space between your ears; I have hard evidence of your extramarital affairs. And what a surprise your wife suspects you already but doesn't want to believe it. All it takes is for me to tune her up to full reality. You think life is a misery now? You're only on the first rung of the ladder to complete damnation. Take a moment to think about your baby, the child you are going to raise. What kind of father are you?'

The colour drains from Matt's sour face, his jaw is set hard, embittered lips pressed together, two ferret eyes staring at her with glowering hostility. 'Touché,' he says, not moving his steely eyes from hers.

Was this his idea of intimidation? All it served was to increase Sophia's anger and determination to bring him to heel.

'Yeah, I didn't come down in the last shower,' she says unemotionally. 'I've paid your gambling debts and you now owe me. It's that simple.'

'So what?' he says.

'I'll show your wife photographic evidence of your affair.'

'What?' he says in disbelief. 'The affair's over.'

'Just the one?' She raises an eyebrow, and he grimaces at her tenacious response.

'Your sister has a limited shelf-life,' Matt sneers. 'What I do in my spare time is nothing to do with you.'

'It's got everything to do with my sister and her child! Teressa may be naïve, but I'm not. I know exactly who you are. You're the one with the problem.' Sophia tries another tack. 'She's already told me about your inability to keep your cock in your pants.'

Matt pulls a face, glancing down at the floor and slowly shakes his head. 'You've got no idea. She's a religious maniac. Joined some strange Christian cult,' he adds. 'Sex went straight out the window as soon as Jesus walked through the door.'

Sophia reels in surprise. 'What the hell are you talking about?'

'She's completely off her head.' He frowns. 'Teressa's out of her mind with bouts of hysteria and temper tantrums. Keeps telling me that God is my saviour. I don't know who the hell she is anymore.'

'Pardon me for not having any sympathy.' Sophia sighs. 'You married her.'

'Enough of this bullshit. Will you give me the extension or not?

'I'll think about it,' she says in a voice laden with dismissal. 'The conversation is over.'

'Don't think for too long,' he quips. 'I wouldn't want your little ruse as a jet-setting world-class interior designer to come unstuck. Your whole career could get blown out to the big wide world.'

Later at the penthouse, Florian and Sophia are immersed in deep discussion.

'Then there's the problem of Matt,' Sophia confides. 'I need to stop him in his tracks. He needs to pay up and move on.' Sophia sounds breathless with anxiety. 'I need both Matt and Willem out of my life, but I must tread carefully.'

'Sure,' Florian mumbles, distracted by the implications of her subversive activity.

Blackmail like this is way beyond anything Sophia has ever considered, until now. She firmly believes the ends justifies the means, and she won't let two men destabilise everything she has built up over many years. Her pulse quickens with fear of exposure and, worse, fear of the unpredictable. She has no idea how far either of these two men will go. A complete unknown. This is something Sophia hates. Highly organised and ordered in the way she plans and manages her private business and domestic life. She can predict weeks ahead when the next client is likely to book. But to have two very different men pose a risk like this, it's unthinkable. She has to take evasive action, cut them both off at the pass to avoid any more stress and worry during sleepless nights. She glances back at Florian's stricken expression.

'Are you absolutely sure you want to go down this path?' he asks, hoping she'll laugh and say this is all an elaborate prank. But she doesn't. Instead she looks determined, tenacious.

'I know Matt's involved with another woman, and of course, Willem is evidently in a clandestine affair with me.' Sophia shrugs, pulling a face. 'Both of them need a fright. If we get compromising video footage of Willem with me in the penthouse and with those photographs of Matt, well, I have some ammo to fight back if things deteriorate any further.'

Sophia turns and smiles at Florian and reaches out to his arm, gripping it. 'Don't worry. It will all be OK. Remember, I have contacts in all kinds of places, carefully cultivated relationships. Let's say I have a few cunning strategies up my sleeve which I'll activate with my contacts if I need to.'

'OK. Let's get everything together so you have a few bargaining chips to play with.' Florian seems incredulous at his own response and wary of being caught up in criminal activity. He decides against saying anything more to Sophia, not wishing to ramp up her distress levels.

'Don't look like that,' she says with a weak smile. 'I'll only use this stuff if I really have to. If Willem gets off-side I can immediately stomp on him. Ultimately, I may have to terminate the contract with Willem but don't want to trigger any fallout,' Sophia explains. 'Do you think I'm being a bit harsh? It's merely a safeguard in case Willem decides to take his menacing act to the next level. I want to be ready and willing to eliminate the risk of any threat to my business and my paying clients.'

'OK then, you're going to have to play hardball with him and Matt too.' Florian sounds more decisive, convinced this is the only option to guarantee a winning solution.

'It's what I want to do,' Sophia says. Yet she fears the two men are unlikely to go quietly.

CHAPTER 43

Entrapment - 2019

Sophia sits scanning prominent newsfeeds in the comfort of her suburban home. She picks up the remote and turns on the air con. Reading from her cell phone screen Sophia sees the summer heat is extreme but not as bad as Nullarbor with a record forty-nine degrees Celsius. Her eyes jump to the next headline announcing, 'Flu On The Rise'. Her thoughts go to Texas and Frank with a booking in ten days. She scans the rest of the article and picks up the basics. Over six million people have contracted flu in America over the past few months and 84,000 are hospitalised. Yikes. She better text him and make sure he has his flu shot before she gets too close. The last thing she needs is a cough or runny nose on the job.

She enjoys keeping up with each client's interests and his local home country's economic, business and political news. Over the twelve years Sophia has regularly entertained her clients with her grasp of current affairs, often astounding them with her sophisticated understanding of intellectually challenging discussions across a wide variety of topics, from politics to scientific innovation. But Sophia believes in compliance. Isn't that what they pay for? So, she's always careful not to defy or belittle her paying lovers' opinions.

At the outset of her career, she used to take notes on topical events in each client's country, but now there's far less swotting and learning on the job. She knows each man reasonably well and makes sure she incorporates his favourite pursuits in their conversations. She'll mention the below freezing temperatures to Frank. That's got to be impacting the oil business at this time of year. Sophia keeps a vague eye on the stock market in case Frank grumbles about the DOW or currency fluctuations. Her clients pay her because it's an uncomplicated and easy arrangement at this stage in their lives. It's an escape from high pressured reality.

Focus on what Frank wants and how to distract him, in fact all of them, she smiles to herself, thinking how most men want the same thing – escape from reality. Who doesn't? Will she ever escape to a better more meaningful life? It's looking less likely as time goes on.

Sometimes playful and cheeky and other times serious and concerned, Sophia always focuses on the client she's with at the time, keeping him relaxed and happy. With an absence of mental stress and a severing of emotional strings, each man basks in her obvious fondness for them, having utter faith that Sophia is devoted to him alone.

Now in her early thirties, each man is confident Sophia is in love with him, believing in the promise of an ideal relationship. Why wouldn't he? The art of adoration and commitment to each man is abundantly obvious. Her mental check list automatically ticks all the boxes as she talks, loves and challenges each client. This is not something new. Sophisticated concubines, mistresses and harems of females have plied their trade to wealthy powerful men for centuries.

Most of Sophia's clients consider their contract with her a considerable bonus, one of life's advantages at a time in their lives when they have accumulated enough wealth and power to secure the services of Sophia for their on-call pleasure. Their contractual obligation is purely transactional, at least it starts out that way, and appeals to her clients, seeking a strict business arrangement. Sadly, some of them are unable to resist falling for her. Managing real emotions, especially love, makes her uncomfortable, unsure how to keep an adoring client at an emotional arm's length.

On Saturday morning, Sophia meets with Florian to discuss progress with the video evidence. They place their orders at the local St Germaine Café on the east side of Sydney, a quiet, well-appointed eatery with a world-class chef that delights customers with every delicious mouthful.

'You do know I love you, and will do anything for you?' Florian says as they wait for another coffee. 'I would merely lurk in the shadows without you in my life.'

Sophia giggles. 'Darling, your shadow sparkles and electrifies everyone around you!'

'Really?' He bursts into laughter. 'That's more like a personal description of you,' he says shovelling in another mouthful of creamy, savoury crepe with crispy free-farmed bacon.

Florian decides to change the topic and get on with the update. He hands her a security protected memory stick with the relevant evidence about Matt's affair. She takes the metal gadget and raises her eyebrows, pressing her lips together, still uncertain if she should risk her relationship with her sister.

'How long are you going to carry on with the business?' Florian asks out of left field. They have discussed this before, but now with recent problems, Sophia repeatedly hints about closing it down and returning to a normal life. In the past he has snorted in disbelief at the thought. But now things have changed.

'I think I'll settle down in my mid-thirties,' she casually remarks. 'Which is only a couple of years away. I need to terminate the whole operation, but it's going to take some time and some delicate handling of my clients.'

'No kidding,' Florian grins, dabbing his lips with his serviette. 'But how are you going to cope financially? Or do you want to become a real interior designer and work alongside me? I think we're a great team.'

She smiles warmly at him. 'Umm, it's tempting, but I still want to find out how serious Hugh is about me.'

'Ahh. Golden Boy, Mr Hugh Rixon to the rescue.' He chuckles and raises his eyebrows, waiting for more details. None were forthcoming. 'Come on, spit it out. I know you had dinner together last weekend. Any progress, darling?'

'There's always progress with me, Mr Fabre,' she teases. 'It was fun, but we got into a few heavy topics.'

'Do tell,' Florian leans towards the centre of the table, inclining his head to hear every exquisite detail uttered by his best friend.

'We actually discussed marriage,' she says triumphantly.

'What? And you kept that from me?' He shakes his head in mock disgust.

'Well, I need time to think it through. I told Hugh that I wasn't marriage material and ...'

Florian interrupts. 'Are you insane?'

'He's a lovely guy. But I had to explain that I can't have children.' She sighs as Florian's face drops.

'How did he take it?' he asks, looking sombre.

'He was silent for about two minutes. I could tell his brain was processing the potential repercussions.'

'And?'

'He says it doesn't matter. That he loves me as I am.'

'Except he doesn't know who you are!' Florian blurts out.

'Yeah, OK. Keep your hair on. One step at a time.' Sophia dismisses his remark, briefly annoyed.

'Talking about baby steps, did you manage to photograph the contents of Willem's briefcase after missing the previous opportunity?' Florian asks, desperate to change the topic.

'I'm seeing him tonight. I'll do it when he's in the shower.'

'You be damn careful,' Florian instructs. 'When he turned up at the penthouse that day, he was definitely casing the place. There's something weird about the guy. He's so disturbing and I can't quite work out why.'

'He's OK,' Sophia says. 'Maybe it's his Dutch accent and abruptness that goes with it. All those Germanic countries have a direct way of speaking. They don't mean to sound aggressive, but it comes across like that to English ears. He's an old softie … apart from his occasional creepy way with words, but English is his second language.' Why was she making excuses for Willem? She frowns, considering what tactics will work best on him.

'All is not well with the man,' Florian interrupts.

Sophia has other suspicions around Willem's potential dodgy property investments and tax avoidance.

'I want to gather more material as insurance if he ever goes rogue.' She smiles at Florian. 'As a prominent politician in the Netherlands, he can't afford for his wife to divorce him with elections so close.'

'Yeah, I didn't realise he was on a trajectory to become the next party leader,' Florian says. 'Talk about taking a risk. Any whiff of a scandal like this in the background and he'll instantly be out of the running.'

Sophia nods, taking another sip from her cup.

'Rather you than me.' He shrugs, watching Sophia, trying to determine if there is any flicker of unease in her expression.

'I think you'll find that he is grateful. He's my client and not yours!' They both force an uneasy laugh.

CHAPTER 44

On the Case - 2020

That evening Sophia enjoys a drink with Willem in the living room overlooking the Sydney Harbour before they leave for the Opera House. He is looking forward to indulging in the latest production of *Carmen*, the story of a soldier seduced by an exotic gypsy of the same name.

'I'm like that poor soldier,' Willem quips. 'An innocent lamb to the slaughter tormented by the erotic wiles of sexy Sophia.'

'Absolutely.' Sophia sniggers, playing along as they continue to sip their drinks. 'It's a wonderful chance to work my magic powers over you Mr Van Howan, especially on the seductive first full moon of 2020.'

'Umm. Don't make wild promises you can't keep.' Willem chortles, clinking his glass against hers.

'Happy New Year,' he says, holding her eyes with his own. 'Even though I wasn't here to celebrate, I know 2020 is going to be a great year for us both.'

Sophia raises a cheeky eyebrow. 'What are your plans then? Remember sir, I always deliver on my promises!'

Willem had accumulated wealth from savvy property investment before entering politics ten years ago. Now a member of Parliament, his popularity has tripled in recent months, according to the Dutch newsfeeds Sophia read yesterday.

Willem stands. 'Another champagne?'

'Sure,' Sophia smiles warmly at her client, 'why not?'

Willem grabs the chilled bottle of French Taittinger 1956 Brut Réserve and pours the golden liquid into her tall crystal glass.

'I better get in the shower, or we'll never make the concert.' He kisses Sophia on the forehead and saunters towards the tiled ensuite bathroom.

Sophia places her untouched glass on the coffee table and

inhales, momentarily closing her eyes. She waits until she hears the water running from the bathroom showerhead before grabbing her cell phone. She walks quickly towards the dining table where Willem left his tan leather briefcase. It is still slightly open after he had removed a photo of a yacht he wants to buy. He had shown the photograph to Sophia earlier. Naturally, she made all the right noises. She now rests her hand on the outside of the briefcase slanting her head, listening for the running shower water.

Within seconds she flips the lid of the briefcase wide open, picks up some of the glossy photographs, placing them on the table surface beside the case. She quickly sifts through other folders and documents before feeling inside the pockets lining the lid and removes two thin transparent plastic files. Opening them and spreading the papers on the table, Sophia hastily clicks off several photos on her cell phone, turns the pages and makes sure every page in the plastic portfolio is photographed.

Sophia grabs a memory stick hidden in a smaller interior pocket, before placing all the papers and photos back in the briefcase precisely as she had found them. Her heart is racing with fear, breath quickening as she gently rests the lid, so it remains in the partially closed position, exactly as she found it.

Willem shouts something unintelligible from the bathroom. Sophia plunges the memory stick into her bra and walks into the hallway. 'Ja, did you call?' she says in smooth even Dutch tones. No one would suspect a thing, but her heart is pounding as she calls out his name. 'Willem?'

He wants another bathmat. Sophia pulls open the linen cupboard in the hallway, grabs a thick white towelling bathmat and moves through the master bedroom to the ensuite. She tentatively knocks on the door.

'Ja!' he calls out.

She opens the sliding bathroom door and smiles at him through the steamed glass of the double-sized shower. 'Shall I leave it here?' she asks, indicating the edge of the hot tub opposite.

'Come in.' He grins, wiping the steam from the glass to look at her more closely. 'Why not join me?'

In a split second it takes for her to smile at him and blow a kiss, Sophia knows she can't oblige with the frightening reminder of the memory stick pressing hard against her left breast. Instead, she shrugs nonchalantly.

'Darling, I've barely got enough time to dress.' She gazes at him lovingly. 'They'll lock us out of the theatre.'

'They better not!' he responds, shutting off the water.

Sophia retreats to her office down the hallway and nervously shoves the memory stick into the port of her laptop and it begins downloading. Now and again, she sticks her head into the hall to listen, gauging Willem's progress. He closes the bathroom door, and she hears his shoes on the floor tiles. He's already dressed!

With a thumping heart and rising panic, Sophia shuts the laptop and urgently unplugs the memory stick. She rams it back into her bra and races past the master bedroom and into her walk-in wardrobe. She should have already been dressed for the opera and frantically grabs her evening attire.

Sophia swiftly undresses and flings her dirty clothes into the laundry hamper before hurriedly slipping an elegant rose-patterned cocktail dress over her head. Turning to briefly face the doorway, where she expects Willem to emerge at any moment, she still has a few seconds and quickly flicks her eyes over the wall of shoes on the shelving opposite. Distracted by anxiety, Sophia grasps the closest sandals, delicate enough to compliment her summer dress. Within seconds she eases her heels into the sling-back straps and stands in front of the mirror. She reaches for a cropped crimson jacket and unexpectedly jumps with fright.

On high alert, Sophia hears Willem drop something in the bathroom. It falls again, a loud clatter as if a plastic bottle top has dropped. The sound of it rolling around the sink is like a rhythmical warning signal to Sophia. She hears muffled swearing in Dutch, Willem cursing under his breath. Does she have time to place the memory stick back in his briefcase? She's torn, fearing being caught with her hands in his leather case, when she already has the evidence she needs downloaded onto her laptop.

She fleetingly considers her narrow choice of options. Maybe she should wait until they arrive home from the opera house? It may be easier to surreptitiously place the stick back in his briefcase while he pours a drink or goes to the bathroom? What if he locks the suitcase before they go out? A rush of adrenaline raises her panic level. She has no idea about the combination lock sequence. Or worse, if he returns home feeling amorous and excited and rips her clothes off only to hear the memory stick clutter to the floor. The very thought makes her heart skip a beat. There's no choice. She must return it to his briefcase now, before they leave for the evening.

Moments later, Willem walks into the living room as Sophia stands, holding her half-finished champagne. She has already poured the other half into the pot-plant next to the armchair.

'Are you not drinking?' he asks.

'I got caught up in reading an article on my phone,' she says. 'All this refugee detention centre drama is looking a bit alarming.' She frowns, hesitating, hoping she's distracted him. 'Are you sure you want to wear that shirt tonight?'

'This?' He turns his hand out to her, confused. 'What's wrong with it?'

'I think you may want long sleeves,' she says. 'It's a bit cooler in the evenings now, and you know the opera house has strong air-con.'

Willem pulls his mouth down at the corners and walks back towards the bedroom to change his shirt. In a heartbeat, she quickly secretes the memory stick inside the briefcase. Sophia can still hear his footfall in the corridor, and promptly moves back towards her drink, picks up the glass and takes a large gulp. She needs to slow her breathing and steady her hands.

CHAPTER 45

Jack Sprat - 2020

Sitting in her study the next day, Sophia downloads Willem's documents, securing them in password-protected folders on her laptop's C Drive. She'll talk to Florian later about moving them onto his private storage hub, so there's no risk of being caught with compromising information. Her body gives an involuntary shiver. There's no time to review the contents, but there were several questionable reports and bank statements on the memory stick. She bites her bottom lip. She plans to go through it all with a fine-tooth comb and put incriminating material in a bank security box.

Her cell phone gives a shrill ring. It's Teressa. Having not spoken to her sister for several weeks, Sophia hesitates, wondering if she should take the call or let it go to voicemail. She sighs and reluctantly answers the phone.

'Hey,' Teressa says. 'Just checking to see if you spoke to Matt?'

'Oh,' Sophia's taken aback at the unexpected question. 'We briefly talked at the barbeque some weeks ago. You were there.'

'What did you talk about?' Teressa asks.

'Nothing much. Matt was saying he has a few stresses with business, a few financial constraints.'

'Really?'

'Yes, really, Teressa. If you have a problem with him, why not ask him yourself. He's your husband.' Sophia recognises her sister's irritation and could, without too much effort, raise the stakes to full-blown rage. Years of a historical conflict between the pair has laid the foundations for short fuses on both sides.

Silence.

'Will that be all?' Sophia asks.

'No. I'm calling about the christening. I sent you an invitation a week ago but haven't heard a squeak,' Teressa says, miffed at being ignored.

Guilt immediately surges through Sophia's body. The last time she saw the baby was three weeks ago. She had been stalling and should have quickly responded. Cuddling baby Jack, walking around with him nestling in her arms and snuggling against her neck, his sweet baby smell, stirred mixed emotions. It sharpened her fruitless desire to have a baby of her own. Her eyes had prickled with unbidden tears as she gently pressed her cheek against the baby's face. Sophia was astounded at her reaction and tried to understand her painful feelings. Jealousy and resentment in equal measure swirled around her heart as she reluctantly handed her baby nephew back to his mother.

Her sister's cosy home had been more shambolic than usual, but it was no surprise given the sleepless nights waking to feed the beautiful, bald, blue-eyed arrival. Sophia had set about loading the dishwasher and washing machine while Teressa slept for an hour. Sophia checked on Jack about a dozen times, watching the sated baby fast asleep in his cot.

'Are you still there?' Teressa's voice interrupts on the phone.

'I'm sorry …'

'Of course, you are,' intrudes Teressa, half expecting some ridiculous excuse to avoid attending.

'I am,' Sophia insists. 'Of course I'll be there. Can I help in any way? You must be shattered.'

Teressa makes an indeterminant noise. 'Yeah it's more exhausting than I imagined.' She sighs. 'Nobody tells you.'

'Isn't Matt helping?' Sophia frowns, clenching her teeth.

'Nah, not much. He's hardly ever at home,' Teressa says quietly, transitioning to her default position, and making excuses for him. 'He's busy working long hours most of the time.'

Sophia silently seethes with anger at Matt Simpson's complete lack of consideration for his wife and baby son but doesn't comment. She needs to avoid ramping up her sister's distress. Sophia decides to distract Teressa and change the direction of the conversation for both their sakes.

'Please tell your gorgeous son that his Aunty Sophia will be there and has a lovely surprise for him.'

Over the past year, the relationship between the sisters has gradually improved. Until Jack's birth, they merely texted one another, avoiding direct contact. With Jack's arrival, both sisters

264

called a truce of sorts, finally accepting their differences and tolerating divergent opinions.

In describing the sisterly reconciliation to Florian, Sophia quotes her best friend back to himself. 'You always say, you can't choose your family, but you can choose your friends,' she explains. 'But now that Jack is here with a daddy who operates below the line, I want to make sure Teressa has the support and do what I can to help her and Jack.'

'Teressa's the only sister you have so it's good you're both reconnecting, especially for Jack's sake.' Florian appears relieved that Sophia has smoothed the bitter angst between the two sisters.

'Trouble is, Matt's proving to be a bigger down-side in the grand scheme of things.'

'Oh?'

'Yes, that prat of a husband, he's still jerking me around about repaying the balance he owes me.'

'I thought it got sorted?' Florian counters with a furrowed brow.

'So did I, but he's missed a couple of repayments again and is ignoring me, at his peril,'

'What are you going to do?'

CHAPTER 46

Swotting for Finals - 2020

Some weeks later, Sophia's grandmother dozes in and out of consciousness in her hospital bed after a nasty fall. Pale faced with a frail bird-like head, her grey hair tracks its own crumpled path in different directions surrounding her fragile paper-thin skin. While there are discussions about a hip replacement, the medical fraternity remain steadfast in their reluctance to operate on Edith, given her advanced age.

'I insist,' Edith demands. 'I haven't lost my bloody marbles!'

Sophia breathes into the cell phone. 'I'll pop over this afternoon, and we can talk through our options.'

'There's nothing to discuss,' her grandmother snaps back with rising agitation. 'I'll be bedridden and a burden to everyone if I can't walk. If there's a reasonable chance, and I believe there is, I want the operation!'

Sophia can't help herself and interrupts, 'Any idea who is going to pay for all of this?'

Silence.

'Look, Grandma, I don't mean to sound brutal, but I've loaned a considerable sum to Matt. He's now stalling over repayments, so I'm in a precarious position.'

'Don't you worry love,' Edith's subdued tone is flattened by fiscal reality. 'I'll take a loan from the bank or borrow from my friend Max Forsyth. He's got more money than he knows what to do with. And your sister seems to think God will provide.'

Sophia rolls her eyes and smiles weakly. 'The realists amongst us have to step up to the plate.'

'Well you never know Sophia. Keep an open mind. God may come to the rescue.'

'Right.' Sophia laughs. 'Those drugs must be working and seem to have suppressed the atheist within.'

'Well, I don't feel much like being an atheist anymore ...'

'OK. Enough with the fooling around. Let's talk this afternoon,' Sophia responds with growing unease at the mention of Max Forsyth's name. 'I'll be there around 2pm, and I'll have a chat to the specialist again too.'

Three hours later Sophia arrives at the hospital and walks briskly to the lift before marching down the long corridor of the geriatric wing. She slows to a sedate, uncertain pace as she approaches her grandmother's room. Holding her ear against the closed double doors, she listens intently to determine if the doctor is talking with Edith. All is quiet. Slowly pushing the swing door open, she leans into the private room. Grandma is propped up in bed, reading a heavy, hard-covered book.

With a shock, Sophia recognises the Bible open between Edith's hands. She appears immersed in every word and oblivious of her grand-daughter observing her from the doorway. Sophia steps forward, smiling, and kisses the elderly patient on both cheeks.

'Umm. I see you're already swotting for the finals!' Sophia giggles as Edith slams the Bible shut.

Her grandmother laughs out loud and playfully smacks Sophia's arm. 'You're incorrigible Sophia Huston,' she says between gales of laughter. 'You'll have to do penance for that!'

'I am already!' Sophia mischievously suppresses more psychological abuse of her elderly grandmother.

While they chat Sophia knows she is the only one who can support her grandmother and financially contribute to the costs and nursing care during her recovery from the hip operation. She'll have to pay. The most irritating aspect is the money Matt is still sitting on could help with this situation. Getting an expert surgeon and extra support care is the only way her grandmother is going to be able to function. She's heard stories about medical personnel refusing to operate on people over eighty, and leaving them injured, drugged up and bedridden until they died. She won't be discussing that aspect with Grandma. All the jokes in the world won't solve this problem. She must make arrangements for Edith to get the best medical care.

The next few weeks fly by in a whirlwind of clients, first-class travel and exclusive social engagements assisting Florian with international interior design projects and typing up reports.

Sophia has several bookings, back-to-back, when Hugh phones her from New York. She immediately takes the call.

'I've missed you,' he says in a lilting Kiwi accent.

'Me too,' she admits. 'It's been a long five weeks of separation.'

'Yeah, I know what you mean. Some good news. I'm flying direct to Sydney for the weekend if you're around? We can spend a couple of indulgent days together before I fly back here for a Wednesday meeting with shareholders.'

Sophia hesitates, knowing Rafe Le Monde arrives on Friday night and Frank Horner on Sunday evening. There's barely enough time to arrange for housekeeping in the narrow timeframe between the two clients.

'Something wrong?' he asks, concerned. 'I don't want to impose but saw this as a chance to be with you, Sophia.'

'Yes, of course,' she says. 'I promised a friend we could go away. You know a girls' weekend up the coast.'

'Sounds totally boring when compared to the fun you can have with me!' He chuckles. 'Can't you drag yourself up the coast some other time?'

She laughs. 'Of course, I can. I can't wait to see you.'

'Excellent!' I'll catch a taxi and be at your place around seven o'clock on Friday night.

As soon as Sophia is off the call, she contacts Rafe and makes an excuse to delay their arrangement for another fortnight. Then she tackles Frank Horner, a man who refuses to entertain compromise or compliance. She braces herself for a tough conversation. To her surprise, he agrees after some light-hearted resistance and confirms the new time in three weeks works better for him.

'At least after the meeting, my mind and body will be all yours,' he jokes. 'But with a massive build-up of orchestral proportions, darlin', especially in my little head!'

She laughs at his crude joke and clearly understands that she better be on form for that appointment.

'Are we talking more than two days or three?' she asks without missing a beat.

'Could be three weeks!' he brags. 'Brace ya' self, Sheila!' He jokes, attempting an Australian colloquialism. 'It could be bigger than Texas!'

'Forewarned.' She giggles, relieved to get off the phone and out of the original appointment.

Hugh calls back during the early evening to rearrange their get-together. 'What do you think about meeting me in Berlin instead?' he asks.

'Of course, if that suits you better.'

'It's winter there, but I've got a lovely little hideaway in the countryside which a friend offered as a holiday escape. We go salmon fishing together, and he always stays over with me at the lodge. Anyway, he said his log cabin is a place like no other. Bit primitive, but who cares? No staff, no interruptions.'

'Why not,' Sophia smiles. 'But I've gotta be back by Wednesday morning at the latest.'

'Sure, no problem. Will organise my pilot to pick you up Friday, say around 2pm.'

'Right, that's fine,' she responds. 'Can't wait to see you.'

Two days later, Sophia is comfortably seated between Hugh's legs stretched out on a large Persian rug in front of the open log fire in the living room. The rustic log cabin, south of Berlin between Konigs Wusterhausen and the Dahme Heidessen Nature Park, is a little more expansive and well-appointed than the remote mountain cabin Sophia envisaged.

They snuggle together after sipping from ceramic mugs of hot Gluhwein, made from cinnamon sticks and cloves soaked in heated red wine, then mixed with fresh orange rind and honey. The delightful smells of the spicy traditional winter drink permeate the entire house. Sophia turns to face Hugh, and he bends forward, gently kissing her on the mouth. The warm, loving kiss radiates throughout her body. This was no ordinary man. Hugh makes her eager for more.

He reaches out for his mug and takes another gulp, then nuzzles his face against her neck.

'I've got something to tell you,' he says.

Sophia turns her head to face him.

'I've left my wife,' he says.

'But hang on. You told me you were divorced,' Sophia says to a guilty-looking Hugh.

'Well, I didn't want to sully our relationship with negative stuff,' he explains. 'My policy is to keep things simple and easy.'

Sophia slowly nods, looking disconcerted at the sudden turn of the conversation.

'Don't get me wrong,' Hugh tries to explain. 'We separated over two years ago. The final divorce papers only came through yesterday.'

A broad smile spreads across Sophia's face, and all anxiety and unease evaporates.

'I see,' she simply says. 'Let's drink to that!'

They tap their stoneware mugs together and smile at each other before swallowing large mouthfuls of the warm, spicy wine.

'To make sure, for my own sake,' Sophia asks. 'Do you have any imaginary children?'

He grins at first, before noticing her steady gaze. She isn't fooling around.

'Of course not, well not yet,' he chortles.

'Remember, it's highly unlikely I'll ever have children,' she says quietly.

'Of course, I know, but we could adopt,' he quickly adds as an afterthought, 'but only if you want to.'

'I do. I'd love to have children. I'm astounded you would even consider it.'

'Evelyn and I didn't have children, partly because we were both so busy in the business over the years. Now, I regret not having any of my own,' he says.

She stares at him with heart-wrenching intensity as he smiles lovingly at her again. She remains speechless.

'I love you with all my heart,' he says simply.

Sophia is astounded. This is a situation she's never visualised. She hears Florian's words ringing in her head. *Sometimes enough is good enough to move on.* In this instant, gazing into Hugh's eyes, she realises this is what she wants. She needs to let go of her past and relinquish the business. Leave it all behind and move onto a new chapter in her life. It will be no easy task, but she knows now precisely what she wants.

Hugh stands up and leaves the room. Sophia straightens herself and flops down onto the sizeable overstuffed sofa facing the open fire. She watches the dancing flames in the metal grate and listens to the occasional crackle as the intense heat warms the room.

A few minutes later, Hugh returns and sits on the floral sofa next to Sophia. He is silent and stares at her for what seems like forever. She holds his gaze as he reaches for her hand.

'Do you love me?' he asks with a tinge of uncertainty. Real love is an emotion Sophia has never truly entertained or fully understood until now.

She nods. 'Yes, of course,' she says, still feeling unsure. 'How can I not love a man as wonderful as you?'

He leans forward and seizes her lips in a long kiss. When they move apart he opens his right hand. Lying in his palm is a magnificent diamond engagement ring, sparkling and twinkling in the firelight. 'Will you marry me?' he asks softly.

Shocked into silence at the unexpected turn of events, Sophia hesitates, breathless and unable to respond.

He inclines his head and raises his eyebrows using his expression, without words, to repeat the question.

'Can I please think about it?' she asks quietly.

'No!' He is emphatic and pulls away from her, frowning.

Her mind races. There's lots to consider, commitments and her business to unravel. Is this even possible? He watches her intently, trying to interpret her hesitation while she deftly attempts to disguise her unease. Why not? It's a few years earlier than she had anticipated. People are sometimes engaged for years.

'I'm not sure how it would all work.' She stalls for time. 'You're overseas a lot on business. I mean, am I supposed to stay home alone?'

'Hell no!' he says emphatically. 'You'll travel with me wherever I go. It's your choice. You wouldn't have to if you want to stay at home. We would be an official married couple, of course. I want you to be part of my life … forever.'

For the first time in her life, Sophia feels an ache in her chest, heart sore at his generosity and sincerity. Unexpectedly, her eyes fill with tears. Hugh's face is wretched with anxiety.

'Say something Sophia,' he pleads.

'Yes!' she announces with angst gnawing at her heart. Hugh

leans forward, slipping the large solitaire diamond onto her ring-finger and kisses her again.

People cancel engagements all the time, so if it doesn't work out, she can still walk away. Everything can change, especially in these dark days with overheated financial markets, refugees being locked up without conviction for years on end. The whole planet seems to be in some conflict or war of words about climate change, pollution and gradients of what's right and wrong. Anything could happen to pull the carpet out from under her perfectly ordered life.

It's time now to make a real change. Wasn't this exactly the right move for her? Over thirty years old and here it is, a chance at a normal life. This is a miraculous chance for a completely new life. At being Hugh Rixon's wife. A devoted and loving wife. Isn't this what she has always wanted? The chance to be a child's mother. So unbelievable. Overwhelming. A quiet, loving happy future with a man who loves her more. More? Didn't Carla tell her all those years ago. 'When you marry, make sure the man loves you more than you love him.' Why? Because he's less likely to stray. Men love a strong woman, and few can tolerate emotionally needy wives, at least not for the long run. Sophia remembers Carla's words and the conversation has replayed in her head many times over the previous years.

'I can tell you're afraid of marriage, of such an infinite commitment.' He interrupts her thoughts. 'I understand, I do. Hell, I've escaped an unhappy marriage myself. But Sophia, I know with every cell in my being that we will be great together, and good for one another.'

She nods, looking at his earnest face and knowing he means every single word.

'Marriage is like a swing in the playground. It swoops up and falls down, depending on how hard you push each other,' Hugh says. 'Other days it simply hangs idle, flat-lining with nothing going on.' He smiles with concern at her worried face. 'But that's life isn't it? Ups and downs. All you can control is your attitude towards it.'

They enjoy a wonderful few days together, walking through the woods, almost ankle-deep in snow, eating delicious meals and sharing lots of laughter. His infectious enthusiasm encourages

Sophia to feel the first seed of excitement about spending the rest of her life with Hugh. Everything about him is comfortable and relaxed. Each morning they sleep in and make love as the winter sun pushes its gentle rays through the edges of the curtains.

Still drowsy from a good night's sleep, Hugh nuzzles up behind Sophia's naked body. During the coldest early morning hours and in a deep sleep, she subconsciously gathers the thick, voluminous feather duvet around her body, pulling it over her head. To guard against freezing overnight and to preserve an ample share of the warmth, Hugh curls up against her body to keeping them both warm. The nuzzling of his face against the back of her neck is the first thing she is aware of on waking each morning. He gently kisses her shoulder, upper back, moving towards her ear, his arms wrapped about her body, sometimes a hand cupping one breast.

Who knew there could be so much pleasure in simply spooning one another in bed? Sophia feels safe. It's a strange sensation, comforting and free in a way she has never experienced. Is this trust? Could this be what love is all about? This overwhelming blissful sense of belonging in this place with this man. Secure and cared for in every word and action. It's a big adjustment for Sophia to accept this possibility. Her entire life has been lived with a guarded pretence, another persona occupying her body and mind so wholly, she struggles to let the call-girl go. Now she's here, deeply immersed in the raw calm acceptance of unconditional love.

She feels Hugh's arousal, a dreamy warmth, a satisfying sense of how she affects him. She stops herself. This is the old Sophia, reading male body language, anticipating every need and want, then calculating his level of desire. She doesn't want to be like this, not here and not now with Hugh. Closing her eyes, a deep sigh escapes from her lips as he runs his right hand over her arm and down across her thighs. It's the same sense of belonging, of comfort fused with her thoughts, Sophia will never forget as she rolls over to face him.

Again, she agonises over her breath, that awful early morning sleep-filled air. Stop. Hugh already joked the previous morning that his stale breath was an overnight affliction too. So what? She lets him kiss her, moving his face against her cheek and ear. Delicate butterfly kisses softly scatter across her smiling face.

Holding the side of her head with his warm hand against her

ear, Hugh gently touches a kiss to each of her closed eyes. Those blue eyes languidly opening and peering at him through dark lashes. He is drawn to her. She emanates everything he finds desirable in a woman. His heart contracts as his fingers reach into the moistened confines of her captivating body. He is hard.

The rush of anticipated pleasure is almost too much to restrain. But he's been here before. He starts to count numbers in his head, batches of threes and multiplies them, controlling his breathing as her hand strokes his keen erection. She moans softly into his ear, and he presses his hungry mouth against her lips, breathing faster as his confident hands seem to possess her in every tender curve and hidden crevice. She is ready. Her body pleads for him to enter.

With one hand on his upper thigh, she presses her fingers into his flesh, like Braille, begging him to slide on top of her. He grasps the signal and broaches the barrier of self-constraint. Lowering his body over hers, Hugh holds her hands in his, resting his weight on his forearms. Sophia is surprised at how connected she feels with her palms pressed against his. It's an intimate connection, something new and astonishing as their bodies move in unison.

He groans, a faint animal sound as her right hand reaches for him. Moving slowly at first, excruciating tension makes her toes curl in delight. Each stroke pulling on the taut strings of an enchanting violin, tugging at an inextricable source, an enticing sexual resonance straining at the limits of enduring bliss. Breathing heavily, they both know the fringes of release are close. He thrusts into her one last time, pitching his head backwards, allowing a loud guttural sound to escape before collapsing on top of her happily occupied body.

Afterwards, both sated, replete with satisfaction, Hugh slowly stands, pulls on his boxers and walks to the kitchen. Every morning he delivers a cup of freshly ground coffee to Sophia, still warm with gratification and the afterglow of his passionate lovemaking. After taking his first sip of coffee, he places his mug on the side table and snuggles back into bed beside her.

'An impressive performance.' She grins at him after propping herself up on pillows to drink from her coffee cup.

'I like to be good at everything I do,' he responds with a cheeky expression on his face. 'As you know I take pride in my work!'

Sophia laughs aloud, and he kisses her once more.

For the next hour, they remain together, propped up on pillows reading their respective books and sipping their lukewarm coffee. They sometimes share exciting passages or quotes from the paperbacks they enjoy.

This was another first for Sophia as she learns to appreciate the blissful peace and simple pleasures in life. Did she need all the drama, the stress and upset of her life back home? The more she thinks, the more she wants to run to Hugh, escape to a loving, calm existence. The big question is, will she ever be accepted in New Zealand? Hugh has made it clear that his home base will always be Lake Wanaka, after all, he grew up in the South Island where Wanaka is his home. But could she seamlessly blend into small-town country living without drawing any unwarranted attention from the locals?

CHAPTER 47

Back to Back - 2020

The ongoing debacle with Matt over the money he owes and the threats he's made weighs Sophia down. In the dark hours of the early mornings, she plays out conversations, extortion and ways of forcing him to heel, similarly with her sister and Edith's friend Max. It's all becoming risky and enormously distressing. How much longer can she maintain a calm exterior and handle the fallout? These are complicating factors she hadn't bargained on when she first set up the business twelve years ago. Not in her wildest dreams. Now the fantasy of her indulgent high-flying lifestyle is fast becoming a nightmare. She is powerless to resolve anything. Her life is closing in, trying to suffocate her very soul and cripple her will to function.

These difficulties hang in the dark recesses of her mind, surfacing in the dead of night to torment her with public exposure and financial ruin. The outside world is cannibalising her well-ordered life, and everyone and everything seem to be conspiring against her. She needs time to think calmly, work out how she can progress without any more drama. She walks into the bathroom and opens the medicine cabinet. Reaching up to a row of bottles, she grabs a small plastic screw-top container of tranquilisers. Sophia hasn't taken any medication for six months and turns the bottle over in her hand to read the label. The expiry date is 4th January 2020. Good, she sighs. They're only a few weeks over the expiry date. Thank heavens she hadn't chucked them out. She tosses a pill down her throat, turns on the basin tap and gulps three handfuls of cold water before turning off the overhead light and returning to bed.

The following weekend, Willem van Howan unexpectedly calls Sophia's cell phone.

'I've been thinking ...'

'Ahh,' Sophia interrupts. 'That's a dangerous occupation.'

'I want to tell you that I'm smitten, *vrouw*,' he says, using kitchen Dutch for the word *wife*, to reveal his domestic familiarity with her.

A flicker of consternation crosses Sophia's face, but she remains silent.

'*Smitten* is the right word, ja?' he asks.

'I'm not sure,' she responds uneasily. 'You can't be. It's not part of our agreement Mr Van Howan.' She uses his surname to shake him back to reality. She doesn't need more complications.

'Argh, you know what I mean, Sophia,' he cajoles.

'You know I'm not your *wife* as you put it. That's not part of our arrangement either,' she says firmly.

'Am I still your captive then?' he questions, frowning playfully.

'When you are with me Willem, you are my guest.'

'And a paying guest,' he reminds her.

'Is there a problem?' Sophia asks, her eyes falling on Hugh's large engagement ring on her left hand. She removed it from the safe to wear around the penthouse while alone. Most days she keeps it locked away, out of sight from prying eyes. The housekeeper has already made a pointed comment about the diamond ring a few days ago. Sophia reminds herself that she can't be too careful.

'Not really,' Willem responds. 'But I was wondering if you would ever consider a more serious relationship?'

Sophia draws in a sharp breath and hesitates before speaking. 'No. I'm sorry,' she says, her mind racing for a way to let Willem down without hurting him or igniting an argument. It dawns on her an approach like this may explain why he didn't confront her over Haruto. Something was amiss after he grilled Florian in the penthouse that day. What is he playing at? Willem would prove a bold adversary, and she has no intention of inflaming any bitterness between them.

Sophia makes an excuse and diverts him from the awkward phone call.

'When will you be here next?' she asks.

'Not for two more weeks. I'm still at the Hague.'

'Maybe you need a mistress in the Hague too.'

He snorts. 'Unlikely, I miss you too much. Maybe I can arrive earlier.'

'No.' Sophia is adamant, replying a little too quickly and is annoyed with herself. 'Did I not tell you I'm at Aitutaki Resort for ten days, so I won't be here any earlier than your booking.'

'Who with?' he asks, the tone of his voice hardening.

'An old girlfriend, Carla Fitzsimmons. Remember? I'm sure I told you last time you were here. We booked it weeks ago.'

'I don't think so,' he says as Sophia feels his unease exuding through the phone.

'I am sorry, *Schat.*' She tries to smooth him down. 'I can't wait to see you in a couple of weeks. I'm really looking forward to having you to myself.'

CHAPTER 48

Casing the Joint – 2020

Less than twenty-four hours later, Willem sits outside Sophia's penthouse, parked in a grey van, in her street. He is disguised by a dark baseball cap pulled low over his eyebrows and continues watching the revolving glass entryway, waiting for Sophia to emerge. Willem's original thinking was to hire a private investigator to track her for a few weeks. But he's uneasy about employing anyone and exposing his deep-seated insecurities and weaknesses. The risk of future humiliation is something he needs to avoid at all cost. After thinking things through it makes perfect sense to do it himself. Willem wants reassurance, something tangible, explaining the secret machinations of this unusual woman. He keeps watching the entryway waiting for Sophia to emerge again. He checks his cell phone.

It's 2.23pm.

Moments later, Sophia materialises from the parking basement seated in her sports car and turns left heading for the motorway. After she passes him without a glance, Willem starts the van, indicates and merges into the busy city street, comfortably remaining two cars behind her. He decides to surreptitiously follow her for a couple of days before he returns home to Amsterdam. He feels confident that Sophia won't notice him as she believes he is in the Hague for at least another fortnight.

Willem toys with the idea of rebooking Sophia next month, once his investigations are complete. He's more intrigued by her lifestyle, and how remote and secretive she seems. Willem is sure there's more to Sophia Hawkins than anyone fully appreciates. It isn't long before he pulls over to the roadside curb as Sophia drives into a suburban home. Once she's inside the two-storey house, Willem taps the street address into his cell phone contacts list. He will get his lawyer to confidentially look up the property's ownership. Two hours later, Sophia emerges and drives off in the opposite direction.

Willem resolves, against all logic, to break into the house to see if there are any clues about Sophia's history or past relationships. He's convinced he will instantly know if anything is amiss and elects to leave the property immediately if he finds anything unusual. He's merely undertaking a tiny bit of surveillance after all, nothing major, simply a little background checking for his own safety. Sophia will never know. She'll remain oblivious. This is easy to achieve in this quiet leafy street when most neighbours have already commuted to their jobs.

He steps out of the unobtrusive van and walks briskly across the tree-lined street before ducking along the hedge out front and makes his way up the concrete driveway. Within moments he easily disarms the alarm on the double metal security gates. Willem quickly finds his way to the back door, after glancing at the tidy yard beside the double garage. He tries the handle, but the door is locked. The backyard is surrounded by a dense hedge which allows enough cover for Willem to crouch and make his way around the back of the house, trying the windows and ranch sliders before stalking along the back veranda. The last door handle he turns, falls open. With surprise, he discovers the laundry door is conveniently unlocked.

As he pulls the handle down, Willem surreptitiously glances back over his shoulders, checking for anyone watching from the adjoining backyards. He sniffs and walks into the house, gently closing the door behind him. The compact laundry room is tidy, with neat rows of washing powder, softener and bleach on shelves above the washing machine and clothes dryer. Willem makes a mental note that the burglar alarm is flashing the word *disarmed.*

He walks slowly and methodically into the open-plan kitchen, touching nothing. While standing in the adjoining living room, he removes a pair of sky-blue surgical gloves he had shoved in his jacket pockets earlier. He swiftly pulls them over his hands. Willem glances around the room, not touching or disturbing anything. In the modern open plan living and dining room, he notices photographs, several with Sophia at the beach or on holiday with friends and family. A grey cardigan is lying over the back of a chair. He walks up to it, bending forward, and sniffs the garment, his nose a mere fraction away from touching it. He can smell her scent. Clearly, this is her home, but why live in two very different properties on opposite sides of the same city? It didn't make sense.

A wave of unease consumes him. At this exact moment, he changes his mind and decides to hire a private investigator to follow her and keep tabs on her movements. He desperately needs to know who she meets or talks to over the next couple of months. Willem wants a full report with plenty of photographs as evidence of her activities. He quickly marches upstairs, hesitating for a few extra moments in the master bedroom, scanning the position of the bed and furniture before hurrying into the other rooms and returning downstairs. So far, everything seems normal, apart from the crazy fact of running two households. Why?

Within four minutes, he is out of the house, locking and closing the laundry door behind him. He peels the bright blue gloves off and shoves them unceremoniously in his back pocket. Willem blows a deep breath from his mouth and hurriedly walks down the driveway, looking furtively both ways. He quickly strides across the road to his van parked diagonally opposite.

He drives off, forcing himself to stick to the urban speed limit. Willem wonders if Sophia will be returning to the same house this evening. Should he cancel the private investigator idea and simply go and meet her? Confront her with the fact that she hasn't outsmarted him. Give her a fright and let her know he is well aware of her private little life in the suburbs.

It's tempting, but what would he achieve? He needs something he can use to ensure she never divulges anything about his identity or personal life. It's risky but worthwhile once he makes it clear to her that he knows all about her own little domestic hideaway. Her vulnerability and fear of exposure will keep her in line. The stability of his political career depends on her always keeping her trap shut, whatever happens, and whenever uncontrollable situations arise. He doesn't want any dirty laundry leaked to online news feeds. This is reason enough to show her he is deadly serious about personal confidentiality.

CHAPTER 49

Caught Unaware - 2020

Willem struggles for some days with the mechanics of how to control Sophia. What is she playing at? Clearly, there is something else going on. At the same time, he's attracted to her but wary of playing his hand, exposing his genuine emotions when he still isn't a hundred per cent sure about trusting her. He's already made a fool of himself by admitting he's smitten. Too much wine! He's embarrassed when he remembers his unplanned admission. No wonder she sounded taken aback on the phone. He can still recall her thinly masked astonishment.

Drawn like an addict, Willem finds himself grasping for another fix, while at the same time, repelled by the possibility of rejection. She could be involved in criminal behaviour and hiding it in the suburban backblocks. She could have a completely different life in suburbia, or far worse, a husband and kids too. He shudders, more determined than ever to find out what the hell she's up to.

Driven by desire and repulsed by anxiety, he'll find out what she's up to without any personal exposure. The more he considers the situation now, the more he resolves to frighten Sophia. Just a little bit. Let her know who's boss. Show her who has the upper hand. He knows he has, of course, and will always control the situation, especially when it comes to women.

Sophia is very self-contained, displaying little emotion and he likes her that way, but a small alarm bell continues ringing in the dark recesses of his mind, persuasive and repetitive. Something's not right. He believes a little bit of fear goes a long way in controlling females. Finding out exactly what she's up to in this cosy suburban home is the easiest solution. At last, his action will secure some credibility and reassurance for himself.

He can't help himself, and two nights later, while maintaining a safe distance, he follows Sophia's car late at night to her two-storey home. She pulls into her garage and walks through the front door of her home. He hangs back, sitting in his parked car camouflaged by the shadows of the tall trees lining the quiet, unassuming street until all her house lights switch off. He glances down at his phone.

11.47pm.

He waits another thirty minutes to make sure she's fallen asleep before walking around the house to the back door. He tries the handle and this time the laundry door is locked. 'Shit,' he whispers harshly under his breath before removing his tie from his collared shirt and wrapping it around his right hand.

Thrusting his fist through the glass windowpane set inside the door, Willem reaches towards the latch before unlocking it and letting himself into Sophia's laundry room. He quickly glances around the darkened space before establishing everything is as it had been the previous time he stood in the laundry room. Washing baskets on top of the front loader, an ironing board stacked against the wall. In the half-light from the streetlamp, he vaguely makes out the boxes of soap powder and plastic bottles of detergent stacked on the shelving to the side of the open kitchen doorway. Briskly walking through the kitchen into the hallway, Willem stands still, listening at the foot of the stairs. All is silent. He flinches at the noise of a wheelie-bin lid slamming shut next door.

He quickly steps back into the shadows, listening keenly before carefully placing a foot on the carpeted tread leading upstairs.

In her bedroom, Sophia jolts awake with a start. Still groggy with sleep and bewildered by a sharp sound. Was it breaking glass? Now a strange muffled noise downstairs? She lies rigid with fear. It is pitch dark as she tries to listen beyond the competing beats of her pounding heart. Maybe a nightmare? A weird image of glistening shards of glass interrupted her dreamless sleep. She concentrates on slowing her breathing, then holding it and listening intently to the night's soundless black. A wall of silence. She releases her breath, realising she must've been holding it for over a minute. Unspecified fear galvanises her stricken body under the bedsheets.

Willem steps onto the third stair; a loud creak groans into the silence. He freezes with fear. Has Sophia heard? Did he wake her? Holding his breath, Willem steps to the side of the stairwell, camouflaging himself in the inky darkness. Waiting. He has enough patience to wait all night. His own breath seems loud, but he dismisses it as paranoia.

There are no other sounds, so he gingerly places a silent foot onto the next tread, gradually making his way towards the upstairs landing. Once there he presses his back against the wall, concentrating his focus on the nearby master bedroom door. Was there fear and anxiety or pure excitement coursing through his veins? A bit of all those things merged into a delicious adrenalin rush. So close to Sophia, asleep and vulnerable, without any knowledge of him standing right here, waiting, yearning, craving the shriek, the terror on her face and in her voice. He slowly grins in the darkness.

Alert, Sophia hears it again. A footfall, a creak on the stairs. With a sharp intake of air, Sophia knows without doubt, someone is making their way steadily towards her bedroom. Can I reach my cell phone on the bedside table? Quick. Do it now. Do it! Text Florian. Again, the unmistakable sound of a slow, ponderous tread creeping closer to the top of the stairwell.

Still controlling her breathing, Sophia stretches her naked arm out towards her bedside table. She immediately clasps her cellphone and presses the speed dial for Florian's number. Before the first buzz, she pushes mute and lies rigid, the darkness and dread growing as the intruder stops. Maybe he's heard the phone vibrate? Sophia clenches her teeth and gradually slides from the side of the bed, soundlessly slumping onto the carpet, crawling towards the wardrobe, the door half open. Smudged, dark shapes of shoes and hanging clothing offer fractured comfort. She can't hide in there.

In the dull light on the landing, Willem can vaguely make out her bedroom door is slightly ajar, and the room is absorbed by complete darkness. Very pleased with himself about taking the time to survey the property earlier, Willem knows his tour of

Sophia's home is about to pay off. He stands outside her door, not quite sure about his next move. Willem always works everything out. He's spent a lifetime planning and manipulating to get his own way and yet here he stands suddenly uncertain.

Sophia crawls along the narrow stretch of carpet between her bed and the open wardrobe and momentarily hesitates, listening. He's close, not quite in the room but just outside the doorway, within earshot. She can hear breathing. Sophia angles her head for her right ear to sense the distinctive sound, capture the regular rhythm. No. There is only black silence. She imagines breathing when it is probably her own pulse thumping in her eardrums. She turns her head again, concentrating her listening. Nothing. Is he standing there waiting to ambush her if she steps through the bedroom door? It's only cracked open. She sniffs. A faint smell clings to her nose. She pulls it into her nostrils again. It's a familiar aftershave with a distinctive scent of sandalwood. It triggers something primal, signalling centuries of anxiety between predator and prey. With an involuntary shudder Sophia's mind races to pinpoint the aroma. He's standing there in the hallway. She knows his body is pressed to the other side of the bedroom wall. Lurking in the heavy darkness. She looks down at the silent cell phone. Florian's mute ringing. Now a text:

U OK?

No! her index finger trembles as she presses the keys. *Call police. Urgent. Intruder.*

Her bedroom door slowly creaks open. It is only halfway, not enough for anyone to get through, but definitely ample for a stranger to push his head into the room and scan the interior, quickly determining if Sophia is asleep in her bed. She holds her breath, feeling her heart pulsating in her face with fear shrieking at every nerve. Sophia turns the cell phone off. She can't risk moving into the wardrobe. The scuffling sounds of moving shoes and shifting boxes would immediately alert the malevolent prowler.

Drawing in a deep breath through her nostrils and holding it again, Sophia sits scrunched up half-way against the inner opening of the wardrobe door. She vaguely sees his outline against the open doorframe. She squints a few times, trying to decipher the night from the shadowy form lurking in the blackness. A man. Could it be her neighbour? He lives alone in the red-brick house next door. She knew nothing about him. But this shadowy figure, a tall, broad-shouldered stranger wearing what looks like a bulky bomber jacket, stands motionless. The white soles of his shoes glow in the blackness with one hand in his right pocket or behind his back, it was impossible to tell.

Where was Florian?

She listens for the police siren. Nothing. Her entire body trembles with terror. She can barely make out the man's steady outline, standing stock-still at the foot of her bed, exploring the room as if infra-red sensors can target her curled-up, crumpled mass near her neatly ordered footwear. His head swivels towards the window. It is a moonless night, thank God. She is an unobservable shape of dread, coiled into submission on the floor.

Closely watching the crumpled mound in the bed, Willem is relieved, convinced she must be out cold. Maybe she took a sleeping pill? He feels a surge of confidence. His head tilts, closely listening for her breathing.

Suddenly Sophia realises the dishevelled bedlinen looks like a body. The profile of an oblivious person in an unconscious sleep. He thinks I'm asleep under the bed covers! What the hell's he doing? Her clenched teeth fight against her screaming body, wanting to expel a lung-full of stale air. Then the unthinkable happens, her clammy hand, clutching her cell phone, loses its grip, and the phone slides with a distinctive thud onto the carpet. A brutal signal to the predator standing motionless in her bedroom. Willem swings around, looking directly at the black mass slumped on the floor in front of the wardrobe. He moves towards her coiled body. She is rigid with desperation, stifling a silent scream as a rush of fear and terror roars through her body.

In the same instant, she hears a car turn into the corner of her street. It speeds the short distance to the house, swerving into the driveway.

He turns, looking directly at Sophia's dark shape scrunched in front of the partially open wardrobe door.

'I won't hurt you,' Willem whispers into the silent darkness.

With a shock, Sophia recognises the stranger's voice. It's

vaguely familiar, something about his accent. She needs to hear him talk again to try and place the familiar tone. It's hard to think straight as her heart pounds against her ribcage. She is aware that she could be knifed or tied up and raped.

'OK,' she replies softly. 'I think you're in the wrong house,' she tries, suggesting a way he can back out of this predicament without further humiliation.

'I'm at the right place, Sophia,' he says.

The shock of his familiarity increases her panic, a dissonance with what she's experiencing from the dissociated voice. He knows me! He knows who I am? How is this even possible? Her mind argues as her heart continues firing off new and more horrifying scenarios.

She calmly modulates her voice as adrenalin continues to flood her body. 'What do you want?' she asks, maintaining her composure. Then she simply stands up, facing the tall, menacing shadow in front of her.

'Surely you can work that out.' He grins, and she catches the accent again, the familiarity and the intonation. Willem? That's too insane! She reaches forward to the bedside table and quickly flicks on the lamp.

'Willem! What the hell are you doing?' she shrieks in horror trying to rein in her conflicting emotions. 'Why did you break into my house?' she says in a calmer voice, tactful, not wanting to further inflame this awkward confrontation.

'I followed you here. I want to know why you have two houses.' Willem explains. 'It doesn't make sense. The beautiful penthouse and a suburban home only twenty minutes away from each other. Why do you live like this, Sophia?'

At that exact moment, Willem hears the car door slam and he shoves the open bedroom window wider. Another man. It looks like Florian. What the hell is he doing here?

Florian fumbles with the bunch of keys and seconds later unlocks the front door. He bursts into the entryway, flicking on the lights and calls Sophia's name as he races up the stairs two at a time. He erupts into the bedroom doorway and flicks on the wall downlight.

CHAPTER 50

Intruder - 2020

'Sophia!' Florian shouts, reaching for her trembling body standing near the double bed. He grabs her in both arms, cradling her before looking up directly into Willem's startled face.

Florian pulls back and stares in shock at Willem Van Howan's familiar figure. 'What the hell are you doing prowling around the house?' he demands of the older man.

'I think I can ask you the same thing!' Willem responds, traces of anger lapping at the edges of his stony expression.

'You're the intruder?' Florian asks, red-faced and flushed with confusion and panic.

Several seconds of stunned silence follows before Sophia gathers her senses and in a composed voice instructs her friend. 'Florian, please wait for us downstairs.'

'But ...'

'Ring the police back and cancel the call-out,' she states.

Florian reluctantly nods and exchanges a baffled glance from one face to the other. 'Can I make coffee and bring you both a slice of *congress tart?*' he asks, still breathless.

'No thanks. I'll be down shortly.'

Uneasy, Florian retreats from the room.

Left alone, Willem and Sophia stare at one another.

'Well?' Willem asks after more than a minute.

'I can explain about the houses, and it's straightforward,' she says with her mind racing to figure out a reasonable response. She must calm down and disarm Willem. The momentary silence between them gives her time to consider a completely different approach.

'I inherited this house. It was my grandmother's home before she moved into a retirement village. I love it here. I have many fond memories from my childhood.' She sounds so convincing

294

Sophia almost believes it herself. She can tell from Willem's sheepish expression he believes her too. His mouth softens and he looks a little humiliated, cunningly masking his usual hard, immovable exterior.

Sophia's face breaks into a disarming smile, looking directly at Willem's dark, half-obscured face. 'Hey, come to bed then,' she offers, keeping her voice soft and unflustered while pulling the duvet and bedsheet back.

'Not yet,' he smiles thinly, his lips pressed together.

'Willem, is this some kind of a joke?' she asks.

'That didn't take you long to figure out,' he says, moving around the bed towards her, fully exposing his face in the half-light of the wall light.

Sophia is only too aware of how situations like this can ignite into uncontrolled volatility. She needs to think swiftly and use her grace and charm to diffuse the tension. Talk him down from whatever weird stunt he's trying to pull.

'Willem let me fix us both a drink,' she suggests, remembering advice from Rape Crisis, years ago, advising to keep calm and use the offender's first name as often as possible. Build a connection. But she already has a relationship with this man, and she can't wait to terminate it. This is way beyond unacceptable behaviour.

'Ja,' he says, converting to Dutch. 'A drink is a better idea.'

Sophia smiles openly, maintaining eye contact with her quarry as strategies to handle the situation race through her mind. A better idea than what? Acutely aware her body is almost naked, she swiftly marches to the armchair opposite and flings a short cotton bathrobe over her shoulders and wraps the robe tightly around her waist, securing it with both ties. Willem remains motionless, watching her in the fringes of the pool of soft half-light from the bedside lamp and the diffused wall light opposite.

'I'll be back in two secs,' Sophia says to Willem before scuttling past him.

He chuckles. 'Two sex sounds good!'

'You gave me one hell of a fright,' she says in Dutch. 'My nerves can't take it!'

'It's OK,' he says. 'I was only playing a prank.'

'Some prank,' she scoffs, moving past him, careful not to risk his anger by tackling him about how he managed to break into her private home so easily. That could wait for another day and time when she was entirely in control. Timing is everything. Too dangerous to go down that path here and now.

Briskly walking through the hallway, down the stairwell towards the kitchen, Sophia finds Florian, flush-faced and seething with apparent anger.

He grabs her shoulder and she gasps with shock. 'Wow you gave me a fright,' he says agitatedly. 'What the hell is going on? Are you OK?'

Her pale face looks directly into Florian's eyes. 'I had no idea it was Willem. I'm as stunned as you are. He's upstairs now waiting for a drink.'

'So am I. How the hell did he get in?'

'Broke in I guess,' Sophia says. 'I thought I heard glass breaking. But can you please wait here? Did you cancel the police? Say it was a misunderstanding or something. Apologise.'

Florian nods, still looking uneasy. 'No congress tart then?' he asks again.

'No. Not yet. But stay down here. Just in case ...'

Dumbfounded, Florian nods again as Sophia grabs two glasses.

She opens the fridge and leans around the door before calling Willem upstairs. 'Would you prefer wine darling or whisky and soda?' She knows his favourite drink and he rarely consumes wine.

'Have you got any Bain's?' he asks.

'Sure, *Schat*, anything you like,' she responds with their shared term of endearment, calmly grabbing a handful of ice and shoving it in a beautiful cut-crystal glass. She may be living in the 'burbs but she still believes in maintaining high standards. 'Soda or mineral water?' she calls up the stairwell again to camouflage her whispers to Florian.

'Soda,' Willem simply replies.

'I'll be on the couch sleeping. Tell Willem I had a bit too much to drink and I'm staying the night,' Florian mouths in a harsh whisper against her ear.

Sophia nods agreement, and Florian clasps her forearm before she heads towards the stairwell with the drinks.

'Hey. Did you explain the two houses?' he asks in a stage whisper, sounding anxious.

'Of course,' she grins. 'I inherited this family home from my grandmother. She's now in a retirement facility, and she sold it to me for a nominal fee. It's an inheritance, darling.' She smiles convincingly. 'So I use it as my little private bolt hole, an escape hatch. I plan to rent it out to paying tenants.'

Florian's brow furrows and he gives a weak grin. 'You're good, but I hope he believes you more than I do!'

CHAPTER 51

Cards On The Table - 2020

'I know you hate disappointment,' Sophia uses her officious, business-like voice on the cell phone to Matt as they discuss the delayed payments on the balance of his loan. 'You've missed two repayments again,' she states in clipped tones.

'I know,' he responds flatly, infuriating Sophia even more.

'We signed a contract two years ago! You stipulated I'd be paid in three months. Then we agreed on a new payment plan for automatic transfers to me on the twentieth of every month. This is getting ridiculous!' Anger rose in her voice, demanding his attention. 'You owe me and need to pay. No more bullshit!'

'Yeah,' he drawls, sounding slightly drunk, stoned or both.

'This is unacceptable! If you don't make arrangements to meet this month's loan repayment and pay-up the shortfall, then I'll …'

'You'll what?' he interrupts sneering. 'Fuck me to death?'

She ignores him, anger almost strangling her words as she demands, 'Pay up or reap the consequences!'

His cell phone dies.

Bristling with pent-up anger, Sophia calls her sister and arranges to meet. It's time to put the cards on the table.

'I want you to myself, without Matt's ears flapping in the background,' she explains to Teressa over the phone.

'OK. I'll meet you at the local on Fraser Street. There're plenty of quiet corners where we can talk without any nosey eavesdroppers. Is it OK if I bring Jack?' Teressa asks.'

'Of course. I'd love to see Jack,' Sophia says.

An hour later, after exchanging initial pleasantries and ordering coffee, Sophia is struck by the pallid appearance of her sister. She's lost some weight too. Maybe the impacts of feeding a new-born. The pair begin to discuss their father before Sophia guides the conversation to Teressa's wayward husband.

'I don't know how to tell you this, and I've struggled with it for a couple of weeks.' Sophia treads gingerly, not wanting the conversation to deteriorate into a cluster of broken eggshells.

'What about?' Teressa asked, feeling slightly uneasy.

'I told Matt I wouldn't tell you, but things have gone too far now and I feel you need to know what he's up to.' Sophia tests her sister's tolerance levels.

Teressa silently regards her older sister but remains expressionless. She lifts two-month-old Jack over her shoulder and rubs his back, comforting herself more than the sleeping baby.

'It's awkward,' Sophia continues. 'But you need to know before you hear from someone else.'

'Are you referring to Matt's affairs?' stony-faced Teressa asks.

'Oh.' Sophia's taken aback. 'You know he's been sleeping with another woman?'

Teressa clenches her jaw. 'No, I didn't!' she snaps angrily. 'I meant his financial affairs.'

'I'm so sorry, Teressa,'

'What?'

'He's also borrowed a large sum of money from me … over two years ago,' Sophia says hesitantly.

'Are you serious?' Teressa is shocked. 'How much?' her sister asks, frowning with annoyance. 'How do you know about the affair? What's the woman's name?'

'Look, it's between you and Matt.' Sophia is wary of causing more significant upset than necessary.

'Evidently it's between you and *my* husband. As you have brought me here to discuss these personal issues you may as well spit it out,' Teressa said inhaling and holding her breath, preparing herself for the worst.

'So did you know?' Sophia responds.

'I had suspicions.' She sniffs, the impact of the information starting to hit home. 'His behaviour in the last six months has pretty much given him away. Maybe he was put off by my pregnancy and then the baby arriving….' Her voice trails off, struggling to absorb it all. 'How much has he borrowed?'

It's a hefty sum.' Sophia tries to carefully position the

discussion to lessen the shock.

'More than twenty grand?' Teressa asks.

'I'm afraid it's a whole lot more.' Sophia pauses, concentrating on her sister's face. 'He's made some repayments, so it's now down to just over half a million. Originally it was only going to be a short term, interest-free bridging loan.'

Teressa gasps sharply, her free hand races to cover her mouth. Sophia reaches across the table and grasps her sister's shoulder, stroking it in an ineffectual attempt at easing her horrified distress.

'How?' is all Teressa can utter, as tears spring into her eyes.

'Here, let me hold Jack.' Sophia takes the baby and hugs Teressa, before they both sit together at the table.

'I'm so sorry,' Sophia says with a furrowed brow, deeply concerned as she cuddles Jack. She glances at the baby's tiny sleeping face, and a rush of emotion surges through her. Sophia can't describe it, love and pain at the same time. With a shock, she tries to avoid a need to cry. She takes a deep breath and holds it, looking back at her stricken sister's sad face. There's safety in preventing the emotional upheaval by sticking to her script.

'I didn't know what to do,' she begins to explain. 'Matt contacted me out of the blue.' She swallows and avoids looking back at Jack, concentrating on Teressa's pale face. 'He had already run up nearly twelve months of gambling losses. I was shocked too, but he made me promise to keep it secret and that he needed a lump sum loan for seven hundred and fifty-four thousand.' Sophia pauses while her sister blinks trying to absorb this information. 'I loaned him the money based on his commitment to making regular monthly repayments. At the time he said the loan would be paid back in three months. It was merely a cash flow issue.'

'Oh God,' Teressa responds. 'This is worse than I thought.'

'I'm truly sorry, but it gets worse,' Sophia says. 'Yesterday, when I talked to him about making the repayments and catching up with the shortfall, he threatened me.'

'What?' Teressa's expression changes to confusion. 'Why would he bite the hand that's helping him?'

Sophia sighs. 'Honestly, I've no idea. I'm telling you all of this because I think he's stressed and not thinking straight. I find it very upsetting. He threatened to ruin my interior design business and tell you that I had flirted with him.'

Teressa's mouth pulls downwards with lips pressed firmly together, sceptical at what she was likely to hear next. 'Did you?'

'What do you take me for?' Sophia is mildly indignant. 'Of course not! Honestly, I can't stand the man. His womanising and gambling is totally abusing his relationship with you.'

Teressa is silent. Tears dry on her cheeks as raw anger takes misery's place. 'Why are you telling me this now?' she asks, frowning and uncompromising.

'I was hoping you could come to some arrangement with him and sort …'

Teressa interrupts. 'I can't deal with this now. It's all too much. I don't know what to do.'

'I want to help you. It's a mess, but we can get through this. What can I do?'

'Things are much worse,' Teressa says quietly, lifting her head to look directly into Sophia's eyes.

'What's wrong?'

'I've been diagnosed with cancer and have already had two bouts of chemo.'

Sophia slumps back in her chair and glances briefly at the sleeping baby in her arms. 'I don't know what to say. Why didn't you tell me?'

'I was hoping to get better. But I feel worse. I don't think the meds are working.'

'When do you get blood test results?'

'Well … I got the results yesterday but haven't told anyone.'

Tears well in Sophia's eyes. 'You're going to be all right. You must believe that. Jack needs you. I need you. I would never have told you any of this if I knew about this Teressa. Forget about it all. It doesn't matter. We need to work on getting you well.'

Teressa remains silent, staring at her half-finished coffee. 'What am I going to do?' she asks and looks directly into Sophia's distressed face. 'The oncologist said I have an outside chance of living eight more weeks. That's it.'

'No!' Sophia says firmly. 'You have a son to think about, Teressa. I'll make some enquiries and pay for the treatment. There are all kinds of things in the world. We just need to do some research. Please don't give up.'

'I need to think,' Teressa states as if embarking on a mission. 'I need some time and deep prayer to give me some guidance. Work out what I need to do in the next six weeks.'

Sophia frowns, taken aback. 'Teressa it's not over. Forget about Matt and the money. We need to focus on you and Jack. There must be some alternative treatments.'

'Honestly Soph, I think it's my time.' She pauses, contemplating what should be said to stop her sister from organising what was left of her life. 'It's God's will.'

'Are you so devoted to religion?'

'Yes, I am. I've had to run my life according to our parents and Matt, and I don't need you to compromise my wishes. Promise me you won't interfere.'

'Teressa, things could be different.'

'Not any more. Not the way my life's turned out.'

'Your baby ...' Sophia glances down at the little chubby-faced child oblivious to the unfolding drama.'

'I need some time to think. God will show me the way forward,' she says, immovable.

'Are you OK?' Sophia leans in towards her sister. 'You don't look well.'

'I'm not. Chemo has knocked me around this time.' Teressa says. 'Matt is the last straw.'

Sophia stands up, handing baby Jack back to his mother before reaching across and hugging her sister. 'I'll do everything I can to help. What do you need?'

'Another life,' Teressa tearfully blurts out. 'Another bloody life!'

CHAPTER 52

Allies at Last - 2020

Standing in the penthouse, looking out across Sydney Harbour, Sophia picks up her ringing cell phone, sees Matt's name and immediately refuses to answer, letting it go to voicemail. Later, listening to her messages, Sophia's heart lurches while listening to Matt's thin wheedling voice.

'Hey, in case you need to know, your sister's terminal and has filed for divorce. I guess both those news flashes will make your day. Thanks for nothing,' Matt sneers.

The cell phone clicks off. Sophia listens to the message again. It's hard to believe she only talked to Teressa a few days ago. How could she not call her sister about progress with treatment? And her divorce? Surely Teressa would tell her about that? Can she even trust Matt to be telling the truth?

She gazes across the city to the horizon where wind-swept ash falls in layers, and the constant smell of smoke delivers the worst bushfires in Australian history. Millions of wild animals are left dead or dying. Thousands of firefighters fight to control the fires through January and February where homes and people are burnt beyond recognition.

While watching these horrific media updates, Sophia becomes aware at the same time, of an unseen viral crisis lurking in the background on unchecked flights of tourists entering the country. The threat of the coronavirus causes an element of disquiet but the bushfires, with more significant visual impact, distract nearly everyone and appear to be a more pervasive threat. She needs to talk to Teressa.

She immediately calls her younger sister, but the call goes straight to voicemail. Teressa still has her effervescent cheerful fake phone voice recording, asking for the caller to leave a message. Sophia snorts with irritation and elects to wait until evening for Teressa to call her back. She doesn't. When Sophia phones again the call goes directly to message service. How could she get hold of Teressa if she isn't taking her calls? She's already suffered a couple of sleepless nights worrying about baby Jack and his now precarious future.

She contacts Florian and asks him to call Teressa. Ten minutes later, Florian phones back.

'Yeah she's taking calls, just not yours or Matts,' he explains.

'Why ever not?' Sophia sounds exasperated, sighing heavily.

'I'll give it to you in a nutshell,' Florian says. 'She doesn't trust Matt and thinks you'll try and dissuade her from the decisions she's making about her treatment. Well, her non-treatment. She's refusing chemo.' He pauses, and Sophia says nothing. It's so unbelievable that someone with a baby would take this option. She can't get her head around it. A type of madness seems to have invaded her sister's head. Some strange, determined rebel has taken over Teressa's mind and body.

'Are you still there?' Florian asks, interrupting Sophia's darkest thoughts.

'Yeah,' Sophia says, drained of all energy. 'What was said?'

'Teressa confirms she's submitted divorce papers. She's in no mood to see or talk to you or anyone else.'

'I see,' Sophia says quietly. 'Does she need help?'

'Hard to tell,' Florian replies. 'You know what she's like. Sounds as if she's undertaking some serious God bothering.'

'Yeah, Matt said she was dabbling in some extremely conservative culty Christian group. I find it hard to believe. It's pretty extreme, don't you think? Is it true?'

'I only spoke to her for about five minutes, but yeah, I'd say on the face of it, she seems to have found the light and the way,' Florian says, pulling a face.

Sophia makes a small sound of disapproval. 'What about her son. Her baby. Is she even factoring Jack into the decisions she's making now?'

'Doesn't sound like it,' he replies. 'Teressa repeated several times about flagging all treatment, saying that she was in God's hands from now on.'

'That's ridiculous! She's always been hysterical and over the top.' Sophia is fed up. 'For heaven's sake, she has a child. Surely she would want to do everything she could to stay alive for her own son.'

'Yeah, reasonable and logical people like you and I would. But we're talking about someone seriously disturbed.'

'How do you mean?' Sophia responds, frowning, concern deepening for her sister and baby nephew.

'I'd say she's tampering with insanity. You need to have a good talk to Matt.'

'No way,' Sophia says emphatically. 'You can, but I won't. That idiot has well and truly sailed for me.'

'Yeah, I get it,' he says, listening to the determination in Sophia's voice.

'Do you think I can take a chance and just turn up and visit her?' Sophia asks haltingly with growing trepidation.

'Sorry, it's impossible to tell. But it's worth a shot given the situation. You need to talk to her. Teressa's not herself, and it's no surprise with the stresses she has to deal with.'

'I'm so terrified for the baby, Florian. Matt isn't a father's arse. Somehow I need to talk to her about looking after the baby until he's old enough.'

'Old enough?' he questions.

'I guess maybe high school age. So Jack can talk to his father and explain what he wants or needs.'

'You need to get real. Matt is never going to be a father to any child. You need to adopt Jack. Here's your chance right here under your nose. Given the situation, why not discuss this option with Teressa. She may be hugely relieved.'

'Maybe you're right. But how do I get Matt on board? He's unlikely to agree given it's me. Let me think about it.'

Sophia diverts the conversation away from Teressa. 'Are you worried about this virus thing going on in China?' she asks while taking a sip of her hot coffee.

'Nah.' Florian shrugs. 'It's like swine flu. It'll blow over. Nothing hits us here, and the only person who had swine flu back then was little piggy Matt and he still has the symptoms.' They both roar with laughter.

'Coronavirus looks pretty bad over there,' she explains. 'It's a lot more serious than anyone first imagined. Numbers keep climbing in Italy now too.'

'Don't worry,' Florian reassures her. 'They know what they're doing and besides only old people are dying from it.'

Sophia is increasingly concerned about the coronavirus outbreak. The death toll and contagious infections are skyrocketing beyond China and into Europe with small pockets now apparent in the USA. There is constant media talk about self-isolation and locking down borders and closing whole counties. It's unbelievable, but she pushes it to the background.

No one seems too concerned in Australia yet. She thinks it may not even reach this far and has more pressing issues to focus on.

She turns up to Teressa's home unannounced.

It's 2pm when Sophia arrives outside her sister's modest home. In contrast to her fears, Teressa seems happy to see her. Sophia is shocked at how grey and almost emaciated Teressa seems. She decides not to comment but can't help feeling distressed at how her eyes seem to have sunken back into her their sockets. While they sit in the living room drinking tea, Sophia tries to control the wave of distress washing over her.

'Where's Jack?' Sophia asks wanting to distract herself.

'Asleep but he'll wake up soon,' Teressa says.

'How are you doing?

'OK. I keep praying for some miracle.'

'Teressa, I've been thinking non-stop about you and Jack.'

'Please don't try and browbeat me into something I don't want to do. I've made myself clear, and I assume Florian explained my stance on treatment.'

'Of course. I respect your decision.' Sophia saw Teressa visibly relax. She must have anticipated an argument. 'Because I understand your decision, I want to offer some help with Jack.' Sophia was heading into uncharted territory and, unusually, felt a lack of certainty and confidence but pressed on with her offer.

'OK,' Teressa responds, carefully.

'We're sisters, and Jack is my only nephew. From the first time I set eyes on him, I felt a strong affinity, a real connection.' She smiles at her sister. 'I don't want to burden you with a discussion around what kind of life his dad will provide for him. All I want to do is offer to adopt Jack. I would always tell him about you and what a wonderful mother you are. He would grow up knowing you loved him and wanted only the best for him.'

'I see,' Teressa said. It was hard to tell if she took this proposal seriously or if was all too much to process.

'How would you cope, Sophia? The design work, the overseas travel. He would need you with him all the time.'

'I've thought about it. I've a little good news to tell you too.

'Oh?' Teressa smiles for the first time. 'Out with it then.'

'A Kiwi guy I met over five years ago, Hugh Rixon, he's a wealthy electronics engineer, and he's asked me to marry him.'

'Wow, Soph! You're full of surprises!' Teressa slowly pulls herself up from the armchair and hugs Sophia. 'Congratulations! But what about your career?'

'I'm thinking of stepping back. Might even chuck it in. Look I don't want you to make any decisions around Jack yet. Take some time to think about it. I will love and care for him as if he was my very own. I haven't fully discussed this with Hugh, but he knows I can't have children and has already agreed, in principle, to adoption. But first, I want you to meet him. You can see for yourself what a wonderful man he is. So, no decisions until you're completely happy.'

'You're the miracle,' Teressa says with watery eyes. 'I can't tell you what a massive weight you've taken off my shoulders, Soph.' The sisters hug again and agree to arrange another meeting giving Hugh and Teressa time to clearly consider the adoption.

During the days leading into early March, political rumblings began to ramp up. It seems inconceivable that entire populations are being forced into isolation and lockdown. A distracted Sophia watches online newsfeeds and starts to feel alarmed. The overseas death statistics and the sheer speed the contagion rapidly spreads through Italy, Spain and France is cause for serious concern. The entire planet is going to be in real trouble.

That night Florian calls Sophia.

'Hell, we're in for some major strife,' she blurts out to her friend. 'I think Morrison is too slow and the horse has already bolted. Why aren't they closing the airports for God's sake!'

'Yeah they'll have to eventually. Too worried about costs. Hey, on a completely different note,' Florian interrupts. 'Got more bad news darl.' His voice is a soft monotone, immediately capturing Sophia's full attention.

'What? Are you OK?' Her voice is tight with anxiety.

'Sure. I've been keeping an eye on Teressa's social media, and I'm so sorry to tell you this over the phone.' Florian's voice tapers off, drifting away from the risk of an emotional outburst.

'And?' she asks with disquiet, holding her breath.

'An old school friend of Teressa's has just put up a message saying she died this afternoon.'

CHAPTER 53

Keeping Mum – March - 2020

After Teressa's funeral, the cold blade of awareness penetrates Sophia's mind. Matt, distraught, overplays his hand at the cemetery, sobbing and being held by his brother and a male friend. He wails and weeps, making a spectacle at the tragic farewell of her twenty-seven-year-old sister. His performance at the burial does little to soften Sophia's assessment of the man.

Wretched with guilt and remorse, Sophia watches Matt from the opposite side of the grave as the casket is slowly lowered. The full horror of her sister buried in a dark, claustrophobic hole in the cold ground hits her hard. She dabs her eyes in silence, wondering how she is going to negotiate with Matt and take care of baby Jack now that her sister has gone. He will never believe his wife agreed for Sophia to adopt Jack. She'd been in tighter spots before and knew Matt could be bought.

A week later, Sophia arrives uninvited to Matt's house. His mother, Ruby, opens the door with Jack warmly swaddled and resting on her shoulder.

'Oh, Sophia,' Jack's grandma says. 'This is a lovely surprise.' The older woman, large-breasted and matronly, had always been impressed by Sophia. The pair had clicked although they rarely found themselves in one another's company. She ushers Sophia into the lounge and thrusts the dozing baby at her. 'Here, hold him for a mo, and I'll put the jug on. Tea?'

'Yes. Thanks.' Sophia is relieved the woman is still friendly and hasn't been poisoned by her toxic son. Ruby bustles into the kitchen to make them both a strong cup of tea.

Sophia gazes at Jack in her arms. He slowly opens his large blue eyes and blinks at her. She kisses his warm forehead and breathes in the baby smell of his soft hair. As she smiles at Jack with his tiny hand clutching her index finger, the baby gives her a broad gummy smile. Absorbed in the moment, Sophia wants to take the baby and run away. She kisses his chubby cheeks and runs her thumb across the back of the baby's hand as he clings to her finger.

'One or two, love?' Ruby asks, putting her head around the kitchen doorway.

'None, thanks. Strong with a little milk.'

Ruby carries the two mugs of tea into the lounge and places them on the small coffee table in front of Sophia.

'That's yours,' Ruby indicates a mug as she grabs the other. 'Poor darling, having to grow up without his mum.'

'Awful,' Sophia comments.

'I don't know how our Matty's going to cope with all this and poor little Jack,' she says unbidden. 'Matt's a good boy, but he has no idea about raising kids.' She shakes her grey curly head and looks down at her mug of tea. 'He's a bit of a lazy bastard too.'

Sophia is aghast, taken aback at the mother's confession about her own son. She's looking for the chance to explain to Ruby, get her onside to herd Matt in the right direction. Is this her chance?

Ruby glances at Sophia and attempts to explain. 'Look darl, I'm his mum, and God love him, he tries. But he's bloody hopeless. I worry about the child.'

'What's going to happen then?' Sophia ventures, almost holding her breath, waiting for a sliver of opportunity in the conversation so she can snatch the advantage.

'I know it doesn't sound right, Sophia, but I'm seventy-two years old and the last thing I want to be doing in my last years on the planet is raising another son.'

'Does Matt know this?'

'I think so. Well, I'm not sure.' Ruby sighs, her hands clasped tightly, resting in her lap, staring directly at Sophia.

'I don't want to cause any more upset, but before Teressa died, only a few weeks ago, we discussed the possibility of Jack coming to live with me.'

'Oh? Do you truly want that?' Ruby transferred her full attention to Sophia's response.

'Yes. I love Jack and promised my sister I would do everything I could to take good care of him.'

'What about your busy life? Can you afford to give it up and raise a child on your own?'

'Yes, of course. But you probably know that Matt and I don't see eye-to-eye. I don't want to go into it all now, save to say, he has been insulting and unreasonable to me.'

'I see,' Ruby says, taking a few moments to process this information. 'But I can talk some sense into him. You do know Matt will probably want access to visit his son?'

'Of course,' Sophia reluctantly agrees. At this point, she will consent to anything. In the cold light of reality, she knows Matt will say all the right fatherly words but is highly unlikely to keep up regular visitation. It's a risk worth taking to secure baby Jack's life. As the words enter her head, the impact, the overwhelming sense of being a mother burns inside her. It's an unreal, compelling inner truth of motherhood she had buried deep and always strove to suppress.

That evening back home, Sophia contacts Hugh. He's surprised and delighted to hear from her. As she unpacks the scenario and the chance to adopt her nephew, Hugh grows quiet.

'Are you still there?' Sophia's voice strains with anxiety.

'Yeah ... Umm ... I don't know what to say. It's a lot to take on board right now.'

'I don't want to pressure you.' Sophia rewinds things a notch or two. 'It's been a traumatic couple of weeks, and as I said, I'm not sure Matt will allow adoption or even consider us fostering his son. It's a long shot given my broken relationship with him.'

'Sure, I understand, and I fully appreciate how you feel, having just lost your sister too.' Hugh treads cautiously. 'Let's discuss it again once you know which way Matt's going to jump.'

'OK. Did you get the photo I sent with me holding baby Jack?'

'Hang on.' Hugh clicks into WhatsApp and opens Sophia's message. A broad smile spreads across his face. 'It's a lovely shot of you both. The baby is very cute. Let's find out what's involved.' He pauses. 'Sophia, in principle, I have no objections, but I do worry about Matt on our doorstep so it would have to be an official adoption to work for us. This is my initial thinking.'

CHAPTER 54

Exit Strategy – March 2020

Two days later, Hugh calls from New York on Sophia's thirty-third birthday. 'I've something serious I need to discuss with you,' Hugh says without any preamble. Sophia's blood runs cold, the colour draining from her face with dread. He's breaking up with her. She knew it. How the hell did she ever think a man like Hugh could want her as a wife? It would never last. He doesn't love her. Her throat constricts as she concentrates on his next words with fear pulsing through her entire body.

'Hey. Are you still there?' Hugh asks.

'Yeah,' she says softly, feeling sick to her stomach.

'I don't know if you've seen the news?'

'Not for a few hours,' she replies weakly.

'New Zealand is going into full lockdown, and you won't get through customs. They've effectively called a state of emergency starting on Wednesday.'

Sophia takes a few seconds to grapple with the meaning of his words as some relief eases its way into her racing mind. 'So, are you ending our relationship?'

'Of course not!' he says impatiently. He didn't have time to explain. 'Listen to me, Sophia, we have less than four days to get you to New Zealand. Who knows for how long. I want you with me in lockdown.'

Sophia frowns, gradually absorbing his instructions as he continues directing the next steps.

'I've asked my PA to organise a plane ticket for you to Auckland and then onto Wanaka. I'll meet you there,' he talks abruptly in his businessman's voice. There is no time for negotiation or emotional considerations. 'It's serious. Morrison will do the same soon, and after that, you won't be able to fly anywhere. It could mean months of isolation.'

'Hugh. What are you talking about?' Her tremulous words sound weak and anxious as she tries to force her speech into usual modality. Fear fades into relief, more than anything, that Hugh isn't dumping her. He still wants her. A reprieve from oblivion and a chance at a real life is still within her grasp.

'Ardern will announce full lockdown starting at level three and by Wednesday level four,' Hugh sounds breathless. 'I haven't got time to talk. Check your emails. Close everything up and get on that plane.'

'But I can't. I need to ...' Panic now overrides any other sensation. How can this be happening? It's impossible! Surely something's wrong?

'I have reliable advice that New Zealand is about to go into full lockdown and will be closing the airports in about five days. You must get there before Monday.'

'How ... er ...what about ...'

'It's OK. You have a day and a half to get sorted and get here.'

'Anything else?' she asks, stunned but compliant.

There was a split-second silence.

'Oh, darling. Happy birthday dear Sophia. We'll be married and living happily ever after in splendid isolation near Lake Wanaka. Get packing. Love you.'

The phone clicks off.

Sophia stands bewildered, holding the mobile device and staring at the blank screen. Like a zombie she walks to the kitchen barstools and sits, taking a few minutes to process Hugh's instructions. She grabs the remote, switching on Sky News to watch the latest reports as she speed-dials Florian.

'Thousands of Australians and New Zealanders could be stranded across the world trying to find a way home ...' the presenter's monotone announcement penetrates Sophia's panic.

'Hey. What's up?' Florian answers her call.

'Hugh phoned just now, telling me to pack up and get on a plane to New Zealand before all the airports close, and all flights are cancelled. He says it'll be happening here soon too.'

'Woohoo! And? Are you going to do as you're told for a change?' he asks, still digesting Sophia's words.

'I'm not sure … it's so left field.' Her voice is tight with worry. 'How can I unravel my entire life in less than two days?'

'Hey, take a deep breath. It's simple,' Florian soothes.

'That's easy for you to say. I have two houses, a business, clients … how the hell …' Her voice rises and the full impact of what she needs to do hits home.

'Listen. I'll pick you up and take you to the airport on Monday, so any last-minute things can be discussed.' Florian channels his highly organised and structured alter-ego which triggers Sophia's need to write lists and swing into action.

'You have the perfect out to close the penthouse. Call your clients and say the business is closing as the country is going into lockdown and there's no way of knowing if there will ever be a recovery, certainly, not soon.'

'How do you know?' she asks.

'Watching the BBC and CNN. Hugh's right. Get your arse over there,' Florian confirms.

'What about the fees, the costs?' she asks, knowing full well that she will be up the proverbial creek like many other businesses in the country.

'I've got your keys, I'll move in, eat your food and drink all your booze and lock the penthouse up for the duration,' he explains with an attempt at laughter before continuing. 'Listen, girlfriend, the best thing you can do now is phone or write an email to those clients and ensure they know you have literally closed up shop!' Florian gives a forced chuckle again.

'What about the house?' she asks, feeling she's completely lost her ability to make any decisions.

'Same,' he says. 'I've got all your keys and will look after it. I could organise tenants to live in it maybe?'

'No way,' she responds firmly, her mojo starting to surface. 'This may only be for a few weeks.'

'I suspect, looking at China's experience,' he sighs, 'we're going to be out of the mix for several months. Worse may be the impact on the economy. Well, let's say it's going to take a few long years to get back up to speed.'

'Oh, my God. I have to be realistic,' she responds, the full onslaught finally hitting home.

'You do.'

'Grounding all the airlines will almost kill the entire industry,' she says. 'What about tourism and hospitality?' The implications push Sophia into getting a grip on Hugh's directives.

'Yup! And you need to get on a plane fast before you're permanently locked out!'

Sophia snorts in disbelief. 'Wow. Never in my wildest dreams did I ever think this would be the way out. I'll close the penthouse business immediately!'

'I'm coming over,' he announces. 'See you in twenty.'

Florian arrives in an agitated flourish, and they both sit on the sofa for the first hour mesmerised by the television news. This is real. It's not some global prank or a crazy nightmare. It confirms for Sophia that it is the end of her business activities.

'It's over,' she says to Florian during an ad break as they both watch the Breaking News and read the ticker tape words about COVID 19 in other countries. Death rates and infections have skyrocketed. Where the hell had she been? Distracted by the small, petty bullshit of her domestic life. This was like a slow tsunami of pandemic proportions, rolling in from afar to slam into all their lives. How had she not taken it seriously?

'Really?' Florian says, astounded by her declaration. He stands still, frozen in disbelief. Is this truly it?'

'Are you going to pour that wine or not?' Sophia asks. 'I must say I'm delighted I still have that effect on you.'

'You're kidding, right?'

'No, I'm deadly serious,' Sophia shoots back, amazed how calm and flippant she seems. 'I feel a huge sense of relief. The burden of deceit and duplicity is finally lifted from my shoulders.'

'Why now?' he asks, filling his own glass before he slumps onto the sofa. Sophia sits in the armchair opposite as they mute the television and continue chatting. She scribbles in her notebook every now and then, making sure she has planned the exit strategy with the least amount of distress to everyone.

'In the past year I've had to deal with snooping Willem, Matt's bad debt, old boy Max looking like a risk in the making and worst of all, Teressa's sudden death.' She inhales. 'Now I have only four days to unravel it all and get the hell out of here.'

Florian's face saddens with regret. 'I didn't think of it like that.'

'Well it feels sudden to me, but I guess for those in the know, it can't be. I'm still struggling to understand how Teressa lost her mind in the process. These are signs from the universe telling me to move onto the next chapter,' she continues, her eyes watery with suppressed emotion. 'I have a flying chance of adopting Jack too, but no time to organise it now.'

'Wow.' Florian takes a gulp of chilled white wine and keeps his eyes on Sophia. 'You've got a lot to look forward to. An entirely different life. You always said you would *retire* in your mid-thirties and here we are …at just thirty-three.'

Florian leaps off the sofa and grabs Sophia's hands, pulling her from the armchair, shaking her from grief and himself from a wave of sadness that his best friend will be moving away. He puts an old favourite song on the UE Boom standing on the bookshelf. Pharell Williams' *Happy* blasts out loudly. Florian sings along, prancing in front of Sophia. After the first two lines, Sophia joins in. They skip around the open plan living room, laughing and shrieking, uplifted by the music and the positive energy seeping into their saddened souls.

They toast one another and their life-long friendship.

'There's one other thing.' Florian looks unexpectedly solemn. 'What the hell am I going to do for excitement without you in town?'

'I'll be back with Hugh.' She smiles at her dear friend. 'It's only a three-hour flight. I'll meet you for lunch when Hugh's submerged in all those business meetings.' She watches his distraught face, still unconvinced. 'You're my *bestest* friend. There's no way we'll ever be out of touch! Besides, I'll have to return to pick up my son!'

Early the next morning, Sophia meets with her business lawyer to trigger terminations of her client's contracts. Swersky's legal consulting fees are well worth it, she thinks, as he presents her with a draft resignation letter to six of her seven clients for approval.

'It's a bit formal,' she comments after perusing through the draft content on the carefully typed single page.

The elderly man frowns. 'These are serious times, and the coronavirus gives you a non-negotiable, credible way out. You mentioned on the phone yesterday that terminating the business permanently was your objective with no wiggle room. Waiving the three-month notice period makes sense too. You need to ensure each client gets the message loud and clear.'

The termination notice refers to the back-out clause in their original contracts and formally terminates their agreement with Sophia. It is polite and business-like, ensuring any prying eyes from personal assistants or wives would think nothing of it.

Sophia nods and rereads the wording, imagining Rafe, Frank, Sam, affable Giles and sweet Haruto, as well as unpredictable Willem, reading these stiff legal words which convey the end of their relationship. The hard lines of the officious typeface punched onto the stark draft suddenly make it all feel real. She is embarking on an entirely different life. In three more days she'll be with her fiancé, a man, just the one, who will be her husband for the rest of her days.

'What's your concern?' Swersky asks, watching his client closely and sees Sophia struggling with some reservations.

'It sounds a bit brutal, in some ways,' she says, glancing up at the determined face of her legal counsel. 'I regard some of these people as friends. It's something I need …'

Swersky draws in a breath, regarding his client carefully, surprised at her reticence. She had been officious and business-like in drafting the original client contract and now hesitates at the finishing post.

'Why not courier the letters directly to their offices?' he suggests, pleased with himself. 'In this instance, I think it would be better than email. Courier them door to door, and it'll be delivered worldwide in less than three days. Costs a bit, but you can afford a hundred and twenty dollars express courier for each client's notice to be hand-delivered surely?' he asks with a grin.

'Good idea. Let's do that.' Sophia is pleased and relieved. 'There's one other thing,' she says and explains the adoption of her baby nephew. Can you draw up the documentation and add a clause cancelling the repayment of a five hundred and thirty-four thousand dollar loan to Matt Simpson, the father of the baby? Obviously, I need this contingent on him signing the necessary adoption papers. But please include his visitation and regular access rights to the child.'

'Right. Are you sure about this?' Swerky's eyes narrow. 'It's a hell of a price for a baby.'

Sophia nods.

'It'll have to be carefully worded to avoid any connection which looks like the illegal buying of a baby. You wouldn't want that!'

'Yeah. Maybe two different documents?'

'Oh, I almost forgot. Has your fiancé signed the papers and agreed to the adoption now?' Swersky asks as an after-thought. 'We can make a draft with both of your signatures already included so your brother-in-law, if he's willing, could in effect sign this copy and we can hit the start button with the process.'

'Yes, absolutely. We had a lengthy discussion late last night and Hugh's fully on board and will sign as soon as we're ready.'

'Let me work on it. You'll need to email me your new contact details, so the domicile of the baby is noted in the papers.'

Sophia rummages in her handbag and withdraws several documents. Baby Jack's birth certificate and identification information for both Matt, Hugh and herself.

'This will take a few months to process ...'

'Oh. Can't I take the baby with me?'

'Well, you could. If you can get a signed temporary order from the father of the child to allow the baby to travel with you. I can email one tomorrow, as long as Matt signs off, but remember Jack is not officially adopted. That's going to take some time.'

'OK, go ahead, and I'll have to meet with Matt first thing, tonight or tomorrow morning and see if he'll sign the travel application for his son.'

'My staff can organise the temporary travel document for the baby as soon as I have those signed papers. Lucky you're only going to New Zealand. It makes things a lot easier. Oh, and I'll need your marriage certificate, that'll make life a lot easier for the adoption process. Courier it to me after the wedding, and we can progress with the documentation ready for signing.'

Sophia stands, her head swimming with panic, so much to do and barely enough time to achieve it all.

'You can't run off yet,' he grins. 'Those notes on your client's letters.'

'Ahh. Of course!'

Swersky leans onto his desk, presses a button and calls his personal assistant to print out copies. At the same time, she ushers Sophia into a private room to seal each client's envelope and check each name and address. She withholds Hugh's letter, folding it carefully and shoving it into her pocket. This one's for personal delivery. She smiles to herself. Each of the others is marked Strictly Confidential. Swersky assures her they will be on the international courier that same day.

Relieved, Sophia also requests Swersky to draw up the relevant property documents to arrange a return of the *gift* of the central city penthouse back to Giles Hamilton. Back in the private room, Sophia dials Giles on her cell phone. She has barely seen him during the past year. At first, he resists taking back the penthouse, but Sophia explains she would sell it and donate the money to the SPCA. The mere suggestion makes him sit up and accept the returned property into his family trust for the princely sum of a hundred dollars. He is delighted to hear all her news and is happy to sign the legal documents.

'Good old Hugh, eh?' he comments. 'The best man won!'

'Do you know, Giles,' Sophia says, 'Hugh's biggest attraction is that he reminds me so much of you.'

'That's so kind,' he responds. 'If only I was twenty years younger, Hugh would have a battle on his hands!'

'And I'd be spoilt for choice!' she quips.

'To express my thankfulness for your generosity, Sophia, I'll donate six hundred thousand dollars to the animal shelter,' Giles says. 'I figure that's the fee the sales agent will ping me for if we organised to sell the penthouse through normal channels.'

'Sorry, Giles, must rush. Have a bit more legal wrangling to do over baby Jack. We'll catch up when I'm back in Sydney which is going to be fairly often. Wish me luck.'

CHAPTER 55

Smooth Operator – Late March 2020

Several disappointed men insist on talking to Sophia but can only leave text messages on her cell phone. The recorded response her clients receive put an end to any further conversations:

This phone is no longer in service. Check the number and try again later.

The only client message Sophia returns is from Haruto Tanaka. It rings once, and Haruto immediately answers.

'Sophia,' he says. 'I am so worried about receiving your letter. Are you all right?'

'Yes, I'm fine,' she says, feeling that sharp pang of regret at losing a friend. 'Haruto do you want the necklace back? I feel awful about this.'

'Won't you have me back' His voice is almost plaintive, the soft vowels of the Japanese language adding emphasis.

'No,' things have changed, and my family need me now,' she states, weighed down with remorse. 'Every Geisha girl has to find a new future.'

'But we could carry on,' he suggests, 'like before. Don't be afraid of the years that have not yet come to pass. I will always look after you, Sophia.'

'I thank you Haruto, and I believe you.' She hesitates, trying to find the right Japanese word. A word that is firm but is gentle in its delivery. 'I have been given the opportunity of marriage,' she says boldly. She hears his sharp intake of breath. 'But now the world is also changing, as I am changing. This virus outbreak has forced my hand, and so I have agreed to marry. I have found my safe haven away from Australia.'

Silence.

Sophia waits, expecting a response of some kind. Could he not congratulate her? Put himself in her shoes, a concept he was unlikely to fully comprehend.

'Haruto?'

'I understand,' he says in a voice heavy with disappointment, mourning the loss of a perfect clandestine escape from reality. How could he ever hope to find this refuge again with a woman like Sophia?

'I will courier the necklace back to you,' she offers.

'No,' he responds. 'It is for you with love from me, and I don't want to take that back from you.'

Sophia hesitates. 'Thank you, my friend.'

Haruto ends the call. Sophia is left clutching the dead phone. Filled with guilt and a rush of shame, overshadowed by the painful loss of their parting.

Ruby calls Sophia and confirms Matt has agreed to meet at her home early on Friday evening.

'Did you have trouble convincing him to talk to me about Jack?' Sophia asks anxiously.

'He was a bit resistant to the idea at first. But I talked him around. He needs to do what's right for his son. I think he gets it and understands,' Ruby elaborates. 'Let me know how you get on and if you need any more help with him.'

By the time Friday evening arrives, Sophia has worked out every eventuality and possible objection Matt may raise. The security gate buzzes, and Sophia lets Matt into the property.

When she opens the front door, Matt is expressionless, standing in front of her saying nothing. She guesses he's angry at being confronted with the inevitable.

She grabs a cold beer out of the fridge and passes it to her brother-in-law. Matt grabs it, grunts appreciation and strolls into the sitting room. Sophia watches him retreat into the adjoining room before he flops onto the sofa. She pours herself a glass of chilled Sav, follows him and sits down in the armchair opposite.

'Well, let's get on with it,' Matt says, impatiently taking a swig from his beer.

'Sure,' Sophia says. They both know the less time they spend in one another's company, the better. 'Did your mum give you the details around the temporary travel document for Jack? It's like a limited passport in circumstances like this. Of course, you need to sign permission for me to take your son to New Zealand in the short term.'

He nods affirmative, saying nothing.

'What's your thinking about us adopting Jack as our own child in the long run?'

Matt looks stony-faced, not giving anything away. He gulps another mouthful of beer and leans his back against the sofa. Sullen and mistrustful, he waits a beat before speaking. 'Frankly, I think the timing stinks. Your sister, my wife, is still warm in her grave and you're trying to railroad me into handing over my only child. My only son.'

'Matt, let's not get off on the wrong foot. Teressa discussed and agreed that Jack should come to me. I didn't act on her wishes as I knew she was very ill and you are Jack's father. I wanted to be honest and transparent. I'm not trying to push you into anything you don't want. Let's discuss this keeping your son's well-being a priority in both our minds. It's easy to fight and argue, the hardest thing to do is to find the right way forward for Jack's sake.'

Sophia sits quietly watching Matt's face as it begins to soften, but he doesn't respond.

'Your mother told me she can't look after Jack forever. She's too old to deal with raising another son at this stage of her life.'

'I know. Mum already told me that.' Matt seems reluctant and unable to express himself. Unexpectedly tears brim in his eyes, and he repeats. 'He's my son!'

'You will always be Jack's father, but you can't be a parent. Do you want a stable life and a wonderful future for Jack?'

'Of course.' He sniffs.

'Can you provide that for him?' Matt rubs his hands over his face, pushing his fingers through his hair. 'I dunno.' He pauses and looks sadly at Sophia. 'I guess not. But that won't be forever. I've got a couple of real good opportunities ...' His voice trails off when he sees the sceptical look on Sophia's face. Who's he kidding?

'Let's think of this another way. It's the coronavirus and lockdown that's forcing the issue. But let's not allow the world to dictate what decisions are made about Jack. You know we finally have something in common, a baby that needs a good home with parents that are always available.'

Matt nods. 'I get that. So what are you saying?'

For now, let's sign the travel documents so he can come with me to New Zealand. I promise to bring him back to Sydney as soon as lockdown is over. It's likely to be in a couple of months. You'll have time to sort out your life and what you want to do. You've suffered enormous stress and upheaval lately.'

'I need to meet this Hugh guy you're marrying, and I want to see where my son will be living.'

An immediate sense of relief washes over Sophia, Matt is finally considering this option, and she needs to accommodate him in every way if it means she can keep baby Jack. 'I'll arrange for Hugh to meet you when we return back to Sydney after lockdown. Jack will be with us so you can spend some time with him too. It's entirely up to you. I think the baby will be safer in New Zealand and with us. It's sensible to let me take him on Sunday.'

Matt nods an affirmation then frowns. 'What about this whole adoption thing Mum was talking about?'

'We can discuss that later and make formal adoption arrangements if you're happy to go ahead. This temporary move gives us all time to calmly think about what's best for Jack.'

'Yeah. If you adopt him, I still want to be able to see him when I want to.'

'Sure. You're his father, and I'll make certain Jack grows up knowing you're his real dad.'

Chances are Matt will get on with his life, meet another woman, marry and have other children. Would he visit Jack that often? Sophia ran through several scenarios. Matt wants to get on with his regular hedonistic existence. Is this the right time to bring up the debt? She looks at him directly in the eyes. Something about him told her he has an ulterior motive.

'I have the draft adoption documentation here if you want to read it? You'll see the visitation and access clauses are already included. In the light of what's happened with Teressa's death, and the huge debt burden you carry, I'm willing to cancel the outstanding loan if you agree to the adoption.' She pauses briefly. 'This is something you need to think about in the coming months. We can talk online or over the phone, if you need to discuss it any further, but I'm prepared to write-off that debt in full.'

'You know Sophia, caring for the baby and cancelling the debt are both generous offers. I'm stunned by the kindness coming from you after all the years of anger and hatred.'

'I apologise,' Sophia simply says, holding her breath in a desperate desire to keep Matt agreeable. 'I want your son to know his father and his adoptive parents, get along with one another. All three of us have his best interests at heart.'

A heavy silence falls between them before Matt speaks again.

'The thing is … I'm really strapped at the moment.'

The real mercenary manipulator can't contain himself. Sophia keeps calm, her concerned exterior doesn't waiver, intent on playing along. She smiles without parting her lips and remains silent, waiting for Matt's next move. She doesn't have to wait long.

'Can you throw me some money to cover the funeral costs and a bit to keep me going while I'm waiting on the business to get the go-ahead?'

'How much?

'Ten thousand, to see me through the next few months.'

Of course.' She nods. 'Sign these travel documents, and I'll double it.'

What?' Matt's stunned.

'Yeah, sign here and here,' she says, passing Matt a pen, and he quickly scrawls his signature on the pages.

'Thanks. I'll transfer twenty thousand dollars into your bank account later tonight. Obviously, I can't cancel the half a million dollar debt until the adoption is finalised, but we'll talk about it again when you're ready.'

Ten minutes later, Matt has left the building. Jack will be delivered to her on Monday, two hours before the flight.

330

CHAPTER 56

Home for the Heart - March 2020

Sophia sucks in a deep breath as she surveys the evening view from her penthouse windows. It's the last time she will look out across the city lights twinkling across the Sydney Harbour Bridge. This has been her entire life until now, and she knows she'll miss her home. But Sophia is doubly excited at baby Jack travelling with her to their new life together with Hugh. It feels right and good to turn her back on all the bad memories of her past. It's so unbelievable she wants to pinch herself to make sure she's not lost her mind and is hallucinating.

She had already anxiously called Ruby twice that afternoon confirming the baby's arrival at her home by 9am.

'Matt's upset of course,' Ruby says in a shaky voice.

'Of course, he would be,' Sophia says, fearing he would baulk at the final hurdle and refuse to deliver the baby in the morning. 'It's a tough time, but he's made the right decision.'

'Yeah, I know. I worry about Matty.'

'Maybe it would be better if you brought the baby here. What do you think? I totally understand what a traumatising thing it would be for Matt to hand Jack over to me.'

There was a pause on the line.

'Yeah that's a good idea,' Ruby said sadly.

An hour later, much to Sophia's relief, she receives a text confirming their arrangements.

She wasn't sure how long she'd been standing there gazing out of the window. Pull yourself together. Hugh is there for you. He loves you and wants you. How fortunate she has choices after the life she's led. How incredible to leave it behind and embark on a new adventure. She must not let the old life leak into her new journey. That part of her existence must remain obscure, buried and never allowed to cast dark shadows over her new dream. The past has gone and is dead and buried. It has to stay that way.

Sophia slowly shakes her head, as if to clear her mind of all emotion. Focus. She makes a mental note to arrange for a new cell phone once she arrives *home* in New Zealand. And once she's married with a new surname, no one would be able to track her. *Sophia Rixon.* She repeats the name several times even though they haven't set a wedding date with the coronavirus lockdown restrictions still in place. Yet it sounds like Hugh wants to get married sometime during the year. She smiled, thinking of little Jack Rixon, smiling at her. She couldn't wait to have him in her arms again and leave the country and the old life behind.

Swersky had warned her, even after Matt signs the official adoption documents that Australian adoption law allows a cooling-off period of thirty-days. So, Matt could revoke the adoption anytime during the first month. Hugh had suggested they send him another twenty thousand dollars after he'd signed the official adoption papers so keep him happy until the thirty-day period had elapsed.

After a whirlwind of non-stop conversations, packing and tying up loose ends, Sophia is relieved to be seated on the Air New Zealand plane on a direct flight to Auckland with sweet baby Jack lying in a flight cot bolted to the wall in front of her. When the plane levels off and the seat belt warning lights go off, she sends a text to Hugh;

I am with child. See you soon. All my love. Sxx

After declaring at customs that she would be in self-isolation for the stipulated fourteen days, she hands over her completed passenger disembarkation form with her new home address. Within an hour she and sleeping Jack transit onto Hugh's private jet bound for Wanaka. It was surprising how trusting the customs officials were, taking her word for her lockdown strategy. But from now on, she will be her word in thoughts and deeds, transforming into a new life as a new wife and the happy mother of baby Jack.

She and Jack are the only passengers on the short one-hour forty-minute flight to her new home. Shattered by recent events, Sophia is comforted by daydreaming about sharing the rest of her life with Hugh. Flying over Otago and Mount Aspiring National Park, the plane circles in the air above the local airfield. Sophia peers out of the small oval window, glancing down at the small town, nestled around the indigo blue waters of breath-taking Lake Wanaka.

Shades of emerald green and early autumn colours, splashes of yellow gold, and deep reds glow in the surrounding sparse scrub-covered highlands. Roads and dirt trails snake their way over stony hills and mountains amongst dramatic rock outcrops, all leading to the lake where the water runs south-east into the Clutha River. As they lose altitude and draw closer to the airfield, Sophia glances outside at a few cars and utes barreling along the roads, with tell-tale clouds of dust spiralling into the clear blue skies.

The mixture of dark and colourful buildings, some traditional replicas of outback cowboy westerns she watched on television as a child, came into sharp relief. Modern timber shiplap two-storey buildings with flat tin roofs and paved pathways seem barren of all human life. It's striking to see only one car parked in the main street with no one walking along the footpaths. The coronavirus lockdown already having an impact.

She looks at Jack's sleeping face and is surprised by the pang of fear for his health and an overwhelming instinctive desire to keep him safe.

Wanaka means obscurity. No one knows anything about her. She packed very little, thinking her new journey would create a new self which needs a new skin, new clothes, demure, relaxed and comfortable gear that conveys contented domestic bliss. She wants to comfortably blend in with the locals and intends avoiding all large social gatherings, an advantage during these restrictive times. Her high-flying Sydney city days are over, and Hugh accepts Sophia hopes for quiet contentment away from the buzz of high society. He had happily agreed to everything she asked, keen to encourage her to move into his home. Hugh loves her. She believes him, and she will do anything to be his companion and wife.

A driver collects Sophia from the small local airport and drives her to Hugh's private retreat on 2,273 acres of New Zealand native bush, sheltered along a meandering mountain gorge. One road in and one road out. She sighs when she arrives at the sprawling, contemporary schist stone and cedar flat-roofed home. It appears almost invisible, sitting camouflaged by native bush and stone outcrops in the surrounding wooded grounds of the extensive farming estate.

Sophia hands Jack to the driver before she knocks on the front door. Hugh bursts through the double doors, scooping Sophia up and whirls her around with delight, thankful that she is finally safely home.

'I stressed myself out thinking something could go wrong with baby Jack, customs or the flights,' he says, smiling broadly. He takes the baby from the driver and kisses Jack's forehead before grabbing her hand and dragging an awe-struck Sophia into the modern living room. One wall of grey schist stone with a massive fireplace above a raised hearth dominates the spacious room. Massive timber beams arch across the vaulted ceiling in the contemporary decorated room.

Her bags are carried to the east wing of the large U-shaped architecturally designed home while they both smile with joy at how their shared future is now forever intertwined. Without fanfare, Hugh holds the baby over his shoulder and pours chilled champagne into two tall glasses, raising a birthday toast to Sophia. She glows with delight at finally arriving at a life she imagined as a teenager nearly fifteen years earlier. She takes a tentative sip, smiling at Hugh seated with the baby on the tan leather couch.

Jack dozes on his shoulder, content after Sophia fed him during the car journey.

Hugh walks his fiancée down the long hall to the baby's room. A local interior designer has set up the baby's bedroom opposite the master bedroom.

'Hugh, it's absolutely gorgeous!' Sophia's heart swells with delight at the perfectly appointed powder blue bedroom.

Hugh walks to the cot and carefully lowers the sleeping baby into his new bed, pulling the merino wool blankets up to the baby's chest.

'Where did you learn your magic baby handling tricks?' Sophia asks astounded at how calm and relaxed Hugh appears.

'My sister has three kids, and I used to love visiting.' He takes Sophia's hand they walk back to the expansive living room. 'We have some celebrating to do,' he says.

That evening, after an afternoon sleep for them all, Sophia and Hugh sit together talking and laughing, delighted to be together.

'You do realise our original business contact remains binding, Mr Rixon.' She smiles playfully before dinner is served. 'It means, of course, that I'll be invoicing you for every night we sleep together. In which case, I'm not sure you can afford to marry me.'

He laughs, deep and resonating. 'Is there no end to your cheeky disposition?' he says, highly amused by Sophia's relentless entrepreneurial focus.

Even in the low evening light, she notices his mischievous eyes glinting into hers. 'I'm making an honest woman out of you, that's got to be worth at least ninety-nine per cent of the cost of keeping you. We might as well do a contra deal.'

'Always closing.' She chuckles. 'Working the sales angle!' And she reaches out and shakes his hand before they both burst into raucous laughter.

Two weeks later they are married on a private beach somewhere along the Otago coast. A sterile celebrant, in a facemask and surgical gloves, has been coaxed into a severely disinfected chauffeur-driven vehicle to officiate at the Rixon nuptials.

Hugh and Sophia stand holding hands on the small private shoreline, facing the celebrant standing three metres opposite. The tall, thin middle-aged celebrant appears to be smiling warmly from behind her mask at the happy bride and groom. She smiles in awe at the massive fee being paid for this short ten-minute ceremony.

There isn't another person for miles. The sandy beach venue is safe, a private enclave under an ancient drooping pohutukawa tree where the beginning of her new life as wife and mother to baby Jack begins.

'You may kiss the bride,' the celebrant says, smiling broadly.

END

ABOUT THE AUTHOR

Nicky Webber enjoyed a successful career as a newspaper and magazine journalist. Born in New Zealand, she lived in South Africa for 20 years before returning home in 1994. In recent years she resumed her original passion for writing, focusing on controversial characters, ordinary people who are living extraordinary lives.

Duplicity is Nicky's fourth contemporary fiction novel. She is currently working on a fifth, full-length book which she expects to publish during 2021.

Nicky lives in Cambridge, New Zealand, where she writes and blogs with excerpts, free chapters and updates of her work. Follow her author page on Facebook or contact her on author@nickywebber.com.

If you enjoyed Duplicity, please consider posting a review on; Amazon.com Amazon.co.uk Goodreads.com or on her website https://nickywebber.com

Other Books Written by the Author:
No Ordinary Man
In the Deep End - Book One
In the Deep End - Book Two
Push Over - a short story about revenge

ACKNOWLEDGMENTS

Special thanks to the professional editing and advice from Tina Shaw and expert proof reading and manuscript correction from ace perfectionist, Nikki Crutchley. I very much appreciated the effort and commitment they both gave in driving this story into a readable state! Also grateful thanks to Bev Robitaille, who, on short notice, performed an emergency rescue on the corrupted final content and delivered a perfectly resurrected file ready for printing.

Thanks to my husband, Hallam Webber, who set up a workstation with two mammoth screens so I could strip and shovel scenes and chapters around with ease. Also, thanks to family and friends who put up with my swearing and cursing over pieces of the puzzle that refused to hang together – thankfully, they suffered early retirement.

Grateful thanks to my team of BETA readers from around the country and the world; Larraine Pita, Deb Espin, Sonja Konings, Shannon Parsons and Carolyn Boardman who waded through early drafts and discussed improvements as the manuscript unfolded. A year ago, they listened to the basic story outline and gave me an enthusiastic thumbs up. Finally, Duplicity is born. Thank you all.

Made in United States
Orlando, FL
21 June 2022

19025067R00211